THE
GHOST
OF THE
REVELATOR

THE
GHOST
OF THE
REVELATOR

L. E. MODESITT, JR.

TOR®

A TOM DOHERTY ASSOCIATES BOOK
NEW YORK

This is a work of fiction. All the characters and events portrayed
in this novel are either fictitious or are used fictitiously.

THE GHOST OF THE REVELATOR

Copyright © 1998 by L. E. Modesitt, Jr.

This book is printed on acid-free paper.

Edited by David G. Hartwell

A Tor Book
Published by Tom Doherty Associates, Inc.
175 Fifth Avenue
New York, NY 10010

Tor Books on the World Wide Web:
http://www.tor.com

Tor® is a registered trademark of Tom Doherty Associates, Inc.

Library of Congress Cataloging-in-Publication Data

Modesitt, L. E.
    The ghost of the revelator / L. E. Modesitt, Jr.—1st ed.
        p.   cm.
    "A Tom Doherty Associates book."
    ISBN 0-312-86426-4 (acid-free paper)
    I. Title.
    PS3563.0264G48   1998
    813'.54—dc21   98-24111
                                                       CIP

First Edition: September 1998

Printed in the United States of America

0   9   8   7   6   5   4   3   2   1

For Bruce, and for Carol Ann,
who made this possible

I

THE late-October New Bruges drizzle—more liquid ice than rain on that Friday night—clicked off the Stanley's thermal finish all the way down from the house into Vanderbraak Centre. Beside me, Llysette sat, drawn into herself, as she always was before she performed.

When you're a professor and retired spy married to a former diva of old France who's been the toast of a Europe now crumbled under Ferdinand's boots, you always hope for peace and quiet. Especially when you've finally turned the disaster of two ghosts in your life into mere inconvenience. And sometimes you get it, but this time even the ice was only the calm before a bigger storm.

"The ice rains . . . at times, Johan, would that we lived where I did not need two coats and wool garments."

"I know." I'd learned early to say nothing controversial before she sang. "I was thinking that over midterms we might take a vacation in Saint-Martine. There's a weekly dirigible from Asten."

"I will not endure that long a time." Llysette shivered. "And tonight, they will applaud like cows. For what do I sing?"

"Because you're a singer. Singers sing. You sing magnificently—"

"Once I did. Now . . . I do not know."

"You'll be magnificent. I know it." I eased the steamer to a stop right opposite the side door to the old Physical Training building, set the brake, and scurried around with the black umbrella to escort Llysette up and inside. I kissed her on the cheek, again. "You'll be fine."

"Fine is for gold, Johan."

"You'll sing magnificently."

"We shall see." She headed up the half-flight of steps to the practice room where her accompanist, Johanna, waited. She'd already warmed up at the house on the Haaren console grand piano. I'd purchased that for her with part of my "bonus" for resolving the governmental ghost crisis. Given what I'd put Llysette through, she deserved the piano and more. Given what Archduke Ferdinand of the Austro-Hungarian Empire and my own beloved country of Columbia had put her through, even a concert Steinbach wouldn't have been the first installment on true repayment to her, but I was trying.

I went back to move the Stanley into a more legitimate spot in the car park, getting even wetter in the process because it was about four times as far from where I parked to the front of the Music and Theatre building.

"Good evening, Doktor Eschbach." One of Llysette's students was handing out programs, but I didn't recall her name—Emelia van–something or other. Then, most of the students at Vanderbraak State University were from New Bruges. Most had a predominantly Dutch heritage—and that Dutch reserve that made Llysette's teaching an exercise as much in trying to bring emotion to singing as to develop the basics of music.

"Good evening."

To my surprise, the foyer was relatively crowded, and I turned toward the theatre itself, but didn't get that far.

"Doktor Eschbach! Doktor Eschbach . . ." Katrinka Er Recchus had the kind of voice that penetrated, but I supposed that kind of penetration was sometimes useful for the dean of the university. Her bright and overly broad smile was dwarfed by the expanse of white lace collar that topped her too ample figure. Although the auburn hair was faultless, I suspected the original shade had been mousy brown, but there was nothing mousy about her—ratlike, perhaps, but not mousy.

"Dean Er Recchus." I bowed to her and then to Alois, her even more rotund husband, a retired major in the New Bruges guard, as was obvious from the squared-off nature of his white goatee, the guard pin in his lapel, and the dark gray cravat and suit. He returned the bow without speaking.

"I had heard that your presentation on environmental politics and policies was masterful," the dean continued. "Doktor Doniger was most complimentary."

"I'm glad David was pleased." Doktor David Doniger, my chairman and head of the newly reformed Department of Political and Natural Resource Sciences, was usually a pain in the posterior.

"Johan." Her voice lowered, but not the overpowering quantity of that floral fragrance that some vain and aging women immerse themselves in under the delusion that olfactory stupefaction will result in visual illusion. "The vanEmsdens were so pleased that you are the first professor to occupy their endowed chair. Peter was particularly supportive of your past achievements and your dedication to Columbia. He served in the Singapore incident, in the Republic Air Corps, as you did. I am so glad that all such unpleasantnesses are behind us now." The bright smile indicated that any such unpleasantness had best remain behind us all.

The Singapore mess, when Chung Kuo had devastated the city, had been well before my time, and Peter vanEmsden and I had merely passed pleasantries at the ceremony where I'd been installed as the first vonBehn Professor of Applied Politics and Ecology. I doubted most knew the ironies involved with my selection to establish the formal legacy of Elysia vanEmsden's father's forebear, and I wasn't about to explain. After all, how could I—a spy carrying on the legacy of another spy?

"I am delighted that they were pleased."

Alois merely nodded, as he did frequently when with the dean.

When I finally entered the theatre that had been the sole lecture hall of the old Physical Training center, I checked the program. At least Llysette no longer had to resort to under-the-table handouts from the Austro-Hungarian Cultural Foundation to make ends meet. Tucked in among the recital pieces, besides *An die Nacht* and Barber's *Monastic Songs,* was Anne Boleyn's aria from *Heinrich Verruckt.* Llysette had wanted to do that aria at her recital the fall before but had done the Mozart Anti-Mass instead. She'd needed the stipend from the Cultural Foundation. The recital had been the night Miranda Miller, the piano professor, had been murdered, and that had started Llysette's and my adventures with several different covert operations, including those of my former employer, the Sedition Prevention and Security Service, more widely and less popularly known as the Spazi.

I shivered a touch. The last thing Llysette and I needed was anything more along those lines.

The house was almost full, with nearly all of the 450 seats filled nearly a half hour before Llysette was due to sing. I paused for a moment before I sat down, about halfway back, on the aisle, still surveying the audience.

In about the tenth row, in the middle, sat a bearded man in dark clothes, not the dark clothes of the Dutch, or even of a conservative southerner, but different, somehow, almost out of the last century. Not too far from the stranger sat Dierk Geoffries, Llysette's chair. On the far side I even saw Marie Rijn, who cleaned the house for us, along with an older man I guessed had to be her husband.

After I seated myself on one of the all too inflexible Dutch colonial hardwood seats, I glanced back at the bearded man. The seats on either side of him had remained empty, even as the house filled.

The lights dimmed.

Llysette stepped onstage, dark hair upswept, almost imperial in the shimmering green gown, and I forgot about the bearded man.

Johanna's fingers caressed the keys of the concert Steinbach, and the sound shimmered into the evening. Then Llysette began, a selection from Perkins, not one from a Vondel opera.

Llysette sang beautifully. She always had, but now there was something else . . . even more of a spark or a lambent flame.

She had the entire audience, even the stolid Dutch burghers, standing and yelling after she finished the encore—something from an opera I'd never heard: *Susannah.* And she smiled back at them. The other thing I'd never heard in Vanderbraak Centre was so much applause from the normally restrained Dutch.

Llysette's department chair—that was Dierk Geoffries—caught me in the aisle. "I didn't think she could get better, she was so good. . . ." He shook his mane of gray-blond hair. "I've heard some of the best—Delligatti, Riciarelli, Rysanek. Tonight she was better than any of them."

I'd never heard better, but I was no expert. From the hypercritical Dierk, that was high praise. "Best you tell her. If I did, she'd just dismiss it as the pride of a smitten spouse."

"I will." Dierk laughed, and I let him head down the aisle first, listening as I did.

". . . better than korfball any day. . . ."

". . . good . . . but . . . don't know about that," murmured the tall blond youth, who probably was on the university korfball team—which had lost badly to Rensselaer the night before.

The bearded man in the old-fashioned suit, except it seemed new, had a broad smile on his face as he bowed to Llysette backstage and murmured something before stepping away and vanishing.

I followed Dierk and a square-faced Hans Waetjen backstage. Waetjen was the chief of the Watch for Vanderbraak Centre, and he'd avoided speaking to me ever since my actions had led to three of his officers being turned into zombies because one had been suborned by an Austrian covert agent. Dierk stepped aside, and the Watch chief bowed to Llysette. "You were magnificent." Then he turned to me. "Almost magnificent enough to forgive you for marrying Doktor Eschbach."

Waetjen nodded and was gone. At least, a year after the unfortunate incident, he was speaking to me, and he hadn't protested, so far as I knew, when the Citizenship Bureau, after years of dithering, had finally granted Llysette her citizen's status. And I'd never known he liked singing.

Dierk shook his head again. "Unbelievable. No wonder you were the toast of the Academie Royale. I was truly blessed tonight." After another incredulous headshake, he, too, slipped away.

"You were wonderful." I hugged her, and I even had remembered chocolates and flowers—but they were waiting for her at home. "You . . . you've never been better."

Llysette smiled . . . shyly, for a moment. "Better we were, and better yet we will be. . . ."

"You, not we."

"We," she corrected me. "And it is good, Johan. Sad . . . but good."

I swallowed and hugged her, knowing my own cheeks were suddenly damp.

"Fräulein duBoise . . ."

With others still arriving to see Llysette, I stepped back to her shoulder, nodding at Johanna and murmuring, "You played well."

"She sang . . . she sang, Johan." The accompanist shook her head slowly. "Singing like that you seldom hear. Seldom? I've *never* heard it before."

"I can see that I have missed too much." Katrinka Er Recchus, Alois stolidly behind her, smiled her broad and false smile. "You were delightful, dear, absolutely delightful." Her eyes went to me. "You have been too modest about her. Far too modest, Johan." As if it were my fault that the former chair of the Music and Theatre Department hadn't bothered to come to Llysette's recitals before?

I forced a smile. "She has always been magnificent."

"Oh, I can tell now . . . but how was I to know?"

I could have asked myself the same. Once I'd thought about enhancing her singing with my ghost-projection equipment, to create supporting "angels," but after what I'd heard, that would have been too great a sin . . . far too great. Then, maybe, any use of the equipment to influence people would have been, and I just hadn't understood then.

"Enchanting," offered Alois, stolidly easing the dean aside, for once. "Wonderfully enchanting." Alois bowed and escorted the dean back toward the foyer.

"Professor duBoise," asked a red-haired student, tears streaming down her face, "how can I ever do the Perkins the way you do?"

Llysette waited.

"Couldn't we change places? I'll never be able to sing like you do."

"You wish to sing, Berthe? Then work you must. I will hear the Perkins on Tuesday." Llysette softened the words with a smile and a pat on the girl's shoulder.

"Your coat," I prompted as the admirers began to thin.

"It is . . . in the practice room."

"Do you need a ride?" I asked Johanna as I started to retrieve the heavy coat.

"Pietr is already getting the steamer." The accompanist smiled briefly at Llysette. "Even was touched, but he won't admit it."

"That, that is *quelque chose incredible.*"

After ensuring that Llysette was wrapped in the coat, I managed to ease the three boxes of chocolates and several sprays of flowers under my free arm and to escort her to the side door. "You wait here, and I'll bring the Stanley around."

"That is fine with me." She shivered, as she often did after heavy exertion, and wrapped the heavy coat around her.

The Stanley started easily, despite the streaks of ice and cold water, and the rain had turned to tiny frozen pellets. Llysette almost slipped getting into the steamer. Before long, the road and car park would be black ice.

The town square was mostly deserted, except for the lights in the Watch station, and I wondered if Chief Waetjen had stopped by on his way home, that is, if he had one besides the station.

"Who was the bearded fellow?" I asked. "I've never seen him before."

"The . . . bearded . . . oh, the man with the ancient cravat?" Llysette shrugged under the heavy wool coat. "Never have I seen him.

He offered his name . . . James . . . Jacob . . . Jensen. He said . . . we would be hearing from him. Then he was gone."

"That's all?"

"He said my singing, it was as grand as any."

"It was." I laughed, but I wondered about Herr Jensen. When unknown admirers promise that you'll hear from them, you have to wonder in what context.

The River Wijk was dark even under the new lights from the bridge. On the other side, I had to go into four-wheel drive once we started up Deacon's Lane because the narrow uphill road had a thin layer of ice and slush. I had the feeling we were in for an early and hard winter, unlike the previous year.

I dropped Llysette by the door while I manuevered the steamer into the car barn.

She glanced up the stairs as we stepped into the front foyer. Force of habit, still, I suspected, from the days when Carolynne, the family ghost, had lurked there. That had been before my efforts with ghosting technology had ended up grafting her into both our souls. It hadn't been planned that way, and it had saved us from worse, but it wasn't always easy living with feelings and memories you knew weren't yours. I felt it was even harder for Llysette and, for that reason, didn't mention Carolynne much.

"Good it is for there to be no ghosts looking down the stairs. I would dread looking up there."

"I know. I always looked first." I locked the door and took off my topcoat, then led her back to the sitting room. "You just sit here in front of the stove." Although I'd loaded the woodstove before we'd left and the sitting room off the terrace was warm, I opened the stove door and added another two lengths of oak. The heat welled out, and Llysette leaned forward to get warm.

"I'll get your wine . . . or would you like chocolate?" As I turned, I could see the piano in the rear parlor—I'd never really used that space before, but it had turned out to be the best place for the piano, and the room was warm.

"The wine. . . . I am warmer, already." She looked up at me, her green eyes wide. "You are good to me . . . to us."

"After . . . everything . . . you say that. . . ." I swallowed. It was still hard. "I love you."

A smile crinkled her lips. "Dutch you are. For all your words, *mon ami,* some you find difficult."

She was right. I did.

"The wine?" Her voice was softer now when she spoke, softer than when we had first met, but neither of us needed to discuss that.

I ducked downstairs—there was a relatively new case of Bajan red, a mountain Sebastopol. Probably not so good as a really good French wine, but better than anything else, and the French hadn't been producing good wines for the last fifteen years or so, not since Ferdinand had reduced the French population by more than 30 percent in his infamous March.

Once I'd opened the bottle, I brought her a glass, with my chocolates. They were the fourth box, but how would I have known?

"Here is the wine . . . and my small offering." I didn't tell her about the roses up in the bedroom. She'd see those later.

"Good." She smiled, and her eyes smiled with her mouth. "French it is not—"

"But almost as good," I finished. Llysette would never admit that Columbian wine would match that of her vanquished homeland, but we could laugh about it—about the wine, not about her terrors, nor the torture under Ferdinand, nor the hard years after.

"Almost."

I sat down beside her on the new sofa—we'd redecorated a great deal in the six months since we'd been married—with my own glass of Sebastopol.

Outside, the ice pellets turned into snow, and the wind gusted. I eased back to enjoy warmth of the stove, of the Sebastopol, of the coming weekend, and mostly of Llysette.

2

THE ice and snow that had intermittently fallen over the weekend and into Monday had long since vanished under Tuesday's sun. Only a light frost remained on the browned grasses of my neighbor Benjamin's fields as I drove the Stanley across the gray waters of the River Wijk and into Vanderbraak Centre just before nine on Wednesday morning. Llysette and I were cutting it close, since she had a student at nine o'clock for applied voice.

"Mercredi, c'est le jour du diable." Llysette had come to speak a bit more French in the months since we had been married, and I wondered how much strain always speaking English had been.

"The midweek peak," I agreed.

"I talk, and they listen, and still I must beat the notes. Nod they do, but understand they do not."

The ever-present Constable Gerhardt waved and smiled above his sweeping mustaches as we slowed on our way around the square that held the Watch building, the Dutch Reformed church, the post centre, and McArdles', the sole full grocery emporium in the area. Then we were past the good constable and headed uphill toward the Music and Theatre building.

"Lunch at Delft's, right after noon?" I asked.

"Mais oui, mon cher." At least I got a dazzling smile before the more somber look clouded her face as she turned toward the Music and Theatre building and her hapless, and probably clueless, young Dutch student.

Dutch students were no different from any other students in thinking that mere mental effort should effect physical results. It doesn't work that way in singing—or in anything—but that's a lesson that almost never can be passed from generation to generation but must be learned the hard way. As Llysette kept saying, "The head, it is smart, but the muscles are dumb." But all too many students didn't want to put in the mental and physical effort required to train dumb muscles.

Before I headed to my own office, I stopped outside Samaha's to pick up the *Asten Post-Courier*. While "Samaha's Factorium and Emporium" had been on the corner opposite the bridge for well over a century, so had far too much of the inventory. The proprietor, one Louis Samaha, not only refused to answer to anything except "Louie," but he was also the only shopkeeper left in town who had individual narrow paper boxes for his special customers. I continued to have a fondness for some traditions, even as I had watched them unravel all around me.

The decor of Samaha's consisted of dark wooden counters and rough-paneled walls that contained fine cracks older than any current living beings in Vanderbraak Centre, perhaps even older than some of the ghosts. The modern glow panels in the ceiling had so far failed to shed light on the store's history or the inventory in the deeper counter shelves.

I ignored the bakery counter and the breads and rolls heavy enough to sink a dreadnought or serve as ballast for a dirigible and pulled my paper from its slot, fifth down in the first row, right below the empty slot labeled: "Derkin." In the three years since I had returned to Vanderbraak Centre, I'd seen Mister Derkin exactly twice.

I left my dime on the counter, since Louie was nowhere to be seen. Although the *Post-Courier* was only seven cents, I kept giving Louie the other three as a fee for saving back issues for me when I was away from Vanderbraak Centre.

The left front-page story above the fold was a rehash—more on the continuing political fight between landing rights at the Asten aerodrome between turbos and dirigibles. I sighed in spite of myself. Some things didn't seem to change.

I folded the paper into my case and climbed back into the Stanley for the short drive to the upper faculty car park, not the lower one where I had dropped Llysette, but the larger one closer to my office. The old Dutch Republican house had been converted to the Offices of the Natural Resources Department—rather, I corrected myself, the expanded and renamed Department of Political and Natural Resource Sciences—dear David's political coup and brainchild.

As I eased the steamer up Highland Street, the clock on the post centre struck nine. Three spaces remained, all in the back row, but what was I to expect when the car park only contained four dozen places and nearly twice that number of faculty lived outside of walking distance? The latecomers parked where they could, but not, of course, around the square. Dean Er Recchus and the town elders had squabbled about that before the magistrates on at least two occasions, and that might recur. The dean's memoranda on the issue threatened to revoke faculty parking privileges for any faculty member so desperate as to occupy a space designed for those shopping at the establishments around the square.

I vented the Stanley before locking it and walking to my office. Gilda, the department secretary, glanced up, her frizzy black hair pulled back into a bun. "Marriage continues to agree with you, Doktor Eschbach. You aren't haunting our halls every waking moment." Her eyes flicked to David's closed and dark door. Gilda never was warm or polite when David was around, but in her position I probably wouldn't have been either.

"I continue to be fortunate." That was true, in more ways than one, and what else could I say?

A single message graced my box, from the esteemed chairman, the most honorable Doktor David Doniger—a reminder of next Monday's faculty meeting, on the special memo paper he used as chairman.

Once in my office, I read through the *Asten Post-Courier* from front to back. Two stories intrigued me particularly. The first was about the reaction of Quebec's president to a fishing rights issue:

Montreal (WNS). Pres. Alphonse Duval announced an "agreement in principle" with New France over the allocation of catches from the Grand Banks fisheries in return for approval of the sale of three New French Santa Anna class frigates to the Navy of Quebec. The frigates are currently under construction at the San Diego, Baja, shipyards.

Jacques Chirac, leader of the opposition Democratic Republicans, denounced the proposed agreement as an abrogation of Quebecois sovereignty over the Grand Banks and an invitation to a Columbian invasion.

Columbian Defense Minister Holmbek refused direct

comment, but Defense Ministry sources indicated that the idea of military action to deal with fisheries matters was "absurd."

The Alliance for World Peace asked Speaker Hartpence to begin an investigation into the charges that the frigate sale agreement was leaked to the media in order to obtain support for an increase in the Columbian military budget for the coming fiscal year.

For some reason, the article bothered me, but I couldn't say why. I read the WNS story again but still couldn't identify why it bothered me. The second story bothered me, too, but for a different reason:

Asten (RPI). The latest development in the Israel Ishmaad murder case is a ghost—the ghost of the child Ishmaad allegedly mutilated and murdered.

Asten City Prosecutor Fridrich Devol yesterday used testimony from Dr. Fitzgerald Warren as key support for his argument that Ishmaad had tortured his six-year-old stepson for an extended period of time. . . .

"In simple terms," said Devol, "young children raised in a normal and loving atmosphere do not develop an awareness of death until they are much older, usually between eight and twelve. The fact that this boy barely six years old became a ghost is the strongest possible evidence that he had been repeatedly beaten, that he was aware of the possibility of death. Not only was he killed, but he was robbed of his childhood long before his death. . . ."

Those close to defense attorney Edward Quiddik have suggested that Devol's argument is "psychological poppycock with no basis in fact" and predict that Quiddik will address the issue with a battery of poltergeistic experts.

The prosecuting attorney's argument made sense to me. Ghosts came from violent knowledgeable death. My son Waltar had lived for nearly ten minutes on that bloody Federal District street, bleeding from bullets meant for me, and he'd been nearly eleven—and he'd never become a ghost. Elspeth had died instantly, too quickly to become a ghost, and, then, I wished I had too. I'd had to learn to live again, and every day, Llysette—and Carolynne—taught me a little more.

At the knock at my half-open door, I set down the paper. "Come in."

"Johan." Wilhelm Mondriaan still remained the junior member of the expanded department. The shirttail relative of the painter continued to inform all who conversed at length with him, in some fashion or another, that he had received his doctorate from The University—Virginia. He had trouble understanding that I had ceased to worship unquestioningly at that or any other altar of higher education, Thomas Jefferson notwithstanding.

"Yes?"

"You know that David is going to bring up the question of putting a zero cap on registrations on Natural Resources Three B?" Mondriaan eased into my not-terribly-capacious office.

Natural Resources Three B was officially the ecology of wetlands course that all the students hated, because none of them wanted a detailed environmental rationale for preserving wetlands when most of them had a tradition of either developing, filling, or "reclaiming" wetlands. The question of what course to cut back on always came back to wetlands ecology. I just sighed. "Are we back to that again?"

"I do not believe we ever left it." Regner Grimaldi stood in the door, chipper as always, in another of his European-cut suits, this one a dark gray chalk stripe accented by a maroon cravat. "Our Doktor David has the persistence of Ferdinand." Young Grimaldi had little love for Ferdinand, and I suppose I wouldn't have either, not if my father had died under the panzerwagens when Ferdinand had contemptuously disregarded the older Grimaldi's surrender of Monaco.

"I take it that our honored chair is elsewhere this morning?"

"He is having another tooth faultlessly capped," added Grimaldi. "But he will return . . . both to us and the elimination of Three B."

"Unlike Gessler to Singapore." Mondriaan attempted to cultivate a rumbling bass, but a mild baritone was all he could manage.

How could Gessler have returned to Singapore after Chung Kuo had thrown three million crack troops into the peninsula? The Aussies hadn't let Columbia use Subic Bay as a staging area against the Chinese assault, not with both Japan and Chung Kuo exerting pressure. Of course, how long Australia itself, let alone its Philippine Protectorate, would last was another question these days.

Mondriaan looked at Grimaldi. "What is the festive occasion?"

"Festive? This is conservative for me, Wilhelm." Grimaldi laughed. "Johan? Will you say anything about the wetlands course?"

"Me? The chairman's favorite bête noire?"

They both waited.

"I'll make my usual point that wetlands are the pivot point of any integrated ecology . . . and I suppose that will get a grudging acceptance that one section will be taught in the spring, and you two can fight over it."

They both nodded.

"I need to finish preparing for my ten o'clock." Grimaldi vanished from the doorway.

"You are the only one Doktor Doniger must listen to," Mondriaan said before he left. "Like the founders had to heed Jefferson. You do know that, do you not?"

I didn't know anything of the sort, only that David and I always clashed and probably always would and that he had the dean on his side. I wasn't sure who or what was on my side, except two assimilated ghosts and Llysette. Having Carolynne as part of my soul hadn't been too bad, but the ghost of justice I'd created with my equipment was sometimes pretty hard for someone trying to deal with departmental politics that had little reason and less justice.

In fact, the whole ghosting and de-ghosting business was as confusing as departmental politics. Supposedly, Heisler, the Austro-Hungarian scientist, had developed a system for systematically removing part of the electronic ego field that comprised the human spirit. Of course, that was the part of the spirit that became a ghost under the condition of knowledgeable violent death. Then, under contract to the Spazi, Branston-Hay, the late Babbage researcher at Vanderbraak State, had developed a similar de-ghosting technology that could either remove the entire spirit from a live person, rendering him a zombie, or destroy any disembodied spirit that had become a ghost. A technology that could turn a healthy individual into a zombie wasn't something I'd wanted to let loose on the world—and I hadn't.

After Branston-Hay's untimely "accidental" death—because the Spazi had discovered he was also selling his knowledge under the table to President Armstrong's covert operation—I ended up as the sole possessor of all his files on the subject. Of course, I'd had to meddle, not that either the Spazi or the president had given me any choice, and matters had gone from less than sanguine to far worse.

Reminiscing over what Llysette and I had survived wasn't going to get papers corrected. So, in the relative quiet that followed my colleagues' departure, I spent the next hour correcting quizzes from Tuesday's natural resources intro course—and trying not to think about the ghost of the child in Asten. I muttered a lot with almost every paper, especially when I discovered that a third of the class couldn't define the water table.

The wind had picked up when I left the office to cross the grounds to Smith, enough that the two university zombies toiling there—Gertrude and Hector—were having trouble raking the fallen and soggy leaves. I smiled at Gertrude, cheerfully struggling with her rake, perhaps because I still recalled her reaction to *Heinrich Verruckt* the spring before. Zombies were those unfortunate beings who had lost that part of their soul that would have been a ghost, or that part of their soul had left them prematurely to become a ghost. Zombies weren't supposed to feel strong emotions, but Gertrude had sobbed, zombie or no zombie.

Hector inclined his head, and I offered him a smile. Hector, one of the few somber zombies, nodded, but it wasn't quite a smile.

Wednesday was usually a long day. So were Mondays and Fridays, since I taught the same schedule on all three days, but Wednesday felt longer, particularly with my eleven o'clock Environmental Economics 2A class. Smythe 203 was always hot, even in midwinter, and Mondriaan didn't help. He had the room before me, and he made sure it was like an oven. Usually I didn't even have to open the windows because the students had done it first. That was about all they were good for on some days.

The blank looks on the faces of those in the front row indicated what kind of day it was going to be.

I forced a smile. "Mister Rastaal, what are the principal diseconomies of a coal-fired power plant, and how can a market economy ensure that they become real costs of production?"

"Ah, Doktor Eschbach . . . I was on the korfball trip, and somehow, I didn't bring the text. . . ."

I didn't even sigh. "Miss Raalte?"

"Doktor . . . the cost of coal mining?"

"Mister Nijkerk?"

"The . . . ah . . . um . . . cost of transporting the coal to the power plant?"

"Miss Rijssen?"

Elena Rijssen just looked at the weathered desktop in front of her. I had to call on Martaan deVaal—one of the few who read the material faithfully.

All this came after an entire class dealing with external dis-economies. Of course, the class had been two weeks earlier, but I tended to forget that retention of material for more than one period was not a strength of the students at Vanderbraak State University. Or any university, I suspected. Why were there so few who really sought an education?

The combination of difference engines and the videolink had given them all the mistaken idea that everything could be looked up and nothing needed to be retained.

After deVaal finished I did sigh. Loudly. "We discussed external diseconomies two weeks ago." I walked to the chalkboard and wrote the question out. Actually, I printed it, because my handwriting is abysmal. "A two-page essay answering this question is due at the next class. It will be counted the same as a quiz."

A low muttering groan suffused the classroom, and several students glared at Mister Rastaal and Miss Raalte. One glared at de-Vaal, as if having the temerity to read the material were a mortal sin. I felt sorry for deVaal, but not enough to let the rest of the class go.

"Now . . . Mister Zwolle . . . would you please define the total pollutant load from a coal-fired power plant?"

Most of them didn't know all of that answer, either, except for sulfur dioxide and carbon dioxide.

It was a very long class.

Afterward, I managed to scurry across the windswept grounds of the university, glad to see that Gertrude and Hector had abandoned their raking, and down toward the square. The post centre clock had struck twelve just as I reached the door.

"Your table is ready, Doktor Eschbach." Victor motioned me ahead of several others and toward the table Llysette preferred—close to the woodstove. I was looking at the wine list when my lady arrived, clutching not only a purse but also a large, brown, bulky envelope.

"Good afternoon, Doktor duBoise." I couldn't help grinning at the ritual as I stood.

"Afternoon, I must concede, Herr Doktor Eschbach. And it is good. . . ."

"If it is good . . . some wine to celebrate?"

At the sound of the word "wine," Victor appeared.

"The chocolate, today, I think. And the soup with the croissants." She smiled.

"Chocolate, too," I decided. "The special, chicken and artichoke pasta."

Victor shrugged at our rejection of the wine but bowed and took the menus.

"What is your news? The envelope?"

"This. . . . It arrived just before noon. I cannot believe it."

"Just now? This noon?"

She smiled and nodded again. "An invitation, a contract . . . to sing in the great concert hall of Deseret. Six weeks from now . . . because Dame Brightman has been hospitalized. That is what I have been asked. Did you know that it is one of the largest . . . perhaps like the Arena di Verona. . . ."

I'd never heard of the Arena di Verona, and my face showed it.

"Perhaps, it is not that large . . . but it is certainly as large as Covent Garden." Her eyes glazed over for a moment, and I wondered which singer within that body—Carolynne the ghost soprano or Llysette the former songbird of fallen France—was reminiscing.

"Deseret?"

"The man who came to see me sing—the one in the ancient coat. . . . I think he signed the letter."

"Are they paying?" I asked, all too imprudently, but lately all too many organizations in New Bruges had been requesting that Llysette perform either gratis or for nominal fees.

"You, you should look." She thrust the stack of papers at me.

So I did, while she edged her chair slightly closer to the wood-stove and watched. Being married hadn't made her any less susceptible to the chill of New Bruges, but perhaps more willing to let me know. The cover letter praised her performance in New Bruges and extended the invitation to perform in Great Salt Lake City. It was signed by a Bishop Jacob Jensen, on behalf of the Prophets' Foundation for the Arts in Deseret.

I'd never cared much for the Saints of Deseret, even as I'd admired their ability to carve an independent nation out in the western wilderness between New France and Columbia. These days . . . Deseret scarcely qualified as a wilderness, not with its coal and iron, its synthetic fuels technology developed from the northern European refugees, and with its carefully guarded monopoly on naturally colored cottons that needed no dyes.

The political problem was that polygamy, even as restrained as it had become in the last few generations, had not set well with Columbia from the beginning. Nor had Deseret done much to allay my concerns about their not-always-so-environmental actions, but I tried not to let my past as a Subminister for Environmental Protection intrude upon Llysette's career.

The contract seemed generous, very generous—$10,000 for three performances at the Salt Palace Concert Hall and two master classes for the University of Deseret. A $5,000 cheque—Columbian dollars—was included as a retainer, drawn on the Bank of the Federal District of Columbia, plus all transportation, including the offer of a first-class cabin on the *Breckinridge,* of the Columbian Speaker Line.

There was another sheet: "Standard Requirements for Female Performers in Deseret." I read it and then handed it to Llysette.

"*Mais non!* Too much it is. . . . I must have a husband . . . as a . . ."

"Chaperon?" I suggested.

"And the gowns . . . no uncovered arms above the elbow, and the covered shoulders? Do they come out of . . . a seraglio?" She jammed the requirements sheet back into my hand. "This . . . I will not do!"

"You certainly don't have to. I did hear somewhere that the Salt Palace Concert Hall is the largest and most prestigious concert hall in Deseret," I said quietly. "If not in the western part of North America."

"My own words you do not have to throw at me." Llysette thrust out her lower lip in the exaggerated pout that indicated she wasn't totally serious . . . not totally.

Victor hovered in the background with the chocolate, and I nodded. The two mugs of heavy and steaming chocolate were followed with Llysette's soup and my pasta and with the hot, plain, and flaky croissants.

I took a sip of the chocolate. "And you could have a recital gown made to their standards from the retainer cheque—"

"Johan!" sputtered Llysette over her mug.

"You did tell me that once your gowns—"

"You mock me!"

"I am sorry. I didn't mean that. I was teasing you, but . . . sometimes you are even more serious than I am." I offered a long face, and that got a bit of a smile. The pasta wasn't up to Victor's normal standards, too heavy by half, but the sauce was good, and I was hungry.

So was Llysette, and we ate silently for a time.

The contract for Llysette bothered me, though. Yes, she had

been one of the top divas in France before it fell to the Austro-Hungarians. Yes, there were few singers in Columbia who could match the performance I had heard on Friday. And yes, the rate offered was probably even a shade cheap for a world-class diva. And yes, it would do her ego, her reputation, her status at the university, and her pocketbook good. But no one had been offering Llysette contracts, ostensibly because of her unsettled status. Why now?

Admittedly, she'd finally gotten her citizenship and gotten married, both of which made her more acceptable to Deseret, but how would the Saints have known that? Or had someone alerted them to it? And why?

None of it made sense, and from the time I'd been a junior pilot in the Republic Naval Air Corps I'd known that coincidences just didn't occur.

"You are thoughtful."

"I wondered about the contract . . . why it arrived now."

Llysette shrugged, then smiled. "Perhaps . . ."

"Perhaps what?"

"You recall the seminars last summer?"

"The ones where all those singers came in?" I did remember them. We'd barely been married a month when dozens of young singers had arrived for Dean Er Recchus's MusikFest, and I'd barely seen Llysette for two weeks.

"A young man there was from the University of Deseret. He was a Saint missionary, but a good bass. The arrangement of the Perkins piece 'Lord of Sand,' he provided that, and I wrote Doktor Perkins. You remember, *n'est-ce-pas?*"

I nodded. Perkins had written a note back, sending several other arrangements and professing enthusiasm about her singing his work.

"This Doktor Perkins, he is well-known everywhere."

"Well known enough to get you a contract, or to want to?"

"*Non* . . . but could he not recommend?"

A noted Saint composer—yes, he could recommend, and the Saints were so hidebound they probably had sent someone to double-check. I nodded. Put in that light, it made some sense, especially with a performer hospitalized. But I wondered. Then, after what we'd been through, I wondered about everything.

I wanted to chide myself. After everything we'd been through? Llysette had been through far more—imprisonment and torture under Ferdinand after the fall of France, a struggle to get to Columbia even after the interventions of the Japanese ambassador who had loved opera and Llysette's performances, and then the unspoken Spazi injunctions against her performing too publicly.

Llysette glanced out through the window toward the post centre clock, then took a last sip of chocolate.

"Late it is. Notes . . . more notes must I beat."

"Don't you have . . . the good one?"

"Marlena vanHoff . . . she is a joy . . . *mais apres.* . . ." Llysette shook her head.

I motioned to Victor, thrust the banknotes upon him, and we were off—me to prepare for my two o'clock and Llysette for yet another lesson of studio voice.

The wind was stiffer and colder, foreshadowing another storm, probably of ice, rather than snow, the way the winter was beginning.

3

LYSETTE didn't run with me before breakfast, and she wasn't exactly a morning person, even on Saturdays when we slept in—except sleeping in for me was eight o'clock, still a relatively ungodly hour for Llysette.

After the strenuous efforts required during the previous year, I'd vowed I'd never let myself lapse back into the sedentary professor I'd almost become after I'd been involuntarily retired as Subminister for Environmental Protection. Of course, my nervous overeating didn't help. Still, at times, it hadn't seemed that long since I'd been a flying officer in the Republic Air Corps, and my assignments in the Sedition Prevention and Security Service had certainly required conditioning. Especially with Llysette beside me, though, it took great willpower to lever myself out of bed, not that I was sleepy.

But I ran—hard—up past Benjamin's frosted fields and well over the top of the hill through the second-growth forest that was beginning to resemble what had existed when the Dutch had reached the area from New Amsterdam.

I was still sweating long after I got back to the house and kitchen, even somewhat by the time the coffee and chocolate were ready and I called up the stairs, "Your coffee awaits you, young woman!"

"You wake too early, Johan." After a time, she stumbled down the steps wrapped in a thick natural cotton robe, disarrayed, yet lovely, and slumped into the chair, looking blankly at the coffee.

"I've already been—"

"Johan . . ."

I sipped my chocolate, then started on finishing up preparing the rest of breakfast—some scones, with small omelets, not exactly Dutch, but tasty, and my cooking has always been eclectic.

"Johan?" Llysette did not speak until she had nearly finished her omelet and half a scone.

"Yes."

"For this concert, I will need a number of things."

"I know. We'd agreed that we'd go down to Borkum today, do the shopping, and have dinner there."

She smiled.

Even after the two years we'd known each other, Llysette still had trouble believing that men—or man, in my case—would carry out promises, despite the fact that I always tried to. Most of the time I did, and I was working on those few times when I got sidetracked.

After I showered and dressed, and while Llysette was finishing dressing, I took the Stanley down to Vanderbraak Centre to pick up the paper and check the post. Mr. Derkin was nowhere to be seen at Samaha's, nor was Louie.

The post centre was another matter. I saw the unmarked brown envelope, postmarked from the Federal District, and my guts churned. I'd never wanted to see another one of those.

Maurice grinned from the window, and I forced a smile as I thumbed through the other envelopes, including the electric bill from NBEI and the bill from New Bruges Wireline. They always arrived on the same day, without fail.

"You always grin when the bills arrive, you reprobate," I chastised him.

"And you never give us credit for the good things, Herr Doktor."

"Such as?"

"The chocolates from your mother and the letters from your family."

"Few enough those are, and why should you get the credit?"

"You're a hard, hard man, Doktor." He grinned again.

I had to smile back despite the tension that gripped me.

Out in the Stanley, I opened the plain envelope. As I had feared, it contained only media clips, and I'd have to read them carefully to determine from their content whether they came from my former employer—the Spazi—or from the office of the President. At least, Deputy Minister vanBecton had sent his clippings under the imprint of International Import Services, PLC. That had given me some warning. The new head of Spazi operations was Deputy Minister Jerome, but I'd only met him in passing years ago. My latest separation from the Spazi had been handled through Charles Asquith, Speaker Hartpence's top aide.

In any case, the clips were less than good news, although I waited to read them until I parked the Stanley outside our own car barn. Llysette's Reo was in the other side. I'd had it thoroughly overhauled and the burners tuned after we'd been married.

I sat in the drive and read through the clippings, all from the Federal District's *Columbia Post-Dispatch:*

Great Salt Lake City, Deseret (DNS). In presiding over the Saints' Annual Conference on the Family, First Counselor Cannon highlighted the church's concerns about the role of culture in developing morals: "We must provide to our youth the finest examples of culture that uphold the moral fabric of our society. Excellence in art must include moral excellence, not mere technical artistry."

Cannon, owner of the Deseret media empire that includes the *Deseret Star, Deseret Business,* and Unified Deseret VideoLink, is the youngest First Speaker of the Church of Latter-Day Saints since the founding of Deseret. He was selected as a counselor 1988, and he has been one of the Twelve Apostles since 1983.

There was more, but it all related to the rest of the Conference on the Family and the emphasis on the need for upholding the "traditional" values, including, I suspected, that of polygamy.

Great Salt Lake City, Deseret (WNS). Former First Diva of old France, Llysette duBoise, will appear in place of Dame Sarah Brightman on November 23, 24, and 25. DuBoise, now a Columbian citizen and performer, is a noted academic as well as a performer. . . . Dame Brightman was hospitalized two weeks ago with an undisclosed ailment. . . .

Doktor duBoise, recently married to a former Subminister of Natural Resources of the Republic of Columbia, boasts an international reputation for both her technique and her sheer vocal artistry. She performed extensively in Europe prior to the fall of France, and recent concerts in Columbia, according to Jacob Jensen, Director of Salt

Palace, have confirmed that "her artistry not only remains unchallenged, but is greater than ever. We are indeed fortunate to be able to secure her performance. . . ."

The article ended with almost a listing of Llysette's credentials, some of it clearly lifted from her recital program. She might be pleased to have been listed as a former First Diva, although I wasn't sure she actually had been—unless it had been while she'd been imprisoned and tortured, simply because the others had fled or been murdered by Archduke Ferdinand's troops.

Colorado Junction, Deseret (RPI). Upstream from this historic Saint fortress today, Deseret's Secretary of Resource Development christened the second phase of the Colorado Power Project, a linked series of three dams designed to provide water for the industrial development spawned by the Deseret Synthetic Fuels Corporation. . . .

In a prepared statement, Premier Escobar-Moire of New France stated that he was "confident" that Deseret would continue to abide by the terms of the Riverine Compact, including the provisions relating to water quality and quantity. . . .

"Deseret risks ecological disaster by this continued unbridled exploitation of river resources," commented F. Henrik Habicht II, the Columbian Deputy Minister of Natural Resources, following a ministerial meeting at the Capitol. . . . Habicht specifically highlighted the Saint diversions of the Snake River as well as the Green and Colorado rivers.

I shook my head and went into the house and upstairs, where I handed the envelope with the clippings to Llysette. She was doing her hair. "These arrived in the post."

Her eyes widened as she read. "First Diva . . . not I. *Mais, ca.* . . . That I will not deny, not now." Then she paused and looked at me. "You said . . ."

"I did. I didn't ask for these. No one has wired me. They're all about you, and about Deseret." I laughed, harshly. "I guess we've been scrutinized a little more closely than I'd thought. You're now national news. Perhaps you should offer a copy to Dierk."

"Rather I would send one to the dean." Llysette's eyes glittered, and I recalled a time when I'd faced that look—and a Colt-Luger—across my difference engine. Then, of course, she'd still been partially ghost-conditioned—a result of Ferdinand's agents' tender treatment. I'd been lucky to escape with a shoulder wound.

"You could do that. She'd probably use it to pry funding out of someone, but you might actually benefit." I paused. "We'll still need to go to Asten sometime this week to start things rolling on your passport."

"A passport, that would be nice. . . ."

"You're a citizen now, and after that story, you won't have any trouble."

"That I should not." She frowned, then pirouetted in the gray woolen suit with the bright green blouse.

"You look wonderful."

"Good. I am almost ready."

While Llysette finished straightening up the bedroom and selecting jewelry to wear, I went down to the study and sat in front of my SII custom electrofluidic difference engine to squeeze in a few minutes on the business of teaching. I called up the text of the Environmental Politics 2B midterm exam that I'd given the previous spring. The second essay question had been a disaster: "Discuss the rationale for Speaker Aspinall's decision to impose excise taxes on internal combustion engines and petroleum derivatives."

The answers had been dismal, ranging from increased revenue to political payoffs—all general and none showing any understanding of either the readings or the class discussion. I'd used a lot of red ink, and I wondered if it had just been me.

It all seemed simple enough to me. Why was it so hard for them to understand that the fuel taxes weren't enacted for either environmental or revenue reasons—but for strategic ones? Speaker Aspinall never met a tree he didn't first consider as lumber or a coal mine that he didn't embrace. He'd pushed the taxes because Ferdinand and the elder Maximilian—not the idiot son who was de-Gaulle's puppet—would have strangled Columbia if we'd ever become too dependent on foreign oil and because it was clear Deseret wasn't about to ship its excess oil and the liquid fuels from its synthetic fuels program to Columbia, no matter what the price, not when New France would pay more and allow transhipment on the Eccles Pipeline for sale to Chung Kuo.

Less than a generation later, my Dutch students were claiming the taxes had been needed for revenue when Aspinall's government had run enormous surpluses.

I looked out the window into the gray and icy Saturday morning, listening as Llysette came down the stairs.

"Johan, a steamer arrives."

"Could you get it? I'll be there in a minute." I saved the question for later thought and flicked off the difference engine.

"Mais oui. That I can do." I could hear the door open. "Yes?"

A feeling like doom looked over me, along with a sense that the part of my soul that was Carolynne clawed in frustration to get out. With that feeling, I ran toward the front door, knocking back the desk chair and literally careening off the wall.

Llysette was faster. The heavy door with its ancient, almost silvered leaded glass pane shuddered closed, simultaneously with the thin whining of a ghosting device that ripped at my soul, trying to tear it away from my physical body. The whining died into silence, and we were both still whole, unzombied, perhaps because of the leaded glass or the door's thickness or both . . . or our previous encounters with ghosting technology.

I held her for a moment, and she held me—as we both shuddered.

"That . . . like the awful . . . what . . ."

"I know." And I did. The feeling was so similar to the time that I had almost used the ghost disassociator Bruce had built for me on Llysette—except the lodestone and the mirror had meant we'd both got a dosage—ghost-possessed, or enhanced. But the soul-shivering and shuddery feelings were the same.

I eased to the kitchen and peered out the side window.

A man stood there blank-faced—zombied. The dark gray steamer stood unattended in the drive.

We waited.

He stood—expressionless, still holding what looked to be a large box of chocolates.

After even more time, I went back to the door and opened it. The clean-shaven and dark-eyed fellow was clearly a zombie, his soul lifted by the device I knew remained inside the pseudo–box of chocolates.

"I'll take that," I said quietly. "Who are you?" I eased the chocolate box from his hands, the box that held some form of the technology that could tear souls from still-living humans.

"Joshua Korfman, sir." His voice held that flat zombie tone.

"Was anyone else with you?"

"No, sir."

"Do you have a gun?"

"Yes, sir."

"I'll take that, too." I paused, not really wanting my prints on it. "Set it down there."

The gun was a standard Colt, not a Colt-Luger. I could sense Llysette's wince behind me. The last thing—the very last thing—I wanted to do was wire Hans Waetjen about another zombie at our house. But there wasn't much choice, not as I saw it.

"Would you call Chief Waetjen?" I asked Llysette.

"I should call?"

"Do you know what he would say if I called?"

"That I can guess. The chief . . . what should I tell him?"

"The truth . . . just not all of it. Tell him that the man raised something and you slammed the door and called and I came running. Then we waited."

"And the box?"

"The box is something that the chief doesn't need to know about. The gun is sufficient."

So Llysette called, and the three of us waited . . . after I tucked the box away in the hidden wall chamber under the lodestone in the study.

The chief arrived in the black Watch car, along with Constable Gerhardt, he of the ample mustaches and thin, always-cheerful face.

"Doktor Eschbach." The square-faced and gray-haired chief snorted. "Why do strange things always happen around you? Why couldn't you have retired somewhere else?"

"This is the family home," I pointed out, although it had only been in the family for two generations before me, and that was a short tradition compared to many in Vanderbraak Centre. "Where else would I go?"

"Anywhere," snorted the chief before he turned to the zombie. "What were you doing here?"

"A man gave me five hundred dollars to kill the people who lived here. Something happened."

"What happened?" asked Waetjen.

"I don't know. I remember reaching for my gun, and she slammed the door. That was when it happened."

"What happened?"

"I don't know." Korfman's face and voice remained expressionless.

"Disassociative ghosting," I suggested. "Strong mental block against murder, but not conscious."

"Eschbach . . . I know about that."

"Sorry."

"Did you ever see these people before?"

"No."

"How did you know whom to shoot?"

"The man showed me a picture."

That bothered me—more than a little—since there weren't any pictures of the two of us together, except for the wedding pictures, and we'd given none to anyone, except for the pair we'd sent to my aunt and mother in Schenectady. They'd come to the wedding, but the pictures weren't ready until later. But someone had a picture.

Waetjen glanced toward me.

"There aren't any pictures except our wedding pictures, and no one has any except us and my mother."

"There wasn't one in the paper?"

I nodded. "I hadn't thought about that. It wasn't very good."

"Good enough for this." The chief glared at me, as if it were my fault that someone had been dispatched to kill us, then motioned to Gerhardt. "Drive his steamer down to the post. Use your gloves and don't touch anything. The wheel won't have any prints but his anyway."

We watched as the two steamers departed.

After the chief left, I turned to my dark-haired soprano. "I'd like to invite my friend Bruce up for dinner as soon as we can. Would that be all right with you? You don't have any night rehearsals yet."

"*Mais oui* . . . and you think he could help with . . . what here has happened?"

"I want him to look at that device, and I'm afraid that they'll be watching me more closely." I shrugged. "I don't even know who 'they' are." I thought about the clippings from the Federal District. "With some of those clippings I've received, it could be any one of a number of different groups involved." What I didn't say was that my past experience had taught me that once one group got involved, so did another, and often another.

"Johan . . . with you, nothing it is simple."

I bent over and kissed her cheek. "Nor with you, my dear."

I picked up the handset and wired Bruce. It seemed like I always wired or saw Bruce when I needed technical support. Then, he'd been the only one I'd been able to trust when I'd been doing field-work and he had been one of the designers in Spazi technical support. He'd been smart and left the Spazi early. Because of Elspeth's—my first wife's—medical condition, I'd stayed . . . and paid dearly. And in the end, the bullets meant for me had taken both Waltar and Elspeth.

"LBI Difference Designers," answered Bruce.

"Doktor Leveraal, this is your friendly environmental professor."

"I should have guessed. It's been one of those days." There was a pause. "What can I do for you this time? No more insurance, please?"

Bruce remained an "insurer" of sorts, since he had all the files on the ghosting-destruction research project that had almost led to my and Llysette's deaths—along with a large number of other un-explained deaths, zombies, and "accidents" across Columbia, espe-cially in the Federal District and in Vanderbraak Centre. He also had the files on my not-so-well-known technology that could repli-cate the electric free fields that defined a ghost. Meddling with that, when Llysette had tried to kill me with her Colt-Lugar, had led to our own "ghost possession."

"A dinner invitation, for you to meet my lovely bride."

"That makes you sound almost human, Johan. I won't ask any more. When?"

"I'd hoped this week. Llysette doesn't have night rehearsals until the week after, and then it's going to get hectic. She's been asked to do a big concert in Deseret—Great Salt Lake City."

"You're going with her."

"There isn't any choice. She's female, and they're Saints."

Beside me, Llysette grimaced.

"Tuesday, Thursday, or Friday. Monday and Wednesday nights I'm the one who stays late."

"Tuesday?"

"I was afraid of that. I did want to meet the lady, and your cuisine is superb, but I worry about the technical details."

"What can I say?" I temporized, knowing everything I said was probably being recorded somewhere.

"I'll see you on Tuesday. What time?"

"Seven. I could make it later."

"Seven is fine. Have a pleasant weekend, Johan."

"I will. And thank you."

"Not yet." With a laugh he was gone.

I set down the wireset and turned to Llysette. "We might as well go down to Borkum and go shopping, as we had planned."

"After this?" asked Llysette. "After someone, they wanted to turn us into ghosts?"

"Do you have a better idea to get our minds off this? We've done what we can right now."

After a moment, she gave me a rueful headshake and nodded.

What else could we do?

4

MARIE Rijn shooed us out of our own house that Tuesday, but I was glad she had decided to stay on as my housecleaner, even after Llysette and I had married, because she kept it Dutch-spotless, and for me or Llysette to have done the cleaning would have taken too much time out of schedules that were already too crowded—and getting worse.

"She likes me now, and she did not," observed Llysette as I waited for the Stanley's flash boiler to heat.

"She didn't know you."

"Different this is. I know, Johan."

I wasn't about to get into that argument. We were both different people from those we'd been a year earlier—far different—and I wasn't certain I had yet learned how different. Every so often, I still recalled a memory image that had to have been Carolynne's or had a shivery feeling about justice that hadn't come from me. How long would I continue to process such additions to my soul? Forever? Sometimes I wondered how I'd managed to add two ghosts to my soul and still survive, but I tried not to dwell on it.

"You are thinking. *C'est vrai, n'est-ce-pas?*"

"*Oui,*" I finally admitted.

She leaned over and kissed my cheek, and I eased the Stanley down the drive toward Deacon's Lane. Despite the clear winter blue sky, there was a crust of skim ice on the Wijk, and a chill wind gusted around the steamer as we crossed the river bridge into Vanderbraak Centre.

As I usually did, I followed my morning routine, dropping off Llysette and then getting my paper from Samaha's before heading back to my office and holding office hours, of which few-enough students availed themselves. While I waited for their infrequent appearances, I corrected papers or worked on various lectures.

Still, when I looked at my desk and the stack of quizzes remaining from the natural resources intro class, I had to repress a sigh. I knew that they would be depressing. So I looked out the window, toward the Music and Theatre building, and that wasn't terribly encouraging either.

Sometimes I do get premonitions, and I was definitely getting one about Llysette's concert engagement. After five years of relative obscurity, why was she being offered the same fees as a Dame Brightman? Or ones that were in the same general area, at least? And why were the Saints making the offer?

That line of speculation didn't go far, because the wireset chimed, and after another deep breath I answered. "Professor Eschbach."

"Professor Eschbach. Chief Waetjen here."

"Yes, Chief. Have you found out anything more?"

"Not much. Have you found anything out of place—or anything that your would-be killer might have left?"

"Might have left? I can't say that I've really looked, Chief. I could search if you want."

"The zombie died this morning—delayed sympathetic bloc, Doktor Jynkstra thinks. But he had mentioned a box of chocolates."

"Chocolates?"

"That's what he said."

"I haven't seen anything like that around lately. I mean I gave Llysette a box after the concert, and there were several she got from admirers, but he couldn't have meant that."

"Eschbach—I know what your real background is, even if no one ever told me. I don't like this sort of thing happening to Vanderbraak Centre."

"I don't either. I give you my word that I don't have the faintest idea what this is all about or even why. I was unconditionally released from all . . . past obligations by the highest possible authority." I paused. "If I learn of anything that will help you, I'll certainly let you know."

"Please do. And I'd appreciate it if you would let me be the judge of whether it is helpful."

"I understand, Chief." My understanding did not mean my agreement, not when two of his Watch officers had previously been suborned into trying to kill me.

Another of my lifelong friends—the chief. I stood and looked out, wondering which was worse, facing the chief or my upcoming intro course in natural resources. Or the ungraded quizzes.

I settled on the quizzes and eased myself behind the desk and took out the pen with the red ink. I needed it. About half of them still hadn't the faintest idea of why food/life complexity distribution was a pyramid or why ancient cities were invariably located on waterways or even of the total extent of the impact of natural resources on the development of human culture.

I groaned after the eleventh quiz. I shouldn't have, because when things get bad, they invariably get even worse. The wireset chimed again.

"Yes?"

"Doktor Eschbach," announced Gilda, "a Harlaan Oakes for you."

My stomach turned at the name—Ralston McGuiness's successor—in essence, the de facto chief of intelligence for President Armstrong, not that the president had too much more than a token operation, but it could be deadly enough, as I had already discovered once before. Had he sent the clippings I'd received on Saturday? Wouldn't Jerome have used the Spazi cover firm?

"Johan here."

"It's good to hear your voice, Johan. The president is having a reception for the arts next week, Wednesday, in fact, and you and your charming wife will be getting a formal invitation. I wanted to let you have some advance warning. He'd like very much to see you both there, and I'd hoped, since you will be in the Federal District, that perhaps we could get together for a few minutes."

"That might be possible," I answered warily.

"The president also wondered if Fräulein duBoise—she still is using that as her performing name, isn't she?—if she might be willing to sing one or two songs."

"I would have to ask her, but I wouldn't see any objection to it . . . so long as she can sing something already in her repertoire. A week's too short notice for something new."

"Anything she would like."

"Should I let you know? She'll need an accompanist and a run-through."

"We can arrange that for the morning of the reception. I can guarantee a good accompanist, perhaps Hatchet or Stewart or even Spillman. We could chat then."

That wasn't a request. I swallowed silently. "I'll wire you later today or in the morning and let you know what she'll sing."

"Good, Johan. Very good. The president would very much like that on the formal program."

"I'll let you know."

"Good. I look forward to seeing you on Wednesday next, Johan."

"I'll be there." As if I had any choice. When the head of government, ceremonial or not, wanted something, it usually meant trouble, especially now that President Armstrong was trying to re-create the stronger Executive Branch once envisioned by Hamilton and using more than a few questionable tactics in his struggle with Speaker Hartpence. Having dealt with the Speaker before, though, I liked his tactics and supporters even less than the president's.

I looked at the wireset. Problems had this way of compounding. If we were to be ready on Wednesday morning, that meant leaving the day before and staying in the Federal District Tuesday night. That brought to the fore another problem that I'd avoided. There are some things you don't want to think about—such as how to deal with former in-laws. But Judith and Eric had been good to me and stuck by me when no one else had. So . . . that was another thing I had to ask and work out with Llysette, and I wasn't exactly looking forward to that either.

With a deep breath and a glance at my watch—ten-fifteen—I picked up the wireset again and tapped out Llysette's extension.

"Is this the charming Llysette duBoise Eschbach? One Herr Doktor Eschbach would like to request your presence at luncheon. He would also like to inform you that word of your talent has spread far and wide."

"Johan . . . I beat notes today. Do not mock me."

"I'm not. You will be receiving an invitation to the big fall arts dinner at the Presidential Palace next week—a week from tomorrow. The president—President Armstrong—has requested that you sing two pieces of your choice at the annual Presidential Arts Awards dinner."

"I do not understand . . . ," she murmured.

"A friend called me. He thought you would like as much advance notice as possible."

"But . . . a week? *Impossible!* I cannot do that."

"I told them it would have to be from your current repertoire. They agreed."

"One year . . . they would forget me. Now, I am to perform before the president?"

"We can talk about it at lunch, but I thought you would like to know. I just got off the wireset."

"Johan . . . what is happening?"

I wished I knew. "You've been rediscovered. That's what. Enjoy it—you've suffered in obscurity all too long." That was all true, and certainly the way I felt, but my guts were still tight.

"Much you have to explain at . . . when we eat. I must beat more notes."

"I love you."

"You are sweet. *Au 'voir.*"

Sweet? That wasn't a word I'd have applied to myself. Devoted, responsible, even hardworking, but not sweet.

Next, I needed to find my hardworking and scheming chair, but Herr Doktor Doniger was out. Gilda promised to let him know I was looking for him. That meant I'd still have to run him down after lunch or after my two o'clock class.

Eleven o'clock came and, with it, Natural Resources 1A, and Mister Ferris.

"Professor Eschbach, will we have to know all of this material about the water cycle for the test?"

"No. About half, but I'm not telling you which half." I turned to the redhead in the third row. "Miss Zand, would you please explain the environmental rationale for avoiding the use of internal combustion vehicles?"

Miss Zand looked blank.

"Mister deRollen . . . why do we use steamers?"

"Professor, that's because when you use a burner, an external combustion engine, you can adjust it so it doesn't pollute, and you get mostly carbon dioxide and water, instead of carbon monoxide. That's really high for a petroleum-fueled internal combustion engine. . . ."

I tried not to smile too broadly, but you have to take your successes and the thoughtful students when you can.

Because of all the questions about the quizzes I handed back at the end of class to avoid too many questions, Llysette actually made it to Delft's before I did and was sipping chocolate.

"You look wonderful, Fräulein duBoise, or Frau Eschbach." And she did, in the gray suit and pale green blouse that she'd found in Asten in August.

"Frau Eschbach . . . in some ways, that I like."

She waited until we had ordered before she finally asked, "This performance . . . at the Presidential Palace . . . you were not joking?"

"No. Harlaan Oakes called me. He said you would be getting a formal invitation. I'll check the post centre after lunch."

"An accompanist . . . I know no one, and Johanna . . . on such short notice—"

"They promised either Hatchet, Spillman, or Stewart."

Llysette's mouth did open at that. "They . . . are . . ."

"The best, I'm sure. You'll have a rehearsal and run-through that morning. Ten o'clock. I'm supposed to give them the pieces, the arrangement details, this afternoon or tomorrow morning."

"Tomorrow morning." Llysette was back to sounding like a diva, if with the softer tone I associated with the overtones from Carolynne. She shook her head slowly. "So strange this is."

"Very strange," I agreed. "I have another problem." And I did— my former wife's sister and her husband.

"A problem?"

"Judith and Eric."

"And?" Llysette raised those dark and fine eyebrows. Was there a twinkle in them?

I wasn't sure, but I'd promised myself—and Llysette—to try not to hide anything. So I didn't. "I normally stay with them in the Federal District . . . but . . . Judith . . ."

"Elspeth's sister she was."

I nodded. "We could stay elsewhere."

Llysette frowned. "Strange it is. . . ." She shook her head. "With that we have no difficulties."

"You don't?" I wasn't sure I wouldn't have.

"Johan, we will stay with them, if they will have us. You are a dear man, and you asked, and that says much."

It said that I was probably stupid, but if I were going to be and stay honest with Llysette, I didn't have many choices, especially since I had a tendency to be so self-deceptive that there remained too many things I didn't catch.

My soup arrived, as did Llysette's croissant sandwich, and we ate quickly, with scattered bits of conversation.

"The dean . . . now she has declared that we will expand the graduate strings program . . . but we may have no more faculty positions."

"What about voice?"

"The voice area, that remains to be seen. Barton, he has returned from his . . ."

"Sabbatical," I supplied.

"And now he talks about a baritone and a contralto we should have." Llysette took a last sip of her chocolate.

"What does Dierk think?"

"Dr. Geoffries, he is of the opinion that there are no funds."

"He's probably got that right."

She glanced from the woodstove to the post centre clock, and I paid Victor.

After walking Llysette back to the Music Building and her waiting student, I doubled back to the post centre to find three bills and, as promised, a heavy embossed envelope with the presidential seal. I decided to save it for Llysette to open, although it bore both our names.

Gertrude the zombie was raking the leaves away from the walk as I marched back to the department.

"Hello, Gertrude."

"Hello, sir. It's a pleasant day."

For her, it always was, but I still remembered her sobbing her eyes out at Llysette's opera the spring before. A zombie, feeling that much emotion? Perhaps . . . could song rebuild a removed soul or spirit? I didn't know, but that confirmed my decision not to mix music and ghosting equipment.

I'd had the idea of using the equipment I'd developed to create "ghost angels" to influence people, but the more I'd thought about it, the more I'd turned from it. Trying to cope with the internalized ghosts of Carolynne and the abstract ghost of justice and mercy I'd created had often left me on the brink of sanity—and I knew what I'd done and faced.

I did catch Herr Doktor Doniger in the corridor as he was heading out.

"David . . . you recall that you and the dean have insisted that I maintain certain political connections?"

"Why, yes, Johan. It does benefit the university." He still had a wary look.

"Llysette and I have been requested to attend an arts dinner at the Presidential Palace next week. She has been asked to perform, and . . ." I shrugged. "I'll work out something for my classes."

David beamed. "I was going over to the Administration building, and I'm sure the dean will be pleased."

"It hasn't been announced yet," I said. "Probably tomorrow." That would make the honorable Dean Er Recchus even happier— that she knew in advance.

"That will be another achievement she can use in presenting the budget to the state legislature in January." David inclined his head. "Funds are looking tight, and that will help."

"Good."

He went off smiling, and I vaguely wanted to smash his kneecaps, but I didn't feel like I wanted to play any more academic politics.

The less I thought about my two o'clock the better, even afterward. Halfway through the semester was a bad time. The students had realized that they were in trouble, that material was piling up faster than they could or wanted to read it because they hadn't read any of it until right before the midterm. You can't assimilate the type of material I provided in midnight cram sessions, and that meant most of the class had received grades of less than a B. For a Dutch burgher's child, even a B was unacceptable, especially with grade inflation.

So the questions became more and more desperate.

". . . would you please explain, Doktor Eschbach, the relationship of the Escalante Massacre on the Deseret synthetic fuels development . . . ?"

". . . I don't understand how the River Compact. . . ."

". . . still not clear on why Speaker Roosevelt rejected the Green River compromise proposed by Deseret. . . ."

". . . I just don't understand. . . ."

". . . don't understand. . . ."

All the questions translated into either desperate attempts to stall the class or equally desperate attempts to avoid in-depth reading and thinking. I suppose that's always been the effort of young adults, except in the past those who felt that way either never got to college or quickly flunked out. Higher-level technology has created a dubious boon of removing much of the old manual labor and requiring more positions where judgment and some thinking are required. People want the jobs, but not the effort required to hold them. Oh, they say they do, but when it gets right down to it, the average student would rather use the university's difference engines for games than number crunching and the library for assignations than assignments.

"Enough!" I thundered, and you would have thought that I'd whipped them. "I am not here to explain every little thing that you find slightly difficult. You are here to learn. That requires thinking. Thinking means working hard. Your questions show that you stop the minute something gets difficult and requires thinking . . . the minute the answer is not written on the page. And who will be there to answer such questions once you graduate?" Assuming that they did.

I wasn't patient, and I felt as though I were getting less so. When you first start teaching, it's flattering to be looked up to and asked, but after a time, you realize that all too many questions are asked out of thoughtlessness and laziness.

Still, I had to remind myself that there was a thoughtful minority in the class who felt, and looked, as appalled as I did at the desperate questions and the failure to try to learn something. That handful was the group I called on when I needed an answer.

Because of them, I'd almost managed to get over being cross when I picked up Llysette.

"You are angry?"

"I'm getting over it. My day was like some of yours. 'I don't understand. . . . I just don't see how . . . Can't you make it simpler? . . . Why do we have to read so much?' "

"To France perhaps we should send them?"

I laughed. Their questions would have them in Ferdinand's concentration camps—except he called them relocation and training camps. That or selectively part-zombied and turned into killing machines for the invasion of Britain that was sure to come in another decade . . . or less. Unless Ferdinand decided to push over the crumbling remnants of the once-great Romanov dynasty in Russia. But no one ever beat the Russian winter, or the Finnish winter, and most of the Scandinavians were building redoubts in every rocky hill and fjord and peak north of the Baltic. The Finns had turned Vyborg into an armory in the Autumn War and continued to upgrade it against the Hapsburgs.

"Oh. Here's the invitation." I handed her the heavy envelope.

For a moment, she just looked. Then she opened it. "A personal note there is." Her eyes brightened, and I could see the hint of tears.

"You deserve it. You deserved it years ago."

"Johan, what we deserve we do not always receive. Because of you, I receive. Not because—"

"You wouldn't have those invitations if you weren't the best."

"*Non. C'est vrai.*" Her green eyes were deep, almost two shades of green simultaneously, as she turned to me. "I would not have them save for you. We know that, and I am thankful to you, and angered at the way the world is. We cannot change what is." She leaned over and hugged me, then kissed my cheek.

I eased the Stanley out of the car park, around the town square, slowly, because McArdles' was crowded with late-day grocery shoppers, and then over the Wijk bridge and up Deacon's Lane to the now-spotless house.

Marie had even set the dining room table and left a steaming apple pie.

I had to scurry to get dinner started, while Llysette assisted with setting out such details as wineglasses and serving bowls. I'd decided on something relatively simple—a spinach linguine pasta with a chicken fettuccine sauce, hot rolls, and the salad.

Before Bruce arrived, I took a few minutes to close the study draperies and remove the ersatz chocolate box from the hidden wall compartment. After I set it on the ancient desk, I went to look for the Watch report that I'd pried out of Chief Waetjen. I thought I'd left it in a file in the second drawer—on top—but it wasn't there. I checked the third drawer, then went back to the stack in the second drawer. It was there, about four files down. I shook my head. Even my memory was going. With the sound of something boiling too violently, I dropped the file next to the difference screen and scurried back to the kitchen.

Even while I chopped the roasted almonds for the curried wine vinegar dressing for the salad, I continued to have less than sanguine feelings about Llysette's invitation to Deseret, despite all the papers—and despite the retainer cheque. But what could I say? "Turn down a five-thousand-dollar retainer; turn away from the recognition you deserve?"

Bruce arrived after dark, well after dark, in his ancient Olds ragtop, and I thought I could hear the beating sound of tattered canvas. My imagination, doubtless.

As he entered, Bruce immediately bowed to Llysette, offering a warm smile. "At last, the beautiful chanteuse of whom I have heard so much."

She blushed. "I have heard much of you."

"Try not to believe too much of it."

I took his coat. "Dinner will be ready in just a few minutes after I put in the pasta."

Bruce looked at me. "So, Johan, business before or after dinner?"

I shrugged. "I'd thought before."

The three of us went into the study.

"There it is." I gestured to the box.

"What is?"

I realized I'd never explained. "A gentleman showed up at the door with this for Llysette. She slammed the door in his face, and he turned into a zombie as a result of the gadgetry inside. I wanted your opinion." I paused. "I did take the liberty of disconnecting the power."

"Thoughtful of you, Johan." Bruce eased open the box and peered and nodded and then fingered his mostly black beard. He took out a small screwdriver, the clip kind, from his shirt pocket and fiddled slightly. Then he nodded and straightened.

"It's the same thing as your first gadget to separate soul from body and then destroy the spirit or ghost. But it's a different approach. I prefer your design. It's a great deal more stable than this."

It hadn't been my design, but one I'd stolen from the difference engine of the late Professor Branston-Hay before his untimely death at the hands of the Spazi covert branch. At least, that was my surmise, although the official cause of death had been a faulty steam control valve in his antique Ford. His house—and all his backup disks—had burned in an electrical fire right after the funeral. So the files and designs I had were among the few left, and probably highly illegal after Speaker Hartpence's announced decision to ban all research and development on ghost-related technologies.

"Good," I murmured. While not relieved, I was happy to know that my surmises had been correct and that Llysette and I hadn't panicked at nothing. I picked up the folder. "Here's the Watch report. It doesn't say anything."

Bruce scanned it quickly. "No, it doesn't."

"I thought so, but you have a more skeptical mind than I do."

"Me? How could you think that?"

"Experience." I laughed, and so did he.

"Is that all?" He held up a hand. "Foolish of me to suppose that, of course."

"Actually, I have a request of sorts. You remember that gadget you built me, two of them actually, that preceded the perturbation replicator and resembled this in function?"

There was a long silence. Bruce glanced from me to Llysette.

I nodded. "She knows." Llysette definitely knew about both the ghost-creation technology and the so-called perturbation replicator, or de-ghoster, although I couldn't remember exactly how I'd come up with the name.

"Those . . . ah, yes. Johan, I had hoped you would get beyond playthings once you married, that kind of gimmickry, I meant."

"You know that Llysette has been offered a concert engagement in Great Salt Lake City; one of the conditions, since she is female, is that her husband or other legal guardian accompany her."

"You are skeptical?"

"She has since received an invitation to perform at the Presidential Palace, and I have received several unsolicited materials that could be construed as background briefing materials."

Bruce held up his hand. "That's enough. More I don't need to know. I'm perfectly capable of creating my own problems. That I can do without assistance—"

"I was wondering if there might be any way to package one of those toys into separate components of an innocuous nature and yet be able to reassemble it into a toy—smaller than the original but equally effective for personal meetings, if you will."

"Johan . . . I rather like the insurance business better than any new ventures, and you *know* how I feel about insurance."

I almost smiled wryly. Bruce didn't like at all the fact that he was one of the two individuals who'd have to release all my forbidden technology if anything happened to me—my insurance, I hoped, against an untimely and early death. "I understand. Can you look into it?"

"How soon? Forget that." He shook his head. "It was a foolish question. I'll wire you tomorrow with an estimate."

"I appreciate it. Now . . . I think we should have dinner. I have some very good Californian wines, a Sebastopol you should enjoy."

"I always enjoy good wine . . . and beautiful women." He nodded at Llysette.

"Careful there," I said with a laugh.

"With you, Johan, I would always be careful. But I can look and appreciate your taste, and your luck." He smiled gently.

Llysette blushed again—more than I'd seen since I'd known her. Carolynne?

I eased the pasta into the big kettle and then brought out the 1982 Sebastopol, around its peak, I thought, and filled the glasses. "We can sit down."

"A toast to your upcoming performances," offered Bruce.

I lifted my glass, and, after a moment, so did Llysette.

"This is a beautiful old house," Bruce said after taking a sip from the wine.

"We've made some changes, and there will be more."

Llysette nodded emphatically, but she could have any changes she wanted except in the study.

"Don't take away the atmosphere," Bruce cautioned.

"That, we could not do. *Mais non.*"

I knew the word "we" referred to more than the two of us, but there was no reason to explain. Who would have understood?

I had to get the pasta and drain it before tossing everything together and serving it, with the rolls. "It's simple."

"He does nothing in the kitchen simple," said Llysette.

"She sings nothing in the theatre simple," I countered.

"I know enough to know that neither of you is simple in any way. Johan always said he was simple. He's simple only in the fact that quiet waters are deep and dangerous."

Llysette laughed softly.

"So is she," I pointed out.

"Like I said . . . ," offered Bruce ambiguously before taking a sip of the wine.

I offered the rolls to Llysette, then to Bruce, and then handed him the serving platter.

"How do you find New Bruges . . . and teaching?" asked Bruce. "Is it that much different?"

"New Bruges . . . it is colder than France, and the people, they keep more to themselves." Llysette lifted her shoulders, then dropped them. "Teaching . . ."

"Is hard," I finished the sentence.

"*Tres difficile, quelquefois* . . . the simplest of matters, and they look as though two heads I had. I cannot do my best if accompany them I must. Do they find an accompanist? *Mais non!* They whimper about how their funds are short and how their lives are hard."

"I can see that you are less than impressed," offered Bruce.

"Ferdinand's prisons they have not experienced," answered Llysette, pausing for a sip of the Sebastopol. "Work, *travail vrai*, they do not comprehend. To find an accompanist? Is that so difficult? To learn the notes?"

"Anything is hard if one doesn't work at it," Bruce suggested.

How well I knew that, and I nodded. Even in the simplest of books, if something did not happened to be explained in two-syllable words, or less, or if they had to think, even in novels, I suspected, they were baffled and claiming that someone *had* to explain. Life never worked that way, I had found. So had Llysette.

"*Mais oui*. But still they whimper."

"Some always will," I suggested. "But you have some good students."

"Marlena . . . a joy she is . . . and Jamella . . . she studies so hard." Llysette smiled faintly. "The good ones, they are few."

"That's true in anything."

"Good pasta, Johan," said Bruce. "After all these years, I finally get to sample your cooking."

"Thank you. You will more," I promised. "Even without agendas."

The slightest trace of a frown creased his forehead before he asked, "Why did you decide to bless me this year?"

I shrugged, not willing to tell him that ghosts of joy and justice and mercy did have an effect. Those I had saddled myself with inadvertently were quietly making me a slightly better person. "It seems like a good idea, even if you are wary of things that seem like good ideas."

That got a laugh. For a time we ate silently. Outside, the cold wind whistled gently and one of the shutters rattled.

"There will be a time when someone needs a ghost . . . badly." Bruce raised his glass of the 1982 Sebastopol, then took a healthy sip. "And I don't want to be around when it happens."

"You, why would you be around?" asked Llysette. "Ghosts, you have said you avoid them."

"Avoid them. What ever gave you that idea? It couldn't be that I never visited Johan until this venerable and ancient dwelling was no longer spectrally inhabited?" Bruce grinned.

Llysette and I smiled back and then at each other. What else could we do? After the fact, it was amusing, not that it had been at the time. Neither Llysette nor I had ever mentioned the details of poor Carolynne's displacement to our own souls. How could we?

How could we tell the world that she'd shot me, under a compulsion from Ferdinand's selective soul-sifting technology? Or that I'd turned all my ghost-creation and de-destruction gadgets on her, except a leaded mirror had skewed everything and dumped the real ghost of Carolynne into Llysette's half-shattered soul and a copy, as well as a ghost that was a caricature of justice and mercy, into mine?

All the world of New Bruges and particularly the enclave that was Vanderbraak Centre knew was that Johan Eschbach's family home was no longer haunted, and a good thing it was, too, now that the black sheep had finally married the French soprano. She might be a foreigner, that Llysette duBoise, and it might have taken a bullet in his shoulder to drive out the family ghost, but he'd finally seen the light.

I almost laughed—it had been a lot more complicated than that, and Bruce was right to worry about ghost creation. I still had the equipment he had created that had saddled me with a simplified version of both Carolynne and a ghost of justice. I was still coming to terms with those forms of possession, but at least it hadn't gone the other way and left me a zombie.

"You two . . . in the Spazi . . . one could not believe it today," offered Llysette.

"They make offers that are difficult to refuse," Bruce pointed out wryly. "If one wishes to work in any high-level position later."

"And how is that so different from Ferdinand?" she asked.

"*Most* of the time," Bruce answered, "the Spazi is content with a few years of your life, and they don't tell you what to think, just what to do."

"My life they have asked years of, also."

"That's past." I hoped it was past. At least she could now perform anywhere in Columbia.

"To many years of rewarding song." Bruce lifted his glass again.

That was something I definitely would drink to, and I lifted my glass as well. "To song and singer." I reached under the table and squeezed Llysette's thigh just above the knee.

That got me a shy and sidelong smile, and a sense of warmth.

5

AFTER my early wirecall to Harlaan Oakes with Llysette's two songs, Wednesday found us in Asten, at the Federal building, and the less said the better about the parking in that convoluted city. The only place we ran into no lines was in the passport office itself.

It was almost as if they were expecting us. They even insisted that, as my spouse, Llysette receive a diplomatic passport—since they had issued one to me when I'd been Subminister for Environmental Protection . . . and let me keep it. Having matching passports with the heavy green covers and the gold stripes offered an additional touch of class on someone's part. The fact that I didn't know whose part twisted my guts more than a little.

We were happy to leave, and even the congested streets of Asten were a relief, despite the excess of dark black steamers that reminded me of the high-tech trupps that controlled the south side around the diminishing back bay.

I took a deep breath once we were clear of the verge-on-verge towns that clustered around Asten and once the Stanley settled into a high-speed glide on the relatively open highway north toward Lochmere.

"You're not only a confirmed Columbian citizen, but you have a passport as well."

"A diplomatic passport—and a year ago they could not find my residence forms." Llysette provided a sound halfway between a snort and a sniff. "Why a diplomatic passport?"

Because that meant that Columbia could scream louder if anything happened to us and because it meant someone expected something to happen. "You are a cultural diplomat, of sorts." My internal ghost of honesty and justice compelled me to add more. "And someone is worried that something might happen. I don't know what."

"My life I thought would be boring in New Bruges. It has not been so."

"There are times I wish it were less exciting." Then, I was beginning to realize that I was never going to escape my past—nor was Llysette.

"Johan?"

"Yes?"

"The zombie who died—was he sent to kill me?"

"I don't know." I eased the steamer around an empty hauler that trailed black smoke, half-wondering why the owner didn't adjust the burners. "He had a gun, and he was told to kill us both. I'd think there are more reasons to kill me . . . but these days, I just don't know."

"A year ago, that you would not have said."

"Said what?"

"You say . . . you have opened your heart more, and I love you for that."

"So have you, and I have loved you longer than I ever let you know." I laughed ruefully. "Matters would have been a lot easier if I had told you."

"*Non, je crois que non* . . . I would have heard the words. The meaning, it would have escaped." Llysette's hand caressed the back of my neck for a time, and I just drove and enjoyed the sensation, trying to forget about assassins, presidential receptions, and the ghost-related technology that was supposed to have been outlawed—and was still being employed.

"We won't know," I said later . . . after leaving two more haulers in the Stanley's wake.

"What will we not know?"

"How things would have turned out."

She laughed, and so did I. We talked the rest of the trip, enjoying just being together—until we drove up Deacon's Lane and into our drive.

Constable Gerhardt was waiting, standing by a Watch steamer, a glum look on his face.

"I'm sorry, Herr Doktor." His eyes went to the house, and he fingered one side of the sweeping mustache.

"Sorry?" I had to shake my head.

Llysette just frowned, her eyes going from Gerhardt to the house and back again.

"Frau Rijn was leaving after her cleaning, and she thought she saw an intruder from the lane. She wired from her house, but by the time we got here, he got away. Smashed the panes in the glass door in back good, he did. Since Frau Rijn said you'd be back this afternoon, the chief had me wait."

"I hope you didn't have to wait too long."

"Less than an hour. Could I wire the chief that you're here?"

"Be my guest." I unlocked the door and let Llysette and the constable enter before me.

The kitchen seemed untouched, the white windowsills clean and gleaming in the late-afternoon light, the floor dust-free, and the faint odor of a meat pie from the warmer filling the room.

"There." I pointed to the wireset on the corner of the counter, the one I seldom used.

The constable dialed something. "Chief, they're here." Gerhardt waited, then said, "Yes, sir." He hug up the handset and turned. "He'll be right up. He asked that you not touch anything."

"I assume we can look?"

"I think so, sir."

"Upstairs, I will check." Llysette scurried up the steps even before she finished speaking.

Gerhardt and I went out into the study. My desk was disarrayed, with the desk drawers pulled out. My custom-designed SII difference engine was on, but only to the directory.

"He ran out the back, we guessed—across the wall," offered Gerhardt. "The Benjamin boy said there was a steamer on the back road there, but he didn't see it very well. He said it was dark-colored."

I walked around the study. Outside of the papers strewn across the Farsi carpet my grandfather had brought back from the Desert Wars and the switched-on difference engine, the room looked as it had when we had left.

The French door to the terrace had a large hole in the double panes next to the lock and glass fragments on the floor and on the stones of the terrace. Print powder lay dusted across the knob and the stones and bare wooden floor just inside the door before where the carpet began.

"Can I?"

"No prints," Gerhardt said. "Not on the glass or knob."

I pushed the door, already ajar, open and stepped onto the terrace, and into the light and cold wind.

The rear yard seemed unchanged—from the compost pile below the garden to the brown grass carpet. The frost-killed tan stalks of the raspberries remained erect, although that would change with the next heavy snow. The only remnant of raspberries until spring would be the frozen pies, freezer jam, and whole frozen berries, more than enough to last through until the next summer.

The second Watch steamer whistled into the drive, and the gray-haired chief piled out, barely pausing at the door long enough for me to open it.

"Doktor Eschbach, you present a problem." Waetjen glared, and I suspected he still didn't care much for me. "When you are here, people get killed and zombied, and when you are not, the same occurs, with thefts as well."

I shrugged. This time, I had done nothing. I tried not to swallow. The last time, when Miranda had been murdered, I hadn't done anything either. Was life trying to tell me that I could not continue being a turtle?

"Is there anything missing?"

"Not down here." I turned to Llysette, who stood in the archway between the sitting room and the study.

"Nothing has moved . . . upstairs." She finished with a gesture.

"Nothing?"

I eased around the chief and let everyone follow me to the study. I pointed toward the desk and the papers scattered across the green Farsi carpet. "I couldn't say that they might have gotten some papers or loose coins or something like that, but there's nothing obviously missing."

"Doktor . . . would there be papers of value here that anyone would know about?" asked the chief.

"Most of the files on the difference engine deal with my writings or my lectures and class notes. I can't imagine any value to anyone but me. I have records for taxes, but why would anyone else care?"

"No valuable manuscripts, anything like that?"

I nodded toward the bookcase. "There are some moderately valuable books there, but it would take a collector to know which."

Waetjen surveyed the long wall of floor-to-ceiling cases. "Are they all there?"

My smile was half-apologetic, half-embarrassed. "I wouldn't know for sure. None seem to be gone, but I couldn't say if a single volume might not be missing."

The square-faced chief touched his gray goatee. "Do you have cash or other valuables in the house?"

"Some of Llysette's jewelry, a few books, some antiques, the silver, some crystal that couldn't be replaced." I tried to think. "The carpet here, the painting in the piano room. But they're all still here."

"You should thank Frau Rijn, then, Doktors. Apparently, we got here before anything of consequence was removed."

"I think so," I answered. "We'll take a closer look to make sure. Did you find any idea who it might have been?"

"The intruder wore gloves, leather gloves. Midheight." The chief shrugged. "Size forty-eight boot—that was in the mud on the far side of the field. Late-model Reo steamer, probably midnight gray."

Constable Gerhardt shifted his weight and looked at Llysette, who boldly returned the look. Gerhardt blushed at being caught and glanced away.

"Let me know if you find anything gone—or added." Chief Waetjen bowed to Llysette, then to me.

After the Watch officers left, I taped cardboard over the broken pane and cleaned up the glass. By then it was dark, and we straggled into the kitchen.

I was getting a good idea what someone was after—but it didn't make sense unless there were two groups involved, because the theft effort came after the attempted de-ghosting/murder.

So . . . someone wanted us removed, but very indirectly, with no connection. That meant it couldn't be the Spazi. Minister Jerome and his minions had ways to remove us without going to low-class thugs. That pointed toward an outside power—someone like the Austro-Hungarians, or the New French, or even Chung Kuo. Quebec could have brought in someone who could pass scrutiny in New Bruges, and Deseret wouldn't go to all the trouble of inviting Llysette, not when such invitations had to be cleared by the Council of Twelve, and then killing her. The Japanese had helped get Llysette released from Ferdinand's prisons and torture . . . and had never called in that favor—or tried.

Someone wanted to steal something I had—that meant they knew or suspected I had ghost-removal technology. That also had to be an outside power, because both the president's office and the Spazi already had such equipment. That bothered me a great deal . . . because no one knew I had that technology, for sure. Jerome and his analysts might suspect—but there wasn't any hard evidence, except in the compartment behind the mirror and in my insurance packages. The file protocols on the difference engine that could capture or create ghosts would have been meaningless, and they were hidden, and the intruder hadn't tripped the counter. But Bruce could have gotten the file without tripping it; so the untripped counter meant only that no amateur had tried.

"How about a salad with the meat pie?"

"*Bien*. . . ." Llysette sat at the kitchen table. "Johan? This is not the same as the zombie, *est-ce-que?*"

"*Non,*" I admitted.

"Who are they? What do they want?" She paused.

I continued to shred lettuce into the salad bowl—romaine, not iceberg.

"The creating and destroying of ghosts—is that what they desire? Your knowledge about such?"

I set aside the lettuce and began to work on a cucumber. "I'm not sure. I think we're seeing two different groups. The first wants us out of the way, and the second wants knowledge, but I'd thought it was more about de-ghosting." The Spazi couldn't have known about the ghost-creation gadgetry, nor could Ferdinand's people. Still, the furor that I'd created before and the latest incident pointed out, again, how ghosts were a real phenomenon in our world, with an impact that couldn't be ignored. Ghosts had certainly made a historical difference in our world—from those that had turned William the Unfortunate's conquest of England from a triumph to near-disaster to all those of women who had died in childbirth and thus prevented early remarriages and slowed the world birthrate.

"Ferdinand . . . could it be?"

"What do you think?"

"*Je ne sais pas* . . . the puppets of that devil Heisler. I know nothing, and they must know more than we do."

I nodded. That was my feeling. Why would Ferdinand or his

mad scientist Heisler bother? But who else would even care? The Spazi could have us imprisoned or eliminated with less fuss.

I set the salads on the table and retrieved the meat pie from the warmer. "It is a puzzle, and we aren't going to solve it tonight, and it is time to eat. Wine?"

"*S'il vous plaît. . . .*"

"That I can do." I could manage wine, just not the spreading web of intrigue that seemed bound to snare us both.

6

ON Thursday morning I was looking at the latest pile of ungraded tests on my desk—these from the Environmental Politics 2A class. I'd persuaded Regner Grimaldi to give it for me while we'd been in Asten. That meant I'd have to return the favor at some point, but I had to admit my schedule was lighter than his. That was always the case with younger faculty. I could afford to tell our honored chair what he could do with an ill-considered idea. Poor Regner couldn't. Nor had Llysette much leverage, and that was another reason why she couldn't afford not to perform in Deseret . . . or in the Federal District—especially when performing might lead to her obtaining such leverage.

I put those thoughts aside, picked up the first test, and began to read: ". . . Speaker Aspinwaald liked mines and lumbermen so he got the excise taxes passed to help them. . . ." I winced at the spelling of the former Speaker's name and the answer, which quickly got worse. I had said that Speaker Aspinall never met a tree or a mine he didn't like, but he pushed through the excise taxes *despite* that. Somehow, about a third of the students never heard the whole story. I picked up the next test, wondering if they had the same problem with whatever else they read, like novels, but before I could concentrate, the wireset chimed.

"It's Watch Chief Waetjen for you, Doktor," said Gilda in the formal tone that indicated David was standing by her elbow.

"Thank you." I waited, then answered, "Yes, Chief?"

"Professor Eschbach, was anything missing?" asked Waetjen.

"Llysette and I have looked, Chief, but neither of us has discovered anything that was missing." I juggled the handset to the other ear and restacked the tests I'd already graded. "There was even a twenty-dollar bill on the corner of the desk—I guess I'd left it half tucked under some papers and the thief fumbled through the papers and uncovered it but left it."

"No thief I ever heard of."

"It could be that was when your officers arrived," I pointed out.

"You said that he left in a hurry."

"I have my doubts, Herr Doktor Professor."

"Doubts or not, Chief, we haven't found anything missing yet, and we've looked." Like the chief, I wasn't exactly happy about the missing burglar or what he'd been rummaging through the house to find. I was afraid I knew—he wanted the information and technologies on de-ghosting—and that meant very big problems, especially with our upcoming trip to the Federal District.

"Do you have any idea what he sought?" pressed the chief.

I tried not to pause in answering. "It could have been a number of things, Chief, but he didn't leave any clues."

"You didn't leave your difference engine on while you were gone, did you?"

"No. He must have turned it on, but none of the files were altered, and it didn't look like he'd copied anything. I can't imagine what he'd want with all those academic records."

"Do you keep your financial records there?" pressed the chief.

"No—nothing like that. I don't need anything elaborate. I get a salary and some consulting income and a modest pension. We're comfortable, but hardly wealthy."

"Let me know if you happen to discover anything else."

I promised that I would, which was a safe promise, because I doubted that I'd find out anything more.

Then it was a dash down the stairs and out to Natural Resources 1A, the previously graded quizzes under my arm.

Gertrude and Hector were turning the flower beds in front of Smythe, spreading bark mulch along the base of the hedges by the walk. The two zombies were turned the other way, and I didn't say anything.

The classroom wasn't too hot, probably because the day was gray and cool, not cold . . . not yet, despite the dark clouds looming to the northeast.

Unfortunately, Mister Ferris was waiting. "Professor Eschbach, you said that we should know all of the material on the water cycle on the test. Does that include the stuff on aquifer and recharge zones? And what about radionuclides in water?"

"All of it." I forced a smile as I continued handing out the quizzes and ignoring the groans.

"Oh. . . ."

"It won't all be on the test, Mister Ferris, as I told you the last time. I'm just not telling you what will be." After shuffling away the three quizzes belonging to absentees, I looked at the black-haired sleeping student in the last row. "Miss Gemert!"

"Sir?"

"Perhaps you would be so kind as to tell the class about upland wetlands."

"Upland wetlands?"

I nodded pleasantly.

"Ah . . . sir . . . I'm on the soccer team . . . and we had an away game yesterday. . . ."

"Those caravan rides are a good time to read, Miss Gemert. And Coach Haarken isn't the one who takes your tests." I kept a smile on my face. "Mister Andervaal?"

"Uh . . . are those the ones . . . the intermittent wetlands . . . with maples and stuff like that?"

"That's a start. What else can you tell us?"

Young Andervaal glanced desperately around, but no one would meet his eyes. It was going to be one of those classes. I repressed a sigh.

Getting an answer to each discussion question took about three students, and I was sweating under my cravat by the time the bell chimed.

Llysette had a faculty meeting at noon. So she wouldn't get lunch, and I wouldn't get to see her. I picked up a nearly inedible sandwich from the student center and, after gulping it down, headed out for the post centre, passing Hector on the green.

The zombie nodded without pausing from his raking, and I returned the gesture.

Another unmarked manila envelope rested in our postbox, and it went into my inside jacket pocket. While I didn't want to open it— more trouble—I did, but only after I got back to the office and closed my door.

Again, only clippings were in the envelope, and there were two.

Great Salt Lake City, Deseret (RPI). An unannounced series of police raids in the warehouse district near the Deseret and Western rail yards early this morning resulted in no arrests but the confiscation of "material of a pornographic and objectionable nature," according to police spokesman Jared Bishopp.

Calls to several foreign legations alleged that the raids were designed to harass businesses whose owners had expressed reservations about recent "revelations" made by President Wilford W. Taylor before the Council of Twelve. Among those revelations were language suggesting that multiple conjugal relationships were a matter of individual choice, not an absolute tenet of the first prophet, for those able to support additional familial units.

Of greater concern was the "clarification" referring to the trade language in the *Doctrine and Covenants* laid out by first president Taylor more than a century earlier. Taylor had revealed that "the people of God should trade only with those who neither threaten nor revile them, who accept the kingdom of Zion, and not with Gentiles who would seek to undo our kingdom. . . ." Although this trade proscription has often been honored in the breach for nearly half a century, the clarification language was seen by some observers as easing the way to permit significant synthetic diesel and kerosene exports to Columbia. New France has never been classified as a "Gentile" or an unfriendly nation, possibly because it supported Deseret against Columbia in the Utah War and again in the Caribbean Wars . . . and because it harbors the Colonia Juarez and Dublan enclaves. . . .

Bishopp denied that the raids were of a political nature.

Heber City, Deseret (DNS). "The ideals of the first Prophet must not fall to the Lamanites of the spirit," cautioned First Counselor Cannon in opening the annual Latter-Day Saints conference. "Nor must we cease in bringing light to a darkened continent or in our efforts to return those of Laman into the fold of God. Our kingdom is of God, and it shall stand forever." Cannon went on to praise the role of the arts in opening man to understanding the need for the coming of Zion to the entire world. . . .

Cannon's language turned more practical in his assessment of the state of Deseret. "Energy and technology are the keys to the next century, and the wise use of water facilitates both. We will continue with the headwaters project." The First Speaker went on to pledge additional funding for the advanced natural gas liquification plants, for water reuse technology, and for additional support of the cotton mission initiatives.

I folded the clippings back into the envelope and slipped them into my case. Great—Deseret was building up its liquid hydrocarbon production industry, which certainly needed more water, I suspected, and trying to ease into more normal relations with Columbia despite nearly a century of unease, a century preceded by thirty years of near-war and border skirmishes where Deseret's independence had only been established through the willingness of New France to provide capital and a trade conduit for technology.

That didn't bother me so much as the fact that someone wanted me to know it—and I still didn't know if that someone was the same someone who'd sent me the earlier clips about Llysette and the arts in Deseret. It had the marks of the Spazi, but the lack of cover address continued to worry at me.

I took a deep breath and sat down at my desk, where, in the hour and a half between returning to my office and Environmental Politics 2B at two o'clock, I would try to put a dent in the tests from Environmental Politics 2A.

I hadn't even started grading the short quizzes that I'd given my honors class in environmental studies. Why did I give so many tests? Because too many of the dunderheads wouldn't study the material unless I did. The attitude seemed to be: "If I'm not going to be tested, I won't learn it."

What none of them seemed to understand was that—at least in my life—the world wasn't too forgiving about what you didn't know. You didn't get second chances—like emergency procedures when flying. If I hadn't known them when I'd been in involved in the Panama Standoff, I'd have been somewhere at the bottom of Mosquito Gulf.

Philosophizing didn't grade tests, and I began to read and to apply the red ink. While some of the students actually made sense, a lot more merely tried to parrot what I'd said, whether it was in context or not.

I looked at the next paper: "Speaker Colmer followed the strong environmental example set by Speaker Aspinall. . . ." Environmental example? Hardly! And I'd told them that, but some hadn't gotten the message. The bottom line was that Columbia was starved for liquid hydrocarbons and the strong Speakers—Roosevelt, Messler, Aspinall, and Colmer, particularly—had recognized that fact and eased through taxes and conservation measures that had immense environmental benefits, but not for primarily environmental reasons. The combination of the high turbojet fuel tax and the astronomical landing fees was really what kept the more environmentally sound and energy-efficient dirigibles and the trains competitive. A lot more people would have been taking turbos and old-style aircraft if it weren't for the fact that those fares were nearly ten times as much.

Except for Alaska, the Louisiana fields, and Hugoton Fields in Kansas and the Cherokee lands bordering Tejas, most of the big North American oil fields lay in either Deseret or New France. Had the Saint wars happened a generation later, I suspected, Deseret would have been a part of Columbia no matter what the cost in lives, but the disasters in the Mexican War, followed by the slavery issue and the *Sally Wright* incident, followed in turn by the first Caribbean War, where the Austro-Hungarians had backed both New France and Deseret, had made a full-scale military effort against Deseret highly unpopular . . . and most impractical. The second and almost abortive 1901 Caribbean War had further reinforced the Deseret–New France ties.

Now . . . with Deseret's chemical and synthfuels industries, and continued militarization, not to mention the so-called Joseph Smith brigades, Columbian military action against Deseret would have been an invitation for deGaulle to strike against the comparatively vulnerable Kansas, Louisiana, and mid-California oil fields, and Columbia couldn't afford that at all, not when Indonesian oil was held by the Rising Sun and the Arabian peninsula by the Austro-Hungarians. There was talk of development in Russia, but the Romanovs didn't have the capital, and Russia was so strife-torn and chaotic outside of Saint Petersburg and Moskva that none of the international bankers would consider it, even with what Columbia and the Brits would have paid for the oil.

Instead, it looked like both President Armstrong and Speaker Hartpence would have to court Deseret for liquid hydrocarbons. Better Deseret than New France, I supposed.

More than a third of the honors class quizzes missed those

points. *Honors class?* I wondered as I set the few remaining quizzes aside and headed for Environmental Politics 2B.

They were presenting summaries of their projects, and that meant I just listened and took notes—thankfully.

I got back to the department offices at three-forty-five. Gilda waved before I got to the stairs. "Herr Leveraal called. The number is in your box."

"Thank you."

Once in my office, I closed the door and wired Bruce.

"LBI Difference Designers."

"Bruce?"

"No. This is Curt."

"I'm sorry. This is Johan Eschbach; I'm returning Bruce's call."

"Just a moment."

I waited. Curt—that was Bruce's brother Curtland. I'd never met him, and until now he'd been a shadowy sort of figure, except he'd never been in the Spazi, unlike Bruce and me.

"Herr Doktor," offered Bruce.

"You wired?"

"I have an estimate on your toys. They should be ready Saturday."

"I take it they're not cheap."

"Compared to what?"

Bruce had a point there. "All right. How much?"

"Say . . . roughly three hundred for a pair. Maybe four at the out-side."

I didn't quite wince. Then, if they were useful in keeping unto-ward things from happening to us . . . how much were our lives worth? "They cost what they cost. Anytime Saturday?"

"You're the customer. I'll see you then, and try to stay out of any more trouble."

"You remain all heart, Bruce."

"Always." There was a pause. "I do have a request."

"Oh?"

"I'd really like to hear your lovely bride in concert. So . . . the next time she performs—somewhere in the seminear geographic vicinity—could you inform me?"

"Of course." I cleared my throat. "It might be a little while, be-cause she just did a recital, but I'll certainly let you know. Some-times she's done concerts around Zuider, but there aren't any scheduled right now."

"I understand."

Why was Bruce interested in Llysette's singing? Was it because he did a lot of work with music systems? I shook my head. I could sense he was interested in her singing, but why? Then, for all the years I'd known Bruce, there was a lot I didn't know, probably because he was private and because I'd never asked. Or was it just that I was getting paranoid about everything?

That raised even more questions I didn't want to consider, not at the moment, although I knew I'd have to, sooner or later.

7

ON Saturday morning, as we lingered over breakfast, Llysette yawned ever so slightly in the warm light from a sun we had seen too little of in the previous week.

"Are you tired?"

"Tired am I all the time. Tired from teaching Dutch dunderheads who believe that singing the wrong notes many times is practice. Vocalises I give them, and they do not use them . . . but for a few, and those, they are too few. A written sheet on how to practice they have, and they do not read it. *Non* . . . they sit and pick out one note after another because the piano they cannot play, and accompanists they will not find. Rhythms they do not learn. . . ." She sighed.

"I'm sorry." I didn't know what I could do, but I was sorry. Even with my pension and salary, I couldn't support her in the style she deserved.

"*Quelquefois* . . ."

I refilled her cup with the last of the chocolate from the pot. "I need to go to Zuider to pick up the gadgets from Bruce. You'd said you wanted to do some shopping. I'm game. Are you?"

"Shopping, that I can always do, even in Zuider."

"I know. We could drive on down to Borkum afterward," I suggested.

"That I would like."

I'd thought she would. "I thought I'd get the post while you finish dressing."

Llysette smiled. "You are good to me."

Sometimes, I wondered. I'd almost gotten us both killed, and she was still having to work far too hard.

The Stanley had plenty of kerosene, and the water tanks were nearly full. I had my own water filter system in the car barn, and that saved a lot of trouble. Then I backed out into the sunlight, under a sky with only a few scattered small white clouds—a good day for a drive.

Benjamin had the whole family out, doing something in the orchards beyond the field that bordered Deacon's Lane. None of them looked up, but I knew they'd noticed. They noticed everything, which had certainly been to my benefit recently.

Who had been behind the attack on us? I had no real idea—or, rather, I couldn't narrow down the suspects. With a half-shrug, I stopped on the east side of the bridge to wait for a long lumber hauler, then took the steamer across.

The square was crowded with Saturday shoppers, but I only had to take the Stanley around once before I could pull into a spot by the post centre. The clock chimed ten as I walked up the stone steps.

I opened the postbox gingerly, only to discover that I had cause for my trepidation. Another of the damned manila envelopes from the Federal District lay there like the miniature bomb it was.

Rather than open it in the post centre, I took it and the letter from my mother and a bill from Dunwijk Plumbing for repairing the kitchen sink lines and eased them into my jacket.

The manila envelope exuded heat in my pocket. It didn't, but that was the way it felt, and I opened it once I'd parked the steamer back in our drive. There was but a single clip from the *Columbia Post-Dispatch:*

> Federal District (RPI). J. Taylor Hunter, assistant president of Deseret, met with Natural Resources Minister Reilly yesterday. The substance of the private meeting was not immediately disclosed, but speculation centered on oil or liquid hydrocarbon exports from Deseret. . . .
>
> The federal stockpile is at an all-time low, less than two months' worth of total Columbian demand, as a result of the refusal of Japan to increase exports from its Indonesian fields to Columbia and the recent oil field explosions in Venezuela, which reduced exports to the Mobile refinery. . . .

The cause of the South American disaster has not yet been established.

I had a good idea about the South American disaster. It had the fine hand of Ferdinand written large upon it.

Since Llysette was still rummaging through the closet upstairs, I set the plumbing bill in the basket on my desk for such and opened my mother's note:

Johan,

I was sorry that you and your darling Llysette will not be able to come down over harvest.

Both Anna and I were thrilled to hear that she will be performing before more appreciative audiences. . . .

You might recall Romer van Leyden. He passed away after a long bout with cancer last week. His son Georg asked to be remembered to you. He works for the New Ostend Water Authority, but I've forgotten what he does. . . .

All our best . . .

Mother still insisted on both wiring and writing, the writing a relic of a more graceful age that I appreciated—and that gave me some pleasurable anticipation in opening a postbox otherwise filled with the mundane business of bills or the chilling manila envelopes that represented a past I never seemed quite able to escape.

Llysette was dressed in a blue jumper, with a white blouse, except she was trying to decide between two jackets—a tan woolen one or a wool one that seemed to match the jumper.

"Mother sent a note." I extended it to Llysette as she hung up the tan jacket.

She frowned in that way that crinkled her nose, and I laughed.

"You mock me," she said.

"You're cute."

"Baby . . . baby ducks, they are cute."

"You are also beautiful and talented."

"Cute, that you called me first."

I groaned.

She smiled and began to read. "She comprehends the Dutch audiences here."

"Backwater Dutch, she's always called them."

"Backwater?"

"Away from the culture of New Amsterdam or Philadelphia, or even Asten."

"*Backwater* . . . a good term." Llysette nodded and handed the note back to me.

"I'm still getting clippings," I said quietly, easing the latest one to her.

"*Mais qui est-ce-qui?*"

"I don't know. It might be Harlaan Oakes—the one who told me about the president's decision to ask you to sing."

"You are not *certain?*" she asked, pronouncing "certain" in French.

"No. The clips and the methods are Spazi, but it doesn't have any of their cover addresses, and I don't know why anyone in the Spazi would be doing this."

This time her frown wasn't cute as she read.

"The oils . . . what have they to do with us?" Her green eyes glinted. "*Quelqu'un crois que* . . . am I to sing for oil?"

"I don't think so. It's more to point out how delicate matters are." I took a deep breath. "Can I explain it on the drive to Zuider?" I forced a grin. "That way we can get through the unpleasant necessities and to the shopping."

"You mock me more. . . ." She gave a pout, lower lip well out, out enough for me to know that she was teasing.

"Absolutely." I hugged her and got a warm embrace in return.

We gathered coats, because despite the sun, there was a chill breeze, and I escorted Llysette out to the steamer, after locking the doors carefully, not that locks would ever stop a real professional. I just hoped they wouldn't break the glass I'd had replaced . . . or worse.

"You would explain?" Llysette said even before I had the Stanley onto Deacon's Lane. The red thermal paint glittered in the bright fall sun, as it should, since I'd washed the steamer the afternoon before while Llysette had held rehearsals for the winter opera.

"About the clippings?" I cleared my throat as we headed down to the bridge. "Columbia is oil-starved. We took certain conservation measures years ago to reduce fuel demands, but there's a cost to all of that. Prices get higher because of the energy component of goods, and higher prices tend to depress investment. Lower investment and higher prices make it harder to develop alternative fuel sources, the way they have in Deseret. We have a lot of natural gas in the Canadian states, but we don't need gas so much as liquids, and liquification and transport are expensive. A good chunk of the western hydropower goes into the aluminum industry." I shrugged. "Sorry. It gets complicated. Higher technology means more energy demand—unless we cut our standard of living. If we could get some oil from Deseret—they're producing a healthy surplus—then we'd have some breathing space to develop our own synthfuels industry more. But Ferdinand doesn't like that, and New France certainly wouldn't like closer ties between Deseret and Columbia. At the same time, I can't believe either New France or the Austro-Hungarians would cooperate in trying to keep Deseret and Columbia from establishing closer relations." I eased the Stanley onto the cutoff leading to Route Five, which would take us to Zuider.

"Cooperate . . . those two? Never," said my soprano.

"Exactly. Deseret wants the best deal it can get. The Saints have been working to become less and less dependent on New France, but it's delicate. We fought four wars with the two of them, but I can see where deGaulle's expansionism would make the Saints very uneasy. If we can open trade more, then deGaulle can't take Deseret's support totally for granted. That also might relieve some of the pressure on the Panamanian Protectorate and the canal."

"And us . . . what of us?" she asked, trying to steer me back to the main point.

"Your singing is a first step. You're now a Columbian citizen, and that one clip pointed out how the Saints see art as a reflection of the world."

"Someone does not wish me to sing in Deseret?"

"Ferdinand, probably. Maybe deGaulle and Maurice-Huizinga, his spy chief. Possibly even the Japanese, since we wouldn't be as dependent on their Indonesian oil." I coughed, then paused to pass one of the ubiquitous and spotless white tank haulers—from vanEmsden's Dairy, of course. "That's the problem. A lot of people have an interest in your singing, and an equal number have an interest in your not singing."

"I thought . . . perhaps they wished for my ability."

"They do." I laughed. "The Saints wanted the best Columbia has. It's a compliment, and the president has reinforced that. It's precisely because you are so good that you're in the middle of this."

"*Jamais pour l'art,*" Llysette murmured and looked out the window. I gave her the space she wanted and kept driving.

After I came off the cutoff onto the new road, Route Five was smooth all the way south to Zuider and Lochmeer, the biggest lake in New Bruges. Route Five shadowed the Wijk south beside fifteen miles of stone-fenced walls enclosing winter-turned fields, stands of sugar maples, and meadows for scattered sheep.

The stone walls exemplified their Dutch heritage, each stone precisely placed and replaced—as Benjamin always had his family doing—almost as soon as the frost heaved it out of position.

After nearly twenty-five minutes, we reached the spot where the Wijk winds west and Route Five swings east toward Lochmeer and Zuider. At the sight of the three Loon Lakes and the well-trimmed apple orchards, I shook my head. I still hadn't gotten around to a proper pruning of my own small orchard.

"*Plus ca change*," murmured Llysette after her long silence. "So hard you try to stay away from what happens in the world, and still they find you. They find me, and, again, my songs are for those in power. But sing I must, or I will beat notes, all my life, and learn the students will not. I do not beat notes, and the rhythms are not there. Half cannot even accompany themselves."

"Will it get better as you get better students?"

"Who would know? Some, like Marlena, they are good. Or Jamella. The others . . . I give them vocalizes. These to train their voices. The brain it is smart, but the muscles, they are stupid. They will not learn vocalises."

"Is that because they feel stupid singing nonsense syllables?"

Llysette shrugged. "Nonsense is in their heavy skulls."

"Thick skulls?"

"Matters it at all? They will not change."

Was everyone like that? I thought I'd learned, but had I? Or was I repeating the same patterns in a different way?

Even on the new road with its passing lanes, it took almost an hour from Vanderbraak Centre into the car park behind the small structure that housed LBI.

The shop was empty, not surprisingly, since LBI wasn't for browsers but for those who knew what they wanted and who could explain it quickly—for busy people—and desperate ones, I reflected.

Bruce bowed to Llysette, then nodded to me. "I would look forward to all your visits, Johan, if you would bring this lovely lady more often."

"I'll see what I can do, but her schedule is far more cramped than mine."

"Truly a pity." He grinned.

A new SII machine stood on the counter, and my eyes went to it.

"It looks good, but it's not that much better than what you have. I'd wait until next year, or longer if you can."

"I can certainly wait."

"What you requested is in my office."

We followed him. A box with the SII logo stood on his desk, beside the small SII difference engine.

Bruce eased the door closed. "We do take certain precautions here, but they don't work against personal eavesdropping, only against electronics."

I offered a faint smile as he opened the top of the box and extracted two silver cylinders.

"These are a pen and pencil set. They work, but I won't guarantee how well or how long." He lifted a squared-off hand calculator from the box and set it on the desk beside the silvered pen and pencil. "This won't do as much as its size says it should, but it does operate." He smiled wryly. "You put them in the jacks at the bottom and point. The delete key is the activator, but it won't work that way unless both pen and pencil are in place. It uses standard batteries, but they're only good for two uses, three at the outside. I'd suggest bringing some spares."

Llysette shivered, and I understood why. I felt like shivering myself. Firearms, bad as they were, felt cleaner, but there was no way I could carry firearms into Deseret. I squeezed her hand.

"Now this. . . ." Bruce lifted the electric hair blower and bowed to Llysette. "Rechargeable batteries in the base, and they'll recharge if you just plug it in. The batteries only work for the special function." He offered a wry smile. "When the temperature switch is down to the 'C' and pushed in and the blower is on low, when you hold the blower trigger you'll get the de-ghosting or spirit removal effect." He looked at me. "I thought your bride should have some protection also, something . . . appropriate."

Llysette could handle a Colt-Luger. I still had several white scars on my shoulder and back to prove it. So I had no doubts that she could handle Bruce's blower/de-ghoster. "Thank you."

"I also," offered my soprano, with a warm but ginger smile.

"Think nothing of it."

"You haven't lost your touch," I said.

"There are definitely times that I wish I had, Johan."

"Me, too—except about that time, I find I'd be dead if I had." I counted out the bills, eight hundred dollars' worth. "I hope that's enough."

Bruce gave a crooked grin. "So do I. I'd rather not deal with your insurance."

"I'd rather you didn't have to either."

"When do you leave?" Bruce asked as I lifted the box.

"Not for another few weeks. Right now, it looks like we'll be there a bit over a week. Llysette's doing three performances and giving some master classes."

Bruce inclined his head to Llysette. "I wish I could be there to hear you."

"You are kind."

"No . . . selfish. One doesn't get to hear the greatest diva of the generation often."

Llysette blushed, but she needed and deserved the praise—it wasn't flattery, but praise.

"This could lead to closer engagements," I pointed out.

"I certainly hope so."

I looked down at the box. "Thank you . . . again. You've been a great help when no one else cared."

"We aim to please."

I let it go. Bruce didn't seem to want to accept my real gratitude, and I'd have to find another way.

The sun was still shining and the white clouds still puffy as I carried the SII box out to the Stanley and slipped it into the trunk. Then I seated Llysette, and then myself, lighting off the steamer.

"To Borkum . . . shopping and a good meal."

She smiled, and for a time we pushed away the implications of the box the steamer carried.

8

ON Tuesday, we boarded the early-morning Quebec Express in Lebanon and rode it into New Amsterdam. We had an hour wait there, spent mostly at a corner table at a so-called café off the main station floor, before we boarded the Columbia Special to the capital. At least, I hadn't received any more of the ominous clips and no one had attempted any more burglaries, but I had few doubts that the respite was more than temporary.

The Special went to the Baltimore and Potomac station just off the new Mall, and even with stops, it was less than seven hours after leaving Lebanon that we stepped out into the seemingly perpetual drizzle that covered the Federal District in late fall.

"That is?" asked Llysette, pointing to the mist-shrouded marble obelisk to the west end of the Mall—almost on the edge of the Potomac.

"The Washington Monument. They finished it five years ago, but it was started more than a hundred and forty years ago."

My soprano shook her head. It was hard for me to believe, too, especially since the Congress was talking about a memorial to Jefferson. Why did they think that would be any different?

The drizzle was warm, steamy, unseasonably hot, even in the former swamp that was the Republic's capital, and I wiped my forehead with the cotton handkerchief. Llysette appeared cool and composed in her pale green suit.

"You like it warmer."

"For me, it is pleasant, like Paris."

I glanced around for an electrocab, finally managing to flag down a dark blue one, bearing the hand-painted logo of "Piet's Cabs."

The driver opened the door. "Where you bound?"

"Upper northwest. Spring Valley—Forty-seventh and New Bruges."

"That's a minimum of five."

"It's usually four," I pointed out.

"Cab commission finally upped the rates," said the ginger-bearded driver with an embarrassed smile.

I showed a five. "I won't argue with the commission."

"Me neither, sir." He stepped out and opened the trunk, and I slid the two valises inside—and the long hanging bag that held Llysette's concert gown.

The driver didn't talk as he headed west on Constitution.

"That, *qu'est-ce-c'est?*" Llysette pointed to the heavy-walled marble monstrosity that the Smithsonian had built to house the Dutch Masters—the remnants of the collection of Hendrik, the former Grand Duke of Holland, yet another casualty of Ferdinand VI's armies in their sweep across the Low Countries. When I'd been subminister, I'd objected to the design, but since Columbian Dutch, the oil people, had paid for the building, the Congress had ignored my objections.

"That's the Dutch wing of the Smithsonian Gallery. I've avoided it—call it a protest, not that mine have made much difference."

"A French gallery is there?"

"They have some vanGoghs and Degas, but no one volunteered to build a gallery the way Columbian Dutch did."

"Always the money."

That was the way it seemed to me also.

The cab turned onto New Bruges Avenue and headed northwest, north of most of the official sector of the Federal District, past the Ghirardelli Chocolatiers and around Dupont Circle.

We passed up Embassy Row, beginning with the huge structures belonging to Japan and Chung Kuo, facing each other across New Bruges Avenue, and I pointed out each, including the still cordoned-off section of sidewalk where the ghosts of ten Vietnamese monks still wailed—fifteen years after they had immolated themselves there in protest. The Chinese could see the ghosts, especially at twilight—but their continued presence hadn't changed anything. In fact, I wondered if the Chinese secretly enjoyed such a reminder of the futility of protest to their endless expansion.

I swallowed as the cab eased around Ward Circle and into Ward Park beyond the seminary. Within a half-dozen blocks, the driver turned off New Bruges and onto Sedgwick.

"The houses . . . they are large."

"Yes." The upper northwest in the Federal District reeks of money, with tile or slate roofs, manicured lawns, trimmed hedges, sculpted gardens, and shadowed stone walks. Once the upper northwest had been far enough from the capital itself that it served as an interim retreat for Speaker Calhoun, but now such retreats were farther, much, much farther, from the Capitol building.

The Tudor house set on a large corner plot was Eric and Judith's. They'd walled the entire back of the property, not long after Elspeth's death and my notoriety in the Nord case. Their car barn had space for three steamers, and the house was thoroughly alarmed.

"This the place, sir?"

"It is." After I reclaimed the bags, I tipped the driver three dollars. "It's a long ride back."

"Thank you, sir."

Judith opened the Tiffany-paneled front doors even before we were halfway up the walk. She'd cut her silver hair short, but she still wore a blue suit, as she often did, from what I recalled.

"Llysette, this is Judith."

"I am pleased to see you, and I am so glad you could stay with us." Judith sounded glad, but I could sense Llysette's wariness. "You are lovely, and that's without singing a note." As always, Judith's words were genuine and warm, as were her gray eyes, and her smile. "As Johan may have told you, I remember hearing you once in Paris, just before the fall of France. You were at the Academie Royale back when I did my fellowship there—one of the last ones before Ferdinand."

"Few remember those years."

"Few want to," answered Judith, half warmly, half ironically. "It was not our finest hour." She gestured toward the dark blue carpeted circular staircase. "I'll lead the way. Johan was the first guest, and you two are the first couple we've had since we remodeled." With a nod, she turned and slipped up the stairs past the large crystal chandelier that hung in the two-story front foyer. We followed her to the guest rooms at the end of the hall, overlooking the front garden.

Llysette glanced from the triple-width bed with the green satin brocade spread to the pair of upholstered chairs that flanked the wall table and then to Judith. "This . . . *c'est magnifique.*"

She was right; it was. Eric and Judith had always exhibited good taste, and they'd made enough to be able to indulge that taste.

"We like our guests to be comfortable, and I especially wanted you to feel welcome."

"*Pourquoi—*"

"Because you and Johan deserve happiness." Judith inclined her head toward me, ever so slightly. "He has had to worry about too much for too long. From what little I know, so have you. I am so glad you will be singing tomorrow. I hope you are."

"The occurrence is strange." Llysette shrugged, glancing toward the window hangings that matched the spread, then back to Judith. "But a singer must sing when she can. These things we do not choose, and . . ."

"After your engagement in Deseret, you will be able to choose where you sing," the older woman predicted.

"One would hope." Llysette's smile was skeptical. "We will see."

"Would you like some *café,* or tea, or chocolate? Or some wine?"

"The wine I would like, but that must come later." Llysette smiled, more warmly.

"Chocolate?"

"Something warm . . . but tea, perhaps?"

"Tea I can do. You'll want chocolate, Johan?"

"Of course."

"If you want to unpack or get settled, I'll be downstairs. Just come down when you're ready." With another smile, Judith turned and departed.

"Little she holds back," offered Llysette.

"They have been supportive when few were." I opened the closet so that Llysette could hang out the gown she would wear the next night. Then I hung up my own suits—one for meeting with Oakes and the formal wear for the dinner.

Once we hung up anything that would wrinkle, or wrinkle more, we went downstairs.

The chocolate and tea were set out in the nook off the kitchen—sunny there when the sun actually shone in the Federal District, but not under the gray drizzle. The old bone china teapot was also there, steam rising from its spout.

In addition to the two pots, Judith had set out the butter biscuits

I was too fond of and *galettes*. Llysette took a *galette* with her chocolate. I had two biscuits.

"Good this is," murmured Llysette after a sip of tea, but I could
see her eyes strayed toward the parlor and the silent Steinbach.

"Something hot is good after traveling, especially when it's so
damp." Judith looked at Llysette. "Have you been in the Federal District recently?"

"Mais non . . . not since first I arrived in Columbia, and little do
I remember."

"I doubt it has changed much."

I agreed silently, taking another biscuit. Nothing happened
quickly, not in a city that had taken more than a century to finish the
monument to the general who had freed the colonies. "The buildings all look the same."

"They are talking about moving the railway station on the Mall,"
Judith ventured.

"Again? Where would they put it?"

"They're talking about refurbishing and enlarging Union Station."

"That would take some doing." I reached for another biscuit.

"Johan. . . ." Llysette paused, and I knew what she was thinking.
I'd gulped down four biscuits in as many minutes. But that was because I was nervous. I always ate too much when I was stressed or
worried—another reason why I needed exercise.

"I know." I grinned.

Llysette smiled faintly. After a moment, her eyes went toward
the sitting room, and she shifted her weight in her chair and set
down her cup.

I got the message, and since Llysette wouldn't ask, I did. "Could
Llysette use the Steinbach in the sitting room to practice a bit?"

"Oh . . . I should have offered. Of course." Judith turned back to
face Llysette. "Let me show you. You are welcome to practice any
time you wish. Anytime," she emphasized with a smile. "You can
close the doors . . . or not, as you please. We do miss the music.
Since Suzanne left, no one plays. The piano is really hers, but she has
no place for it, and we keep it tuned."

The two headed for the parlor, and I let them, listening as Judith
tried to make Llysette feel welcome.

When Judith returned, after closing off the doors so that we
wouldn't distract Llysette, I poured more chocolate. "Would you like
some more?"

"A half a cup. Let me check dinner. Eric should be here before long."

I poured the chocolate and waited, listening to Llysette. Even through the doors, she sounded magnificent. She'd finished a run-through of both pieces before Judith slipped back into her seat.

"I hope that didn't get too cool."

"It's fine."

"I appreciate your trying to make her feel welcome. . . ."

"She's beautiful. She plays well, too," Judith added as her eyes went toward the closed French doors.

"She's always telling me that a singer needs keyboard skills, and she's always bemoaning the fact that her students never want to work on the keyboard. I did get her a piano—a Haaren, nothing compared to yours."

"You spent more than you had, knowing you."

I had, but . . . what else was new?

"Most of our students couldn't handle the training she's had," said Judith. "I can tell it wasn't easy for her."

"No. Not much has been, and I've been no bargain in that department, either."

"You've been hard on yourself, Johan."

"With some reason," I pointed out.

"You've never had too many options."

I heard steps and stood as Eric entered the kitchen.

"Like the proverbial clipped coin, you've returned." He held both his case and a folded copy of the *Post-Dispatch* but leaned over and kissed Judith. "You look and smell good."

"You had a hard day, then."

"Such a skeptical woman after all these years."

The piano stopped. Llysette came to the parlor door, and I opened it.

"This is Eric. Eric, Llysette."

"Johan is indeed a lucky chap." He bowed in that charming way he had, with that boyish and disarming grin.

I reseated Llysette and poured more tea into her cup. Eric took the empty chair but did not pour himself anything.

Judith slipped out of the nook and back into the kitchen.

"It's really amazing," Eric continued. "Here I am in my own house, sitting across from one of the great divas of the century. I'd count myself lucky to meet her, let alone find she's married to this . . . shirttail relative."

I suspected Eric had wanted to say more but realized it might raise implications.

Llysette blushed. *"Non . . . pas de tout. . . ."*

"After your last recital, I'd have to agree with Eric," I told her.

"You . . . you favor me, and so you do not listen. You hear what you would hear."

"If Johan says that," Eric interjected, "he means it. He's never been known for undeserved flattery."

"Thank you," I told him. "What other words of welcome do you have?"

"I could have told that you'd arrived." Eric added, more soberly, "Just from the news."

I groaned, half in mock-anguish, half with concern. "Now what?"

"Secret talks between Deseret and the Speaker, the reappearance of the famous Llysette duBoise, and more speculation about the man she married—rumored to have been a top assassin in the Spazi foreign branch. . . ."

"You're kidding, of course." Eric had been known to stretch matters.

"I wish I were, Johan." He shook his head. "They don't want to leave you alone."

I swallowed. "Who . . . when—"

"This afternoon's *Post-Dispatch.*"

Llysette glanced at me and smiled, as if to say that it didn't matter, and, now, between us, it didn't. But it wouldn't help her if the rest of the world thought I was a former killer dog.

I forced a shrug. "They can say whatever. An assassin is one of the few things I haven't been, and heaven knows, I've done enough of which I'm not exactly proud." And that was certainly true.

"It's time for dinner," Judith said firmly. "Such serious subjects require nourishment." She glanced to Llysette. "Unless you need more time to practice."

"Mais non . . . I have practiced enough."

Dinner consisted of a rack of lamb with a rosemary glaze, potatoes in a cheese soufflé, and green beansamandine, not to mention breads and salads.

At first, the conversation dealt with the trip, passing items, and praise of Judith's cooking. Mostly I ate and listened.

Then Judith asked, "What are you singing?"

"Debussy, the aria of Lia from *L'Enfant du Prodigue,* and Mozart,

Exultate Jubilate. Two is but what the president requested." Llysette glanced at me.

"I haven't heard the aria," said Judith, "except through the parlor doors, but it sounded beautiful."

"Everything she sings is beautiful."

"You can't tell he's in love or anything," said Eric.

I took refuge in another bite of lamb.

"You're different, Johan. More mellow, I'd say," Judith offered.

"More there is that he feels," opined Llysette. "And he will speak more."

"The original Sphinx—he actually speaks about how he feels?" asked Eric.

"Quelquefois."

"If I don't, she waits until I do." And the waiting had gotten very cold at times before I learned.

"With this trip to Deseret, are you up to being spy, manager, bodyguard, and general flunky?" asked Eric.

"That's about it, isn't it? Except you forgot target. I don't mind the others, but I worry that we're being set up for something, and I don't even know what."

"They won't let you be, will they?" said Judith, shifting her weight in the Jefferson spiral-back chair.

"Not when they need us." I explained why I thought we— Llysette, actually—were being used as one of the cultural pawns to open energy trade.

"It figures," added Eric, turning to Llysette. "The fact that you're French will make it harder for deGaulle to say anything openly."

I wasn't sure about that, but Eric might well have been right.

Llysette yawned.

"You need some rest," suggested Judith. "What time are your engagements tomorrow?"

"Ten," I admitted. "I have a meeting, and she has a rehearsal."

"Then you should be resting or relaxing, not sitting stiffly around a table with a pair of fossils," said Judith.

"Fossils? Hardly."

"You have been most kind, and for that I am grateful." Llysette stood. "Perhaps you could visit us?" She laughed. "You could wait until the spring. The winter in New Bruges I would wish on no one."

"That would be nice," Eric said. "You know, we've never been there. It's strange, but somehow . . ." He shrugged, and I appreciated his words.

"Shoo," said Judith with a laugh. "We'd keep you talking all night, and while Johan wouldn't suffer, Llysette would."

I had to grin.

Llysette used the whirlpool tub in the overlarge guest bath, and I sat on the tiled edge in my undershorts, enjoying the warm steam and the view.

"You . . . are . . . *impossible* . . . ," she said slowly, accenting the French *"impossible."*

"Me?"

"Toi!"

"I'm impossible," I agreed, not averting my eyes. "How was the piano?"

"Magnifique . . . almost a concert instrument it is, and to have no one to play it . . ."

I wished I'd been able to afford one for her that good, but ours—hers, really—was a rebuilt thirty-year-old Haaren, good, serviceable, with a nice tone, but definitely not in the class of the grand Steinbach in the sitting room below. I wished I'd been able to give her something like that.

"You, you have given me . . . us . . . much. Do not worry yourself," she commanded, as if she could read my thoughts, and perhaps she could. Or my face, anyway.

I tried not to, too much, and got her one of the big cream-colored Turkish towels instead.

She didn't need it for long, and I wasn't that impossible. Neither was she.

Later, after I'd turned out the lights and we'd climbed under the covers of the triple-width bed, Llysette snuggled up beside me. "Good people, they are," she murmured sleepily. "I am glad we came."

I was pleased that she was glad, less pleased that my Spazi past had shown up in the *Post-Dispatch,* and even less pleased that I'd been termed an assassin, since I hadn't been. Even though I'd killed, as had most Spazi field agents being hunted by Ferdinand's Gestaats, it had been only for self-preservation. Even as I reflected on that in the darkness, I had to ask myself—or had Carolynne's ghost prompted me?—how much was self-justification. I tried not to shiver and wake Llysette. She needed her sleep.

9

THE next morning Eric insisted on dropping us at the Presidential Palace, and Judith insisted—equally firmly—that she would pick us up whenever we wired. Judith's parting words had been: "I've taken the day off, and I expect you two to take full advantage of that."

I presented the government ID I still retained to the guards by the wrought-iron fence that surrounded the Presidential Palace. Llysette proffered her university card.

"One moment, sir and madam."

I glanced eastward, toward the Capitol, the domain of the Speaker, its lower reaches blocked by the turrets of the B&P station on the Mall, the whiteness of the recently restored west front of the Capitol a contrast to the dingier structures that flanked an increasingly run-down Pennsylvania Avenue. The Capitol had been restored three times, but it had taken a century to finish the Washington Monument. Somehow that said something about the relative priorities of the Congress in dealing with politicians and soldiers.

"They're expecting you both, sir and madam."

I didn't know about both of us. When we got to the east entry, a young man in a dark suit, with a goatee that looked glued on, immediately hastened up to Llysette. "Fräulein duBoise?"

Llysette nodded as if there could not possibly be any doubt, and I wanted to grin. Instead, I did the answering, like any good manager. "Yes. Who will be accompanying her?"

"Fräulein Stewart. She is already in the Green Room."

We followed the goateed young fellow, and then I bowed to Llysette as she entered the Green Room, where a full-size concert Steinbach had been set up at one end. "I'll wait somewhere if I'm done first."

"And you, sir?"

"I have an appointment with Harlaan Oakes."

"Very good, sir." The goateed fellow and the functionary in the butler's outfit let me head toward the east entrance, except I doubled back and headed for the lower stairs. I didn't get far before another fresh-faced young man, with the telltale bulge in his jacket, found me. "Minister Eschbach?"

"Yes? I presume Harlaan is where his predecessor was."

"Ah . . . yes, sir. If you would follow me . . ."

No, they weren't about to allow me to wander through the Presidential Palace by myself.

Harlaan, wonder of wonders, was actually standing in the lower hall. Like all political functionaries, he wore a gray suit so dark it was almost black. His maroon cravat blended with the faintest of stripes in the suit. "Johan. You are punctual, as always, as in everything."

That bothered me. "I try. Sometimes circumstances don't allow it, but today worked out."

Harlaan gestured toward the small office that had been Ralston's, and I followed him. His goatee was square, with a hint of gray. No trace remained in the small office of Ralston, the man who was now a zombie, the man I had turned into a zombie to protect Llysette and myself, to cover up one murder, and to, in the end, ensure that I took on the burden of two other souls.

The door closed behind us, seemingly of its own volition, and I took the battered wooden captain's chair on the right of the desk. Harlaan looked at the chair behind the desk, then took the one in front, as if to admit we were equals, another less than wonderful sign.

"I caught a glimpse of your wife. She is beautiful."

"She'll also sing beautifully."

"That will please the president . . . no end."

"Good. What did you have in mind, Harlaan, since this isn't really a social call?"

The president's adviser cleared his throat. "Johan, you're also going to be contacted by some people on Minister Reilly's staff, and we've been requested to ask if you would visit Deputy Minister Jerome after you're done here. Reilly's people are going to want you to do some sightseeing—or keep your eyes open for violations of the Colorado River Compact."

"And see what else I can steal of environmentally friendly or synthfuels technology?" I shifted my weight in the old chair. "What does my friend Minister Jerome want? Or is it Asquith?"

"Officially, it's Minister Jerome."

I waited.

"And officially, he wishes to apologize for past discomforts."

Worse and worst. That meant even more disasters to come.

"You scarcely look pleased, Johan."

"Would you? In my position?"

Harlaan laughed, once. "Possibly not."

"And why is the Spazi going to such lengths?"

"Because the Prophet, Revelator, and Seer of Deseret has requested your wife's performance, and because Minister Holmbek is disturbed by the disruption of Venezuelan oil exports."

"I presume you have been the one enlarging my exposure to the print media?"

Harlaan shrugged. "One is never sure whether what is printed here reaches New Bruges."

"Do you know who made that attempt on our lives?"

"An attempt on your lives?"

"Harlaan." I waited.

"No. We suspect Maurice-Huizinga or Ferdinand. You might ask Minister Jerome."

That was all I'd get, and I changed the subject. "What else will Minister Reilly's people want?"

"A written report, I am sure. They always want something in writing. I can't imagine you have any problem with that."

Not too much of a problem. Just writing a report doubtless of an adverse nature on a neighboring country for which I wouldn't get paid. And if I did, the amount wouldn't be near enough to cover the real costs.

"What do you want?" I asked, another foolish question.

"A copy of whatever you report would be appreciated, of course, although you're certainly under no compunction to provide one."

"Harlaan . . . a little more, please."

"The president is concerned, Johan, deeply concerned."

"That's apparent. Why?"

"Deseret is almost a closed culture. Great Salt Lake City is the only place where they really allow outsiders, in any meaningful sense, you understand. The world has changed in the last century since the death of Prophet Young, but Deseret has not."

I had to frown at that. "What about their advances in drip farming, the natural cottons, their synthetic fuel plants, their specialty steels? Or the results of their partnerships with the Bajan difference engine suppliers? Or their success in building on the original Fischer-Tropsch designs? Those aren't exactly products of a backward culture."

Harlaan raised his eyebrows. "As you know, all of those are derivatives of others' ideas, not original in nature. That is the essence of Deseret, and why our concerns are social and political. The president is deeply concerned that any measurable unrest in Deseret will invite greater New French involvement under their mutual defense pact."

"Those concerns wouldn't have anything to do with the growing oil shortages, would they?" I asked. "This great interest in lack of Saint creativity and originality seems to have appeared from almost nowhere."

"Those are more concerns of Minister Holmbek and Speaker Hartpence."

"They're real concerns," I pointed out.

Harlaan shrugged. "Our concerns are political."

"How can you have politics as we know them? Deseret is a theocracy, and from what I know, their Prophet, the Twelve, and the First Speaker have close to iron control."

"Exactly." Oakes's smile was anything but pleasant. "And in this modern world, social change is going to occur, either peacefully or from the barrel of a firearm. There have been rumblings about something called the Revealed Twelve. We don't know much about them, except that they feel that the Twelve in power are rejecting the real teachings of their prophets."

"Whereas you and the president hope that Deseret decides to move into the twentieth century before the rest of North America moves into the twenty-first? Perhaps so that you can reduce conflict with Deseret while tensions are building to the north and south— and, of course, with Ferdinand and our commitments to the Brits."

"Something like that."

"I'm somewhat confused, Harlaan. While I may understand the international implications, what does all this have to do with a retired subminister?"

"With a retired subminister . . . nothing. With a former Spazi

agent who is familiar with some of the latest developments in . . .
shall we say . . . the proliferation or de-proliferation of psychic realities . . . a great deal."

"Oh?" I didn't like his reference to the "proliferation" of psychic realities, not at all.

"We all have our sources, Johan. The decision to offer your
Fräulein duBoise a contract to perform was not made purely on
artistic grounds." He held up his hand. "She is certainly well qualified, and as a Columbian citizen now, she certainly meets the requirements of the Cultural Exchange Act, which is the ostensible
political rationale for the invitation. Artistically, the choice is im-
peccable, and now that she has married you, the decision conforms
to the policies of the Twelve, which restricts female performers to
those underage or married and accompanied by their husband. We
and Minister Jerome have been offering, and will continue to offer,
a modicum of, shall we say, residual and residential oversight, as we
have for all of those associated with the recently discontinued projects of former minister vanBecton."

The more I heard, the more superficial sense it made, and the
less real logic Harlaan's words held.

"Who is interested in such illegal psychic research?" I pressed,
not wishing to admit much of anything. "Ferdinand knew it all to
begin with, and vanBecton—and Minister Jerome—certainly knew.
As do others." Meaning the president and Harlaan.

"Certain equipment has been traced to Deseret. It's a closed society, as I pointed out. We don't know who or why, but your invitation
wasn't exactly by coincidence. Minister Jerome has doubtless come
to the same conclusion." Harlaan smiled grimly. "None of us like
the idea of advanced psychic technology in a potentially unfriendly
theocracy with an energy surplus on our borders—and on New
France's borders."

I did wince slightly.

"Now . . . you understand that, under other circumstances, the
president merely could have gone to the Speaker and suggested that
your trip to Deseret would not have been in the national interest."

I understood. President Armstrong and Speaker Hartpence were
waging a silent but ongoing war for control and direction of Columbia, and any concession or request for cooperation would have
been seized upon as a weakness. At the same time, they both agreed
that anything that could destabilize Deseret or allow greater New
French involvement there was in neither's interest.

"So . . . what do you want from me?"

"What you want for yourself, Johan. Peace and quiet. Your pledge to avoid becoming entrapped in the politics of Deseret. That's all." Harlaan rose from his chair with a smile.

That was hardly all—hardly it at all—and we both knew it. Harlaan proved that with his next words.

"Minister Jerome's limousine is waiting for you. They'll bring you back after your meeting."

I could hear Llysette and Fräulein Stewart still practicing as Harlaan escorted me to the less obvious west exit, where a dark gray Spazi car waited.

With just me and the driver, the short trip to the Sixteenth Street Spazi building was silent. I still swallowed when I entered the underground garage of the building officially called the Security Service building, for all that the entire world knew it as the Spazi building. Another young fellow in dark gray, with one of those new ear sets, was waiting for me and escorted me to the elevator and up to the fourth floor.

Neither the flat gray ceramic tiles and light blond wood paneling designed to hide the darkness behind each door had changed. The smell of disinfectant was particularly strong in the garage subbasement. Even in the elevator, the odor of disinfectant, common to jails and security services the world over, lingered, although it vanished when I stepped onto the dark rust carpet on the corridor leading to Deputy Minister Jerome's office.

His clerk, though young, had a narrow, pinched face under wire-rimmed glasses and presided over a large wireline console. She nodded and tapped a stud on the console. "You are expected."

The young Spazi agent waited, and I stepped through the paneled door alone.

Jerome, blond, expansive, and blue-eyed—and younger than vanBecton—stepped forward, extending his hand. "Minister Eschbach—"

"Minister Jerome, those days are past. I'm more of a simple professor, married to a woman far more famous than I am."

"Nonsense, Johan. You two are perhaps the most visible couple in Columbia today."

And whose doing was that? I wondered, considering that no one had even heard of us a month previous.

"Please." He gestured to one of the leather-covered chairs before the desk, then took the other. The blue eyes weren't as friendly as the smile, but I supposed that had been true of every Spazi director I'd known.

"What can I do for you?" I asked.

"I've been reading your file, Johan. I rather suspect you know, in general terms, but I will spell it out. We have reached an ostensible accommodation, tacit in nature, with Ferdinand, on the issues surrounding ghosts. He won't keep it, and he doesn't believe we'll keep it. We need to attain a better energy trade with Deseret, and this performance of your wife is one of the tools for, if you will, de-ogrefying Columbia in Great Salt Lake City. The problem is that Ferdinand's people suspect you know something about the de-ghosting technology." Jerome smiled coldly.

I frowned. "Why is that a problem? Assuming I did, they'd like nothing better than for me to be in Deseret. But if I did, the last people I'd give that technology to would be the Saints."

"I'd hoped that would be your view . . . especially given the sensitivities to, shall we say, psychic proliferation or destruction." The Spazi minister gestured toward the briefcase on the desk. "We would feel more . . . comfortable . . . if you would be willing to borrow what you need. Just take the case. Call it a loan of equipment necessary to protect your lady."

"A loan." Almost the last thing I needed was a loan of that kind of equipment, yet if Jerome were correct, and he probably happened to be, I couldn't afford anything less. "Does this also have to do with the attempt on our lives? Was that Ferdinand?" I waited. "Or Maurice-Huizinga?"

"We don't know."

"Comforting to hear," I said. "Such certainty in this uncertain world."

"There is one other matter."

"Yes?"

"Deputy Minister Habicht—Natural Resources—has requested that you spend a few moments with him."

"I'd been told that was a possibility."

"You can pick up your 'loan' on the way back. His security people might get a little concerned." Jerome stood. "I do sincerely wish your wife well, and look forward to her success. You may not wish to convey that. The blessing of the Spazi is certainly not always looked for, but you two will have it where it can be provided."

I stood as well. "Thank you. I understand." And I did. He honestly wanted Llysette to do well, and he wished I'd drop off the face of the earth, except that no one could afford that because of the "insurance" arrangements I'd made previously, which would release too much ghost technology if I died.

"I'm sure you do, Johan. We all do what we must."

That was that, but I wanted to chew my nails down to the quick.

Since Natural Resources was only across the street, the young Spazi agent and I took the tunnels. Deputy Minister Habicht's office was on the eighth floor, on the south end of the east side, with an unobstructed view of the Capitol dome.

Habicht looked more like a Spazi chief than Jerome had—with deep-set dark eyes, narrow face, and a smile as false as deGaulle's word. He put me on the leather couch, deep blue, and stayed behind his desk.

"It's good to meet you in person, Johan. Minister Watson spoke of how dedicated you were."

Dedicated—that's such a weaseling word. It means someone worked hard but either doesn't agree with you or is ineffective or both.

"I've seen in the paper that you've also obtained a reputation for dedication," I countered.

"According to our records, you were also rather effective at a time when most of your contemporaries were inclined to disregard environmental protection. Would you mind telling me why?"

"Because over time you can't separate environmental protection from either defense or survival." That was obvious enough. "What do you need?"

"A man who gets to the point." Habicht smiled. "We understand Deseret intends to continue massive expansion of both its synthfuel plants and its related chemical industry. Currently, our emissions control technology would not support that kind of expansion. That means that either Deseret is going to increase downriver emissions in the Colorado—which has certain strategic considerations—or they've achieved a better system. Any information you could provide would be more than welcome . . . more than welcome."

I tried not to frown, and that disturbed me. Was it me or the circumstances? I was trying not to frown all the time. "I would think that you would have better sources than a casual visitor to Deseret."

"Let us just say, Johan, that your in-depth technical background has been overlooked by Deseret in the interests of obtaining your wife's services. We're confident that anything you can add will be more than useful." Habicht smiled, and I had to wonder why they all smiled and why I felt very much the opposite.

"I'm not sure I'm as confident as you are, Minister Habicht, but any environmental and technical information I may run across will certainly be yours."

"That is all we could ask."

And all he was going to get.

Then it was back through the tunnels to the Spazi building. The loaned equipment briefcase was waiting with the electrolimousine. I took a quick look before closing it. There actually were a few items I might be able to use, and that was somewhat disconcerting.

Minister Jerome wanted my help and Llysette's success badly. That made me more nervous than I'd been in years—except perhaps when I'd found Llysette pointing a Colt-Luger at my forehead. I wondered just how bad the energy supply situation was getting.

As I rode back to the Presidential Palace, another thought crossed my mind. Should all my equipment on ghost disassociation and replication be removed from the house in our absence? Or would it be safer there in our absence? Either way, that would pose a problem, not insurmountable, but a definite problem. Then again, I had this feeling that what I'd thought secret wasn't nearly so hidden.

When I reentered the Presidential Palace, Llysette stood near the east entrance with a small, dark-haired woman. Small the woman was, but so determined-looking that I could scarcely have called her petite.

"Johan, I would have you meet Terese Stewart."

"Johan Eschbach. I'm pleased to meet you, Fräulein Stewart."

"Terry, please. If for nothing else, I'm glad you married this lady so that the rest of us will be able to hear her sing again." Terry Stewart paused, then fixed me with those intense eyes. "Were you really a spy?"

"That was a long time ago. But . . . yes. Not an assassin, a spy." There wasn't much point in lying. My record had been laid out in the media.

"And they still made you a government minister?"

"What else could I have done?" I asked. "I did have a doctorate in environmental engineering. Were you really young and foolish once?"

She did laugh, and Llysette smothered a frown.

I'd learned, probably too late, that a cheerful attack is a lot better than detailed explication.

"You might have what it takes to be married to a prima donna at that." She turned to Llysette. "Until tonight."

"Tonight," affirmed Llysette.

Even as she finished, one of the functionaries in dark gray eased up. "Your limousine is waiting, Minister Eschbach, Fräulein duBoise."

Indeed it was. A substantial black limousine stood in the side drive of the palace, with a driver holding the door.

"*Comme ca, c'est etrange* . . . last year I cannot sing, and now . . . the limousine of the president . . ."

Put that way, it *was* strange, but we'd already learned how life twisted.

Once again, we were driven up New Bruges, past Dupont Circle and the Japanese and Chinese embassies and the old observatory. The trees were gray in the light drizzle. I felt as though the entire world were gray.

The limousine didn't bother me quite so much as the small gray steamer that was parked back on Sedgwick—just barely in sight of Eric and Judith's. Harlaan hadn't been jesting about protective details.

I wanted to shake my head. VanBecton—Jerome's predecessor—had tried to eliminate me, and now everyone was doing their best to protect us. Protection meant danger, and I still hadn't a very clear idea of exactly what that danger was—except that something in Deseret was very dangerous and everyone wanted Llysette and me there.

Judith opened the door before I had a chance to knock. Her eyes went to the black limousine that slowly pulled away. "That's very impressive. I forgive you for not wiring. Have you eaten?"

We both shook our heads.

"I am famished, also," announced Llysette.

I didn't announce it, just ate everything that Judith put on the table. None of us said anything, really, while we wolfed down the croissants and soup. Then the three of us sat in the sunroom for a time after lunch.

"What did you think of the Presidential Palace?" asked Judith.

"*C'est magnifique, mais triste d'une maniere ou d'une autre* . . ."

Sad somehow?

"In what way?" asked the silver-haired woman who had been my sister-in-law.

Llysette shrugged. "That . . . I could not say. It could have been greater, but I know not how."

It could have been, I supposed, if Washington had not died before taking office, if Adams had been a bigger man . . . if Jefferson had not been so opposed to a strong executive. . . . So many ifs, but we had to live the lives we led, not those that might have been, and that went for those who came before us and for those who would follow. Somehow, that thought made me feel uneasy—or did it make that part of me that was still Carolynne uneasy? Or both of us?

Judith glanced at Llysette. "What would you like to do now?"

"To rest, perhaps . . . ," ventured Llysette.

"Then you should."

I went upstairs with her but, after I tucked her in, came back down. She definitely wanted just rest.

"Beneath that cheerful exterior you're worried," Judith observed. "Would you like some more chocolate?"

"Yes, and please."

We went back to the sunroom, and the warmth of the chocolate was more than welcome. I worked at curbing the appetite engendered by nerves and only had two of the butter biscuits.

"You're thinking like a spy again, Johan. That may be the immediate problem, but it's going to be very small in the future."

"Assuming we get to the future."

"I have every confidence that your talents will see you two through the web of intrigue. Yours and Llysette's talents, anyway."

"What do you mean about the future?" I was afraid I knew, but I asked.

"You've always been the star, so to speak. The spy, the minister, the noted professor and commentator. Llysette could be a far brighter star. How do you plan on dealing with that?"

"I hadn't thought about that. What would you suggest?" I took a long swallow of chocolate and refilled the cup.

"It might not happen, but I think it will. Times are troubled, and people look for heroes. They want a symbol, someone who has triumphed over adversity." Judith shook her head. "She's a singer, possibly without equal. A beautiful singer, a woman who has survived Ferdinand's prisons, married to a handsome war hero, spy, and politician. All of the ingredients are there."

I wanted to protest, to say that Judith didn't know any of that for sure, but I didn't. After having heard Llysette's recital last year and the one weeks earlier, I knew there was no comparison. Good as she had been, now she was outstanding, brilliant . . . and if I—and the Spazi—could keep her safe, the world would find out soon enough.

"You already know it," Judith pointed out. "You're fighting it, but you know it. It makes you nervous. You ate practically half a tray of butter cookies."

She was right, and I had, despite my initial resolve to eat only two. I didn't have any real answers, either. Llysette deserved everything, and I'd have been deceiving myself if I didn't wonder where that would leave me, because I was essentially a has-been.

After a time, I went back upstairs when I heard Llysette getting ready.

Another of the president's black limousines was waiting at five-thirty outside Eric's and Judith's.

Llysette wore the shimmering green gown we'd gotten in Borkum, although she'd almost balked at spending that much, retainer or not, until I'd pointed out that she could use it both in Deseret and in the Federal City.

"I'm impressed," I told Llysette as we walked out to where the driver held the door for her. "In all my years in government, I never got a limousine to take me anywhere. You've gotten us two in a single day."

It got worse—or better, depending on the viewpoint.

The limousine took us to the north front entrance of the Presidential Palace, and they'd opened it to the media types—and there were a half-dozen, more, again, than I'd ever seen as a subminister.

"A little to the left, Minister Eschbach. Thank you."

I moved, and that meant they got several shots of Llysette all by herself. She looked radiant, even with the green cloak over the full gown.

We were seated together, midway down the table, but on Llysette's right was Hartson James. Besides being the head of Columbian TransMedia, he'd also bankrolled the president's early campaign when no one ever thought a politician from West Kansas stood a chance of becoming president, whether the office was considered largely ceremonial or not.

James immediately monopolized Llysette.

"You're the one William is so determined to hear sing. Well, if you sing half as good as you look, we're in for a rare treat."

"You are too kind," murmured Llysette politely.

"Kind? Never call a media man kind. We always want something. If you're that good, I'll be badgering you to perform, and if you don't, my commentators will be questioning the president's judgment. Either way, we win." He laughed, and I disliked him.

Llysette continued to listen politely.

I was seated beside the artificially red-haired Deanna Loutrec, otherwise known as Madame D—of the artificial "Madame D's Gems" and the slogan "no one will know but your jeweler." To my surprise, she wore but a single ring, and I would have bet it was real, for all its size and sparkle.

"So you are the mystery minister?" asked Deanna.

"Hardly—just a university professor who was once a junior subminister and who had the fortune to marry a beautiful soprano."

"Beautiful and talented soprano's don't marry nobodies or no-talents," she observed, "even handsome ones."

Handsome? I doubted that.

"No false modesty, Minister Eschbach. You are handsome." Deanna laughed, not quite raucously. "You're also very off-limits. If I batted an eyelash at you, your lovely diva wouldn't leave enough of me for a one-minute commercial."

I almost nodded at that. Of Llysette's determination I had no doubts.

"See? You don't even protest."

How could I?

After a bite of the green salad orange and amandine, I turned to Llysette, who had barely taken one small bite. "How are you feeling?"

"Nervous . . . I feel *tres* . . ." She shook her head.

"You'll do fine." I squeezed her knee under the table. "You will."

Before we finished the fillets, Llysette slipped away to join Terese Stewart. Even I couldn't eat the remainder of my dinner, and I wasn't the one singing.

"I have persuaded one of our guests—the lovely Llysette—to sing a pair of songs for us," the president finally announced, "and I won't even try to pronounce the names of either song, except to say that the first one is by Mozart and the second, naturally, by a French composer. Fräulein Llysette duBoise, accompanied by Terese Stewart."

Llysette said nothing by way of introduction, just nodded to the pianist, waited for the music, and launched into the Mozart. I'm no musician, but it seemed to me that her voice floated, soared, and yet carried a depth that was beyond depth.

The stillness between songs was absolute, the hush of an audience afraid to break a spell, the sort of hush seldom heard, especially in New Bruges, I reflected absently.

Then came the Debussy.

After the Debussy, the entire table was silent. The silence of shock, the silence of having heard something so great that all else paled. Then the staid burghers and astute politicians cheered and clapped . . . and clapped and cheered.

Just before Llysette sat down, Deanna turned to me. "The idiots . . . why did they keep her from singing for so long?"

I shrugged. "We tried. It took a while." A while, two ghosts, and too many zombies and deaths.

Llysette eventually slipped away from the impromptu stage in the corner of the room, and I stood to seat her.

At the end of the table, as we sat, President Armstrong rose, and the clapping died. He held up his water glass—he'd never touched anything alcoholic, the rumor went. "Even if it's water, the thought is champagne. To the greatest singer I've ever heard. . . ."

Another round of applause followed the president's toast.

"You were wonderful," I whispered.

"You were absolutely magnificent! Absolutely!" insisted Hartson James. "You should do a special for TransMedia."

Llysette nodded. "You are too kind."

"I mean it. After your Deseret engagement . . . perhaps something for Christmas . . . at least a few songs for one of the Christmas specials."

I had the sinking feeling that he meant it, really meant it.

Somehow, we got through the rest of the dinner, and Llysette smiled politely again when the President and Frau Armstrong made their way to Llysette as we were departing.

"I meant what I said, young lady. If I were more articulate, I would have said more." His practiced smile was warm.

"I so enjoyed your singing," offered the strawberry blond First Lady, and I trusted the warmth in her voice more than the practiced voice of the President.

Then we were escorted back to the limousine—or another one—for the drive back to Eric and Judith's.

Llysette almost cuddled against me in the limousine on the way through Dupont Circle and up New Bruges.

"Both of us . . . we wanted to sing so much, and . . . we sang for us . . . and for you, Johan."

For me? I could sense the tears, and I just held her. What else could I do?

I kept thinking about Bruce's pen and pencil set and about the case under the wide bed in Eric and Judith's guest suite—and about the deadly words *psychic proliferation.*

10

THE Friday after Llysette's appearance at the Presidential Palace was the first full day we were back in Vanderbraak Centre. I dropped her off at the Music and Theatre building, as usual in our routine, and went to Samaha's to pick up the papers that had accumulated in our absence.

I scurried through the fitful drizzle that had replaced the early-morning snow flurries, but, barely four steps into that dark emporium, I ran into the proprietor.

"Doktor Eschbach . . . that was some picture of your lady," offered Louie. "And right on the front page, too. Saved a couple extras for you. Rose says we'd best go to her next recital."

"I'll tell her. Thank you."

"Fancy that—one of the world's greatest, and right here in Vanderbraak Centre."

"You never know," I said as kindly as I could after picking up the papers and paying Louie for the extras. My stomach twisted at the mention of the front page. Even the annual Presidential Arts Award dinner shouldn't have made the front page—unless someone important in the capital wanted it there very badly.

"Right here," Louie repeated.

"It does happen." I slipped the papers under my arm and made my way out into the damp.

Back in the Stanley, I read the story before heading up to the faculty car park. I thought I'd better know what had been said. Louie had understated the press—page 1, if below the fold, of the *Asten*

Post-Courier, with the picture taken outside the Presidential Palace, one of the ones that didn't show me.

> Federal District (RPI). "The greatest singer I've ever heard"—that was how President Armstrong characterized soprano Llysette duBoise after her performance at the National Arts Awards dinner at the Presidential Palace.
>
> "Magnificent performance," commented honorary National Arts chair Benjamin Kubelsky. "I only wish she'd had time to do another piece by Mozart—*L'Amero e Costante.*"
>
> DuBoise's performance marks the return of the French soprano once hailed as the next Soderstrom, and those who heard her were unanimous in their praise. . . .
>
> DuBoise had been imprisoned after the fall of France, released after the intervention of the Japanese ambassador to Vienna, and granted asylum in Columbia. With an earned doctorate from the Sorbonne, rather than return to opera or the concert stage, she took a teaching position at Vanderbraak State University in New Bruges in 1989. Last year, she married another distinguished faculty colleague there, former Subminister for Environmental Protection, Doktor Johan Eschbach. Eschbach, a decorated pilot in the Republic Naval Air Corps and rumored to have once been a Spazi agent, was the most notable figure in the Nord scandal, when a still-undisclosed assassin wounded him and killed both his wife and son.
>
> Sources in the capital indicate that duBoise felt she could not perform publicly in the uncertain status of an artistic refugee, but once she was granted Columbian citizenship earlier this year, the way was open for her return to the stage, and what a return it was and will be.
>
> DuBoise is scheduled to present a demanding and full concert at the Salt Palace Concert Hall in Deseret in early December, where she will be accompanied by the noted composer, arranger, and pianist Daniel Perkins.

I shook my head. The story was nearly a duplicate of the one that had run in the Federal District's papers, both the *Post-Courier* and the *Evening Star,* although there it had merely led off the entertainment and arts sections. Merely? More people read those than the front page.

With all the publicity, someone definitely wanted a target. That was clear. Why they did wasn't so clear, for all the explanations.

I hadn't even gotten inside the office before David practically swarmed over me. "Johan, the dean called over, and she was most pleased about the story."

They both should have been. Although Llysette had gotten top billing, as she deserved, the story had mentioned both of us and suggested that Vanderbraak State University had a distinguished faculty.

"And a spy, Johan? I never would have guessed beneath that scholarly exterior."

That was a purely political disclaimer, but I smiled. "The story noted that it was *rumored* I was a spy, David. I was a pilot and a subminister, however, as you know."

David let my own political statement slide. "We shouldn't go on rumors, I suppose."

"No. The dean wouldn't like it if people insisted that the rumors about her and Marinus Voorster were true."

"Ah . . . no. That is true."

"I'm glad that's understood." I smiled more broadly. "I need to get ready for my classes and talk to Regner and Wilhelm about what happened in the ones they took for me."

"Of course."

The papers in my box were mostly junk—textbook announcements and cards for perusal copies—but there was one envelope in the dean's cream-and-green stationery.

I opened that as I walked up the stairs.

All it said was: "Bravo, Johan!," with a scrawled "K" beneath.

Bravo for what? Having the sense to marry the woman I loved? To let her do what she had been born and trained to do? That merited congratulations?

Regner caught me opening the door to my office. "Oh, that was beautiful. Such a slap in Ferdinand's face."

"What?"

"Llysette's performance. It makes him look like the uncultured barbarian he is." Regner then glanced around the empty hallway. "About what they wrote about you . . ."

"I was a pilot and a subminister, Regner. I am a full-time university professor, and would like to stay as such. Let's leave it at that."

"As you wish, Johan." Unfortunately, the young fellow grinned, but I didn't want to lie outright. So I let it pass.

Nowhere could I escape the questions, not even in my environmental economics class.

"Ah . . . Professor Eschbach . . . is it true you were a spy?"

"Mister Nijkerk, you can't believe everything that the newspapers print. I was a pilot and a subminister, and that's enough for any faculty member." More than enough.

"But they all wrote—"

"I believe what they wrote was that it was *rumored* that I was a spy. That is not quite the same thing," I pointed out, trying to avoid an out-and-out lie but also not wanting it broadcast across the campus that I'd admitted to having been a spy. In my vanity, I'd rather have been classed as a Spazi covert operative, not a common run-of-the-mill spy, but they wouldn't have known the difference. "The newspaper speculations will not assist you in discussing the impact of taxation on the consumption levels of environmentally sensitive goods. Mister Dykstra, what does the location of the Tejas oil fields have to do with the development of the current steamer technology in Columbia?"

Mister Dykstra swallowed.

After forty minutes more on the impact of transport technology on the environment, I escaped to Delft's. I made it there before Llysette.

"Herr Doktor Eschbach, will the lady be joining you?"

"Yes, Victor."

"Then you must have the table by the stove."

I nodded toward the door. "Here she comes."

Victor turned and gave a deep bow to Llysette. "I did not know, but I am pleased that it was a French soprano that the president did praise."

"*Merci.*" Llysette smiled.

Victor ushered us to Llysette's favorite table, and that was a good thing, because she was almost shivering from the damp cold.

"Do you know what you would like?" he asked.

"The New Ostend cheddar soup, with the green salad, and chocolate," I ordered.

"The croissant with the salad, and the wine, the good white."

"With pleasure. With much pleasure, mademoiselle." Victor bowed again, as if Llysette's presence had made his day.

"You are certainly the belle of Vanderbraak Centre," I said with a laugh. "What did Dierk say?"

"I should apply for full professor. That is now before they forget."

"He's probably right. That assumes you want to keep teaching."

"Johan. I have one paying concert."

"So far."

"We shall see."

She was right about that, but she hadn't seen the local paper.

"Here you are, prima donna of Columbia." I passed the newspaper across the table to her.

Llysette still flushed ever so slightly. "This, it is . . . *tres difficile*—"

"Hard to believe? For the diva who was supposed to replace Soderstrom?"

"Long ago, that was so long ago . . . or it seems so."

"*Voilà!*" Victor presented Llysette with the shimmering white Sebastopol, followed by my chocolate, and flashed another smile. He was clearly enjoying himself.

"Did anyone else say anything?"

"The dean, such a letter she wrote me." Llysette gave a sound that was too feminine for a snort and too ironic for a sniff. "The butter, it would not melt in her mouth."

I got the idea.

"She only told me, 'Bravo.' " I lowered my voice slightly, not that it mattered. "David was worried that it said I'd been a spy."

My diva smiled broadly. "Worry he should, the . . . weasel. He and the dean, they are similar."

Weasel was probably too kind a description, but I was feeling charitable and let it pass.

II

~

Outside of the gray steamers that appeared in and around Vanderbraak Centre, especially in the vicinity of Deacon's Lane, the next complete week after Llysette's appearance was surprisingly quiet. Both Llysette and I actually managed to catch up on missed teaching and lessons, at least mostly.

No strangers appeared at our door with odd boxes, and the newspapers were temporarily silent on the subject of either Llysette or me.

That lasted until I picked up Llysette the following Friday, a clear late afternoon so cold that her breath was a white fog as she slipped into the Stanley in the twilight.

"I'm glad you don't have any rehearsals tonight," I said casually, easing the steamer out and around the square past McArdles' and toward the Wijk River bridge. "It's been a long week. Anything interesting happen?"

"Doktor Perkins—he sent me an arrangement, a special arrangement, to see if it would I like." Llysette's words ran together, the way she did when she got excited. "And he writes that he looks forward to playing for me, and would I send the arrangements I would prefer. . . ."

"Doktor Perkins?" I pulled up to wait for a hauler to cross the bridge.

"The composer—he is the one who put Vondel to music. But his art songs, they are so much better. I sang the one."

I frowned, trying to recall her recital. For only a few weeks ago, it seemed even longer. *"Fragments of a Conversation?"*

"Exactement!"

"He's a Saint?"

"For me, he wishes to play. . . ."

"He should. Who could he play for that would be any better?" I had to smile. Sometimes she still didn't realize just how good she'd gotten.

"You are kind."

"This time, I'm just accurate." The Stanley slid a bit, and I eased the steamer into four-wheel as we headed up Deacon's Lane in the dimming light.

Llysette swallowed. "And my concert, they wish to record. There is . . . an agreement. . . ."

"A contract?"

"I have it here." She held up what might have been an envelope, but I was concentrating on driving.

"I'll look at it when we get home." I paused as it hit me. "A recording contract? That's wonderful! Maybe you won't have to teach Dutch dunderheads for the rest of your life."

"Mon cher . . . sweet you are, but even I, I know that people, they must buy the recordings, and who will buy the songs of an aging French singer?"

"About half the world, once they hear you. And you're certainly not aging. I can attest to that."

Llysette laughed. "You are *impossible.*"

I probably was, in more ways than one, but I had this feeling. Llysette had needed only one break, and she'd gotten it. With her determination, she wouldn't fail—not unless someone stopped her. And that led to the other feeling—the one that said she needed protecting more than I did.

Once we were inside, and after I'd stoked up the woodstove against the chill created by the cold and the rising wind, I did read the contract while Llysette sat in front of the stove and watched.

"It looks all right to me. Would you mind if I called Eric? I think they have someone in his law firm that does this sort of thing."

"He would do that for me?"

"I am sure he would be more than happy. More than happy, but I probably can't get an answer until late Monday or Tuesday."

While Llysette changed into more casual—and warmer—

trousers and a sweater, I went into the kitchen and started on dinner: a ham angel-hair pasta with broccoli that wouldn't take too long, with biscuits and a small green salad. First came the water, since that took the longest to heat, and then I went to work on the sauce, digging out the butter, a garlic clove, the leftover ham and the horribly expensive broccoli crown. Fresh vegetables were still costly in the winter in New Bruges. Then I got out the milk and the dash of flour I needed.

I had the sauce ready, the biscuits ready to go into the oven, just about the time the kettle was boiling. So in went the angel-hair. I set the kitchen table, but the pasta wasn't ready—still far too al dente.

Because watched pasta never boiled, not for me, I slipped out of the kitchen and into the study for a moment, taking the mail from my jacket pocket and setting it on the desk.

I looked at the mirror on the wall, with the bosses that opened the concealed storage area that contained not only the old artificial lodestone but also the de-ghosting equipment and, now, the equipment case from Jerome.

Strange . . . a year before I hadn't even known about the hidden area, not until Carolynne—then known only as the silent and enduring family ghost—had pointed it out to me and begun to murmur Shakespeare and art songs. Now, from within me, sometimes I could almost hear the songs in my ears, not just in my thoughts. Llysette, I knew, heard more than I did.

When I'd attempted to develop a copy of Carolynne, assuming that's what you could call a difference engine–generated replication of a ghost of a singer who'd been murdered more than a century earlier, I'd failed until I'd used the scanner to replicate her actual being. Did that mean there had been two Carolynnes until each joined with me and with Llysette? Did that mean technology would someday be able to clone bodies and each body's soul? I wasn't sure. The metaphysics was beyond me, and I didn't want to think about it all that closely.

I shook my head, eyes refocusing on the mirror and the equipment it hid. The Colt-Luger from Jerome wouldn't help at all, but some of the other items might, such as the detector-transparent rope. I had my own plastique, but there was no point in turning down some from Minister Jerome, and the miniature homing beacons might come in useful somehow. I'd have to consider what to take to Deseret—and how I could conceal it, although most of the equipment was radar- and scan-transparent.

My hand brushed the difference engine as I turned. Was it warm? I frowned, checking the desk. I hadn't recalled the stack of papers beside the console being quite so neat.

After the screen cleared, I ran a check, but there was no sign that the machine had been used since the night before. I shook my head. If strange agents with de-ghosters didn't get me, paranoia would. I switched off the SII machine.

With the hiss and smell of pasta water that had boiled over, I hurried back to the kitchen. I still hadn't managed handling both cooking and worrying simultaneously, and I doubted that I ever would, all Llysette's comments about my being a chef to the contrary.

12

After another week of chill and occasional snow flurries, the temperature had climbed again until it was nearly springlike, although the scent of damp fallen leaves permeated the entire campus. My nose itched. The clock had struck four o'clock as I'd left Smythe after my last class for the week, and the wind—suddenly colder—gusted around me as I walked downhill toward the post centre.

Most of the parking spaces on the square were taken, and the small car lot beside McArdles' was filled with the steamers of those who wished to do no grocery shopping on the weekend.

"Good afternoon, Constable." I nodded to Gerhardt as I passed the Watch station and turned up the walk.

"Afternoon, Doktor. A good one." He looked to the fast-moving clouds coming in from the north. "So far, but the clouds look nasty."

"They do. Maybe I'll get home before they get here."

The post centre lobby was deserted, and my dress boots echoed hollowly on the stone floor. In our box were three envelopes, and one was manila. The manila envelope was exactly the same as the earlier ones postmarked in the Federal District. From Jerome, I suspected more and more. I shook my head and put it and the two bills into my inside jacket pocket.

On the way back to my office from the post centre, I took a detour. I walked by the Science building, noting that the blackened windows remained where Gerald's concealed laboratory had been.

I'd seen the equipment lugged out and even toured the empty spaces that had been refurbished for a new difference engine center for the students.

I'd been so concerned about de-ghosting, but what about creating psychic proliferation, as Minister Jerome had put it? Was there a military application to creating ghosts?

I snorted. There had to be. The military could pervert anything. Then it struck me, and I swallowed. He'd mentioned it. I never had to anyone in the Spazi—ever.

The sky darkened, and I looked up as stiff gusts of cold wind buffeted me. The clouds had swept in and covered all but the lowest part of the western horizon.

Branston-Hay's equipment hadn't been destroyed, no matter what Speaker Hartpence had said. It was doubtless somewhere else, with some other Babbage type attempting to refine the selective de-ghosting procedure already adopted and implemented for Ferdinand's crack commando troops.

Pellets of ice bounced off the stone walk as I headed back to the Natural Resources building.

I also wondered who or what branch of government might be working on Gerald's project to create ghosts. So far as I knew, I'd been the only one to actually implement that feature of his research, but if Bruce and I could, it certainly wouldn't be a problem for any number of researchers, assuming anyone had the material . . . and that was the question. I'd erased the files from Gerald's difference engine, and his backup disks had supposedly gone up in flame with his house. Had anyone else seen his material—all of it? I just didn't know, and wouldn't if or until strange ghosts started popping up places where they shouldn't be.

My own efforts had indicated that matters didn't usually turn out as planned, and while Llysette and I had survived, we certainly weren't the same people we'd once been. Still, those considerations wouldn't stop others, and both Harlaan and Jerome were hinting that they hadn't.

Hunched up in my overcoat, I trudged through the intermittent ice pellets and wind gusts to the Natural Resources building. Gilda's desk was empty, and David's door was shut and locked—not surprising on a Friday afternoon.

I sat at my desk and extracted the manila envelope that held a single clipping:

Great Salt Lake City, Deseret (WNS). Denying reports that
New France had sent a strongly worded note protesting the
planned diversion of more than 10 percent of the annual
flow of the Colorado River, First Counselor Cannon reemphasized the close and continuing ties between Deseret and
New France. "Allies in the past, and allies in the future . . .
there is no room and no reason for discord in a world
haunted by the spectre of Austro-Hungarian imperialism."
      Cannon refused to discuss specifics of the so-called
Green River revitalization program, only saying that the
amount of water involved was "vastly overstated". . . .
      Usually reliable sources indicated that the First Coun-
selor was delicately suggesting that Deseret needed calm relations with both New France and Columbia.
      In a related development, scientists in the water reuse
program at the University of Deseret announced an improved metering technology for drip irrigation systems.

      Water, diplomacy, and strained relations between Deseret and
New France. The clipping seemed to be something that Deputy Minister Habicht would be more interested in than Jerome or Oakes—
but the envelope had come from Jerome's operation, and that still
bothered me.
      Then, everything about Llysette's scheduled performance in De-
seret was beginning to bother me, and we still had another three
weeks before we got on the dirigible for Great Salt Lake City.
      Still . . . there wasn't too much I could do that I hadn't already
done, and I had papers to grade. There were always papers to grade.
Papers, tests, and quizzes. I almost didn't know which stack to tackle,
but I settled on the quizzes from Environmental Politics 2B. That was
because I could make a dent in that stack before I was due to pick up
Llysette at five o'clock.
      By then, we'd be the last on campus. We usually were.
      I actually got through the quizzes, but I didn't have time to
record the scores in my grade book, so both grade book and quizzes
went into my case, as did the other ungraded materials. I had to lock
the building and turn out the lights, and that meant it was slightly
after five before I pulled the Stanley up to the Music and Theatre
building.
      Even so, I waited almost ten minutes before Llysette arrived, pre-

ceded a few minutes earlier by the dejected form of a student I did not know. I never knew who the first-year students were until close to Christmas.

"That was a discouraged student," I observed as Llysette hoisted herself and two large bags full of papers and books into the front seat.

"Discouraged she is? Ha! I should be the one discouraged."

"Oh?" I waited as she settled herself.

"To sing, that she wishes with but two hours of practice a week."

"Don't they know better?"

"They think they are busy, too busy to practice, yet to learn music, to major . . . they say that they desire." Llysette snorted. "So few understand."

"Most young people have to learn about work," I temporized.

"Work . . . *non* . . . I have talked of school too much. . . ." She shook her head. "So much warmer it was this morning, but now. . . ."

"It didn't last long," I observed. "All of a day and a half. It feels like it's going to get colder, a lot colder, and soon."

Llysette shivered at the thought, even while ice pellets resumed their pinging on the Stanley's thermal finish and glass. The square was half-deserted by the time I drove the steamer past McArdles' and the post centre. Truly amazing how a good ice storm emptied the square so quickly.

After we crossed the river bridge, I glanced at Llysette. "I think we ought to ask Bruce up for dinner."

"*Pourquoi*? You have need of his services?"

"No. I don't need anything. Not that I know of. But I've always contacted him when I wanted something, and that's really not fair or right. Besides, he's got a good sense of humor, and he likes music." I eased the Stanley up Deacon's Lane, taking a little extra care in the heavy gusting winds.

I let Llysette out by the door, then opened the car barn and put the Stanley away. I definitely didn't want to expose the thermal finish to the ravages of an ice storm.

While Llysette changed, I went into the study and lifted the wireset. There was a good chance Bruce was still at the shop. He always was.

"LBI Difference Designers."

"Bruce, this is Johan."

"Don't tell me."

"I'm not telling you anything. Llysette and I wondered if you'd like to come up for dinner on next Friday or Saturday. Not tomorrow. . . . I wouldn't drop an invitation on you with no notice."

"It must be worse than I'd thought." His voice was dry.

Had I been that inconsiderate? Probably. "It's not bad at all. I don't need anything. No one's attacked anyone. No strange messages."

"That might be worse."

"Bruce, it's a dinner invitation. Good food, and I hope good company."

"Saturday would be better."

"Good. We'll see you at seven a week from tomorrow." After I hung up the wireset, I glanced around the study. I swore I could feel heat from the SII machine, but when I checked it, it was cool, although not so cool as I would have thought.

With a sigh, I fired it up and checked the accesses. Nothing. Then, on an off thought, I checked the backups. One was something I hadn't recalled accessing in a while, some notes on the wetlands course. In a moment of whimsy, I'd entitled the notes: "Politics."

Maybe I'd called it up, but I didn't recall it. Besides, how could anyone even get into the house without Jerome's people noticing? And they wouldn't be interested in ecology notes.

I shook my head. Paranoia? Or was Jerome playing a deeper game? Probably, but what, and what could I do about it at the moment?

With a snort, I walked back to the kitchen, wondering what I would fix for dinner. I hadn't really given it the faintest thought.

13

Friday's ice storm turned to snow, more than a foot, which was followed by rain and then a hard freeze that turned everything to ice on Monday. Tuesday, the wind changed, and by Wednesday morning the temperature was springlike again, not at all like the last days of October, and foggy, but not bad for running. I went all the way to the top of the hill and out into the old woods a ways, my boots crunching through the crusty snow.

After breakfast, a shower, and dressing, I made my way to the car barn to light off the Stanley. Although the day had gotten foggy with the sunlight and warm, moist air, the glare was intense even through the intermittent fog.

Standing outside the car barn, I glanced to the south, across the glittering iced snow and through the leafless trees of the orchard. Between the drifting patches of white, I could see a gray Spazi steamer on the back road. Jerome was certainly keeping his promise about surveillance.

I shook my head and opened the car barn door, then unplugged the heater, before starting the steamer and backing out. I'd closed up the barn, turned the steamer—avoiding Marie's old black deSoto—and even had the Stanley warm inside before Llysette struggled out of the house and into the seat beside me, clutching her bags of music and books.

"Winter, for this I am not prepared." Llysette shivered.

"It's warmer than yesterday." I eased the Stanley onto Deacon's Lane and headed downhill toward the river and Vanderbraak Centre.

"That is like comparing the icebox and the freezer."

"Wait until it really gets cold."

"I cannot believe I leave the stove to beat notes to dunderheads." Llysette half-sniffed, half-shivered in her heavy coat. "Even to the good ones."

"You will. You'll just complain more." I laughed.

"You mock me."

I could feel the pout. "I wasn't mocking you, just stating what I thought would happen." When I stopped at the bridge, I bent sideways and kissed her cheek.

She raised her eyebrows, and I knew what she was thinking.

How did I get out of being condescending when I had been? By not opening my mouth in the first place. "Lunch?"

"*Mais non* . . . auditions we have for the festival. Did I not tell you?"

"You did. I didn't remember that was today."

"Johan. . . ." She shook her head but then spoiled it by smiling shyly, as if to ask how I ever could have been anything other than an absentminded professor. Maybe she was right.

After dropping Llysette off at the Music Building I made my morning pilgrimage to Samaha's for the paper, before heading back to my office to scan it and prepare for my classes. There was little enough in the *Asten Post-Courier,* except a tiny blurb about the Austrian ambassador being recalled to Vienna for consultations. I wondered why, but the story was just a wire blurb without details.

The big story was the latest revelation about the Asten midtrupp ring and the turbo-dirigible controversy. One of the trupp chiefs had invested heavily in the governor's brother's construction business, and lo and behold, the business had been awarded the contract to extend the obsolete aeroplane runways to accommodate turbojets.

After shaking my head, I surveyed the environmental economics papers I had to hand back—not really terrible, but methodically mediocre. They'd all realized that I wanted facts and analysis, and most had gone through the exercise, but without either insight or inspiration. I picked up one.

". . . taxes raise the price payed for fuels, like steamer kerosene so when Speaker Aspinall pushed through the excuse taxes . . ." I couldn't read any farther again after "excuse taxes," not without wanting to add comments about proofreading, assuming Miss Lyyker knew the difference. So I set it aside before I lowered her grade more.

Eleven o'clock came and went, and environmental economics was about as I feared—multiple hidden groans over the grades, followed by sullen glances when they thought I wasn't looking.

The class discussion was subdued, because it had begun to dawn on them that they weren't getting A's or, in many cases even Bs— clearly my fault, in their minds. After all, I was there to teach them, to spoon-feed them what they needed to know, if necessary, so that they could obtain the magic diploma and entrance to the occupation or graduate school of their choice.

Did I feel cynical?

The frightening part was that I believed my analyses were objective. So I plunged into trying to ignite some interest.

"Mister Deventer, would you rather be a north woods logger or a New Bruges fishing boat captain?"

"Ah . . . sir?"

"You heard me. A north woods logger or a fishing boat captain?"

"But, sir . . . I would prefer not—"

"To be either? I can understand that. Humor me, Mister Deventer. If you *only* had those choices, which would you choose?" I smiled and waited, ignoring the sigh. If you don't ignore such sighs, you go slightly mad.

Mister Deventer surprised me. "If I had to choose, Doktor, I'd try to be a fishing boat captain. . . ." He went on to explain in logical terms how he could invest more in equipment to seek out fish while as a logger he would be limited in what he could log and where.

"Very good. Now what about the impact of the Blue Water Laws?"

Mister Deventer knew that, too, explaining how the combination of the water and wetlands laws retained the quality and quantity of marshland breeding areas for various species in the food chain and thus increased his putative profitability as a fishing captain.

Somehow, ignoring the handful of sighs and focusing on those students who appeared interested, I struggled through the examples of how environmental issues and changes impact basic economics and even society's structures.

Water from the melting ice and snow covered the stone walks outside Smythe by noon. Given New Bruges's variable weather, the water would probably freeze at night, leaving a death trap for the early-morning classes. I pushed aside that thought.

Instead of lunching with my spouse, since she was otherwise occupied, I went to the post centre. When I opened the postbox, I wished I hadn't, but not totally. Besides a letter from my mother, there was a manila envelope, thicker than any of those I had received earlier. I swallowed and carried it and the letter from my mother back up the hill to my office, stopping to get a sawdust sandwich and powdered chocolate that wasn't quite a uniform solution from the student center.

Between sandwich bites and sips of cool and dusty-tasting chocolate, I read the friendly letter first, not that it said much except that life went on for Anna and my mother and asked, again, when Llysette and I would next visit Schenectady.

I could have worked out some times before semester break, but Llysette couldn't, not with the load and schedule she carried and not with the time she was taking off to sing in Deseret.

Outside my window, I could hear the post centre clock chime the half hour. Twenty-five minutes before I had to go another round. I finally choked down the sandwich before opening the manila envelope:

> Newport (FNS). Defense Minister Holmbek represented Speaker Hartpence at the keel-laying ceremony for the *Hudson*. Holmbek's remarks were brief, but he did state that the *Hudson* would provide the first step "to ensure freedom of trade and freedom of passage."
>
> The *Hudson* and the *Washington* will be the first nuclear-electrosubmersibles in the Columbian navy and are projected to be launched nearly simultaneously with the second Japanese electrosubmersible, as yet unnamed. . . .
>
> The first Japanese nuclear submersible, *Dragon of the Sea,* completed her maiden voyage more than a year ago, but the three newer ships will incorporate updated technologies from both Columbia and Japan.

The second clip put the first in proper perspective, even if I didn't care for that perspective:

> Vienna (WNS). Minister of State Franz Stepan announced that Ambassador Schikelgruber is being recalled "for consultation" with the emperor and his government. . . .
>
> Sources close to the State Ministry have reported "dissatisfaction" with the Japanese-American technology

sharing that resulted in the development of nuclear-electrosubmersibles. . . .

In a related development, the Austro-Hungarian Southern Fleet has closed the Arabian peninsula to non-Austrian-flag shipping "indefinitely" in the wake of Islamic fundamentalist riots in Makkah and Madinah. . . .

The closure was protested violently by the Indian Mogul Shaharrez, who suspended iron and textile exports to Europe "indefinitely."

I rubbed my forehead, not that I could do anything about a world situation that seemed to be getting worse and worse, and slowly studied the next clipping:

Citie de Tenochtitlan (NFWS). "In time of trouble, we of mid-America must help each other." Those were the first words of Marshal deGaulle in announcing a loan of 300 million new pesos to Venezuela for the refurbishing and repair of the fire-ravaged Lagunillas oil depot.

DeGaulle went on to pledge continued New French support for embattled President deSanches's efforts to strengthen Venezuela's industrial base and trade balance, noting that "we must decide our own destinies, based on the needs of our people, not upon transatlantic agendas."

Reports from the Bolivar naval yard indicate that two New French cruisers and the carrier *Buonaparte* are already on station "somewhere in the vicinity of Aruba."

Great—deGaulle was protecting the South American oil fields, while Ferdinand was exerting complete control over the Middle East and Columbia and Japan were racing to build and deploy technology that would make obsolete conventional military vessels, presumably to give them the ability to interrupt oil shipments, among other things. I picked up the last clipping:

Federal District (RPI). "The recall of Ambassador Schikelgruber confirms Ferdinand's effort to make Columbia an Austrian dependency," stated Congresslady Alexander (L-MI). . . .

Alexander, known for her outspoken opposition to any

form of accommodation or compromise with Austro-Hungary, also released the text of a purported communiqué from the Ministry of State in Vienna. The alleged communiqué orders the ambassador to "take all steps necessary to convince the Columbia government of the severity of the decision to implement a nuclear-powered armaments race." Alexander's revelation was dismissed by Ambassador Schikelgruber as "a political ploy designed to disrupt efforts at peaceful resolution of difficult issues."

I noticed that captivating, charming, and cultured Schikelgruber hadn't actually denied the communiqué. It was an interesting situation, since Alexander and the president were of the same party and these clips had come from Jerome, who was a Reformed Tory to the heart.

At least, there weren't any clips from Deseret . . . this time.

With a look at my watch, I began to gather my notes for my next two classes.

14

By Saturday, we'd had both another freeze and another thaw, but the driveway was clear, and so was Deacon's Lane when I headed down to McArdles' and the post centre. That gave Llysette time to practice by herself. She continued to fret about the Perkins pieces, probably more than she would have otherwise, because Perkins would be playing for her in Great Salt Lake City.

With the square crowded, I tried the post centre first, using one of the short-time parking slots for the Stanley. Getting out, I slipped on a patch of ice and almost tripped over the raised stone curb.

The postbox contained a few bills and advertising circulars, no more manila envelopes from the Federal District, and a flat package wrapped in brown paper—addressed only to "J. Eschbach, Vanderbraak Centre, New Bruges," with no postbox or other identifier. The post cancellation was from the Federal District. The return address on the package stated: "International Import Supply, 1440 K Street, Federal District, Columbia," and both address and return labels were plain white with standard-difference printer typefaces. Was this a new Spazi cover firm? The paper wrapping was similar.

I put it in the rear trunk—uneasily, especially since it was heavier than it looked. After that, I had to circle the square twice before there was a space behind McArdles' in the small car park lot.

"Professor Eschbach," said a young woman carrying a baby, someone I should have known but didn't recall.

"Good morning. How are you doing these days?"

"I was going to come back for my master's work." She shrugged and looked down. "But one of us in school is about all we can afford right now. Terrence should finish his premed courses by spring."

"It's hard with children." The reference to Terrence jogged my memory. Terrence Maanstra had undergraduate degrees in music, engineering, and political science. Rachel had been a promising pianist—until she met the intelligent, charming, and totally unfocused Terrence. "But don't wait too long. Professor duBoise thought you could have a good career as a coach-accompanist."

Rachel smiled, almost sadly, as she shifted her weight to catch the child, who had suddenly lurched awake. "We'll see."

"You take care," I told her as I headed into McArdles'.

Her smile faded slightly as she turned away.

Why did so many of them think marriage solved problems or that they could avoid facing themselves by getting married? In my life, at least, marriage had just made facing myself more imperative—and simultaneously harder. Much as I loved and had come to love Llysette more and more, facing up to myself, that part wasn't getting that much easier.

I'd decided to fix flan for desert for Bruce—and for myself, I admitted, since I was trying to be less self-deceptive—but flan required more in the way of heavy cream and eggs than we had. Picking up a basket, I walked to the back corner of the store. As I lifted the quart of cream and two dozen eggs—not that I needed that many, but better too many than too few for a cook who liked things too rich—I couldn't help overhearing fragments of conversation from two women an aisle over.

". . . that Professor Eschbach . . . the one who was a spy . . ."

". . . you think she was a spy, too . . . why she was imprisoned?"

". . . Delia heard her sing . . . must have been a spy . . . too good for here . . . say she was the mistress of the Japanese emperor once. . . ."

"Patrice said she was doing a big international tour now that she's a citizen . . ."

". . . maybe I'll go the next time she sings."

I tried not to wince as I walked back to the checkout stands. The truth was bad enough without gossipy elaboration.

After I parked the Stanley in the car barn, eased the suspicious package into the empty storage locker on the side of the car barn, and put the cream and eggs into the refrigerator, I pondered what to make for lunch to the strains from the Haaren's keyboard and Llysette's throat. I also wondered if I were being paranoid about the

package. Still . . . better paranoid than injured or dead, and I wanted
to let my subconscious chew on the problem.

Llysette was still practicing as I puttered around the kitchen—
the Perkins piece I thought. It wasn't Latin. That meant it couldn't
be the Mozart, and it was an art song in English.

Deciding on a mushroom quiche—dinner would be the lamb
that had been marinating for two days—I tried not to clank as I got
out a baking dish and the eggs and cheeses. The crust came first, and
I was in such a hurry that it was probably going to be too thick and
not flaky enough. Once it was in the baking dish, I blotted my forehead with the back of my arm.

The white enamel sills of the kitchen didn't seem quite so
sparkling. I'd probably have to get around to repainting them once
the spring semester was over. Like my mother, and all the Dutch,
much as I muttered about the endless cleaning and painting, I still
started squirming at chipped paint and hints of grime.

Instead of worrying about spring cleaning, I threw together a
small green salad for each of us, then quickly sliced and sautéed the
mushrooms while the oven heated.

Everything took longer, and it was well past one o'clock before I
could announce, *"Mademoiselle la chanteuse . . .* your midday repast . . .
c'est pret."

The piano stopped. "In a moment, Johan . . . but a moment."
Then her fingers went back to the Haaren's keyboard.

I wondered whether to turn the oven on low to hold her lunch.
When she practiced, a moment might be a half hour, but that was
one of the traits I respected and—sometimes—loved.

Then she bustled into the kitchen.

"The other Perkins. . . ." She shook her head as she sat. *"Tous les
annotations . . .* he is less . . . conventional . . ."

From what little I'd heard, the esteemed Doktor Perkins was less
than the perfectly conventional Saint. He'd waited to get a doctorate before undertaking his mission, then been asked to leave Fin-
landia during that mission because he insisted on playing music
rather than trying to convert locals. From Vyborg he'd gone to the
Netherlands, where he'd dug Vondel's plays out of the depths of
the libraries and started turning them into operas, again ignoring
the preaching business. After receiving an award and some solid
cash from Hendrik—one of the last such grants before Ferdinand
and his jackbooted troops arrived, the good Doktor Perkins had

trundled home to Deseret, where he had married his childhood sweetheart—and only his childhood sweetheart. He'd been periodically quoted, from what I'd been able to dig out of the Vanderbraak State University library, as saying that music was his mission.

"Did he write anything conventional?"

"*Mais oui* . . . but no longer. The more recent . . . they are better, but *tres difficile.* "

I cut her a healthy wedge of quiche, a second for me, and then opened a bottle—table-grade Sebastopol, but better than tea or chocolate with quiche. I set the glass before her and seated myself.

"A chef you should have been," Llysette said after her first bite.

"I don't know about that. It's hard for me to handle more than a few dishes at once, and chefs have to oversee dozens."

"*Une petite brasserie. . . .* "

"Very *petite.* Such as the size of our kitchen here."

The quiche was good—even if I *had* cooked it.

While I did the dishes and thought, she wandered back into the music room. I wondered what to do about the package. I was 90 percent sure it was trouble, but with the strange mailings I'd had . . . who knew? And if it happened to be trouble, was it an amateur effort or a professional one? Also, did the package contain anything of value if it weren't trouble? There was no way of knowing without opening the package.

Finally, I went out to the car barn and began to fiddle with tools until I had what I wanted.

It took me a long time, but using a mirror and a razor knife fastened to a cross arm attached to a rake, I had a tool I could use around the corner of the stone-walled car barn.

Then, trying to open the package carefully was tricky. I'm one of those people who has trouble directing actions in a mirror. It must have taken me a dozen attempts to make the first cut in the heavy package tape and almost as many for the second.

I only started the third attempt.

Crummtt!

The explosion ripped my rake-tool out of my hands.

There were only fragments of confettilike cardboard and shards of paper-thin metal—those and a depression next to the car-barn wall.

"Johan!" Llysette came running from the house.

"I'm fine. Just stand back."

She didn't.

"The ground explodes, and you are here, and I should stand back?"

"Yes."

"Johan." Her green eyes flashed.

"I didn't want to worry you."

"You still are *impossible.*"

"You're right." I had to smile sheepishly. I hadn't been careless but stupid, and I didn't feel like admitting that totally openly. "I do need to clean up the mess."

"The . . . mess . . . will it explode?"

"There's nothing big enough left to explode."

She shook her head.

She was right about that, too.

After Llysette went back into the house, I searched the area but found little except for a larger assortment of shreds of the thin metal and what looked to be the remnants of some form of pressure sensor. Basically, the idea had been to shred me with the metal, had I been stupid enough to open it. Well, I had been stupid enough, just not in direct range, and I suspected I'd hear from someone, sooner or later.

But I just collected the mess and tucked it into the rubbish bin. There wouldn't be anything traceable, scientific forensic work or not.

Then I went back to the house.

"Johan." Llysette put her arms around me almost before I closed the door. "I did not mean—"

"I know. You were worried, but I was trying to keep the Watch out of this. What would Chief Waetjen say if I'd handed him a bomb?"

"You could have been killed."

"If I'd opened it in the normal way . . . but if it were a professional job, the chances were less, assuming I took precautions." I shrugged. "I did. If there's a next one, we call in someone else." I knew there wouldn't be. There might be something else, but not another bomb. The bomb was almost an admission that Jerome's people in the gray steamers were doing their job very effectively.

"That you promise?"

"I promise."

She kissed me, and the kiss was warm enough that one thing led to another and that Llysette didn't get back to practicing.

As a result, I was still struggling to catch up on dinner when Bruce's ancient Olds's convertible whistled through the darkness and up the drive to the side door. I had extracted a promise from

Llysette not to mention the explosive nature of the afternoon, the explosive nature of either the early or later afternoon.

Bruce stepped up to the door at six-fifty-eight, with two bottles of wine in a basket. The wind had picked up and was swirling snow-flakes across the drive, the light kind of flurries that wouldn't stick.

"Greetings, Johan." He handed me the basket. "And Llysette." He turned his head and smiled.

Standing by the foot of the stairs, she returned the smile. "Good it is to see you."

"Greetings and thank you." I glanced at the wine. "Yountville. You're definitely spoiling us."

"I am not spoiling you, Johan," he said with a grin as I took his coat.

"I wondered about that."

"New Bruges has too few cultural adornments to risk losing one." He inclined his head to Llysette. "This is part of my small effort to persuade her to remain."

The shy smile that crossed her face was part Llysette, part Carolynne, and an expression I treasured.

"Business?" he asked briskly.

"Strictly social." I shook my head. There was no way I was going to tell Bruce about the bomb—no sense in ruining his evening. "Except I'm running a little behind."

They followed me into the kitchen while I checked the pepper-roasted potatoes and the steamed mixed squash and tasted the mint-apple-plum sauce for the lamb.

Somehow, I got it all together, and we sat down at the table by seven-thirty.

Bruce took one bite of the marinated rack of lamb, then a second. "Very good, Johan. Very good."

"Thank you."

After a sip of the Yountville, he tried the potatoes and nodded. "Tasty."

"They are good also," Llysette offered. "In France, Johan, he could have been a chef."

"I don't question his cooking, dear lady." Bruce paused. "Then again, the best chefs have also been known to be handy with knives and other weapons. Perhaps he would have been a well-known chef."

"You are so complimentary," I told him, passing the hot croissant rolls to Llysette.

"With whom else can I be so honest?"

He had a point there.

"Have there been any new . . . developments?" he asked.

"Outside of a few clippings to ensure we are fully informed of the tense international situation? No."

Bruce took a roll and set the basket in the middle of the table. His arm fanned the air, and the three candles in the silver candelabra flickered, then recovered. "Technology interests?"

"More energy and water, from what I can tell. Energy is the big thing."

"With imports up to forty percent of fossil fuel consumption, I would think so. I wonder why it took so long to get the Speaker's attention?" asked Bruce.

"Oh, it might have to do with the Red Sea embargo . . . or the accidents in Venezuela. Or even the Japanese refusal to divert some Oceanic oil to Columbia. Then, it might be that energy is just the issue of the month."

"You also believe that Ferdinand is Kris Kringle and that mechanical brass difference engines represented the peak of computing technology," suggested Bruce.

"Compared to deGaulle, or that fellow in Quebec—Chirac, is it?—he might be."

"Frightening thought."

"The good Saint Nicholas, more coal he should bring to the stockings of Dutch children," added Llysette.

"I agree." Enough of international politics, which none of us could ever control. I refilled her glass, then lifted mine. "To friends and forgetting international disasters."

Bruce nodded, but he drank. After a moment of silence, he asked, "What are you singing in Great Salt Lake City?"

"The pieces . . . they are from many sources." Llysette shrugged. "Mozart, Debussy, Perkins, Barber, Exten—"

"It has to be difficult getting an accompanist," ventured Bruce, his hand touching a dark beard that had rapidly grayed in the past several years. I wondered how much I had contributed to the gray . . . and why he was asking about accompanists. Bruce seldom ventured idle questions. "You said it was a problem the last time I was here."

"Johanna . . . she is . . . good."

"But not outstanding?"

"On some pieces." Llysette shook her head. "The students . . . they . . . they are the difficulty . . . not Johanna."

Bruce frowned, his brows creasing slightly.

"It's hard for Llysette to play for them and teach them, and a lot of the piano students think accompanying is beneath them." I snorted. "There's more demand for accompanists than for virtuoso pianists, but they don't seem to understand that." I paused, then turned to Llysette. "I forgot to tell you. I ran into Rachel . . . the one who married Terrence Maanstra. They have a child."

"A waste. A great accompanist she could have been. Now . . . she will have children and wonder."

That was one of the few things I had learned young. You seldom regretted the opportunities you took that didn't work out, but you always regretted those you turned from.

"Is having children so bad?" murmured Bruce, then added with a smile, "It wasn't so bad for us that our parents did."

Llysette raised both eyebrows momentarily. "An *artiste* who children has before . . . before . . ." She paused. "To turn from the art, that is a choice. *Mais, point de chanter . . .*"

"You're saying that a singer can turn from singing after she knows what singing is all about, but to abandon it before she really starts is wrong?" pressed Bruce.

"It creates a different kind of ghost," I said dryly.

"I respect your opinion on ghosts very deeply," Bruce replied deadpan.

"It's one area where I have a range of experience."

"*Assez des revenants . . . ,*" suggested Llysette, and she was probably right. "The students, they do not understand the need for the accompanist, and too many notes must I play. Wine, lager, they can afford, even steamers, but not the music, not the accompanist."

"Students haven't changed much, I see," answered Bruce with a laugh.

"I suspect they're a bit more spoiled than we were," I suggested.

"*Un peu?* Spoiled you never were, Johan." Llysette gave me a broad smile.

She was wrong, but I appreciated the support. Compared to her, compared to Bruce, compared to many, I'd been spoiled, though I flattered myself that at least I knew all the advantages I'd had in life.

"*You* were never spoiled," I finally said.

Bruce remained silent.

"Oh, *mon cher?* And was not to sing before the *Academie,* was that not being spoiled?"

She had a point. There, unlike New Bruges, the audience knew great music when they heard it, but most of those who had heard her then were probably dead, except for those few who had survived Ferdinand, either physically whole or as ghosts.

"Being able to enjoy culture is a form of being spoiled," observed Bruce.

"So is being able to perform without fear of starving," I added. "The highest-paid forms of singing these days are pop-singspiel and Philadelphia lip-synch."

"They're reviving *Your Town* again, I saw." Bruce finished his goblet of Yountville, and I refilled it.

"That's because a flop of the thirties is better than anything being written today." I hadn't cared much for either Pound's poetry or his sole play, satire as it was of *Our Town*.

"*C'est si triste . . .*"

From there we discussed theatre, poetry, and, of course, music.

The Yountville had long since disappeared when Bruce finally rose. "I don't live around the corner."

"You could come more often if you did," I pointed out.

"I couldn't afford to. No one up here except you, Johan, buys what we sell."

I nodded and reclaimed his coat from the front closet.

"It's been a lovely evening." Bruce looked vaguely puzzled as he paused by the door.

I could understand that, but I couldn't say a word. It was probably the first time I'd offered Bruce something without asking for something, or expecting it, and that bothered him.

"I've enjoyed it," he added, as if he were surprised that he had.

"We're glad."

Llysette nodded with me.

With a nod, he was gone, into the snowflakes that still swirled but hadn't stuck on grass or drive.

"Lonely, he is," said Llysette as we watched Bruce back the Olds around and head out into the darkness, back toward Zuider.

I knew that. I'd been there, and I tightened my fingers around hers, glad that I was no longer lonely, that our ghosts had left us filled and together, rather than empty and alone.

Llysette squeezed my hand in response.

15

Not a great deal happened over the next week, perhaps because of the pair of ubiquitous gray steamers that parked in out-of-the-way lanes and perhaps because nothing would have happened anyway.

That is, nothing of cosmic import occurred. I did get a brief call from Minister Jerome in which he suggested that the disposal of suspicious packages might be better handled by some of his experts, assuming I preferred not to involve the local Watch.

I thanked him and told him that I would certainly keep that in mind.

Llysette still practiced and beat notes into students, worried about the student opera production she had to leave six weeks or so before it went up, even while the students thought six weeks was an eternity. And she reminded me, more than occasionally, to be aware of suspicious packages. But we didn't get any more, and mostly, her worries centered on the Perkins pieces.

"So . . . so . . . precise . . . they must be."

I'd heard that phrase more than once.

As for me, I continued to struggle with my own Dutch dunderheads, as well as study the occasional clips from various news sources that periodically appeared in our postbox. I had to admit that the clips were interesting and that I'd missed that aspect of my job two positions previously—I did like learning new and differing things . . . and always had.

On that Wednesday, after scanning the local paper, I'd reluctantly plunged into grading papers, half-enjoying the bright sunlight pouring through the window, sunlight that had been rare in recent weeks.

The papers were on the issue of converting external diseconomies into market forces. I had asked each student to come up with one example of government success and one of failure and then compare and contrast them.

I glanced at the top paper and began to read: ". . . the fuel taxes imposed by Speaker Aspinall's government represent a case in point where a successful use of external diseconomies was achieved . . ."

At that point I began to wince. Despite lengthy explanations, Mister Anadahl had apparently failed to grasp the distinction between the specific external diseconomy and the policy designed to remedy the problem.

Several other papers cited fuel taxes as a success without ever explaining the diseconomy they were supposed to remedy. Then I came to a gem, by one of the quiet ones—Miss Gaarlen. She'd actually gone beyond the assignment and compared legislation that had attempted to remedy environmental diseconomies, such as the Wetlands Equalization Act, with other legislation designed for different objects, such as the fuel taxes, that had achieved the same result. Several of the following papers cheered me up with their understanding of the subject.

In a way it puzzled me. They were all in the same class, with the same teacher, yet a disparate handful understood, and another larger group, with no noticeable difference from the first group, hadn't seemed to learn anything and had failed in exactly the same way. Had the second group all worked on their papers together? Who knew? What I did know was that they hadn't had the brains to work with someone who did understand the problem I'd posed. Or they didn't care, which was more disturbing.

I tried to take comfort in the half a dozen fairly good and good papers, toiling with papers, and red ink until ten-forty-five and then packing them away and extracting my class notes.

"You're leaving next Friday?" David cornered me as I left my office for Environmental Economics 2A with a stack of papers under my arm.

"Saturday. Friday I teach a full schedule."

He cleared his throat. I waited.

"Johan . . ."

"You're wondering if I have to go the whole time?" I shrugged. "If I don't go, Llysette doesn't sing. Those are the terms of the contract. The Saints don't want unattached attractive females in Great Salt Lake City. Especially singers, I'd guess. So if the dean wants the publicity, I have to go."

"Ah . . . it wasn't that."

I waited again.

"I just received the latest issue of the *Journal*—"

"The one with my article on environmental realities?" I continued to be surprised that the *Journal of Columbian Politics* continued to seek my articles and commentaries, given the outrage they often provoked.

David nodded.

"What was it that disturbed you about this one? My analysis of the practical impossibility of compliance with the legal terms of the Safe Water Sources Act?"

My chair shook his head and cleared his throat. "I was . . . somewhat concerned by the flippant definition—"

"Of an environmentalist? Someone who throws his trash in your backyard and proposes to split the cleanup taxes with you?" I laughed. "I could have used almost the same definition for an industrialist, except he leaves the trash where it is and calls it previously used raw materials. Maybe, in my next article—"

"Johan . . . the vanEmsdens would not be pleased."

"Donors or not, David, they won't read the article. The most they read is the *Dairy News,* or whatever their trade press is." I shouldn't have been so hard on David. I suppose I should have been grateful to occupy the vonBehn Professorship, but I doubted that the legendary and outspoken Aphra would have minded my independence.

"Johan . . . ," he said almost helplessly. "What about the students?"

"They won't have read it either." Had any of my students ever read the *Journal?* If they did, not a one had ever mentioned it or used the material. Besides, why would they ever read anything not assigned? Or read a book that wasn't enjoyable?

Last year, one Mister Paulus had blanched when I'd suggested that the criteria for greatness of a book included far more than the level of enjoyment of the readers. The poor fellow had been honestly shocked.

"You'd say that about our students?" David was honestly distressed, or counterfeiting distress well.

At times, I had to wonder why he got so upset about such comparatively minor things—but I wondered about too many things too often. "We have some good students, David. Then we have the others, and I'd say more than that about them, and you know it. I'm hopelessly outspoken. Use it as an example. . . . On the other hand, you'd better not. None of them regard outspoken honesty as a virtue." I smiled. "I need to go, or I'll be late for class."

I nodded and stepped around him. With the endowed chair had come tenure, and that meant David could rant and rail, but that was about it. I only wished Llysette had tenure, but I hoped, even with all the complications, that her singing in Deseret would give her the stature to negotiate something like that.

Environmental Economics 2A was predictable, especially after having read their papers. Predictable and totally inexplicable. An environmental diseconomy is very simple. It is effectively the negative environmental impact of any cultural or societal action for which no individual or group of individuals bears either the cost or the responsibility—such as air pollution from the old internal combustion engines or wastewater discharges from manufacturing plants before the Blue Water Laws.

So why did I get questions like Miss Fanstaal's? "Professor Eschbach, I don't understand why you said the federal grazing fees created external diseconomies. Can you explain that?"

"Because the fees don't cover the maintenance costs of the grasslands. The degradation isn't anyone's specific responsibility."

She still looked blank. So did four or five others. Miss Gaarlen managed to conceal the same wince I felt.

All in all, it was a long class, and I kept wondering where I'd gone wrong. So much of what I taught seemed simple enough to me—and to about a third of the class—but for the others it was as if I were teaching Boolean algebra in Sanskrit with Greek footnotes to explain the underlying concepts . . . or something.

Llysette was actually coming out of the Music Building before I got there.

We both looked at each other, and then we began to laugh in the mist that wasn't quite a freezing drizzle.

"It's been one of those mornings," I finally said.

"Dunderheads, they are," she agreed.

We walked slowly down to the square, arm in arm.

"The diva and the doktor." Victor bowed deeply as we walked into Delft's.

From his tone, I had the feeling both terms referred to Llysette.

"The doktors and the diva," I replied with a smile.

"But of course." Victor's smile was bland.

We got the table by the stove. That had effectively become Llysette's table once Victor had ascertained that she was *the* diva of Columbia.

"Wine, the good red," said Llysette.

"Chocolate, please," I added.

Victor nodded and hurried away.

I offered the basket of bread to Llysette. She shook her head. I took a piece of the crusty bread and ate it all even before Victor returned with our beverages.

"Your wine, mademoiselle."

"*Merci.*"

"Thank you for the chocolate, Victor."

"It is nothing."

I wanted to add, "*Et comment!*" But I refrained, showing the self-restraint David was convinced I lacked. Instead, I said, "I'll have the small pasta primavera." I didn't need the large serving, not with my battle against midlife bulge.

"The special soup," Llysette added.

Victor bobbed his head and slipped away.

"You had a bad morning?" I prompted.

"They are so slow." She paused to sip the wine, then looked at the glass. "This . . . I should not. *Mais* . . . I dread the afternoon rehearsal. Soon we must go to evenings."

Llysette was doing a short comic opera, something I'd never heard of—*The Spinster and the Swindler,* by a composer I'd also never heard of, Seymour Barab.

"Why?" I thought I knew, but I asked anyway.

"To them, six weeks, eight weeks, it is forever. One week and more I will be gone, and for two they have the holidays. They should be off book, but still they must hold their scores. So . . . we must rehearse more. Only in rehearsal do they look at the music."

"You can't sing with your nose in the score."

"Sing? They cannot sing, except three; they cannot act; they cannot think. And I must beat notes and walk them from the one place to the other." Llysette took another long swallow of the wine, then set the goblet down as Victor reappeared with her cream of broccoli soup and my pasta primavera.

For a time, we ate silently. We were both hungry. We always were, it seemed, or was it nervousness?

Later, I walked Llysette back to the Music Building and her waiting student, then went down to the post centre.

The manila envelope in the postbox was briefing book–sized and thick. Unlike the others, it had a printed return address, the Spazi one, International Import Services, PLC. From the feel, it contained briefing papers and clippings, and I could definitely feel the contents. I swallowed hard but didn't open the package or the two bills. Packages gave me a queasy feeling.

David was out—or still at lunch—when I got back to the department offices.

"Is our esteemed chairman expected back soon?" I almost bowed to Gilda, but that would have been too much of a mockery.

"Doktor Doniger has left to attend a meeting of the Association of Columbian University Professors in New Amsterdam." Gilda smiled. "His return is not imminent."

"But return he will," I predicted.

Gilda nodded, her fingers on the calculator. The sheets of difference engine printouts before her indicated she was trying to catch up on the departmental budget, something she never did while David was around.

I'd never bothered to join ACUP, since the one meeting I'd attended had convinced me that the group catered to the lowest common denominator, and that was complaining. I hadn't regretted the decision, not yet anyway.

For once, I actually locked my office door while I was inside—before I opened the heavy envelope . . . carefully.

More than a dozen clippings lay on top of the stapled document that had no letterhead, nor any identifying marks. After setting aside the clips, I flicked through the document, noting the section heads:

"Deseret: Current Government Structure"
"Deseret: Economic and Market Structure"
"Deseret: Internal Security Forces"
"Deseret: Church Security Forces"
"Deseret: External Security Forces"
"Deseret: Dissident Influences"

"New France: Intelligence Operations in Deseret"
"Quebec: Intelligence Operations in Deseret"
"Austro-Hungary: Intelligence Operations in Deseret"
"Japan: Intelligence Operations in Deseret"

I noted the obvious omission—"Columbia: Intelligence Operations in Deseret."

I had a lot of reading to do in the few days ahead, and I doubted that I'd enjoy any of it.

In the meantime, my two o'clock environmental politics class was nearing, and with it the stunned looks on about half the earnest Dutch faces. What would they look like if I showed them the material I'd received from Jerome? I shook my head—just the same stunned looks. Anything outside their universe was incomprehensible.

Had I been that dense when I'd been their ages? I could ask my mother, but I wasn't sure I really wanted to know.

I slipped the briefing materials back into the envelope and the envelope into my case. The case was going with me to class and everywhere else until its contents reached my study at home.

At least the Spazi was overseeing the house, for which I was becoming increasingly, if reluctantly, grateful.

16

 $\backsim$

SUNDAY afternoon before we were due to leave, I finally faced up to the unpleasant task of determining what I should take to Deseret. Of course, if I decided on Sunday, that also gave me almost a week to reconsider.

The briefing materials from Jerome had given me enough pause, but what they hadn't addressed was who had made the attack on Llysette and me or sent the package bomb. From what I knew, and from what Jerome had sent, it was clear that the first attack had to have been directed by either Quebec, New France, or the Austrians. Quebec made no sense, crazy as some of the Quebecois were, unless it was as a favor to New France.

Most of the operatives on the other sides, the ones I'd known in passing over the years, wouldn't have used that sort of a high-technology bungle. A good long-range slug thrower was far more effective and simpler. Only the Austrians seemed fascinated with the use of de-ghosting devices. But Maurice-Huizinga of New France was perfectly capable of using that sort of device to implicate Ferdinand's people—and that would have been foolproof, because the implication didn't require the success of the technology, only its discovery. In fact, it would have been better if the technology failed, because that would have me and the government looking.

The bomb was another question, but it fit the same pattern, either Ferdinand or New France trying to pin it on Ferdinand. Except that I really didn't know. It was all educated guessing, and guessing was guessing.

The other thing that bothered me was the continuation of subtle signs that someone had been looking through the study—and that meant Jerome's people. Why, I didn't know, because they had all the information about ghost technology that I did, and a lot more besides—that they could have known about. Or had they figured out more from the supposedly destroyed backup disks of Branston-Hay? But if they had, again, they didn't need what I had.

I shook my head. I didn't know enough. I never did, it seemed.

The array of equipment and material spread across the study was impressive, even to me, and I was glad I'd drawn the blinds before I'd started.

Yet after what Jerome had sent me in the briefing package, how would what I could take possibly be enough? Every major power in the world seemed to have a presence in the Saint theocracy—and each had an agenda as to who should get the fuels and chemicals from the Saint factories.

The international situation was worsening, as if it could do no less. DeGaulle had reinforced New France's naval forces in the Azores and Madeira—both seized with the fall of the Iberian Peninsula a generation earlier. An Austro-Hungarian garrison had been bombed in Madinah and another in Aqaba, and nearly six hundred soldiers had died. Claiming that the explosives were of New French manufacture, Ferdinand had extended the prohibition on non-European shipping, and that meant non-Austro-Hungarian ships, in the area around the Arabian oil fields. Ferdinand's Mid-East governor had also rounded up and summarily executed over a hundred known Muslim activists.

I swallowed and shook my head. I couldn't handle the whole world, or even a corner of it. I just needed to figure out what would best protect us in Deseret.

Deseret didn't sound all that stable, from the briefing materials. There was supposedly a schismatic group called the Revealed Twelve, sort of a shadow First Presidency. The First Presidency was the effective governing body of Deseret, composed of the Twelve Apostles. From what I could tell, the president and assistant president were almost religious heads of state, while the real power was the First Counselor, who was also a member of the Twelve.

The Revealed Twelve were underground, the actual names and members unknown, but they had been circulating materials claiming that the First Presidency had corrupted the true teachings of the original Saint prophets. The warehouse crackdown mentioned in one of the clippings had apparently been a Saint government attempt to seize materials printed by the Revealed Twelve. One of the Twelve Apostles had been killed in a steamer accident under mysterious conditions three months earlier and another hospitalized for undisclosed ailments.

Of course, that wasn't all. There was a Women's Party, but they circulated nothing, except a verbal de facto veto of names for replacement elections to the Seventy—equivalent to the Columbian Congress—and to the First Presidency. According to Jerome's materials, the women hadn't been terribly effective in influencing choices for the presidency, but several candidates for the Seventy had, in fact, been rejected. What I still didn't understand was how women could vote in a patriarchal, polygamous society and yet how they clearly voted to support the theocracy.

At the whisper of feet on the floor, I looked up from my reverie.

Llysette stood in the doorway from the sitting room, her eyes going from the case provided by Minister Jerome to the three dusty cases that had rested in wooden wine boxes, each under two layers of bottles of Sebastopol. I hadn't even brought down any of the clothing or taken out some of the special equipment that fit on the difference engine—or the large de-ghosting projectors in the compartment under and behind the mirror.

"That . . . you cannot bring it all."

"Hardly." My voice seemed dry, even to me. "I'm not even sure where to begin, except that metal firearms are out." Of course, that suggested that I should bring the plastic dart gun with the tranquilizer darts—the pieces probably would fit in the special boots. Probably plastique, because I could conceal that in innumerable places and could rig up detonators from common elements obtainable in Deseret. I sifted through Jerome's case and found the vest—the standard-issue Spazi vest that was essentially pure plastique and undetectable. There was also a vest liner—proof against most bullets and sharp objects, provided they were aimed at your torso and not your neck and head. The thin synthetic cord might come in useful, because it always had.

My eyes turned to the difference engine, and I swallowed. Just in case . . . I probably ought to bring some of the codes I'd developed— Bruce had predicted that someone would need a ghost, and I'd always regretted it when I hadn't listened to him. Of course, he'd also said that he didn't want to be anywhere around when that happened.

Even those decisions still left a lot to be determined, and I shook my head.

Llysette's eyes went from case to case, from deadly item to deadly item, and then back to me. A faint smile played across her lips. "If your David . . . or the dean this could see . . ."

"I'd rather they didn't, thank you." David was paranoid enough without absolute proof that I really had been a covert agent.

"If I had seen . . ."

"It wouldn't have changed anything."

"*Mon cher*. . . ." Her tone said I was lovable but deeply mistaken.

I didn't argue. I just walked over and held her for a time.

17

IN the end, I hired a public limousine to take us to the aerodrome in Asten, since with our newfound visibility I really didn't want to leave the Stanley exposed in the public car park. I did make the limousine reservations in Marie's name, with our street address—a small protection, but better than none, and besides, since I didn't have a published street address anywhere, anyone looking for us was more likely to key on the name.

The driver who pulled up on that cloudy Saturday morning was a sandy-haired woman—she could have been a lady trupp with the hard planes of her face and the gritty voice. "The Rijns here?"

"This is the place. Asten Aerodrome?"

"Be fifty."

I flashed the fifty, and she loaded the four valises and Llysette's hanging bag into the dark gray deSoto, a vehicle far more square than my sleeker Stanley. The faint odor of kerosene emanated from the deSoto, the sign of a mistuned burner.

Rain pelted the deSoto briefly as we passed through Zuider before taking Route Ten southeast.

"You two taking a dirigible or a turbo?"

"Do we look like spendthrifts?" I asked, forcing a laugh.

"Never know these days. If I could afford to go anywhere, I'd take the dirigible—first class. Be nice to sit on that fancy deck and watch the world go by."

"That it would," I answered.

"They have a gourmet café, too. That's what the *Post-Courier* travel section said." The driver's voice was firm.

With a shrug, I let it pass, since I'd never traveled first class on a dirigible, not except for a few short trips between New Amsterdam and the Federal District when someone else paid the freight.

"You think your students will miss you?" Llysette asked somewhat later, just before we entered Zuider.

"I doubt it. What about you?"

"They will be most pleased. For a week, no one will make them practice." Llysette shook her head. "Nor will I beat notes." She smiled.

"You need this time away from teaching," I said.

"Plus du temps . . . that I do need."

We talked about teaching and about the weather, but I didn't feel comfortable about much else, not with a strange driver. In the end, neither Llysette nor I said that much, and I kept worrying about all the questions raised by the briefing materials sent by Jerome. A tense international situation, enough domestic unrest in Deseret that the police were conducting raids against the so-called Revealed Twelve, and enough international concern that someone had tried to turn both Llysette and me into zombies and someone else had tried to blow us up, while someone else had been prowling through my study but taking nothing.

With those happy facts constantly intruding into my thoughts, we arrived in Asten around eleven.

The driver deposited us before the white-and-gray awning of the Speaker Line, and a porter appeared with his cart.

"The first-class departure lounge."

"Yes, sir." The porter nodded his square-bearded face, and we followed him to the smooth stone ramp to the second level, past the lower lounges and the smoke that drifted from them.

The landing and loading tower dated back nearly a half-century, although it had certainly been refurbished over the years and doubtless would be again, especially after the dirigible–turbo battles were threshed out.

The first-class lounge was paneled in dark walnut, with heavy but slightly faded green hangings. The windows were clear, shining, spotless, like every window I'd ever seen in New Bruges, and through them I could see the shimmering white length of the *Breckinridge,* with the twin gray stripes. A direct dirigible flight from Asten to Great Salt Lake City, on the Speaker Line yet.

The brunette in the trim gray uniform with the winged dirigible with the "SL" superimposed inclined her head. "Might I see your passages?"

I extended the folder.

She glanced from me to Llysette. "Oh . . . you're the famous singer. The one who sang at the Presidential Palace."

"*Mais oui.*"

The scanners hummed, and I tried not to swallow, hoping that none of the various assorted tools for committing or preventing mayhem would register. The potentially most dangerous "tools" were Babbage code sheets tucked into Llysette's and my professional papers, but they were meaningless to about anyone but me and the late Professor Branston-Hay. Or so I hoped.

"You may board now. We won't be allowing coach travelers on yet." The sniff indicated what she thought of coach travelers, those who would spend days in mere seats.

A first-class cabin on the *Breckinridge*, of the Columbian Speaker Line—clearly, someone had gone to a great deal of trouble for Llysette, or us, although I wondered if I were just being paranoid and jealous of the attention and whether I were really suited to be the spouse of a true diva.

The dirigible was named after the short-termed Speaker who was assassinated more than a century earlier by a disgruntled Irish immigrant whose sister had died in the *Falbourg* disaster, along with nearly a thousand others fleeing the Great Tuber Plague.

Breckinridge had been a compromise Speaker, I recalled, because he had the support of the old Anglo-South. He'd also been a terrible strategist, because he'd misjudged the strength of Santa Anna and ignored the northern provinces of what had then been Mexico, fearful that attempting to annex California would have upset the slave-nonslave state balance. I sometimes wondered what would have happened if General Scott hadn't died of ptomaine poisoning, but wondering didn't change history. What had happened had happened.

The *Breckinridge* was not the largest airship, but it was impressive enough—a shimmering white cigar, floating from the docking tower, visible through the windows as we walked up the circular ramps, the porter following with our luggage.

The steward almost clicked his heels as he studied the passes. "Yes, sir and lady. Lower promenade four—one of the most charming. If you would follow me?"

We did, down the central corridor and up a gentle ramp to the next level, the porter and baggage cart behind us. The corridor walls were a cream damask, probably over thin aluminum sandwich with honeycomb sound barrier between.

At the door, we received an old-fashioned bronze key. "Enjoy your trip with us, lady . . . sir."

I tipped the porter, and Llysette and I were alone, the door ajar. I closed it.

Like all dirigible cabins, ours wasn't terribly large, but the bed, covered in immaculate white lace, was double-sized, and our window was beneath the promenade deck. We stepped up to the double-pane glass, sparkling even in the gray morning light, glass framed with shimmering blond paneling that glistened with care.

"There's the river." The *Breckinridge* seemed to swing into the wind, and I could hear the slow-speed turbine fans whine.

"This . . . I cannot believe . . . *la premiere classes*. . . ."

"You can't? Not even after the praise of the president?"

"Les mots, ce sont seulement les mots. . . ."

She had a definite point there. Words were but words, while the cabin represented another two to four thousand dollars for a round-trip. Rather than dwell on that, I stepped behind her and put my arms around her, then kissed her neck slowly.

"You are *impossible*. . . ."

"Not totally."

For a moment she relaxed; then she opened her eyes as the airship lurched ever so slightly, and the ground began to recede slowly.

"Could we . . . the promenade deck?"

"If it's open. You want to watch as we leave lovely industrial Asten and the mills and factories?"

"Mais oui. . . ."

So I locked the cabin, not that a lock would stop a real professional, and we climbed the circular golden pine staircase to the promenade deck, itself also polished and varnished golden pine. Stowing the luggage could wait. We'd have plenty of time, and then some.

Asten lay spread out beneath us as the *Breckinridge* eased westward and skyward on a level keel. Intermittent drops of rain from the higher clouds splattered against the transparent semipermeable windscreen, and the impact and screen combined to create a thin fog that shifted unpredictably just above the polished wooden railing of the deck.

Most of the spotless and white padded lounge chairs were already taken, but we did find a pair of chairs near the stern, closer to the rushing whine of the turbine-powered airscrews.

A heavyset man in the business brown of a commercial traveler looked across the space between his table and our chairs. His eyes dismissed me and centered on Llysette. I couldn't blame him, but it bothered me. Would it be more and more like that?

I didn't know. So I pointed. "There . . . way down there, you can almost see where the Brit colony failed. I was in charge of that preservation effort, you know?"

Llysette's lips crinkled. "Somewhere, you have told me that."

I got the message. I'd told her more than once. So I laughed.

That got a smile in return.

"You are not so serious now, Johan, not about yourself."

That might have been, but I felt serious about everything else around us. I did notice that the traveler in brown had shifted his attention to a female steward who was half my age, or less, and I didn't know whether to be relieved or concerned.

So I signaled for refreshments, and we got an older male steward who immediately made for Llysette.

"Fräulein?"

"Wine . . . do you have any from Bordeaux?"

"Alas, fräulein . . . no. We do have some excellent Sebastopols and a red Yountville—a cabernet."

"The Yountville."

"Make that two," I added.

The *Breckinridge* continued to climb as it soared westward, well south of Vanderbraak Centre, and even Zuider, and we sipped the Yountville before ordering lunch—also on the promenade deck—although it was really more of a midafternoon chocolate or tea by the time we were served. Still, we weren't exactly in a hurry.

The traveler in brown left, only to be replaced by a wrinkled lady in purple, whose lavender perfume wafted around us intermittently.

18

ON the second night, with the dirigible soaring across the Columbian midwest after our afternoon stop at the Chicago aerodrome, Llysette and I sat at an outside corner table in the dining salon, with a view of the darkening plains to the south. The salon was small, with a dozen tables, compensated for by three sittings. The menu was equally restricted—four entrées.

The waiter, in his green-trimmed gray coat and gray bow tie, bowed. "Have you decided?"

"*Coq au vin* . . . with the pilaf."

"The same," added Llysette. "And I would like the basil dressing also."

I nodded. "And we'd like a bottle of the chardonnay—the ninety Sebastopol."

"Very good, sir." He bowed and was gone.

At the nearest table—the one behind Llysette—sat the commercial traveler in brown and another younger man in a charcoal gray suit.

". . . probably another fool's errand. The Saints really don't want to buy our stuff, just steal it," said the man in brown, his voice barely carrying to me.

"Hervey, the boss wouldn't send you if he didn't have a reason. Besides, they can't steal something as big as an industrial boiler system."

"They can steal damned near anything, and don't you forget it,

Mark. Or copy it." The man in brown snorted. "Try the wine. . . . Worry about the Saints tomorrow."

A smile crossed my face.

"You smile?" asked my singer.

"Singers and salesmen," I whispered. *And spies who don't want to be.* "It's just interesting. You still nervous?"

"I have not sung a concert this large in many years."

"You probably sang for a lot more important people at the palace."

"They would not know a . . . an aria from an art song."

"You have a point there. But do most audiences? Except for the critics?" I stopped as the waiter returned with the wine and poured a bit of it into my wineglass.

I sipped and nodded, and the waiter half-filled both glasses, leaving the bottle.

"It's good."

Llysette took a small swallow. *"Mais—"*

"Not as good as a really good French wine," I finished with a grin.

We both laughed. My eyes rested on her for a moment, then traveled the salon as my singer took another sip of wine.

Dark mahogany arches were draped with green hangings, as were the faintly tinted salon windows that framed the darkness of the night, a darkness broken intermittently by pin lights from the communities below and by the reflected glow of the airship's green and red running lights.

Pale green linen covered the table, and the white bone china and heavy silver glimmered in the muted illumination from the chandeliers. Low voices from the other tables merged, just enough that only a few distinct words emerged, here and there.

On the surface, I reflected absently, little different from a private club anywhere in Columbia—stolid, heavy, ornate, and relatively tasteful—yet a total illusion. The paneling was a thin veneer over plastics, the hangings lightweight and fireproof fabrics, the tables fragile frames bolted in place over a deck that was more cunning braces than solid polished wood. Even from all the conversations came only a few words rising above the rest.

Was the *Breckinridge* a metaphor for all Columbia? I wondered. Or the world? Didn't Columbia have its conflicts, and was the power struggle between President Armstrong and Speaker Hartpence any different from that apparently beginning between the Twelve Apostles of Deseret and the Revealed Twelve?

"You are thinking?" In her teal traveling suit with a green scarf and a cream blouse, Llysette looked cool in the salon's muted light, young, and very beautiful.

"You are beautiful." I could only shake my head.

"*Belle . . . parce que . . .* you said that because you love me."

"I do, but that doesn't mean what I say isn't true. It is."

She shook her head. "Once. . . ."

"Now."

She finally smiled.

Always, behind the clink of silver on china, the low drone of merged voices, behind the walls and hangings, was the thin whistling of the turbine airscrews as they pushed the *Breckinridge* westward across the high plains, through the darkness.

I definitely felt pushed through the darkness, trying to see what would happen before it did, wishing for a better light.

But there wasn't much I could do except enjoy the time. I lifted my wineglass. "To now . . . to us, all of us."

Llysette's eyes weren't even puzzled, but clear, and her lips smiled in acknowledgment as she lifted her glass to touch mine.

19

L LYSETTE and I had a continental breakfast on Monday morning—
that was all that was available—at a table on the promenade
deck.

In the night, we'd passed well north of the Kansas Proving
Grounds and the legendary White Sands, so called because the first
nuclear device tested there had turned the sand hills white. There
hadn't been many atomic tests in Columbia—no place was really
suitable, even for the underground tests that had followed.

That problem hadn't hindered either Chung Kuo or Ferdinand.
Ferdinand had just cordoned off a section of the Sahara and turned
it into various forms of glass. I didn't know exactly what the Chinese
had done, but then, few did, even Minister Jerome.

"Would you like some more chocolate?" The steward, in crisp
gray, bowed from the waist yet managed to keep the tray level, a tray
containing both a teapot and a chocolate pot.

"Yes, please." I glanced toward Llysette. "Chocolate?"

"Je crois que non." Her voice was languid, relaxed as I seldom
heard it, and I was glad the trip had been relatively leisurely.

"No more for the lady," I said.

"Yes, sir."

The mug of chocolate, rimmed in gold, and a butter biscuit went
on the lightweight wooden table, anchored to the composite deck
beside my lounge chair, and the steward slipped toward the heavyset
businessman at the larger table, surrounded by assorted stacks of
paper.

Through the transparent and semipermeable windscreen I could see clouds to the south and feel the slightest hint of a breeze on my face, cooling it from the heat of the winter sun.

As I sipped the heavy chocolate, reminiscent of my Aunt Anna's, I leaned forward in the chair and looked over the polished blond wooden railing that circled the *Breckinridge*'s promenade deck. Below were the dry lands, another of the flat plateaus of eastern Deseret, and a thin strip of green that was a river I didn't know. In the shaded places and on the north sides of the low hills were patches of snow, apparently remnants of an early winter storm.

"Are we over Deseret yet, Johan?" asked Llysette sleepily, stretching and rubbing her eyes as she straightened in her chair.

"I think so. Deseret starts before the Rocky Mountains actually end. In fact," I pointed back eastward, "all of that is part of Deseret."

"It is not a pleasant-looking land."

"No."

"That, what is it?" She pointed to a squat and sprawling complex of buildings that sprawled across the hills just west of the peaks we had skirted in coming down from the north.

"It's probably one of the new synthetic fuels plants."

She wrinkled her nose.

The synthetic fuels plants were just another far-reaching result of the unfortunate Colfax incident, or the circumstances that had led to it, really. Prophet Young, the second and apparently greatest Saint prophet, had set up fur-trading stations on the eastern side of Deseret, all along the Colorado River and well into the Kansas territory of Columbia, at least that part of it claimed by Columbia after the Kansas Compromise, which had averted—along with Lincoln's speeches and maneuverings—a civil war over the slavery issue.

The Saints had used that time of unrest to consolidate their hold on the wilderness, but Columbia had protested the fur stations.

The Saints had rejected the protest and sought aid from Santa Anna and his French advisors. They'd obtained, somehow, Brit-built Gatling guns and secretly fortified the so-called fur stations. Columbia then sent Colonel Colfax to rout out the Saint invaders, but Colfax and his troops had disappeared without a trace. So had most of the soldiers in the ill-fated Custer expedition, except for the stragglers who had claimed the Saints and Indians had used a white parley flag as a ruse to lure the Columbians into a Gatling crossfire.

Looking down on the rugged terrain, I could see how even a large mounted troop could disappear . . . or fail to see an ambush.

With the later infusion of the French forces behind Maximilian and the threat of a retaliatory invasion beyond the boundaries of Tejas and into Columbia from what was becoming New France, despite Maximilian's Austrian origin, the Colfax and Custer incidents were laid aside, if not forgotten, and the Saints retained most of the former Kansas territory west of the Continental Divide—except that Columbia had held onto the headwaters and the first fifty miles or so of the Colorado River.

At the time, no one had known of the oil, coal, and natural gas held there—and now the area accounted for most of the liquid and gaseous hydrocarbon production of Deseret. The Saints had become pioneers in another way, in the development of producing liquid hydrocarbons from both coal and natural gas.

Of course, it hadn't hurt at all that the arms genius John Moses Browning had been a Saint and poured his considerable ingenuity into weapons development.

"Johan, *qu'est-ce-que c'est?*"

"Oh, sorry. I'm just thinking about history. How things could have turned out very differently."

"You think that Columbia, it might have conquered Deseret?"

I had to laugh at that. "*Non.* If New France had been weaker, Deseret might control much of Tejas and all of California. Somehow, I can't see Deseret and Columbia in the same political system."

Llysette shrugged. "One never knows."

"That's true." There was a lot I'd never anticipated, and that was in a world I knew, or thought I did. "I suppose we should finish repacking. Then we could come back and watch the landing."

"I would see the landing."

So we abandoned our table and went down to the small but elegant cabin. I had wished it had more than a tiny sink and toilet, but I knew that water had to be limited—it was heavy. Still . . . after three days, I wanted a good hot shower.

Once we'd packed, we made our way back up one level to the promenade deck and an unoccupied set of lounge chairs.

The dirigible had changed course and was approaching Great Salt Lake City from the south, coming over a long, low ridge. Below were houses, and more houses, all set on streets comprising a pattern largely gridlike, except where precluded by the hills and occasional gullies.

We stood at the railing of the promenade deck, not more than a meter from the windscreen, as the *Breckinridge* eased northward.

The city lay right under the Wasatch Mountains, far closer than I had realized from my self-gathered briefing materials, and far more polluted, with a thin brownish cloud veiling the city itself. The air pollution bothered me, because it seemed unnecessary. The Saints had advanced water treatment technologies and a chemical industry second to none.

"The air, it is not clean."

"Must be some sort of inversion," I speculated. "I'd bet it's more common in the winter."

"I must sing . . . in that?"

"It looks that way."

Llysette frowned slightly.

Ever so slowly, the *Breckinridge* eased down into the valley, across the miles of houses, and toward the dark iron pylon that was the Great Salt Lake landing tower.

In time, a slight shudder ran through the deck, and then lines sprang from everywhere to steady the dirigible.

Llysette and I exchanged glances.

"I haven't been here before either," I pointed out. "We might as well gather up our luggage."

As we walked down the single set of steps to the lower promenade deck and our cabin again, a crackling hiss came from the corridor speakers, followed by silence.

"We are docked in Great Salt Lake City. Local Deseret time is eleven o'clock. We will be debarking shortly. Please check your seats or cabin to make sure you retain all personal items."

I opened the cabin door. The suitcases and Llysette's long garment bag for her gowns remained as we had left them. Since no porters or stewards appeared, I hoisted three of the bags and managed to tow a fourth.

Llysette struggled with the garment bag—at least until we reached the promenade deck, where someone had lined up some luggage carts, all bearing a strange logo that was comprised of an intertwined "Z" and "M" within a golden oval.

I gratefully commandeered a cart, cutting off a pair of commercial travelers, and stacked the luggage on it. The garment bag went on top.

"First-class passengers are requested to de-board through the left forward doors," crackled over the airship's speakers. "Left forward doors for first-class passengers."

We headed toward the port side, following a handful of others.

I could see that while the first-class debarking doors were open, the starboard side doors were not.

"Just first class here," said the steward.

Llysette favored him with a look somewhere between a sneer and a glare, and he swallowed. I didn't blame him.

At the end of the glassed and enclosed ramp to the tower itself, through another set of doors, stood two figures in gray.

"Non-Deseret citizens to the right for customs and immigration clearance, please. To the right, please. Take your luggage with you. Deseret citizens to the left. . . ."

We headed to the right, behind perhaps twenty others, near the rear of the group. We'd taken longer because I'd stopped to load the bags on a luggage cart and because the others traveled lighter. Then they probably weren't bringing concert clothing either.

I stopped the luggage cart on the polished brick floor, and we waited behind a short line of several men.

Llysette had her winter coat, hardly necessary in the warmth of the landing tower, draped over her arm. I was perspiring in mine and took it off, laying it across my arm as we waited. Waiting always reminded me of my time with the government.

Five flat podiums stood at the end of the long room, and behind each was a gray-uniformed figure. All the customs officers were male, and four had square beards.

"They do not look happy," observed Llysette in a low voice.

"I never met a customs official who did," I whispered back.

"You never will," murmured the short man in front of us without turning. "Especially here."

Then, as the Deseret customs types began to ask for the passports of the first-travelers in each of the five lines, a bearded figure in an antique-looking brown suit stepped up to the customs/immigration officer on the far left, whispered something, and pointed. The officer nodded, and the man stepped forward, past the travelers before us, and bowed to Llysette, then nodded to me. "Fräulein duBoise, Minister Eschbach . . . if you would come with me."

Belatedly I recognized the man and grasped mentally for his name. "Herr . . . Jensen, is it?"

"Here it's Brother Jensen," he said with a smile. "But I'm gratified that you did recall me."

"You were most complimentary," said Llysette, "at the recital."

"You deserved every word," answered Jensen. "We need to clear your luggage. I have a steamer waiting below."

As we were escorted past the other travelers, I could catch a few words.

". . . said there was some opera star on board. . . ."

"She looks like an opera star, she does . . . and to think . . ."

". . . called him Minister. . . ."

"Like to get fancy treatment like that. . . ."

Jensen led us out through a side door, and I could sense more than a few eyes on our backs as we followed him into another office with both a desk and chair and a podium, behind which stood an older customs official.

"Your passports, if you please?"

We presented them, and the white-haired official compared pictures and faces, then returned the passports.

"You aren't carrying any firearms, are you? Any religious materials that are not meant for personal use?"

I must have frowned.

"You can bring in a Bible or Koran or that sort of thing for your own use, but commerce in religious publications is restricted," the official explained.

"Music . . . that is all," Llysette said.

A faint smile crossed the white-haired man's lips. "If you would open your bags?"

We might be getting special treatment, but even opera stars apparently weren't exempted from customs. Or maybe opera stars whose husbands were former spies weren't.

The inspection wasn't quite cursory, but the inspector probably felt it didn't have to be more than that, since the platform was actually a scanner of some sort. I didn't worry—not too much—since the valises had passed Columbian scanners of a more sophisticated nature and since every single item I'd brought was scan-transparent.

"Thank you."

The scanners passed us. I managed to keep the same bland smile in place.

"Thank you, Brother Harrison." Jensen smiled, and Harrison smiled back.

"Now . . . to get you settled."

We followed the stocky Jensen down the dull red-carpeted spiral ramp and through the nearly deserted main level and out under a portico. I pushed all the luggage on the cart, walking behind Llysette and Jensen and drawing up when the Saint stopped. The wind was chill, if not quite so cold as it had been in Vanderbraak Centre when we'd left, and bore the faint odor of chemicals.

"Here we are." The Deseret official gestured to a shiny brown steamer.

It was a make I'd not seen before, a Browning, and far more square and angular than my Stanley, but effectively the size of a limousine, even if Brother Jensen hadn't called it that. Was it named after or another development from the arms makers? I didn't know. I wondered what else I didn't know and would find out.

Jensen opened the square rear door and helped me load the bags. I laid the garment bag on top.

"Performing clothes, I'd wager."

"To Deseret standards," I added.

"Good. Some folks have trouble with that."

"When in Rome . . ."

Jensen closed the rear door. I turned, wondering what to do with the cart, but a man in a brown jumpsuit had already collected it and several others and was wheeling them back inside.

A clean-shaven young man sat behind the steamer's wheel. He wore a dark green jacket, almost a military blouse, but with no brass and no insignia.

Jensen opened the door and inclined his head to Llysette for her to enter.

"*Merci.*"

The Browning had bench seats in the section behind the driver, the kind facing each other. I sat by Llysette, and Jensen sat across from us.

"I'm afraid that the route to the city isn't the most scenic," apologized Brother Jensen. "The aerodrome has to be here in the flat south of the lake. Because of the winds, I'm told." He smiled. "I understand that neither of you has been here before."

"You understand correctly."

"I'd like to go over a few basics. It avoids misunderstandings. I assume you read the background materials I sent with the contract."

"*Mais oui,*" said Llysette politely, not quite coldly.

"Yes."

Jensen turned and nodded to the driver. The Browning eased away from the aerodrome building.

"Good. We won't have to go over those. You'll see women with hats—that's a tradition, but not a requirement."

"Unlike the business of no bare shoulders?"

Jensen nodded. "I should also point out a few other things. Profane language bothers people here, even if it's casual and accepted language elsewhere. Also, although it's common in Columbia, it would be better if"—he inclined his head to Llysette—"you were accompanied in public, by either Minister Eschbach or Doktor Perkins or myself, if they're unavailable."

Llysette's face hardened ever so slightly, although she merely nodded.

"Now." Jensen cleared his throat. "On to a few more mundane items. The city is on a grid system. All the towns and cities in Deseret are. The main north–south street is always Main Street, and the main east–west street is Center Street." Jensen laughed. "Except here in Great Salt Lake. The north–south street is Temple, and the part north of the Temple is North Temple and the part south—"

"Is South Temple?"

"That's right. So if an address is two hundred west, two hundred south, you can tell that it's two blocks south of the center of the city and two blocks west."

I nodded. That seemed simple and logical—too logical for a sect that was supposedly based on mystical revelations translated from golden tablets that only three or four people had ever seen, none of whom had lived past the Nauvoo Massacres.

Then again, given the hostility that had driven the Saints from Columbia out into Deseret, I couldn't say I blamed them for some of what they'd done.

Jensen gestured out the window again. "There is the Temple. The building with the rounded roof is the Tabernacle."

"Is that where the Saints' Choir—?" ventured Llysette.

"Yes. They practice and broadcast from there. Also the General Conferences are broadcast from there as well."

"Once I heard them, in Orleans." Llysette nodded. "Many years ago when I was young."

The Temple was all I had expected, its towers white and shimmering on the hillside, immediately surrounded by what appeared to be white walls, browned grass and leafless trees, and a few evergreens. The Saints had emphasized the Temple's grandeur by keeping the buildings around it low.

The uniformed driver eased the Browning off the expressway and onto a wide boulevard heading north in the general direction of the Temple.

A series of interconnected white stone buildings appeared on the left.

"There's the Salt Palace performing complex, where you'll be singing. The Lion House Inn is where you'll be staying," offered Jensen. "It's straight ahead, but I'm having Heber take you around the Temple just so you can get an idea of the area. The original Lion House is a museum. It was the home of Brigham Young. We'll pass that after the Temple."

"He was the second prophet? The one who founded Deseret?"

Jensen nodded before continuing. "You can change your money, as you need it, at the Inn." He shifted and handed an envelope to me but looked at Llysette. "This is just a hundred dollars, but that should hold you until you get settled." His eyes flicked back and forth, as if he were unsure as to whom he should be addressing.

Since it appeared expected, I opened the envelope. There were ten notes, each ten Deseret dollars. Each note held a picture of the Temple on one side, with a bannered motto beneath that read: "Holiness to the Lord." On the other side was a likeness, but it wasn't that of Joseph Smith or Brigham Young but of someone called Taylor.

"Thank you." I slipped the envelope into my jacket pocket. "We can return it later—"

"Please . . . it's just a courtesy, and we'd feel better about it."

I didn't protest, and I doubted Llysette would either.

The driver turned the Browning again, onto West Temple South. Two blocks later, we passed the Temple, surrounded by white stone walls and heavy wrought-iron gates, all swung wide open.

"Here's the Temple."

The Browning came to a brief halt, and I could see that the Temple wasn't quite so white as it had looked from a distance, but it was impressive nonetheless, especially with the gold angel suspended above one tower. I could see perhaps a hundred figures in groups scattered around the walks and gardens, despite the chill winds. After a moment, Jensen nodded, and the Browning pulled away.

Just beyond the Temple, where the street signs changed from West Temple South to East Temple South, we passed another turn-of-the century complex, with interlocked buildings and covered walkways.

"The Lion House."

Right past the Lion House was a bronze memorial, a monument

apparently to a bird, but I didn't want to ask. Abruptly the houses grew larger.

"*Pourquoi* . . . why is that house . . . many houses?" Llysette pointed toward a compound, almost, surrounded by a white iron fence that was head-high. Four good-sized houses surrounded an even larger structure.

"Oh, that's the older Eccles house. Each wife has her own house, but the main house is where the family gathers for home firesides and family home evenings and the like."

I could see the reasoning, particularly if the custom had started with the polygamy of more than a century earlier. Effectively, the ghost of a wife who died would be restricted to her own house.

Llysette's face remained calm, but her hands tightened around her purse and her gloves.

After several blocks more, the driver turned north again.

"Up the hills in that direction"—Jensen pointed generally eastward—"that's where the University of Deseret is."

We passed more of the oversize and well-established dwellings. "A number of the Seventy reside in this area."

"The Seventy?" asked Llysette.

"The Quorum of the Seventy," answered Jensen. "That's the body below the Apostles, in a way."

Llysette offered a Gallic nod.

The Lion Inn was a squarish white marble building, of perhaps six stories, less than three blocks from the Salt Palace complex. The awning under which Heber pulled the Browning was a forest green, trimmed in gold, and a doorman in a green suit, piped in gold, was unloading the bags even as Llysette stepped out onto the polished bricks of the walk.

Another doorman held wide the golden wood and brass-trimmed door that led into the carpeted and hushed lobby.

The concierge looked up expectantly as the three of us neared. "Brother Jensen."

"This is Doktor Llysette duBoise and her husband, Minister Johan Eschbach."

"We are pleased to have you as our guest." The clean-shaven blond concierge nodded to Llysette.

"The performance suite."

"Yes, Brother Jensen. The nonsmoking one?"

Jensen turned to us.

"Definitely," I said.

A faint smile crossed the concierge's face. Approval, I thought.

Even the interior of the elevator was paneled in golden oak and trimmed in shimmering brass. The floor was a white marble tile. Jensen pressed the "six," and the lift hummed upward.

Brother Jensen turned left off the elevator, and we followed. He paused at the door to the suite, then bowed and handed a folder to Llysette. "This has the rehearsal schedules, as well as Doktor Perkins' wireset number, and some information about the hall and an advance copy of the program—the one you and Doktor Perkins approved. The master classes will be held in the small recital hall. It's marked on the map." He unlocked the door, then handed the two keys to me.

We stepped inside and onto a thick pale green carpet. My boots sank into the pile. The walls were a cream damasked rose pattern, and the crown moldings were cream as well.

The performance suite was capacious indeed. The space contained a master bedroom with a triple-width bed and two separate attached bathrooms, a living room, and a small kitchenlike area, with an eating nook overlooking a balcony. From the windows and the balcony it looked almost like I could have thrown a rock and hit the northernmost buildings of the Salt Palace performing complex.

The suite was definitely for performers. There was even a console piano on one wall of the sitting area—a Haaren. I had to smile at that. I just hoped it was tuned.

"I've taken the liberty of including several bottles of wine in the cooler. Alcoholic beverages aren't permitted for Saints, and they're not served in the restaurants, but there is a dispensation for visiting dignitaries."

"We appreciate the consideration," I said politely, "and all your arrangements."

"You have been most kind," Llysette added.

"If you wish to eat in the Inn, just put the meals on the room bill, and we'll take care of them. That is a standard part of the contract. If you wish to eat elsewhere, leave the receipts for me with the concierge, and I'll ensure you're reimbursed—for the two of you." Jensen frowned momentarily, then continued. "I think I've covered everything, but if you have any questions, please feel free to wire at any time." He bowed at the door and was gone.

I glanced around the suite, certainly more palatial than anywhere I'd ever stayed. "They certainly are treating you like royalty."

"No wine?" Llysette snorted.

"You get wine. You'll just have to enjoy it here and not in the restaurants. He even got that right." Except how they had known? . . . That was another question that bothered me, unless they did it for all outsiders. "Do you want to eat, or do you want to clean up?"

"A bath, I would like. Is there any food here in the room?"

I crossed to the kitchen area and opened the cabinet—only a small range of china and glasses. Then came the cooler—where there were five bottles of wine and some cheeses and packages of crackers and two apples wrapped in foil.

"Apples and cheeses and crackers."

"*Assez.* I will bathe, and you can shower in your own bath."

"I forgot that."

So I started slicing apples and cheese to the background noise of running water.

20

L LYSETTE'S first rehearsal was scheduled for ten o'clock, and that meant not sleeping too late on Tuesday. She wore a dark green dress with a tan jacket, both tailored, but loose-fitting enough for her to sing. She'd end up removing the jacket. I knew how hot she got once she was really working.

Singing was athletic, and I'd never appreciated that until I'd met Llysette and watched her work.

"Are you ready?" I glanced toward the door of the suite.

"Mais oui."

"Do you mind eating downstairs?"

"Non. I do not like staying in a room, even one as large as this."

I understood. She even hesitated about closing the bedroom door, or any door. At times, I hated, really hated, Ferdinand. Then, probably a third of Europe still did.

She smiled. "You wish to observe?"

She was right about that. We hadn't observed much the day before, just taken a short walk in the wind up to the Temple, only to find the grounds were closed on Monday afternoons for maintenance. So we'd just wandered back to the hotel and taken a nap and eaten and slept. The dirigible trip shouldn't have been that tiring, but it had been. I could tell that because nothing seemed quite real, foreign country or not, despite all my worries and all the Spazi briefing materials.

No one else was about on the sixth floor where we waited for the elevator. Perhaps no one else was staying on what seemed to be the suite floor—or they weren't up yet.

Then, I had noticed the black seals on one door. I wondered how having a ghost-inhabited suite impacted on the bottom line of the Lion Inn. Hotels might provide a good market for de-ghosting equipment. I pushed that thought away. The last thing anyone needed was de-ghosting equipment available to everyone—since it also had the property of turning healthy individuals into zombies. My hand strayed to the calculator in my jacket pocket. The silver pens were in my breast pocket.

Llysette frowned but said nothing.

When we stepped out of the elevator into the lobby, I looked around for a moment before spotting the brass letters that spelled out: "The Refuge."

"There."

Llysette's heels clicked on the marble as we crossed the long lobby to the Inn's restaurant. The Refuge was white-walled, with dark green upholstered chairs and a dark gray carpet.

We didn't even have to wait.

"This way, Fräulein duBoise."

"Someone's briefed them," I whispered as we trailed the young woman to a corner booth, and a table with crisp white linens and shining silver, and a serving tray with six covered silver dishes of assorted jellies.

The menu, as expected, contained no references to coffee or tea, but they did have chocolate, for which I was grateful.

"Chocolate?" asked a smiling waiter, also fairly young, perhaps the age Walter might have been.

"Please," I answered, gesturing to the cups.

He filled both and left the pot on the table.

The dining area was half-filled, but whether that was because it was nearly a quarter past eight or because the Lion Inn was not filled on a Tuesday—or because the food was not that good—who knew?

"Have you decided, Fräulein duBoise?"

"The second breakfast, if you please."

"The Deseret Delight? How would you like the eggs?"

"Poached."

He turned to me.

"I'd like the number four, but could I have eggs Bruges instead of eggs Benedict?"

The waiter raised his eyebrows. "Sir?"

"Béarnaise instead of hollandaise."

"I can ask, sir."

No promises there.

He returned immediately with two large orange juices and a plate of croissants. "Your breakfast won't be long."

"Thank you."

Llysette sipped her orange juice and glanced around the dining room area. I had more chocolate and refilled my cup.

"There are no men with two women," said Llysette.

She was right. There were men alone, men with other men, and men with a single woman, and one family that appeared to be traditional—husband, wife, and three children.

"I can't explain that one way or another." I offered a smile. "There's probably a lot I couldn't explain about Deseret."

Llysette sipped her chocolate, then lowered her voice. "The women . . . I do not understand them."

I didn't either. They had secret ballots and the right to vote, but they seemed to accept a secondary status. Then, maybe the elections were a sham, except Jerome's briefing materials indicated that the elections for the Seventy—a sort of theocratic parliament—were real and that the unofficial Women's Party had effectively blocked several candidates.

"Your breakfast, fräulein, Doktor." The waiter's smile seemed pasted in place as he set the orders before us.

I had eggs Bruges—they actually had them. A lot of restaurants think that béarnaise goes only with meat, but the Lion Inn either didn't or was under orders to cater to us.

"Thank you," I said.

"Is there anything else?"

Llysette and I looked at each other.

"No, thank you."

We were both hungry, and we didn't talk that much.

After breakfast, we went back upstairs.

As Llysette washed up, I glanced through the *Deseret Star*—"Proclaiming the News of Zion and the World." The paper had been laid out on the table outside our door.

In the Arts section, there was actually a small article:

. . . the noted Columbian soprano arrived in Great Salt Lake yesterday to prepare for a series of concerts with Doktor Daniel Perkins, the world-famed composer and accompanist. . . . The first concert will be Thursday evening at 8:00. . . . Among the works presented will be several of Doktor Perkins's compositions, including the well-known *Lord of Sand* . . . based on a poem by F. George Evans. . . . First Counselor Cannon hailed the concert as a "widening of cultural horizons" . . . he is expected to be present.

Another article also caught my eye:

Great Salt Lake City (DNS). Police arrested yesterday two men wanted in connection with the vehicular homicide of Second Counselor Leavitt last September. Pending full identification, their names were not released.

Although the two were arrested in a hideout in the warehouse district, police spokesman Jared Bishopp denied that the arrests had anything to do with the "pornographic material" raids that have been ongoing in the area. . . .

Bishopp also denied that the raids had any connection with the death of Deseret University professor R. Jedediah Grant. Grant, a difference systems expert, burned to death in a mysterious fire in his steamer last week.

"I'll bet," I murmured to myself. "All coincidence." I couldn't help but think about the fact that the press had referred to Llysette, again, as a noted Columbian soprano.

After she touched up her makeup, I got out our overcoats—it was still cloudy and cold-looking outside. Then we took the elevator down to the lobby.

Llysette tucked the black leather music folder under her arm, not that she'd need the music, except to go over with her accompanist, who was supposed to be the composer. I wondered if he'd use music for his own pieces.

The morning was gray, with brown overtones from the polluted air, and a cold wind whipped around us as we walked down First Street West. According to the maps Brother Jensen had left, we would enter the concert hall through the second door.

A single white-haired guard in green sat at a kiosk just inside the single unlocked glass door. "Hall's closed, sir."

"This is Llysette duBoise. She has a rehearsal this morning with Doktor Perkins." I offered a smile.

"Be a moment." The guard straightened, then rummaged

through a folder and looked at something, then at Llysette. "Looks like you, miss." He smiled. "I'll bet you sing as good as you look, little lady."

I could feel Llysette stiffen, but she managed a smile. "We do try."

The foyer inside the doors stretched nearly fifty meters in each direction and was covered in a green pile carpet. The dimness of the light and the Corinthian pillars, mixed with what I would have sworn were Egyptian half-obelisks, imparted an air of a museum—or a ruin.

I guided Llysette toward the one door to the hall that was propped open. The concert hall proper was enormous, big enough for nearly three thousand people, I guessed, as we walked down the maroon carpet past dark upholstered seats toward the lighted stage where two men stood.

I strained to listen as we neared.

". . . don't care . . . let the music be good and so will the concert . . ."

". . . make it good, Brother Perkins . . . too much rides on this . . ."

"If I could make . . . that should not . . ." The clean-shaven Perkins shook his head and turned. "Doktor duBoise!"

Llysette acknowledged his words with a nod.

"There's a set of temporary steps at the side there."

We took them and met the two men by the end of the concert Steinbach.

"And this must be the famous Minister Eschbach." Perkins smiled warmly.

"Scarcely famous," I protested.

"I'm Dan Perkins. It's so good to meet you, Mademoiselle duBoise." He looked first at Llysette and then in my direction. "Or is it Fräulein or Frau?"

"She sings as Fräulein or Mademoiselle, but technically she's both a doktor and a professor." Somehow I'd thought he'd be bigger, but I was nearly half a head taller than he was.

"A professional in every sense of the word." He offered a boyish smile that belied the tinge of white in his blond hair and gestured toward the man with the blond beard beside him. "This is Brother Hansen. James V. Hansen. He's with the culture people for now."

Hansen bowed from the waist. "A pleasure to meet you both." His smile was friendly and almost as practiced as a politician's. "You are punctual . . . unlike some . . . artists. . . ."

I took Llysette's overcoat, and she opened the folder.

"Some questions . . . before we commence?"

"Of course." Perkins almost sounded happy that she had questions.

I retreated back down to the hall. Standing around would only make them uncomfortable, or me, and slow things down.

I sat in the darkened third row, just out of the lights. Hansen sat on the end of the front row, where he could survey both the empty hall and the stage, and his eyes were never still. He was solid, blond-haired like so many of the Saints seemed to be, and wore a gray suit that was conservative in cut but with a fine green stripe that would have been considered almost frivolous in Asten. I hadn't missed the slight bulge in the coat either or the thickness around the waist. He was also older, possibly even older than I was, and that bothered me.

Good covert agents, and I'd liked to think I had been one, had to go on feelings as much as on cold logic, but that was always hard to explain in debriefs. I'd have hated to explain in writing, even in something as frivolous as a spy novel. They always make spies out as either cold calculators or dashing romantics, when most of us were men trying to handle impossible jobs any way we could—like Hansen apparently was.

Brother Hansen, for all his charming smiles, was the Saint equivalent of a Spazi agent, and he'd been talking to the composer and waiting for us. I tried to think as Llysette and Perkins began to go through the concert schedule but found myself drawn into the music. I could tell Perkins was as good an accompanist as I'd ever heard, and even after a few minutes I could tell the concert was going to be something special.

When they got to his pieces, several times he stopped and talked to her, but I couldn't really catch the words, except that he seemed to be explaining what he'd had in mind. Like most artists, he explained with his hands and his intonations, perhaps more than with his words.

Once, right after we'd been married, I'd wondered what would happen, what could possibly happen, to two upcountry academics. Well . . . something had, and I wasn't quite sure I was ready for it. The rehearsal just reemphasized the feeling I had that Llysette duBoise was about to be rediscovered—and then some.

Hansen sat and listened and watched, seemingly ignoring me, and I sat and listened and watched all three.

After they finished, and it must have taken nearly three hours,

Llysette turned backstage, apparently heading for a dressing room or a ladies' room or both. After a moment, Hansen walked up to Perkins. I listened in the darkness at the side of the stage, just short of the temporary stairs. I had both overcoats across my arm.

". . . you were right. . . ."

Perkins grinned boyishly again and shook his head. ". . . better even than . . . they've got quite a surprise coming. Wait until she has an audience. I can tell."

"There may be a few surprises all around."

Perkins looked hard at the older man. "They had better all be pleasant ones, *Brother* Hansen." He stressed the word "Brother."

"The First Counselor has already told me the same thing, Doktor." Hansen cleared his throat. "I only meant that sopranos are supposed to be boring. I enjoyed it, and this was a rehearsal."

"She's got the artistic soul or spirit of two singers—and the artistry. She could look like . . . a duck . . . and no one would notice."

"She's no duck, Brother Perkins. Like I said, surprises all around."

I could hear Llysette's heels coming from backstage, and the two stopped talking. She was pulling on her jacket as she walked into the light, and I stepped up onto the stage, holding her coat.

Hansen frowned as he saw me, as though he'd forgotten I was there. I held in my own smile. One trick I had learned in the Spazi was blending into the background when I wanted to. Sometimes, though, I felt I blended whether I wanted to or not.

"This afternoon, then?" Llysette asked as she neared the big Steinbach.

"At four," Perkins answered.

I wondered if they'd scheduled another rehearsal, but I didn't ask. Llysette would tell me, and it was her voice and concert.

Llysette didn't speak until we were outside, walking back toward the Lion Inn. "Doktor Perkins, he is not what I expected."

"How is that?"

A messenger in a heavy coat dodged around us and kept running south.

"He is not cold, the way his letters were, and he says what he thinks."

I had to wonder how Perkins had survived in a theocracy. Through absolute talent? If so, that said something about Deseret, but exactly what . . . I wasn't sure. Then, I was getting less and less sure about more and more—like who wanted whom dead and who wanted Llysette to succeed and who to fail. I saw too many possibilities—one of the dubious benefits of age and experience.

"We practice again this afternoon—at four. A short time."

"Here?"

"*Non.* In our room. I wished . . . the phrasing in two of his songs. I must think. He played them, and we were not together . . . not how I would like."

"That's fine with me."

"You are good."

I still doubted that but didn't speak for a moment, as a fiercer gust of wind whipped around us and tossed scattered snowflakes along First Street West.

We turned the corner toward the Lion Inn, and I added, "I forgot to tell you. There was another article in the local paper about you and the concert. Brother Hansen reminded me about it when he talked to Perkins while you were backstage. Hansen was talking about a surprise, and I got to thinking about a different kind of surprise. There's one thing you haven't really prepared for. It might not happen." I shrugged. "But it might."

"*Qu'est-ce-que c'est?*"

"What if some reporter or videolink type corners you?"

"*Moi?*"

"Don't be coy, my lady. You're getting better and better known, and even the First Counselor here apparently wants a success. What better way than some sort of interview?"

"And they would ask what?"

"Anything." I laughed, then coughed from the cold wind. The hotel was less than a half-block away. "Something like . . . why are you returning to performing now? Or . . . what do you make of singing in two national capitals in less than a month? How do you like Deseret? Was your husband really a spy?"

Llysette shook her head. "Those, they will ask, you think?"

"Some of them have no shame. Most of them," I added.

"I am performing now because they have let me."

I winced. "*Non.* . . ."

Llysette grinned, and I realized she'd just been teasing. "That, I would not say, save to you. What I will say . . . A person who has no country has few choices. I am happy now. I will perform so long as people wish to hear."

"What about the spy business?"

"*Mon cher* . . . he is a very good professor, and he was a war hero, and he is a good man. He is no spy."

That was true as far as it went. "If they ask more?"

"I will say that they should ask you if they do not like my words."

"What is the message behind your concert, Fräulein duBoise?" I asked in the snide way I'd heard from too many linkers.

"Message?" Llysette shook her head. "You have suffered from them, Johan."

"Probably. But it's the kind of question some will ask."

"Then I would say that music is beauty, and there is too little beauty in a cold world." She paused, and I could see that her face had lost most of its color.

"You need something to eat."

"*Je crois que oui.*"

"Is the hotel all right?"

"What is close is best."

We made it to The Refuge, and Llysette had chicken noodle soup, while waiting for a salad, and I munched on crackers.

"The soup is good." Her face was still pale.

"I'm glad." We didn't have a corner booth, but, again, no one was seated at the adjacent tables, although we had a waitress, an older and gray-haired woman.

"He is a good accompanist."

"As good as he is a composer?"

"At both he is good. His art songs, they are better than the Vondel operas."

"The lyrics are better than Vondel's?"

"Dutch . . . it has the charm of Russian and the efficiency of Italian."

My Dutch ancestors would have protested, but Llysette remained pale, and I had more to worry about than Dutch opera lyrics composed centuries earlier and set to music by Doktor Perkins.

"Like French, you mean?" I said with a grin.

"You. . . ." Then she shook her head and smiled back.

As she took another spoonful of soup, I glanced around the dining area. Most of the diners were male, in groups of two to four, and most wore gray or brown suits, especially dark brown. None looked in our direction.

The color was beginning to return to Llysette's face by the time the salads arrived. I'd eaten three large soda crackers. Would I have been better off with the soup? Probably, but I'd had too much soup as a sickly child.

The salads disappeared quickly, as did the rolls that came with them. I'd barely finished when the gray-haired waitress reappeared.

"Would you like some dessert? The lime gelatin pie is good. So is the double chocolate death cake."

I passed on the lime gelatin pie, and my waistline wouldn't have stood the cake.

"Do you want to see the Temple grounds?" I asked after signing the bill for lunch with: "duBoise/Eschbach, Room 603."

Llysette shrugged, then answered, "I ate too much, and a walk would be good."

The wind had died down by the time we left the Inn's lobby, and with the sun out, I ended up loosening my coat after the first block. Llysette did not do the same, but she wasn't shivering either. I did not point out the snow on the mountains to the southeast.

To the east of the Lion Inn rose the white stone spires of the Temple and, below them, white stone walls. The air easing in from the northwest carried the faint tang of petrochemicals and of salt.

I squeezed Llysette's gloved hand, and she squeezed mine.

We slowed at the corner, behind a woman with a double stroller carriage.

Both fair-cheeked children smiled at Llysette as she bent over. "They are beautiful."

"Thank you." The woman smiled, then pushed the stroller across South Temple.

I caught the brightness in Llysette's eyes as we waited for the signal to turn to allow us to cross the street. "I'm sorry."

A flash of green blotted away the incipient tears. "You did not—"

"I can be sorry." I reached out and put my arm around her shoulders as we walked and squeezed her gently.

"That . . . it was not meant to be."

I didn't know about that, only that Ferdinand had a lot to answer for, and that there wasn't much I could do about that either. My neck twitched, an unpleasant and too-familiar feeling, and I casually looked toward the street and the maroon Browning that steamed by silently.

Two men wearing green jackets, from what I could see, under their gray trench coats eased up the street after us, keeping well back, but you never lose the feeling of eyes on your back.

More Danites? I kept the half-smile on my face as we crossed to the walkway that bordered the park surrounding the Temple square proper.

Although Great Salt Lake City had to hold more than a quarter-million souls, the streets were not thronged with steamers or steam buses. I craned but saw no haulers. Were they banned from the area around the Temple?

The browning grass in the park around the Temple was trimmed and raked and without leaves, despite the winds of the morning and the day before. Nowhere did I see even the smallest bit of litter.

A small group of young adults, less than a dozen, followed a young man in a charcoal gray suit, without an overcoat, who periodically stopped. For a time, we trailed the group, discretely back.

"The building here is the genealogy center." He gestured toward the two-story gray stone structure that bordered the street on the north side of the square. "The difference engines there have everyone's ancestry on record. You'll learn more about that later."

Then came a churchlike building.

"This is now the performing hall. It's called Assembly Hall. There are three concerts a week broadcast from here all over Deseret. . . ."

Llysette shook her head and looked at me.

"I know," I whispered.

The group marched toward another building, with a keystone declaring it the "Visitor Center," but I didn't feel like declaring us as visitors, even though we were.

I glanced back. The two Danites had split up, but they were clearly continuing their vigil.

A higher stone wall encircled the Temple proper, and those gates were barred with black iron gratework. The dome-roofed Tabernacle squatted across a flat rectangular area, half-filled with raised stone enclosures that were turned bare-earth flower beds. The flower beds were bordered with low juniper hedges.

We walked up to one of the Tabernacle doors, where a too-hefty young man in a charcoal black suit stood. He wore a rectangular name tag that proclaimed him as "Brother Marsden."

"Can we look in?" I asked.

He smiled and opened the door. "The choir won't be practicing until tonight. There are some schedules and pamphlets on the ledge along the wall."

The Tabernacle was impressive—essentially an amphitheatre around a series of tiered risers and a huge organ. The walls were white and gold, and the woodwork glistened under the dome. The recording equipment was still in place, with microphones hung strategically.

I could hear the whispers from a couple standing just before the front row of seats, a good ten feet lower than where we stood at the rear, and more than a hundred feet away.

". . . Prophet Young preached right here . . . before they built the Temple. . . ."

". . . so did Jedediah Grant and Cannon."

"Good acoustics," I murmured to Llysette.

She nodded, her eyes still on the massive organ pipes and the tiered seats for the Saints' Choir.

". . . booms when the Saints' Choir sings—"

"I would go," Llysette said abruptly.

I took her arm. "The Tabernacle bothers you."

"For singing it should be, not for the preaching."

"I don't know how much preaching they do there now."

She shook her head.

We walked slowly back to the hotel and our suite, where Llysette eased off her shoes and stretched out on the bed. I found the hotel-provided *Guide to Great Salt Lake* and began to read.

I got as far as the winter recreation areas by the time four o'clock came. The rap on the suite door was firm, and I opened it. Doktor, or Brother, Perkins stood there.

"Come on in. She's expecting you."

Beyond the composer, where the corridor turned toward the elevator, I saw a gray coat with a fine green stripe and a blond-haired head vanish around the corner.

Perkins saw my eyes and nodded.

I shut the door without comment. "Could I take your coat?" I wanted to see what the composer said.

"Brother Hansen is concerned. He insisted on ensuring that I arrived . . . without incident. He worries that admirers will waylay me— as if any of them would recognize me outside of formal wear." The composer's laugh was ironic, with a hint of what I would have called self-mockery, as he turned to Llysette. "You, lady, will re-invent my career. If you sing as you did this morning . . ." He shook his head.

Llysette's slight frown disappeared with his words, and she said, "I am but a singer, not a composer."

"People listen to singers, not composers."

Llysette shrugged, indicating that she didn't agree, but that she wasn't going to argue.

I retreated to the corner chair when the slender blond man sat at the piano and played several bars—something I didn't recognize. "It's even in tune." He opened one of the folders he had brought in and set the opened music on the piano's rack.

"Good," answered my lovely wife, and I wished I could play. But whatever gods or ghosts determine our heritage ensured musical talent was something I lacked.

"I thought we might try the 'Fragments' part first. Here. . . ."

"*Oui*. . . ."

There was a difference between their efforts in the concert hall and the suite, but one so slight to my ears that I wouldn't have caught it without Llysette's explanation, and I wondered how many people really would have caught the difference.

They continued for a time, then switched to the second song. After two attempts, Perkins paused and turned to Llysette. "Could you hold this just a little longer?"

"I did not read the phrase so. Could we sing that phrase both ways?"

"Of course."

So they did.

Afterward, the composer frowned.

Llysette remained straight-faced.

"I think you were right," Perkins said. "It sounds better. That could be because no one else has . . . the vibrancy you do."

Llysette looked down. Sometimes, she still didn't fully understand what she had become. "*Encore* . . ."

They went back to working on the song—*Lord of Sand*, I thought, the Evans poem.

In time, Perkins stopped playing and stood, stretching.

Llysette almost shook herself and glanced toward me. "I feel better," she said with a faint smile.

"I am glad you do," the composer answered, bending over and folding up the music. "I think a great number of listeners, even those few who heard you years ago, will be surprised." He looked at me.

"I haven't doubted that," I said, "but I'm not a musician."

"I am, and I know that they will be surprised." He offered that boyish grin again.

I brought him his coat.

"How have you found Deseret?"

"We've not seen that much, except what we saw on the airship and the Temple grounds."

"And the Salt Palace," added Llysette.

"I hope you get to see more after the concerts. You might ask if you can get farther south. There's so much there—Cedar Breaks, Ankakuwasit . . ."

Llysette nodded.

I decided to ask. "We're strangers here, and some things aren't obvious. When Herr Jensen picked us up, he had a driver who wore a green jacket. The coat looked like a uniform, but it had no insignia." I spread my hands. "I might be mistaken, and I would dislike having an incorrect impression."

"I doubt your impression was incorrect." The composer smiled wryly. "The Danites wear green, and I wouldn't be surprised if Brother Jensen's driver were a Danite." He turned to Llysette. "The Danites were the original militia in the first Saint war back in Columbia. Now . . . they're more of a . . . something like the Masons in Columbia."

According to Jerome's briefing papers, they were far more than a fraternal order, more like a paramilitary order, if not a secret but official arm of the church.

I didn't have to force the frown. "That seems odd."

Perkins laughed. "Why would it be odd? Deseret is surrounded by Columbia and New France. Until comparatively recently, Columbia kept trying to annex us, and now Marshal DeGaulle has the same idea. We can't afford a large standing army. That's why the First Presidency has always supported the Danites and the Joseph Smith Brigades."

I shook my head, then decided to push a little more. "No, I didn't mean that. I meant his having a driver who was a Danite."

"That's no more strange than my having Brother Hansen as an escort." Perkins paused. "Surely you understand that we all want this concert to go well and no one wants either this lovely lady—or, unfortunately, me—to be distracted. Music is far more highly regarded here in Deseret than in Columbia." He smiled. "This lady would not have had to wait for citizenship to have sung here. Her concerts would have been mobbed."

I got the message and felt guilty for pushing so far. "I guess I didn't realize just how celebrated you two are here. I got into the arts business late, and by marriage." I put on a sheepish grin and looked at Llysette. "In New Bruges, people are not exactly the most enthusiastic of music lovers. Sometimes . . . I'm not so bright . . . as I should be."

"My lady." Perkins turned to Llysette. "You are indeed fortunate to have a husband who is not a musician."

"That I know." She smiled fondly at me. "He worries about me, not about the notes."

I tried not to sigh. I just hoped she wouldn't analyze the conversation too closely, praying she was still thinking about the music.

"My wife is probably asking where I am." Perkins turned to Llysette. "Tomorrow at ten?"

"That would be good."

With a last boyish smile, the composer left. The gray coat and blond hair told me that Brother Hansen was waiting by the elevator.

I closed the door and turned to Llysette. She'd slumped into one of the armchairs.

"You're tired."

"*Oui.*"

"And hungry."

She nodded.

"I'll dig out some of the cheese and crackers. It's hard working with a composer."

"*Non* . . . he is easy to follow, but to sing his words . . . as well as one can . . . *c'est tres difficile.*"

"Do you want to rest? A glass of wine before we find somewhere to eat? Or should I order dinner up here?"

"The wine. Then I will decide."

I went to extract one of the bottles from the cooler and to get her some cheese and crackers. Perkins was honest, and he didn't want Llysette worried, and he was worried, and we were definitely under protective surveillance—all of us. All in all, a pattern was emerging, and I didn't care for its shape in the slightest.

"Do you think you have . . . whatever it was . . . worked out?"

"I should think so. Tomorrow, then we will see."

That we would, except I knew tomorrow was but the beginning.

21
_ᔕᓄ_

A FTER breakfast on Wednesday, while Llysette reviewed her music
again and warmed up some, I went through both local scandal
sheets. In addition to a small article about the decision by Escobar-
Moire to send another New French naval battle group to the Azores,
the _Deseret News_ contained an article mentioning the concert. That
meant both papers were being fed material. I had my doubts that
they had teams of reporters seeking it out.

> Great Salt Lake City (DNS). A select number of University of
> Deseret voice students will get the chance of a lifetime this
> coming Friday and Saturday—an opportunity to show off
> their talents to world-famous Columbian soprano Llysette
> duBoise. . . .
>
> In addition to her three concerts this week at the Salt
> Palace (see Entertainment Calendar) with Deseret's own
> world-renowned Daniel Perkins, DuBoise will be conduct-
> ing two master classes for the top female voice students at
> Deseret University.
>
> "It's a great opportunity for our students," said Joanne
> Axley, the Director of Voice Studies for Women at Deseret
> University. "They're really looking forward to working with
> Doktor DuBoise. . . ."

I flipped to the Entertainment Calendar, and, as indicated on
the front part of the Arts section, all three concerts were listed, with

THE GHOST OF THE REVELATOR

three stars, presumably indicating a recommendation of some sort. I pondered the story, carefully placed below the fold, but on the front page of the Arts section in the lower right corner. Neither the place nor the times for the classes were mentioned, either.

The *Deseret Star* only mentioned the concerts in the section headed "Upcoming Cultural Events"—in bold type—but the *Star* had offered the earlier story.

"Johan?"

"I'm ready any time you are." I stood and handed the section that had the *News* article to Llysette. "You're getting even more famous. Show this to Dierk and the dean. 'World-famous Columbian soprano.' "

She read the story slowly, then looked up. "I am not good enough for their men?"

"I don't know that it was meant that way," I said. "They seem to keep men and women almost separate." I picked up my coat and donned it, then extracted hers from the closet.

"Women are not so good as men?" There was a glint in her green eyes.

"I don't believe that, but I can't control what the Saints do or believe," I pointed out.

"So long as you do not become a Saint. . . ."

"There's not much chance of that." And there wasn't. Who wanted to join a faith based on imaginary gold tablets translated by a prophet who had never been to school? While the idea of dying and becoming God sounded all right, I had my doubts about what it really might be like. Besides, I was having enough trouble learning how to be a real person with one wife, and polygamy had to be even harder. Then, maybe I was spiritually polygamous, with the fragments of Carolynne's ghost welded to my soul and being married to a singer who was somewhere between one and two separate women trying to be one. And people out there were considering creating more ghosts?

"Quiet you are," said Llysette.

"Sometimes . . . I just have to think." I held her coat for her, then opened the suite door.

Llysette shook her head at herself and walked over to the piano and picked up the black folder with the music and then her handbag.

The concierge nodded as we stepped out into the lobby, and I returned the nod, although I wondered if his gesture were really for us.

Outside, even under the canopy, the wind was chill again. The sky was clear and a chilling blue. Cold as the air was, it smelled clean for the first time since we'd arrived, and for that I was grateful.

Llysette fumbled the top buttons of her heavy coat closed and clutched her music.

A green steam bus, trimmed in gold paint, hissed by and stopped at the corner ahead and disgorged several dozen people. All were fairly young, less than thirty, and most were men. The younger men were uniformly clean-shaven. Did beards come with marriage? Doktor Perkins was clean-shaven, but he had a reputation for being a nonconformist. On the other hand, Brother Hansen was bearded and he was definitely older and, given the Saint culture, probably just as definitely married for, as they put it, "time and eternity."

A different pair of Danites followed us to the concert hall. I didn't mention them to Llysette. What was the point in possibly upsetting her before her first big concert in years? Especially when they seemed to be there to protect her?

Still, my fingers curled toward the calculator in my jacket pocket, and I wanted to touch the pen and pencil set. There was also the plastic blade in the belt, but that would have taken too long to get out.

"Good morning . . . Doktor," offered the white-haired guard. He struggled slightly with the "Doktor," but someone had clearly briefed him.

"Good morning," said Llysette cheerfully.

"They're waiting for you."

"Thank you." She bestowed a dazzling smile.

I held the door for her, noting the slightest of headshakes on the part of the guard, almost as if he felt someone that beautiful didn't belong in public—or something like that.

The two Danites had dropped back as we'd entered the Salt Palace complex, and I lost sight of them as we headed through the dimness toward the hall itself.

Doktor Perkins and Brother Hansen were waiting at the base of the stage, at the waist-high dark green curtain that circled the pit.

"Are you ready?" asked the composer.

"Yes." Llysette started to unbutton the heavy black coat, and I stepped forward to help her out of it. "It is cold today."

"We're in for some snow later, only an inch or two, they say." Perkins grinned. "Just so it's over by noon tomorrow."

Llysette shivered.

"It's not any warmer here, or not much," I pointed out as I folded her coat over my arm.

"That explanation, Johan, I could do without."

I shut up. She was tense enough.

"What would you prefer?" asked the composer. "Would you like to warm up?"

"*Non* . . . already have I. . . . The two songs . . . first. Then the program as we would sing it."

Perkins nodded, and I backed away as silently as I could, followed by Hansen. Llysette and the composer/accompanist moved toward the big Steinbach.

"How do you find Deseret?" asked Hansen, smiling his politician's smile, when we reached the space at the foot of the temporary steps.

"With Llysette's rehearsals and practice, we really haven't had much time to sightsee. We did tour the Temple grounds and the Tabernacle, and the small performing hall and the park and the gardens. They're all very impressive." I smiled. "It's always been amazing to me to read about how much you Saints have accomplished. To see it is even more amazing."

"People work hard here." Hansen paused, his eyes going to the stage, where Llysette and Perkins stood by the Steinbach. The composer gestured to the music, then seated himself and played several bars before looking up. Llysette nodded.

"You're a professor now, aren't you? Have you published many books?"

"Environment and natural resources. And no, I haven't published many books, just a handful of articles. Most of them upset people." I laughed softly, not wanting the sound to carry, but I supposed it did anyway, because Llysette looked in my direction.

"Time to sit down and be quiet," I said wryly, moving back up the aisle and into the darkness.

Hansen again took a position in a seat on the end of the first row, from where he could watch both stage and seats.

I watched, but it took only a few attempts before Llysette and the composer appeared satisfied with the two sections they'd rehearsed the night before. Then they went into the program itself. Although it was only a rehearsal, it was still better. I wanted to cry and shake my head, understanding a little bit more why not performing had hurt Llysette so deeply.

Before I really knew it, the rehearsal was over.

As Brother Hansen stood in the open area below the stage, Perkins gestured to me. So I climbed up the temporary steps on the right-hand side, carrying Llysette's coat with me.

Because she was perspiring slightly, I just held the coat.

"I realize that it is very short notice, but Jillian and I would like to know if you both would join us for dinner this evening." Perkins's eyes went fleetingly in the direction of Hansen, so fleetingly that I wouldn't have caught the movement if I hadn't been watching. "A very bland meal, a chicken pasta, if that's all right," he added. "I wouldn't want to upset a singer."

"That would be wonderful," said Llysette. "Johan and I would enjoy that." She paused. "I would prefer . . . cilantro I do not like."

"This recipe doesn't feature cilantro or much garlic."

I supposed we could enjoy a dinner away from the Lion Inn. "Would you care to have lunch with us?"

"I wish I could." He shook his head and checked his watch. "I still have a class to teach."

"You teach also?"

"At the university." He grinned again at Llysette. "I'm the one who set up the master classes for you. I hope you don't mind if a few of my students sit in."

"*Mais non.*" Llysette smothered a frown.

"If that would bother you . . ."

"*Non* . . . I enjoy teaching men."

"Tonight. I'll pick you up at the Inn just before seven?"

"That would be fine."

He nodded and then gathered up his music and headed down the steps and for the open hall door, his strides long and quick, as if he were already late. Hansen looked at us, then hurried after the composer.

"Do you want your coat?"

"*Pas encore . . .*"

We walked slowly out of the hall, not because Llysette was tired, but because she wanted to cool off before going out into the cold. My thoughts kept flitting to the business about his teaching and his students and the newspaper article that mentioned only female stu-

dents—yet more pieces to a puzzle that got more and more complicated.

"Lunch?"

"Please."

The two new Danites, or whatever they were, followed us back to
the Lion Inn and The Refuge, where we were escorted back to the
corner table—again with a healthy space around us.

Llysette didn't feel like talking, and I didn't press. As every performance neared, she drew more and more into herself. That was
one reason why I'd been surprised that she'd accepted the dinner invitation. But her instincts were good, and if she accepted, I'd follow
her lead—with a look over our shoulders.

The rest of the day was uneventful. After lunch, Llysette napped,
and then . . . well . . . we both napped after that.

When we woke, she took a bath, and then I showered and
dressed and she fussed over one of the songs at the piano before she
dressed. I opened another bottle of wine, but she only had one glass
while she dressed, and I read the hotel-provided guidebook from
cover to cover once more.

At five to seven, we were down in the lobby. At three before the
hour, a red steamer pulled up under the canopy—unsurprisingly, a
Browning—and we stepped into the night air.

Despite their ornate wrought-iron shapes, the streetlights were
energy-efficient glow throwers that penetrated the gloom without
searing the eyeballs. Again, as I sniffed and smelled chemicals and
air pollutants, I had to wonder why the Saints had installed the most
environmentally friendly and energy-efficient lights while only undertaking considerably less effective air pollution controls.

As Perkins guided the steamer eastward and uphill, I glanced
back through the twilight, convinced that the same pair of head-
lights that had pulled out from the Lion Inn was still behind us, if a
block back. There's a thin line between occupational caution and
paranoia. I wondered if I was crossing that line.

Doktor Perkins drove quickly, except when he neared what
seemed to be a school, where he slowed down. That seemed odd,
since it was well past any normal school hours.

"There's a ghost of a young woman there. She was killed in a
steamer accident several months ago, and her family visits her every
night."

We peered through the darkness. Sure enough, several figures seemed to group around a white shadow. I shivered, and Llysette reached out and squeezed my hand. How many ghosts were on my soul? I tried not to think about it.

Perkins turned right, downhill, then pulled into a bricked driveway another hundred yards past the turn.

The two-story house was nearly a century old, made of hand-formed yellow-brown bricks. The light on the wide front porch revealed that the trim was almost a forest green, accented with gold-painted gingerbread.

A double car barn had been added later, although some attempt had been made to match the house brick.

I held the steamer door for Llysette, feeling dampness on my face. Scattered flakes swirled down around us for a moment, then vanished.

Perkins led the way up the antique brick steps and across a wide-planked and roofed porch to a golden oak door, which opened as we neared.

"That didn't take long," the petite blonde woman said to the composer.

"They were waiting." He gestured, and we stepped inside. "This is my wife, Jillian. She's a pianist."

"When I get time." Like the composer, Jillian Perkins was blond and slender, except her hair was more of a strawberry blonde shade and very curly. She had a pixielike face, and her eyes sparkled. She wore a tailored blue dress that set off her eyes and hair. I liked her.

"If you'd say good night to the children, Dan? They're waiting."

"Excuse me." The composer bowed and headed up the narrow staircase, shedding his overcoat as he hurried upstairs, his shoes slapping on the polished wood steps.

"We can sit down for a moment." Jillian nodded toward the front sitting room, which contained a couch and two armchairs, as well as a small grand piano, something called a Ballem, but I didn't recognize the name. I walked over and studied the piano.

"We inherited that. Dan hates it. It's good furniture, but the internal works leave a little to be desired." Jillian offered a short laugh. "I teach youngsters on it. It's hard to keep in tune, but it's good practice for my tuning business. The good piano is in the study."

I sat on the couch beside Llysette, our backs to the filmy lace-trimmed curtains that framed the small bay window overlooking the front yard and street.

"How do you like Deseret?"

"It is . . . different." Llysette smiled gently. "Very . . . clean."

"The Temple is impressive. So is your husband," I added. "Llysette had told me about his music. She's sung some of it for years. But he's much younger than I expected."

"Dan does have that boyish look," Jillian replied, brushing a strand of curly hair off her forehead. "Would you like something to drink? We have hot or cold cider, hot chocolate, and orange and grapefruit juice."

Llysette smiled. "The hot chocolate, if you please."

"The same, thank you."

"Make yourselves at home. I'll be right back."

Alone momentarily, we glanced around the sitting room. From what I could see, it was the largest space in the house, and the only one capable of holding even a small grand piano. The house was actually smaller than ours in New Bruges. A large brick fireplace stood in the middle of the outside wall at the end of the room away from the small entry space and stairs. On each side of the fireplace were built-in bookcases.

I scanned the titles, those I could read, starting with the shelves on the left side. The few titles I could read told of the subject matter clearly enough—*History of the Latter-Day Saints, Witness of the Light, Sisters in Spirit, The Gathering of Zion, Brigham Young: American Moses,* and several volumes entitled *Doctrine and Covenants.*

The books on the right side were radically different: *Principles of Voice Production, Dynamics in Scoring, A Brief History of Music, The Complete Pianist, Vondel: A Guide, Henry Purcell,* and two shelves of what looked to be scores, some hand-bound.

The mahogany side tables, while akin to Columbian revival, were more spare and were scarcely new. Neither were the chairs and the couch on which we sat, although the room was as spotless as any well-kept Dutch dwelling. I definitely got the impression that composers, at least in Deseret, were not all that well compensated. And from what Llysette had indicated, Perkins was one of the better-known North American composers.

From the couch, we looked into a dining room not much larger than the eating space in my kitchen, at an oval table set for four.

"Modest . . . ," I murmured to Llysette.

She nodded.

Doktor Daniel Perkins needed Llysette as much as she needed

him, perhaps more, and the recording contract made a great deal more sense—a great deal.

"Here's your chocolate." Jillian returned with a small tray and four cups, all steaming.

"*Merci.*"

"Thank you."

At the sound of shoes on the steps, she turned.

"They're all tucked in," Perkins explained as he passed the piano.

"It's cold out. I thought you might like some, too."

"Thank you, dear." He took the cup and settled himself into one of the chairs.

She set the tray on the side table and took the other chair but perched on the front.

"How many children do you have?"

"Three," answered Jillian. "Two boys and a girl."

"Ages ten, six, and two," he added. "And they're going on forty, fourteen, and two."

I must have frowned slightly.

"You wonder about the stories of large Saint families? And multiple spouses?" asked Perkins with a smile.

"It had crossed my mind," I admitted, "but you really never know, and it hasn't been that easy to learn more than the basics about Deseret. At least until recently." I was pushing it, but too many loose ends were dangling about, with too much at stake.

"Deseret is no longer a farming nation. We're growing, and we need more hands, but they have to be guided by an educated mind. Minds take longer to train than bodies."

"So the 'magic number' is no longer five?" I asked blandly.

Jillian winced, but Perkins grinned, a little self-consciously, before answering. "The church believes that while five children is an ideal, ideals don't necessarily fit all families."

I got that message—immense social pressure to have large families, but not an absolute written declaration.

"I'm curious. We saw a large house near the temple—with separate dwellings. . . ."

"The old Eccles house. It's almost a museum," Perkins said with a nod. "There were more housing complexes like that even twenty-five years ago." He shrugged. "Times change." Then he stood. "I need to finish up with the dinner."

"Dan's a far better cook than I am," Jillian said with a smile as the composer vanished in the direction of the kitchen. "He's not totally traditional."

Not totally? I was definitely getting the impression that Perkins was very untraditional in a traditional society, maintaining the mask while straining against it. Was that the reason why Brother Hansen was trailing Dan Perkins? "Are any composers traditional?"

"I don't know any others personally." Jillian smiled. "Most biographies of composers show they have a certain . . . flair."

"That is true," averred Llysette.

I would have had to agree.

"Here it is." Perkins held a large serving dish, then lowered it onto the small oval table.

We rose and inched toward the archway to the dining room.

"If you two would sit here and here," said Jillian, pointing to the two chairs away from the archway to the living room and the door to the kitchen. "That way, we can get to the kitchen."

I held the chair and seated her, and Perkins seated Llysette.

The dinner was simple—the chicken pasta with portabella mushrooms, flaky rolls, and a green salad.

"The white pitcher has ice water, the gold one cider," Jillian added.

I decided to try the cider and lifted the pitcher, looking at Llysette.

"*Mais oui. . . .*"

Then I tried the pasta. Not only was Perkins a composer, but he was also a good cook. Straight-faced, I asked Llysette, "Do you think he should have been a chef, too?"

"Together, you should open a bistro."

"And you'd sing?"

"The café songs, I heard them first, and when I was small, *tres petite,* a café singer I wanted to be." Llysette took a swallow of the too-sweet cider and managed to get it down straight-faced.

"You've come a long way," I pointed out.

"She really has," added Perkins.

"Your husband said you were a pianist," I said to Jillian.

"He is much better, but I teach part-time at the university, and I play at the ward services." She smiled. "I enjoy it."

"I wish I had that kind of talent," I answered.

"You have other talents, *mon cher.*"

"Listen to your lady," suggested Perkins.

"I always do."

"Maintenant . . ."

"It took a little while, but not long, to realize I got into trouble for not listening."

That got a smile from both Perkinses.

"So," I asked, after a moment, "how do you think the concert will go?"

Llysette frowned over a mouthful of salad at my boldness.

Perkins finished chewing before he answered. "If our rehearsals are any indication, it should be good."

"What about the recording?"

"That's easy. The hall has a permanent recording system. Deseret Media will record all three performances, and we'll take the best version of each song. Hopefully . . . everyone in Deseret and Columbia will want a disk, and we'll all make lots of money."

Jillian nodded. "At least to cover the deposits."

"You made deposits?" I asked.

"Even in Deseret, artists have to pay," he pointed out. "It seemed like a good idea."

"Everywhere we pay," added Llysette.

I wondered if Llysette and I could get the loudmouthed media type at the presidential dinner—Hartson James, had that been his name?—to push Llysette's disks in Columbia. That would have to wait. "Artists pay everywhere."

"So true," said Jillian wryly.

I reached for the rolls, then offered them to Llysette. She declined.

"Maybe you could answer a few questions for me," I offered tentatively. "I've been a few places, but I've never been here, and Deseret is strange because, on the one hand, it's very familiar, I suppose because we speak the same language, dress similarly. On the other hand, words and terms don't quite fit."

"Such as?" The composer held his cider glass without drinking.

"Well . . . don't you call steamers Brownings?"

Jillian smiled.

"We generally call them steamers, or sometimes Stanleys, even though there are other kinds in Columbia." I took a small sip of the cider, very sweet. "And you have chocolate, but not tea or *café*. You have cider, but not wine." I shrugged. "I suppose I could come up with others, except I don't know enough yet to point them out." I offered a laugh. "A measure of my ignorance."

"You said you had questions . . . ," prompted Perkins.

"I suppose I do," I said ruefully, "but it's hard even to ask what you don't know. I guess I feel like I have some, but when you ask me . . ." Actually, the problem was even more basic than that. I needed to know things, but I didn't want to upset any of the three before the concerts. Yet I'd not have this chance again. It was frustrating, and I've never been that good at drawing people out. Llysette could be, when she wasn't worried about performing, but she was worried now.

My words—or my acting—got smiles from the others.

"Maybe . . . it's just that all the terms I read in the papers are confusing. I read about counselors and presidents and a presidency and apostles, and I see the same name being so many things." I shrugged.

"The same name?" asked the composer.

"Cannon, I think. He talks about culture, and he's a counselor to someone, and then I read that he's an apostle, or one of the Twelve. But he's also a businessman." I shrugged, then grinned. "I've done a lot of things, but I don't think I've ever done four separate jobs all at once—and been in the media as well."

Perkins nodded, an amused nod. "He does get around, but it's simpler than you think. The same people are members of the Twelve and the First Presidency. Counselor is one of the titles within the Presidency. We've never really had a full-time government separate from the church and business. For Deseret, they all go together."

"So the Twelve Apostles are like the apostles of Christ, except that they're more of a government, like, say the ministers of government in Columbia?" I paused, then added, "But what's the difference between the First Presidency and the Twelve Apostles?"

"Same people, but different functions," answered the composer. "As the apostles, they guide the church. As the Presidency, they guide the country."

I frowned, not dissembling in the slightest. "Is the President also the . . . Prophet, Seer, and . . . ?"

"Revelator?" Perkins took a sip of cider. "Actually, the First President—that's the official title—is usually the head of the church, the Prophet, Seer, and Revelator, but in his government role, he's more like the president of Columbia."

"The head of state? Then who functions as the real head of government?"

"That's the First Counselor."

I shook my head. "So the same people wear different hats." I added another frown. "Now what's the difference between the Twelve and the Revealed Twelve? Is that another set of hats, too?"

Both Jillian and Llysette exchanged puzzled glances, then looked to the composer.

"No," he said. "The Revealed Twelve . . . that's some sort of underground schismatic religious movement. No one seems to know much about them, except they're claiming that they're the true Saints and that the current Apostles have betrayed the Prophet. I've seen some fliers around the university, but they don't last long. The Danites get rid of them pretty quickly." Perkins grinned wryly. "Some people always think the rest of the world is out of tune."

Somehow I wasn't certain whether he was referring to the Danites or the schismatics.

"Oh," I answered. "I just thought . . . with all those interlocking names . . ."

He shook his head. "The Revealed Twelve, or whatever else they call themselves, are just disgruntled outsiders afraid to appear in public and make their case."

I nodded. From what little I'd seen, I wouldn't have given much for their chances if they did appear.

From there we talked of cabbages and queens, ships and sailing wax, so to speak, through a heavy chocolate cake for desert and more chocolate to end the dinner.

In the end, Perkins drove us back to the Inn, and I noted that another pair of Danites watched us from the back of the lobby.

22

∽

THE less said about the hours before the first Deseret concert the better. Llysette was as touchy as a caged cougar, not that I expected any less, with all that was riding on her performance.

The fewer words I offered in such circumstances, the smoother matters went. So I massaged her very tight shoulders and then confined my conversations to inquiries about what and when she wanted to eat, any chores I could run for her, and reading the favorable story in the *Deseret News.*

"The headline is good—'World-Renowned Pair Open Concert Season.' "

"They did not write our names?" said Llysette from the piano bench, where she looked at the music.

"The rest of the story is good, too." I began to read:

" 'Great Salt Lake City (DNS). With one of the world's top vocal piano and vocal duos in Llysette deBoise and Daniel Perkins, the Salt Palace performing complex opens its fiftieth consecutive season tonight.

" 'Perkins, recently awarded the Rachmaninov Award by Czar Alexi, is also the recipient of numerous other honors, including the Hearst Arts Medallion and honorary degrees from the Curtiss Institute, the University of Virginia, and the Saint Petersburg Conservatory. His arrangements and compositions have been played by every major symphony orchestra in the world. He is the composer in residence at Deseret University.

" 'DuBoise, most recently featured at the Columbian Presidential

Arts Awards dinner, where she won rave reviews, has returned to an active performing career, interrupted for several years as a result of the instability in France. Former First Diva of France and featured soloist at the Academie Royale in Paris, she has appeared in most of the major opera houses of Europe. With a doctorate from the Sorbonne, she is director of vocal studies and opera at Vanderbraak State University in New Bruges, Columbia. Last year, she married former Columbian Subminister for Environmental Protection Johan Eschbach.

" 'The program will feature works by Mozart, Strauss, and Handel, as well as several new arrangements of Perkins's own work written specifically for Fräulein deBoise. The concert will begin at 8:00 P.M.' "

"About the Debussy they said nothing."

"They didn't," I agreed. "That's one of your best pieces."

"You do not like the *An die Nacht?*"

"You know I love that, and you do it beautifully. But," I sighed, "you do so much so well that I'd spend all day categorizing them." I shouldn't have mentioned anything by name, not before a performance.

"I am difficult. *Je sais ca. Mais . . .*"

"I know. There's a lot at stake."

"*Trop . . .*"

We had eaten a late breakfast—room service—and from what I knew, a late lunch/early dinner would be the order.

"A short walk might do us good."

"*Peut-etre.*" Llysette didn't sound convinced.

"There were some shops on the other side of the street from the Temple, a woolen shop for one."

She pursed her lips. "A short walk?"

"Three blocks each way."

"Three. I can do that."

We stopped by the concierge's desk and converted 300 Columbian dollars into Deseret dollars. The two red hundreds also had the "Holiness to the Lord" motto, but the face on the bills was of someone called Grant.

It had snowed or rained earlier, and the streets were wet under high gray clouds. A steady cold wind blew from the northwest. Llysette fastened her collar.

Another pair of young and bearded Danites followed as we walked eastward on West Temple South.

Deseret Woolen Mills occupied a small red brick building practically across from the Temple grounds. In the window were woolen coats and brown and black woolen scarves.

Llysette wrinkled her nose. "Brown is for cows."

"They might have other colors inside."

"*Peut-etre.*" That was one of the more dubious "perhapses" I'd heard, but she consented to turn toward the door, which I opened for her.

"The ladies' section is to the right," offered a woman with braided gray hair, although I doubted she was much older than I.

Llysette marched in the direction indicated, as if to determine quickly that the Deseret Woolen Mills had little to offer her.

I paused by a small rack of men's coats—jackets without matching trousers, almost blazers, except they were tweed and the upper part of the chest and back were covered with soft gray leather.

"Those are popular with the ranchers." A gray-haired bearded man eased up beside me.

"Ranchers?" I hadn't thought there were many left, with the energy developments.

"They do wear jackets, but they're particular about what they wear. Why don't you try one on?"

The jacket was comfortable and probably warm—definitely necessary in New Bruges. In the end, though, somehow I just couldn't see myself wearing tweed and leather to class or anywhere else.

I replaced the jacket on its hanger, put my own suit coat back on, and went to find Llysette.

She was in the rear corner of the store, holding a woman's suit. She glanced at the pale green woolen skirt, then finally took off her own coat and tried the jacket.

"Looks good." I tried to keep my voice enthusiastic, even as I saw the Danites on the sidewalk, waiting. "Why don't you put on the skirt?"

"I do not know. The skirt is long."

"Try it on. I think it would look good."

The saleslady, the only other woman in the store, nodded.

While Llysette was in the fitting room, I walked toward the front of the store and studied the pair outside. Young, short-haired, but bearded, wearing the dark green overcoats, eyes hard with that look common to all too many fanatics.

At the creak of the ancient fitting room door, I turned and stepped back toward the women's section.

Llysette pirouetted in front of the full-length flat mirror.

Although the skirt was long, slightly below midcalf, the lines flattered her.

"You look spectacular."

"*Le prix*, that also is spectacular."

"You deserve it."

"I do not know."

"I'll buy it."

She shook her head. "Now . . . should I wish, I can purchase my own clothes."

The outfit took most of our cash, but I had pressed because it was warm and looked good on Llysette and she needed both, particularly with another cold New Bruges winter nearing.

The streets were still damp as we walked back to the Lion Inn, but the air seemed even colder.

After hanging up the green woolen outfit in the closet, Llysette took out the music again and sat on the piano bench.

My stomach growled.

After checking the menu and running it by Llysette, earning a raised eyebrow for interrupting her, I ordered the plainest form of pasta from room service, with the sauce on the side, to be safe about the whole thing.

Nearly forty-five minutes later, Llysette glared at me. "*Le dejuener* . . . it is where?"

"It's supposed to be here." I picked up the wireset and dialed in the number.

"Lion Inn, room service. May we help you?"

"Yes. This is Johan Eschbach. I ordered a dinner nearly an hour ago, and we still haven't seen it. Suite Six-oh-three."

"Yes, sir. Just a moment, sir."

I waited.

"He's already left, sir. Let us know if he's not there in five minutes."

"I will."

I turned to Llysette. "It's on the way."

"On the way? And how proceeds it—by airship from Paris?"

"By Brit rail—wide slow gauge."

"Humorous that is not."

A rap on the door saved me from having to make further attempts at humor. The server wore the livery of the hotel and pushed a cart table.

"I'll take it in," I told him.

"But—"

"I'll do it." I smiled.

He backed away.

Llysette watched as I set up the table, then went to the cooler and extracted a bottle of wine and set a glass beside her plate.

She looked at the wineglass, then shook her head. "A half a glass, that is all."

"You can have the rest when you celebrate later." *Unwind,* that would be more like it.

"Then, I will need the wine."

After we ate, Llysette started on her hair.

In the end, I opted for the formal concert dress, black coat and black tie. As the consort to the star, it was better to be overdressed than underdressed.

I still brought the plastic blade, and the calculator and pens, as well as a few other items, such as the dart gun sections in my boot heels.

Llysette warmed up and did her makeup. She didn't put on the performing gown at the inn but wore a plain dress. I carried the garment bag, and we walked the block and a half through the gray gloom to the hall—a good hour before Llysette's curtain time.

Her dressing room was marked—in large red letters—and there were two flower arrangements there.

She read the cards and handed them to me with a smile:

Break a leg, or whatever—Bruce.

Best wishes. Jacob Jensen.

Then I helped her into the gown, and she went back to a few slow warmups. I stood in the corner, slightly away from the waist-high and oversize ventilation grate, half-wondering if that much cooling were necessary in the summer in Great Salt Lake. I shook my head. The big grate covered an air return. The inbound air register was near the ceiling and about one-tenth the size of the big return duct.

I'd seen several of the large grates as we wandered around looking for her dressing room, and I supposed, with the heat from the stage lights, at times there was a need to suck out that hot air quickly.

A knock echoed from Llysette's dressing room door. I walked over and eased it ajar to see who was there.

The brown-bearded Jacob Jensen stood outside, wearing a formal outfit. I was glad I'd worn my own formal dress. Jensen bowed, then extended an envelope to me. "Your tickets, Minister Eschbach."

Strange as it seemed, I hadn't really thought about tickets. For a moment, I just stared.

"The fifteenth row. After I heard your lady . . ." He paused and shook his head. "Her voice is too powerful to sit too close. There are two tickets. That's so you don't have to sit next to anyone if you'd rather not."

"Thank you." Why two and not three? Still, it was Llysette's show, and I wasn't about to upset anything.

"Does she need anything?"

I looked toward Llysette. She shook her head.

"No." I added, "But thank you for the flowers."

"I'm most grateful she's here." Jensen cleared his throat. "If she does need anything, let me know. I'm in the small office at the corner there." With a nod and a smile, he walked briskly toward the back of the stage, behind the rear wall of the stage.

Llysette looked at me, and I got the message. "You're ready to be alone."

That got a nod.

I stepped over to her, hugged her, and whispered, "I love you. You'll be wonderful." Then I left, closing the door behind me.

I hadn't realized just how big the concert hall was until I saw it lit. Llysette hadn't been exaggerating, not much. There had to have been two thousand seats in the three tiers. Even a half hour before the performance, more than half were taken. It was strange to think that more people would hear her in one night in Deseret than had heard her in six years in Columbia. Strange and wondrous and sad all at once.

My seat was beside Jillian Perkins, who wore a maroon dress with a white lace collar. The seat on the far side of her was vacant, and I understood why I'd gotten two tickets, rather than three.

"Good evening," I said as I eased in beside her.

She smiled, an expression pasted on under concerned eyes.

"Worried? They'll do fine."

"Dan . . . he's worked very hard for this."

I understood, I thought. Everyone needed the concert, for very different reasons. Llysette needed it to rehabilitate her career and give her leverage toward more security and tenure . . . and financial independence. Dan Perkins needed it because . . . I suspected he and Jillian required the money for a growing family, and he needed another boost for his career, perhaps because his music wasn't simple singspiel trash or lip-synch monotony, but complex composition based on good verse and possibly better music. The Saint theocracy needed the concert as an opening wedge toward wider relations with Columbia, and Columbia needed Saint oil and energy exports.

Then . . . there had to be others who needed a disruption, like deGaulle, or Ferdinand. I hoped the Danites and the others were up to containing anything along those lines.

Jillian blotted her forehead.

"He's invested a lot in this?"

"Not in the concert, but in the recordings."

"Llysette will sing well."

"He says she is the only one who can do justice to his art songs." She swallowed.

I patted her shoulder, just once. "She says he's the only one that understands the music and the piano enough to let her sing her best." Llysette hadn't actually said it, but I understood that was how she felt. Llysette didn't have to say it, not to me.

Either my words or gesture triggered the slightest frown.

"I wish I could play for her." I laughed ruefully. "But I've got as much musical talent as a frog. It's hard to watch her, to be able to appreciate it, and to add nothing."

"You have done a great deal, Dan says. Weren't you an important government official?"

"It's not quite the same," I protested.

"You love her . . . almost more than time and eternity." Her words were not quite a question.

I nodded.

"That makes it hard. Very hard," she said.

We understood, sitting there as the hall filled, each of us wishing for the best for someone we could do little to help. I'd liked Jillian from the moment I'd seen her—almost like the sister I'd never had, and never would.

The stage remained empty until nearly ten minutes past eight, when the doors to the hall were closed and the lights dimmed. The house wasn't quite filled, but close to it.

My eyes took in the suspended microphones, and I swallowed.

Then two figures stepped forward and bowed. The applause was polite, modest, but certainly not overwhelming.

First there was a light, but florid, aria by Handel—light for

Llysette, anyway, *Lusinghe piu care.* After a brief silence, the applause was strong, much stronger. Then came the Mozart, *Exultate Jubilate.*

Llysette's voice intertwined with the notes from the piano yet remained separate, floated yet dropped inside my head, separated me almost from breathing. I wasn't the only one, because when she finished there was a gasp from the entire audience. The applause was thunderous, or close to it.

During the applause, more Saints filed in, filling many of the remaining seats.

Then came the Debussy aria, Lia's air from *L'Enfant du Prodigue,* and there wasn't any doubt about the volume of the applause. A few more listeners straggled in, and I began to wonder about Saint punctuality.

All in all, by intermission I was sweating, and the hall was still slightly chill. Beside me, Jillian was equally damp, and her teeth fretted on the linen handkerchief clutched in her hands. Then I understood. The Perkins pieces were after the intermission.

"They're better," I offered.

"What?" Her eyes weren't really focused.

"Dan's pieces. They're every bit as good as the last Strauss and the Mozart. They could be better. You'll have to see."

She offered a faint smile and went back to worrying the linen.

I tried to listen to the whispers and low voices around us, despite wondering whether I really wanted to know what they were saying.

". . . heard Rysanek once . . . said she was the greatest. Not anymore . . . and I'll bet we haven't heard the best yet. . . ."

"I don't understand. Where did she come from? Why is she here?"

"Don't fret, Jefferson. Just enjoy the music. You won't hear this again, not when the rest of the world finds out."

". . . get tickets for your folks?"

"Never heard Debussy sung like that, and Debussy never did either, poor man."

My guts were tight, and I wished I had something to chew on. I wanted to go backstage, but that was the last thing Llysette needed.

Finally, I stood up, just before my seat, to stretch my legs. I looked at Jillian, but she didn't even glance up.

Then the lights flashed, and people began to file back into the hall, and I sat down.

Jillian fretted with her handkerchief again and twisted in her seat, her eyes downcast.

The first song after intermission was from Puccini's *La Bohème,* in Italian about Paris, and then came a short and humorous Wolf piece, *Mausfallen spruchlein,* before Llysette launched into the three Perkins pieces.

They got another resounding ovation, and she completed the concert with *An die Nacht.*

The last piece wasn't the end, though, not after the audience kept applauding and standing and screaming.

Jillian and I just stood with them. I think we were both numb, in the way that you get when the emotional overload is too great to feel any more.

Finally, the audience sat, and Perkins settled himself at the piano.

The encore had to be partly Carolynne's, although only two of us would have known that as Llysette finished and as the applause and cacophony cascaded around me.

Jillian and I didn't speak. What could we have said that wouldn't have been banal after the performance of our spouses?

Bright lights surrounded Llysette's dressing room, and I had to ease around the crowd, but I wasn't getting very far.

"There's Minister Eschbach!" boomed a voice, and Jacob Jensen and his driver, Heber, pushed aside some of the well-wishers and their bouquets of flowers—just flowers; apparently chocolates weren't *de rigueur* in Deseret—and escorted me behind the video-linkers and their lights, all focused on Llysette.

"Fräulein duBoise, why did you wait so long to return to the stage?"

"For many years I had no country. A person who has no country has few choices. I am happy now in Columbia. I will perform so long as people wish to hear."

"Some people have said your husband was a spy, and that he still might be."

"*Mon cher* . . . he is a very good professor, and he was a war hero, and he is a good man. He is no spy." She offered a wide and sparkling smile, and I thought she had seen me.

"But do you know if he once was a spy?"

Llysette smiled. "You do not like my words, then you should ask Johan. He is there." She gestured toward me.

I had to give one of the young linkers credit. He dodged around Heber and had the videocamera in my face.

"It's said you were a spy. Is it true?"

"I don't think it's any great secret that I once was employed by the Sedition Prevention Service—that was a long time ago. I was also once a military pilot, and a government minister, and my family was killed, and I was wounded for that service." I forced a smile. "But all of that was a long time ago, and I'm a professor of environmental studies married to one of the greatest singers of the age. She's your story. You'll see a lot of retired officials. There's only one of her."

Surprisingly, the young fellow smiled and turned the camera back toward Llysette.

"You've sung in two national capitals in less than a month after years of no public performances. How did this happen?"

"Doktor Perkins. He sent a student to a clinic. There I sang one of his songs. He sent me arrangements." Llysette shrugged. "He is a great composer, and his student led to the concert."

"Is there any message behind your concert, Miss duBoise?"

"Message?" Llysette laughed. "The beauty of the music will last when we are gone."

"How do you like Deseret?"

"Many of the people, they are friendly. I have not seen much. I have prepared for the concert."

"That's enough!" announced a bass voice, and the lights dimmed, and the media scuffled away, slowly.

Blinking in the comparative gloom, I stepped forward and hugged my wife, gently, then kissed her cheek. *"Magnifique!"* I whispered. "And that's understating it."

A few steps away, Dan Perkins was hugging Jillian. Her eyes were wet. After a moment, they stepped toward us.

"There aren't many nights . . . like this." His voice barely carried over the noise of another group that seemed headed toward us and the mutterings of the departing videolinkers.

"Non." Llysette squared her shoulders. "But twice more we must perform."

Perkins nodded, then grinned. "We'd better enjoy it."

"Here they are!" boomed the bass voice again, which I finally attached to a blocky man not much taller than my shoulder who gestured toward an older man at the head of the new group.

"This is the First Counselor, the Most Honorable J. Press Cannon." The bass-voiced man gestured.

First Counselor Cannon had white hair and beard, a cherubic face marred slightly by childhood acne that had never totally healed, and warm bluish-brown eyes. He inclined his head. "You were absolutely superb, Miss duBoise."

His voice was full and concerned, and I distrusted him on sight. He was the kind of man who was always honest, forthright, supportive, and able to use all three traits to his own advantage to be deadlier than most villains.

"I thank you."

"Don't thank me. I'm thanking you for an experience that comes all too infrequently, if ever."

Llysette flushed.

He turned to me. "You have had some experience with the media, I notice."

"Me?" I shook my head.

Cannon laughed. "Minister Eschbach, someday we'll talk." He turned back to Llysette. "Unlike your president, I have heard many singers. I've never heard one like you." He shook his head. "We have been truly doubly blessed with your presence. I will be here tomorrow and Saturday." With a last cherubic smile he nodded, and he and his entourage marched off like some religious band ready for another revival.

Eventually, most drifted away, and Llysette changed back into the simple dress. I eased her performance gown into the bag.

The Danites, and there were four now, escorted us both back to the Lion Inn, right from the dressing room. One carried the half-dozen bouquets that had been pressed upon Llysette.

Outside the concert hall, a dozen people stood in the swirling snowflakes that weren't sticking to the sidewalk or the street.

"Miss duBoise . . . please . . . would you please sign my program?" The girl barely came to my shoulder. "Please?"

I fumbled in my pocket and found a pen, not one of Bruce's set, and extended it to her.

Llysette smiled and asked, "Do you sing?"

"After hearing you . . . I . . . I'm afraid to try."

"So was I once, when I heard Tebaldi. Learn to sing, child."

The girl looked down, then slipped away.

A white-haired woman eased a book toward Llysette—open to a picture of a much younger Llysette duBoise. "I never thought . . . You're better than all of them, and I've heard them all."

"You are kind." I could see the moistness in my diva's eyes as she signed the picture, moistness that glistened in the reflections of the street glow throwers.

When the woman closed the book, I caught the title—*Prima Donnas: Past and Future.*

Llysette signed all fifteen programs, with a kind word and a smile for each. But she was silent, withdrawn deeply into herself, as we walked the last half-block to the Lion Inn and took the elevator up to the suite.

The Danites followed silently, and I wondered why, half-musingly, still in a detached state myself, until we reached our door.

"Miss duBoise? The flowers, ma'am?" asked the Danite who had carried them all the way from the dressing room.

We both looked at the flowers held by the Saint. What could Llysette do with them?

Finally, she took the one bouquet with the pale white roses, barely more than buds, and looked at the young Danite. "Have you a wife?"

He nodded.

"And the others?"

"Some do, Miss duBoise."

Llysette smiled. "I cannot have too many flowers around me. Perhaps you could take them . . . if you would wish . . . for all of you, and for watching out for us."

"Thank you." A momentary smile cracked the pale face under the blond hair.

"We thank you," she said.

After they left, I closed the door and took Llysette's coat, then hung up her gown.

She stood almost where I had left her, in the sitting room area, staring blankly in the general direction of the windows.

"Johan . . . you have not said much."

I shook my head, and my eyes burned again. "What could I say? I've never heard . . . no one had ever heard . . ." I looked into her green eyes, saw the pride and the incredible pain. "I don't have the words. I feel anything I say is so little to describe how you sang." What could I have said that would have been adequate to describe that incredible performance?

"You know."

"I know." And I did.

"Some wine. It might help."

I filled her wineglass, and she took it and nearly drained it in one swallow.

I wanted to tell her to take it easy, but I didn't. Instead, I set the bottle on the table and stood behind her and squeezed her shoulders, sort of an awkward hug, then kissed her neck.

"The critics, they are not the audience." She stood, unsteadily, and walked to the window, looking out at the snow-flurried and misted lights of Great Salt Lake.

Well I knew that. The critics were like David and the dean, unable to do much, but always faulting everyone else. "Even the critics were impressed." *Enough, I hope . . . enough.*

"Never like this . . . and I must sing tomorrow . . . and Saturday."

I understood the pressure more, now. She had conquered, and she had to do it again . . . and again, never letting down, never letting up, and every critic would be wondering, first, if her performances were just a singular occurrence and, then, when she would fail.

"You'll do it." I put my arms around her, gently.

She sobbed softly, and I held her for a time, a long, long time.

23

THE next morning, while Llysette was still sleeping, after running through my exercises as quietly as I could, I sneaked down to the lobby and bought copies of both Great Salt Lake City papers, each one in its polished wood stand. No plastic or metal in Deseret, almost a throwback in some ways to the New Bruges of a half-century earlier.

The news stories—if there were any—should have been favorable, but I'd learned a long time ago that critics were a species alien to reason, common sense, or public appeal.

Llysette was still asleep when I got back to the suite, and I eased the bedroom door closed and sat down in the wide-armed and overupholstered chair that almost resembled a padded throne. After opening the *Deseret News,* I turned to the Arts section, holding my breath as I saw a picture of Llysette and Dan Perkins just after taking a bow, Llysette with one bouquet of flowers in her arms. I'd been there, but I hadn't even seen those flowers. Then I read, slowly, waiting for some bombshell. There wasn't one. Were the Great Salt Lake City critics a species slightly less alien than their Columbian brethren?

> Great Salt Lake City. "Magnificent is too weak a word" to describe the performance of Llysette duBoise and Daniel Perkins, said Salt Palace concertmeister Jensen. For once, if possible for a man who praises everything, Jensen underpraised the artists he hired for the Cultural Series.

"Never has Deseret heard such a presentation of classic and art songs!" added Grant Johannsen, conductor of the Deseret Symphony. They were both right, even conservative, in their praise.

DuBoise offered depths, shadings, tones, textures in a shimmering and seamless weave of sound that melded perfectly with Perkins's sure touch on the keys. So perfect was the match of keyboard and voice that every number ended with stunned silence—followed by thunderous applause.

My eyes burned as I struggled to the end. It hadn't just been me. Everyone had sensed and felt that impossible energy, that emotional torrent encased in sheer perfected discipline.

The *Star* commentary was of the same timbre, and both ended with the recommendation that would-be listeners sell their dearest possession, if need be, to get one of the few tickets remaining.

Like all critics, the *News* reviewer did have a few nasty digs after the one at Jensen:

> While the concert itself was an unimaginable improvement over past offerings, so much that Jensen will be hard-pressed to repeat such a triumph, even should he live so long as Methuselah, the Salt Palace management still manifests a carelessness of detail in other ways. There were far too few souvenir programs, and the concession areas were grossly understaffed. Likewise the warning bells for the intermission were weak and lost in the hubbub as listeners rhapsodized happily about the music. Fortunately, the warning lights were adequate, if barely.

The *Star* reviewer attacked the parking and the lack of concert-related transport and the lack of programs. I was just glad that everything about the performance itself was glowing.

I took a deep breath.

The bedroom door opened, and Llysette, tousled and beautiful in her robe, stood there. She squinted against the light pouring through the wide window. Then her eyes went to the paper.

"What said they?" She frowned. "*Non.* Do not tell me."

I couldn't help but grin from ear to ear. "No one has ever gotten a review this good. Ever."

"You jest."

"Not about this." I folded back the *News* review, stood, and handed it to her, then went to heat water for the chocolate that was apparently the only warm morning beverage permitted in Deseret. The suite had the powdered kind, but it was better than the alternative, which was nothing at all.

"*Non, c'est impossible.*"

"That's what they wrote. It might even sell a few of those disks your friend Doktor Perkins is having recorded."

"He is having all three nights recorded."

"That's good, but he won't need them—unless it's because of technical problems." All problems were technical in one way or another, as I'd learned in the Spazi.

The wireline chimed.

"Hello," I answered cautiously.

"Minister Eschbach . . . this is Orab on the front desk. Ah . . . we've received a considerable number of flowers. . . ."

"How considerable?"

"Fifteen arrangements, but the florist said there would be more coming."

"Could I wire you back in a moment? I'll need to talk to Fräulein duBoise."

"Yes, sir."

"Now does someone want what?"

I turned to Llysette. "You were a hit. The concierge reports that you have more than a dozen flower arrangements and bouquets downstairs."

"Oh."

"That many flowers. . . ." I paused. "And the florists told him more were coming.

"With so many, I will sneeze and not sing." Her eyes went to the pale white roses, barely opening, that I'd placed in a glass pitcher taken from the minuscule corner that substituted for a kitchen.

I nodded.

"What will I do?"

I shrugged. "Keep the cards or notes. Maybe you could donate the flowers to a hospital or home or something."

"You do what you think best, Johan." She reached for the *Star,* stopping short of the paper.

"It's just as good," I reassured her, picking the handset back up. "Concierge."

"Orab? This is Minister Eschbach."

"Yes, sir?"

"Fräulein duBoise is overwhelmed at the thought of all those flowers. Unfortunately, she's also somewhat allergic to many of them. She wondered if she could have any cards or notes that went with them, but if we could send the flowers to a hospital—for children or for older people?" I paused. "We'd be happy to pay the florists or the hotel for the transportation. It's just not something we can do personally, and it would be a shame to waste such a lovely gesture."

A brief silence followed. "Why, yes, sir. I'm sure we could arrange that. Would you want to send cards from Miss duBoise?"

"No. Make it anonymous."

Llysette nodded from across the room, her eyes lifting from the *Star* Entertainment section.

I took the liberty of ordering breakfast that was half-lunch from room service, getting another nod as I did.

Llysette read each review several times.

After a meal that was probably too hearty, Llysette decided to immerse herself in hot water. She liked it hot enough almost to boil lobsters. Once she was safely in the tub, I experimented with the videolink set. I did find a noon news program after a half hour or so.

". . . speaking on behalf of the First Presidency, Counselor Cannon was clear about the path Deseret must follow." The screen shifted to the white-bearded Cannon.

"Deseret deplores the Austro-Hungarian action in further militarizing Tenerife, but neither can we condone the seizure of the Cape Verdes by New France. . . ."

I winced. That action hadn't gotten into the papers yet.

"In related news, another squadron of the Columbian navy has been deployed to the Bermuda Naval Station. The Austrian ambassador to Columbia made his protest to Columbian Speaker Hartpence simultaneously with a protest by Ambassador Rommel to British Prime Minister Blair. Schikelgruber's protest came immediately upon his return to the Federal District. Austro-Hungary claims the action violates the Neutrality Treaty of 1980 between Great Britain and Austro-Hungary." The videoscreen showed a Columbian cruiser, accompanied by two frigates, in a blue expanse that could have been any warm-water ocean.

Abruptly the screen shifted to a happy family, five children gathered around a table, with a clean-scrubbed woman serving them and the beaming bearded father.

"For that special family time . . ."

From the family image, the screen shifted to a blue book lying on a white cloth. The gold letters proclaimed *The Book of Mormon, Another Testimony of Jesus Christ.*

"Help your family better understand the eternal truths of the Book of Mormon."

The screen shifted to an oblong box, bearing a stylized figure in a white robe and another set of gold lettering: *The Book of Mormon Family Game.*

"Bring the values of faith into your home in a fun and cheerful game the entire family can play. *The Book of Mormon Family Game.* Sold at LDS Bookstores everywhere. Here's how to bring the Scriptures to life for the whole family."

Another oblong game box appeared on the videoscreen, one with what seemed to be two stylized cobalt roads meeting at a golden intersection.

"The Missionary Game! Exciting and entertaining for Saints of all ages. A fun way to teach your younger children about missionary work. Everyone will catch missionary fever from this entertaining new game for the whole family."

I had to wonder where the Saint missionaries were going. It couldn't be to Europe. Ferdinand and his crew had treated the Saints as badly as the Gypsies and other dissidents. There were some Saints in the western parts of Columbia and in New France and in Oceania and South America. But were they trying to convert New France? Or would the loosening of relations with Deseret mean an influx of Saint missionaries?

Another video cut revealed still one more family, this time with four children, two boys and two girls, all blond, all seated around a table, caught laughing with bowls of popcorn in their hands, and an open blue-covered book on the table. A set of chimes rang, and a cheerful voice proclaimed: "Family . . . more important now than ever."

With that, the video flicked back to the news studio and a bespectacled man in a dark blue suit and a cravat wider than the Mississippi.

"That classical concert at the Salt Palace last night? The one featuring our own Daniel Perkins and Llysette duBoise. Some had questioned, quietly, just how good it was going to be, since Miss duBoise hadn't performed before a large audience in more than five years."

"No one's questioning now. This is the first time in five years a classical performance has generated the level of enthusiasm that approached—no, it almost exceeded that of gospel music in the Cannon Center. Word's gone out, though. The remaining tickets were gone in less than a half hour after the box office opened this morning.

"She can sing, and he can play, and it's just that simple. Of course, it doesn't hurt that she's beautiful. Here . . . take a look."

The image shifted from the announcer to one of Llysette before the interviewers.

"Is there any message behind your concert, Miss duBoise?"

"Message?" Llysette laughed. "The beauty of the music will last when we are gone."

"How do you like Deseret?"

"Many of the people, they are friendly. I have not seen much. I have prepared for the concert."

Llysette's smiling image remained on the screen, frozen, as the commentator added, "For those of you who haven't any idea of how beautiful this music truly is, here's a brief excerpt."

Of course, the excerpt was from Perkins's *Fragments of a Conversation,* but even over the degraded videolink speakers, Llysette sounded gorgeous.

The one news announcer looked to the other. "She seems very gracious."

"She is. After she sang last night, she signed programs and talked to admirers waiting outside in the snow. And if you think all entertainers are elitists, she walked—that's right, walked—back to her hotel. No limousines. If you haven't seen her and Doktor Perkins, beg a ticket if you can. You sure can't buy one now."

"Oh." Llysette's voice was somehow very small.

I turned and flicked off the set, then walked toward her, but she sat in the other armchair before I could give her a hug.

"Are you all right?"

"To get ready for the master class I must."

"That, my lady, didn't exactly answer the question."

She smiled, wistfully, sadly, and with restrained happiness—all at once. "So many I . . . we . . . would have liked to see this, and now it happens in a foreign land. Only you understand, and that is sad."

"Your father?" I asked.

She nodded.

"Your mother?" I didn't ask about the deacon—Carolynne's deacon. I knew.

"She loved me. She did not understand." Llysette stood.

I did hug her—tightly—and for a moment, we clung together. Then she blotted her eyes. "Still I must ready myself for the classes."

"What do you do at these classes?"

"I must listen, and then I must offer instructions. You will see."

She dressed, and I showered and dressed, and we were ready about the same time.

We walked the short distance to the complex, and I held the map in my hand, occasionally noting that the Danites continued to trail us. How were they different from the Spazi? I wasn't sure, only that it felt like we'd been shadowed for half our lives when, in reality, it had been something like two months. Or had it? Weren't we shadowed by government most of our lives, one way or the other?

Outside, the sky was mostly clear, but the wind blew, far more than in New Bruges, but not quite so cold. Llysette still shivered within her coat.

An oval-faced woman was waiting in the lower hall outside the lecture room, neither pacing nor totally composed but worrying her lower lip. A smile of relief crossed her face as she stepped forward. Her long blue skirt nearly swept the floor, but I could see that she wore stylish boots that matched the belt that was mostly covered by the short suit jacket. Her cream blouse was silklike.

"I'm Joanne Axley, professor of voice at Deseret University."

"Llysette duBoise," I said for my diva, "and I'm her husband and escort, Johan Eschbach."

"I'm so glad you could spend the time with us, Doktor duBoise. I've limited this group to graduate students in voice." She smiled apologetically. "Doktor Perkins did prevail on me to let several of his graduate students sit in as well."

"I would be happy to hear all, and offer what I might." Llysette's smile was professional, her voice slightly warmer than cordial.

The procedure was relatively simple. A student got up. Llysette was given a copy of the music and a little time to glance over it. Then the student went over beside the piano and sang one song and then stood and waited for Llysette's comments.

Llysette wasn't at a loss for words, not in teaching.

"Your dipthongs, you are letting them change the pitch."

The blonde young woman nodded.

"When you shift to the second vowel, the pitch changes. Stay on the first vowel. . . . Touch lightly only the second."

That got another nod, but I wondered about the comprehension.

"One more time. . . ."

The blonde cleared her throat gently and then sang.

"*Non!* . . . Like this. . . ."

Llysette sang the same phrase, and even I could sense the difference.

After a time, Llysette gestured toward the next student. The dark-haired girl/woman almost trembled as she stood beside the piano. I could tell that the student's tone was good, better than that of most of the students Llysette had at Vanderbraak State, but there was no life in the song.

Apparently Llysette agreed. "Stop!" My singer shook her head sadly. "What does this verse mean?"

"It's in Italian."

"*Ca,* we know. But what do the words mean? Tell me with your own words . . . what does this mean?"

"Ah . . . Doktor . . . she's singing about how she is sick and everything is hopeless."

"Do you sound hopeless?" asked Llysette with a smile.

The dark-haired student looked confused. In the background, Joanne Axley nodded, and I understood one of the reasons for master classes. After a while students tune out their instructors. When someone famous and important says it . . . then the teacher— sometimes—regains credence.

"You must sing the words *and* the emotions. A voice, it is not a piano. It is not . . . a drum."

The next student had trouble with something that Llysette called "the anticipation of the consonant."

"The body . . . it knows the next sound is the consonant, and it desires to sing that consonant. That closes off the vowel. You must stay on the vowel longer. . . ."

The comments continued with each student.

"You squeeze your breath too much here. . . ."

"A nice touch there . . . delicate, and that it should be. . . ."

"Do you know the style? How must one sing this style . . ."

"Your neck, it is tight like a wire cable, and you have no breath on the long phrases. . . ."

What got me was that these were *good* students. I almost shuddered at what Llysette—or most voice teachers—had to go through with the others.

She motioned to one of the young men, dark-haired. "You, have you a song?"

"Ah . . . yes, Doktor."

"Then sing it for me."

She nodded as he launched into some aria I didn't recognize, but, then, I wouldn't have recognized most of them.

The "one-hour" master class lasted more than an hour and a half before Llysette heard the last song from the last male graduate student and Joanne Axley walked with us to the door of the lecture room.

"You've been very gracious . . . and very helpful." Joanne Axley's smile was warmer than the one she had offered when Llysette had arrived. Another case of Jensen—or someone—leaning hard and people being surprised after the fact?

"I would try," Llysette said. "You have taught them well."

"Thank you. I try."

"They do not always listen," Llysette added dryly. "That I know."

"You made quite an impression." Axley smiled brightly. "Gerald and I will be at your recital tonight. We're looking forward to it."

"Thank you."

We stepped into the hall, and Axley turned back to the group, perhaps for some summary comments.

"She's nice, but a little on edge." I was trying to be diplomatic.

"That I understand. She is a singer. She has worked hard. She has told her students much of what I tell them. More than that, I do not doubt. They do not listen *toujours*. I come, and they listen." Llysette shook her head slowly. "The students, they are so stupid at times."

"They are, and you need to eat," I said as we walked up the carpeted stairs to the main level.

"I must rest, and I worry about the second piece of Doctor Perkins. Last night . . . I was not my best."

For a singer, I'd decided, or for Llysette, nothing short of perfection was acceptable, even when a performance was close to fantastic.

So we walked back to the Lion Inn and the performing suite, where she sat at the Haaren with the music while I ordered a lunch/dinner from room service.

I did manage to drag her from the piano when the cart table was wheeled in, partly by starting to pour some wine.

"Half a glass. That is all."

That was all she got. I took a full glass—just one.

Llysette went through several mouthfuls of pasta before she paused.

"That class took a lot out of you? Why did you agree to it?"

"The opportunity . . . the performance. . . ." She sipped the half-glass of wine she had allowed herself.

I understood that part. It had been presented as a package deal. "But did you have to work so hard?"

"How could I not? When was I their age, no one would listen to me, not someone . . . like I am now."

"You?"

"Then, in France, in the provinces . . . every girl would be a diva. My parents could not afford the best in teachers, and I learned the piano too late." She paused and took a mouthful of pasta.

"At what, age twelve?"

"Twelve," she affirmed. "Eight, it would have been better. So you see, that is why I must teach—"

"And why you get irritated with students who aren't serious."

"*Mais oui.* . . . They waste my time, and that time I could give to others."

Others like little Llysette duBoise had been dying for a chance. I just swallowed and took a small sip of wine.

Between one thing and another, we got backstage at the concert hall forty-five minutes before curtain time.

Dan Perkins met us with a smile as we went backstage. "Joanne wired me," he said. "She was pleasantly surprised at your master class. Very pleasantly surprised."

"She should not be surprised," said Llysette.

"I told her that." His smile widened to a boyish grin. "And I told her that I'd told her earlier that I'd be telling her just that."

That got me smiling, and Llysette as well.

"James B. Bird, one of my students, wired me to tell me you were outstanding."

"Your students were better," Llysette said.

"Don't tell Joanne that." He glanced toward the stage. "I need to warm up."

"Then you should."

He bowed and departed.

Once Llysette was settled in her dressing room and once that look crossed her face, I kissed her and eased myself out. From somewhere, I could hear the sounds of a piano—Doktor Perkins warming up.

After hearing Llysette from the audience the first night, I decided to view the proceedings from backstage the second night, although I couldn't quite have said why. A feeling, more or less. I hoped Herr, or Brother, Jensen wouldn't be too displeased.

I found a stool, which I appropriated, and stationed myself in the wings on the left side of the performing area, on the left looking at the audience.

Of course, I couldn't stay on it and found myself pacing in tight circles behind the angled partitions that provided slit views of the performing area.

Brother Jensen paused as he walked past. "Just stay behind the tape that marks the sight lines, Minister Eschbach."

I glanced down. The stool was a good ten feet back of the red tape on the stage. "I think we're well clear."

He nodded, then walked on to continue his survey of the backstage area. About that time, I heard the murmurs and rustles that signified that they'd opened the house to the audience.

In time, the five-minute lights blinked, and then the chimes warbled. But the murmurs continued from the hall as more Saints filed in—late—and it was nearly fifteen minutes later before Llysette came out from the corridor from the dressing rooms, accompanied by Dan Perkins. I smiled as they neared and got a warm but puzzled smile in return. "You are here?"

"I thought I'd watch from here. Less company." I grinned. "Your admiring public is waiting."

"Jillian didn't come tonight," said Perkins. "She said it was too nerve-racking, with all the crowds. It's easier to perform than watch." He offered that boyish grin. "For me, anyway."

"I don't know. I can't perform." I reached out and squeezed Llysette's hand.

As they stepped toward the stage, I had to wonder why they'd both gotten tied up with people who weren't thrilled with crowds. Then, my experience with the Spazi and in politics had inevitably led me to the conclusion that crowds tended to bring out the worst in people.

Llysette and Perkins stepped into the light, and the applause built and slowly died away. They waited until the hall was perfectly still before his fingers drew the first notes of the Handel from the big Steinbach.

I turned to my left, where a stagehand had eased up slightly more than a dozen feet away, partly shielded by one of the side partitions, apparently to watch the concert. He wore, like most of them, dark trousers and shirt and the ubiquitous leather equipment belt.

Llysette's voice rose with and over the Steinbach, but I couldn't concentrate on her singing.

The stagehand was dark-haired, and he watched Llysette intently. Too intently. Even with my poor sense of rhythm I could tell he wasn't following the music.

He eased forward, still well out of sight of the audience.

My fingers felt like thumbs as I got out the calculator and fumbled the pen and pencil into the rubber-screened holes, even while I slipped from my stool and edged toward the black-shirted figure, slow step by slow step.

Llysette's voice glided across the Handel and toward the end.

With the applause, the dark-haired stagehand took another step toward the stage, his hand straying toward the shirt that was too loose, Deseret or not.

With the glint of metal and the thundering applause, I jammed the calculator's delete key.

The thump of his body and the dull clunk of the dropped revolver were lost in the applause, for which I was thankful. Bruce's disassociator beam was so tight I didn't even feel that shuddery twisting. I hoped Llysette didn't either, but I hadn't had much choice.

The calculator went into my jacket pocket after I reached the unconscious figure and bent down. I shook my head—another zombie.

A dark-suited figure appeared beside me, one with that air that signified professionalism. His fingers checked the prone stagehand. "Neatly done, Doctor," he said in a low voice. "I didn't think you'd reach him in time. He'll have quite a headache, I imagine."

"Who are you?" I asked, keeping my voice low but straightening and stepping back. Who knew who else might be around?

"Danite Johnson. First Counselor Cannon asked us to keep a watch on the performances. This one slipped by." His eyes continued to survey the backstage area.

Two more Danites appeared and quietly carted the intruder off.

Llysette went to the Mozart, apparently undisturbed—and that got another powerful ovation. So did the Debussy.

After the first half, I slipped out of sight, back along the rear wall, still watching Llysette's dressing room, but placed so it would be hard for her to see me. I didn't want to interrupt her concentration or to let her see me too closely. She'd know that I was upset. One of the uniformed guards remained by her door from the entire time she entered until she headed back toward the stage with Dan Perkins.

The audience got more and more enthused with each song in the second part of the program, and it wasn't clear if the ovations after the encore would ever end.

I hugged Llysette once she cleared the stage. "You were wonderful." And I meant it.

"I wasn't sure how it could be better than last night," added Perkins, "but she was. We've got some incredible recordings, if they didn't have technical problems."

That was about as far we got at that moment, because people began appearing from everywhere. There were more admirers and a lot more guards, both those in serge blue uniforms and Danites. And I could see the hidden and portable scanners. While I admired the efficiency, I got an even colder feeling, because it was clear someone had let the presumed Austro-Hungarian agent in. Then, he could have been one of deGaulle's as well. Either way, his presence had been permitted, and that meant Deseret was no different from Columbia or anywhere else.

When the last admirers finally left and Llysette was beginning to sniffle amid another pile of flowers, I looked at her.

Should I tell her? If someone else did, that would upset her even more. I took a deep breath.

"You had another fan backstage," I finally said.

"A fan?"

"I think he was invited by your former friend Ferdinand. He's now getting a rest cure, courtesy of the Saints."

Llysette's eyes widened. "Backstage you were. . . . Was that why?"

"Just a feeling," I admitted. "I didn't think anyone would try something opening night. People let down their guards after opening night. So. . . ." I shrugged.

"There was a coldness after the Handel, but I sang."

Brother Jensen, nearing with a pair of Danites, frowned at her words.

"I tried to be quiet, and I hoped it wouldn't upset you."

"What drew you to the intruder?" asked Brother Jensen.

"He just didn't feel right." What I didn't want to say was that, for some reason, the Saint security had let him into the backstage area. Were they watching me? If so, I'd fallen for the trap, and that meant trouble . . . but how could I have risked letting Llysette get shot?

Someone clearly knew that, as well, and that left me feeling even more helpless.

"Tonight, you must take the steamer," Jensen insisted.

Neither of us was about to argue, and after Llysette changed we followed him down a long ramp, flanked by Danites, two of them carrying more of the flowers. With Llysette's garment bag over my shoulder and my fingers concealed by it, I checked the hidden belt knife, then the calculator components.

We needed neither. A shimmering Browning—brown, of course—waited below with Heber at the wheel.

We sat back in the dark leather seats of the Browning as it crept from the garage underneath the performing complex up a concrete ramp and around two corners and onto the street, going around the block to bring us in under the canopy of the Lion Inn.

"It is sad. One concert, and now I can no longer walk a few meters."

It was more than sad. I nodded.

24

I was awake well before eight, and I finally eased out of bed before nine, leaving Llysette to get the sleep she needed. My back was stiff from trying to be quiet and still when I was wide-eyed. I never could sleep as late as Llysette, but I wasn't under the same kind of strain that she was, nor was I undertaking the more strenuous kind of workout that a full recital or concert happened to be.

After closing the bedroom door, I did struggle my way through my exercises again—twice. They weren't a substitute for the running up the hill and through the woods, but the mild workout helped both body and mind. I wasn't about to go running off, literally or figuratively, not while she was sleeping or after the various attempts on either or both of us.

I did go downstairs and retrieve the papers, but no stories appeared in either daily, even concealed, about the assault by the phony stagehand or about Llysette. Most of the news that wasn't local was focused on the Atlantic naval buildups and the increasing tension between the Austrians and New France and Columbia, although Ambassador Schikelgruber had met with Minister Holmbek to assure him that Austro-Hungary had no intention of beginning a naval war in the Atlantic.

"Just like Ferdinand had no intention of annexing France or the Low Countries . . .," I murmured to myself.

I had two cups of the powdered hot chocolate while I studied the papers, even the advertising, but there wasn't even a hint in the police reports about the attack on Llysette. Should I have been grateful? I wasn't sure.

Then I read through the cards that had come with the flowers. A few were recognizable, one way or another, like the formal card from Walter Klein, the Columbian ambassador. He was one of President Armstrong's few political cronies who had actually gotten rewarded. I might have met him once or twice. There was one from Hartson James, the TransMedia mogul, who definitely saw something in Llysette. I just hoped his interest was purely commercial. The rest were from people, presumably Saints, whose names were unfamiliar.

Finally, I flicked on the videolink, keeping the volume down, and sampled the five channels, trying to avoid the endless family-centered commercials and to find something resembling either news or a cultural program.

Llysette kept sleeping and I kept switching channels. After probably another hour, I picked up the wireset to order a brunch for us—Llysette needed to get up before long and eat.

As I did, I thought I saw a video image of the Salt Palace, and I put down the handset and eased the video volume back up.

". . . Columbian soprano Llysette duBoise, in the midst of an acclaimed series of performances at the Salt Palace, has shown a side that most women in Deseret would find closer to their hearts than navigating the treacherous slopes to a high C. DuBoise was apparently inundated with flowers from admirers. While she has kept the cards, she sent all but a single bouquet to those in hospitals and homes."

The video showed the same clip of a flushed Llysette taking a bow with Perkins and then one of the interview clips with Llysette speaking.

"The beauty of the music will last when we are gone. . . . Many of the people, they are friendly."

The video went back to a group of three around a low table in a studio setting designed to resemble a sitting room. A blond man sat with a redheaded woman on his right and a brunette on his left.

"She sounds like a woman who has her heart in the right place," commented the redhead.

"She probably does," answered the man. "What's more interesting is that she insisted on paying for the transportation of the flowers and that the donations of the flowers be anonymous."

"Does she have any children?" asked the brunette.

"No . . . her marriage to Minister Eschbach is her first, and they've been married only about a year." The blond announcer paused. "For those of you who only know that she's a high-paid diva and sings beautifully, you might also be interested to know that she spent several years in an Austrian prison. Reportedly she was tortured before she was released."

"So . . . you're saying, Daniel, that this is one singer who isn't just an image and a pretty face?"

"Does it sound that way?" asked the smiling blond man.

"No. She sounds like quite a lady. Have you heard her?"

"Last night. She and Perkins are wonderful. You're going tonight?"

"I already was, but after hearing all this, I really wouldn't miss it."

"You won't regret it. Now . . . we'll be right back with a heart-warming story on the Heber City playground."

With that, the video cut to another smiling Saint family and a sickeningly perky jingle. I switched stations, then turned the video-link off.

The story on Llysette was planted, so firmly I could smell the odor of manure seeping from the silent video set. I hadn't checked the station, but I would have bet that it was the one owned by First Counselor Cannon.

The story was pitched to women, in a sickening way, and even cleverly suggested that Llysette was both to be admired and pitied—admired because of her pluck and talent and pitied because of her childlessness.

I almost wanted to retch. How many other stories were out there—ones I hadn't seen? And why? Was this a crash effort in humanizing the former enemies? Or something else?

The silence about the intruder was deafening. No one had wired, and there was nothing on the videolink news or in either paper.

I felt isolated.

The bedroom door opened, and Llysette stepped out, eyes squinting even in the indirect light of the cloudy late morning.

"Johan . . . how you can chirp like the bird so early, that I do not know."

"Heredity. You should see my Aunt Anna."

"*Toute la famille?*"

"Not all. My father was more like you." I glanced toward the window. "I was about to order something to eat."

"Another meal in this room . . . *non* . . . that will not do."

"That's fine. Do you want me to wire Jensen and find another restaurant?"

"*Non* . . . the bird in the cage will I be." She sighed. "But the cage downstairs, *du moins*. I will not be long."

Her definition of *long* was another comparative I let go, especially since I also needed to shower and to get dressed. First, I did fix Llysette a cup of chocolate, before I climbed into the shower. The hot water felt good, and despite the chocolate I'd had, my stomach was growling by the time we stepped into the elevator.

The lobby was more crowded, but no one gave us more than a passing glance, and a tall blond waiter escorted us to a corner booth in the Refuge—not the same one we'd had before, but a corner booth that was relatively isolated, and I got hot and steaming non-powdered chocolate, which I sipped most gratefully.

The family at the long table nearest our corner of the Refuge kept looking at us. I tried to concentrate on whatever a Deseret skillet was—a concoction of red potatoes, various peppers, eggs, and slabs of ham all served in a miniature cast-iron skillet set in a wooden holder or plate.

"That's her . . . know it is . . . saw her on the link."

"Must be her bodyguard with her. . . ."

I winced at that.

"Her husband . . . say he was a spy once."

". . . looks pleasant enough."

I felt like glaring but didn't.

"Do you expect a spy to look like a Lamanite, Ellie?"

"A spy you do not look like." Llysette's eyes twinkled, and she raised her water glass. "Even when you are spying."

I decided to eat more and eavesdrop less.

The Saturday afternoon master class was nearly a repeat of the Friday one, except the students were more nervous and Joanne Axley gave Llysette a more glowing introduction.

Afterward, several of them clustered around.

". . . will you be back to give more recitals here?"

"I must be asked," said Llysette politely. "The arrangements are made years before, at times. This was not planned."

I'd almost forgotten that.

"You were so good. . . ."

Llysette nodded toward Joanne Axley, who stood talking to a redheaded young man. "Your professor, she is very wise. You are fortunate."

The slightest frown crossed the student's forehead.

"So easy it is," Llysette continued, an edge to her voice, "to forget. Do you know of Madame Rocza?"

"Ah . . . no, Miss duBoise. Is she a singer?"

Llysette shook her head. "She taught many of the best when they were young. Now . . . some, they scarcely know her. Do not do that." She smiled politely.

"Ah . . . thank you."

"You are welcome."

Joanne Axley slipped over toward Llysette as the conference room emptied. "I overheard your words to Bronwin," she said to Llysette with a small laugh. "I appreciate the thought, but I don't know as she'll listen."

"The students, they are dense."

I could vouch for that.

"Weren't we all?" asked Axley.

Somehow I doubted that either of them had been. I had been, and I knew it, and I'd had to learn far too much the hard way. My only grace in that department was that I knew I'd been dense and spoiled—and fortunate enough to survive both.

After the master class, we walked eastward, through the light and chilly gusting breeze. I glanced ahead toward a large building taking up an entire block. "Zion Mercantile" was spelled out in shimmering bronze letters.

"Shall we?" I asked.

"Mais oui."

The first stop was the dress section.

Llysette frowned at the long-sleeved, almost dowdy, dress on the mannequin, then went to the next one—equally conservative, with another ankle-length skirt. Her eyes went to the shoppers.

A tall, graying redhead passed us, her camel overcoat open to show a high-necked cream silk blouse and dark woolen trousers. With her was a younger woman, also a redhead. After them came a stocky blonde, with a wide, if pretty, face and sparkling blue eyes. Each hand grasped a child's hand—both blond and blue-eyed like their mother—and neither boy was over five or six. The mother wore a blue turtlenecked blouse, also of silk, and a skirt that reached nearly to her ankles. Under the skirt I could see blue leather boots. All three women had their hair in French braids. In fact, most of the women in Deseret had long, braided hair, I realized.

Silk blouses? They didn't look synthetic, unless the Saints' synthetic fibres were far better than those of Columbia. Then, the Saints had developed a silk industry early in south Deseret.

I followed Llysette into the coat department, where a well-dressed and gray-haired woman stood with three girls who looked to be of secondary school age. All four had their hair braided, and the girls tried on coats.

Llysette picked up several coats, among them a dark green woolen one.

"That looks nice."

"At least, you do not tell me when I sing that it is nice."

I winced. Llysette hated the word *nice*, but I didn't always remember.

She handed me her coat and tried on the green, then walked over to the flat mirror on the wall before shaking her head. I handed her back her coat and returned the green one to the rack.

The next stop was lingerie, and I tried not to frown at the filmy garments in every shade of the rainbow. While the coats and dresses had been solid and conservative, not even the theatre district of Philadelphia showed undergarments like some of the Zion Mercantile offerings.

Llysette saw my face, clearly, and a wide smile crossed her lips as she lifted a black lace teddy from a rack. "This one . . . you would like?"

I could feel myself flushing.

"*Oui.* . . ."

I had to grin.

"About some things, Johan, Dutch you are still."

She was probably right about that, too, and I wasn't sure whether I was relieved or disappointed that she didn't buy any of the lingerie. Nor anything else except a small jar of a body cream. All in all, we spent nearly an hour roaming through the store, and I spent as much time thinking as looking.

The store bothered me, and I wasn't sure why, exactly. There hadn't been more than a handful of men anywhere, and the women in the store were well dressed and well-groomed, and a number of them were smiling. Not exactly what I would have expected in a rigid theocracy.

"Johan?"

"Oh . . . sorry. I was just thinking."

"We can go. I have found nothing that I could not do without *absoluement.*"

As we walked slowly back to the Lion Inn, toward a sun low in the sky, with the wind ruffling my hair, I watched the people even more closely. A woman with braided blond hair coiled into a knot at the back of her neck walked with an older white-haired and bearded man. Neither looked at the other. She wore a long camel coat, as did he. Two women in short wool jackets and ankle-length skirts shepherded six children, all fresh-faced and scrubbed, in the direction of the Temple park. A young man, clean-shaven, strode briskly past us.

"Downstairs or upstairs?" I asked when he stepped into the inn's lobby.

Llysette shrugged.

"Are you hungry? Pasta? Soup?"

"To finish the concerts, that is what I wish." She marched toward the elevator.

I followed but said nothing until the couple with the three children exited at the fourth floor. "Are you angry with me?"

"Mais non . . . I am angry with this place."

"It is different. It—"

"Did you not see?"

"What? That there weren't any women by themselves, unless they had children?"

"You did see," she answered with that tone that indicated that what she meant was perfectly obvious.

With a slight *cling,* the elevator stopped at the sixth floor.

"You're angry that the only place you're getting a chance to sing is one where women are treated this way." I paused, then decided against pointing out that the women I'd seen hadn't seemed depressed or oppressed. It could have been that I wasn't seeing those women.

"I cannot sing in France. It is no more. I cannot sing in Columbia, except to make . . . someone look good." She left the elevator with a shake of her head. "These things . . . I must wait. Tonight, I will sing."

"Did I do something?" What had I missed?

"It is not you."

I wondered, but she did smile, and I opened the door. A large stack of cards lay on the small side table under the mirror—more, I supposed, from flowers sent to Llysette.

With my diva's touchiness, I tried to remain in the background, guessing at the pasta she wanted for dinner and making the arrangements, fielding Jensen's wirecall to notify Llysette that a limousine would be waiting to avoid problems.

The Browning limousine, with Heber at the wheel, was waiting, and we rode silently the long block to the underground entrance.

"Thank you." I opened the door for Llysette one-handed, her gown in the bag I carried in the other.

"You're welcome," answered the driver.

We followed another functionary in a green coat up the ramps. "How do you feel?"

Llysette didn't answer, and I didn't press. Once she wanted me out of her dressing room, I went to find Jensen. He wasn't in the corner office, but I tracked him to a lower level where he was talking to three men in gray jumpsuits carrying tools and wearing equipment belts.

When he saw me, he turned and hurried over.

"No matter how you plan, some technical thing always goes wrong in a concert hall." He laughed. "What can I do for you, Minister Eschbach?"

"I wondered if anyone has found out anything about the man who tried to attack Llysette last night."

"No. We haven't heard anything much. One of the . . . security types . . . said something about his being zombied." He shrugged. "I just don't know." After a pause, he added, "We've put on another fifty guards, half in plainclothes, and the city police have doubled their patrols in the area around the complex."

"Is there any other reason to worry?" I asked pleasantly. "Besides last night?"

"Not that I know of." He glanced back toward the workmen.

"I won't keep you."

I decided to remain backstage, but I positioned my stool a little differently—where I could watch the approach area to Llysette's dressing room, and the stage. That meant I would see Llysette performing from the side and behind.

Despite the dimming lights and the chimes, the concert was even later in starting than the previous two nights. Saints seemed to have this proclivity to be somewhat tardy. I had peeked earlier, and the hall was going to be standing room only. It made me wish that

Llysette were getting a percentage of the tickets, because someone was going to make quite a stash.

With the lights down, the notes rose from the Steinbach, and Llysette's, and Carolynne's, voice shimmered out of the light and into the darkened space. I could almost imagine the notes lighting the darkness.

The Handel was good, the Mozart better, and the Debussy extraordinary.

Again, I kept out of the way at intermission.

The second half was every bit as good as, if not better than, the night before. Llysette's voice seemed at times to rip my heart from my chest and at others to coax tears from me—or from a statue.

If I'd thought the applause the previous two nights had been thunderous, I'd been mistaken. The stolid Saints stood and clapped and clapped and clapped, and clapped some more.

Llysette and Dan Perkins finally capitulated and did a second encore—another Perkins song, simpler, but it didn't matter to the crowd. They stood and cheered and clapped, and they kept doing it.

Llysette deserved it—more than deserved it—both for what she'd endured to get there and for the sheer artistry of what she had delivered.

I met her at the back of the stage. "You were wonderful. More wonderful than before."

"My head, you will turn, but you love me."

"You were wonderful," added Dan Perkins. "And I'm not married to you."

At that she did flush, and the blush hadn't quite cleared when the admirers began to appear.

After several anonymous well-wishers, a familiar face appeared.

"You were wonderful." Joanne Axley smiled at Llysette, then turned to Dan Perkins. "You were right."

"Magnificent," added the short man with the Deseret University voice professor.

"I wish more of my students could have heard you," added Axley.

"They should listen to you," said Llysette. "I told them all those things which you—"

"Thank you." Joanne Axley and her husband slipped away.

Was she upset? I wasn't certain. I just stood back of Llysette's shoulder and surveyed the small crowd lining up to say a few words to either Perkins or Llysette.

THE GHOST OF THE REVELATOR ∾ 223

"I'm sorry about Joanne," Perkins said quietly.

"I would be upset, were I her," answered Llysette quietly. "She has sung here?"

"A number of times, but she's never moved people the way you did."

"That is sad."

A heavyset woman with white hair stepped up. "You remind me of that Norwegian. You were wonderful. Are you any relation?"

"Thank you. I do not think so. All my family, they come from France."

"*Magnifique, mademoiselle, magnifique!*" That was the thin man with a trimmed mustache. "Claude Ruelle, the former French ambassador here in Deseret. After the Fall . . . I stayed. You, you have brought back all that vanished." With a few more words along those lines, and a sad smile, he was gone.

Counselor Cannon appeared at the very end of the line of well-wishers, and he bowed to Llysette. "You have sung magnificently, and your warmth and charitable nature will do much for all of us. Thank you." The voice and eyes were warm, but I still didn't trust him.

Beside him were two other men I hadn't met before. The dark-haired one bowed to Llysette, marginally. "You were outstanding." The other nodded.

"Thank you."

"Might we have a word with you, Minister Eschbach?" asked Cannon.

"Ah . . . of course."

Llysette raised an eyebrow. "I will be changing."

"I'm sure I won't be long."

She slipped toward the dressing room, not quite in step with Dan Perkins, and I watched for a moment.

"Minister Eschbach?"

"Oh, I'm sorry. You were saying?"

"She is truly amazing," said the First Counselor. "You must be very proud of her."

The idea behind Cannon's words nagged at me. Was all of Deseret like that? Llysette was amazing and I certainly respected and admired her and loved her, but it really wasn't my place to be proud. Her parents should have been proud, but I hadn't done anything to create her talents or determination or to give her the will to succeed.

"Minister Eschbach . . . now that your wife's concerts are completed . . . we had hoped that you would be willing to tour the prototype of the Great Salt Lake City wastewater tertiary treatment plant," suggested the heavier-set man beside Counselor Cannon. "That way, you could report to Minister Reilly on our progress in water reuse and the continued progress on meeting the goals of the riverine agreements."

Wastewater treatment? Minister Reilly might like that, but did I really care? "What did you have in mind?"

"Perhaps early tomorrow. We understand that you will not be leaving until Wednesday."

"That might be possible."

"We had also hoped," suggested the thinner, unnamed man, "that you might be free to see the water reuse section of the new stage-three synthfuels plant near Colorado Junction."

What half of the Columbian government wouldn't give for me to see that. "I hadn't even considered that possibility."

"We would be honored," added Counselor Cannon.

At that instant, I heard—or felt or sensed—something chill and menacing. A faint scream? A cold feeling gripped me. "Excuse me."

"Minister Eschbach . . . but . . ."

I pushed past the wastewater man, sprinting toward and right into Llysette's dressing room. I also ran into something else, barely getting an arm up in time, and that was enough to send me reeling back into the door.

I staggered up, but the dark-shadowed figure literally disappeared.

My head throbbed, and Llysette's dressing room was empty. Her gown lay on the floor, and her dress was gone. So was she. A few drops of blood led toward or away from the corner of the room.

I stood there fuzzily for a moment. No one had gone past me. Then I saw the air return grate, unattached and leaning against the wall. A man-sized section of the metal on the left side of the air grate ductwork beyond and behind where the grate cover had been had been cut out.

I didn't bother to wait for whoever it was who charged into the dressing room behind me but scrambled through the grate aperture and then through the opening in the air return duct and into a room filled with pallets of paper products or something. I almost tripped but half-ran, half-tumbled out that door into a back corridor—just in time to see two black figures sprinting down a ramp.

I sprinted after them, but by the time I got to the lower garage, a steam van had hissed up the ramp and vanished into the darkness.

A pair of Danites and a uniformed policeman pounded up behind me.

"They're gone." I wanted to shake my head, but it might have fallen off if I had. I touched my forehead, and my hand came away bloody.

I followed them back to a small conference room in the center, where Brother Hansen and two other blue-uniformed officers waited. I didn't wait to be asked but dropped into one of the chairs. I just looked at Hansen. "I couldn't catch them."

"This was on her dressing table." A grim-faced Brother Hansen handed me an envelope. It had been opened, and that bothered me in a way.

I looked at it. In block letters that could have come from any of a dozen difference engine printers was inscribed: "MINISTER ESCHBACH."

The message inside was short—very short.

You will be contacted. Be ready. We do not want your wife.

I had a good idea what they wanted, and someone knew me well enough to understand that I was far more vulnerable through Llysette.

"What has anyone discovered?" I asked tiredly.

"Brother Jensen was surprised, bound, and gagged," said Hansen coldly. "His keys were taken, with all the master keys." Hansen seemed to have taken over the investigation, and the uniformed officers looked at him as he talked. "The steamer the kidnappers took was a common blue 1990 Browning, and the tags were covered. There are more than ten thousand blue 1990 Browning in Deseret. They wore gloves, it seems, and the security system was disabled on a lower garage door. Bypassed, actually. They wore standard staff working uniforms, and we think they wore flesh masks as well."

"In short," I said, "they left no traces at all. What about the tools?"

"They were all taken from the cribs on the lower levels. That was why they made the attempt tonight. They probably had all afternoon to get organized."

"No working on Saturday afternoons?"

"Right. When did you last talk to Brother Jensen?"

"Before the concert, I talked to him briefly, but he had some problems. Maintenance problems, I gathered, because he was briefing or listening to several workmen."

"Do you have any idea what they want from you?"

That was the question I'd been dreading, in a way. I took a deep breath. "It could be anything. Something about government in Columbia, information about . . . people I've worked with." I shook my head. "Most of that I'd think they could get from other sources. I've been out of government long enough that things have certainly changed. And why they'd kidnap Llysette I don't know."

"There are some indications that they settled for her," Hansen said. "You can't think of anything else?"

I could think of plenty. "Let me think about it. There's probably something, but my wife's been taken, and I'm not thinking too clearly." That part was definitely true. It's different when matters are personal. I'd found that out with the Nord incident and with van-Becton's games last year.

I stood. "So far as I can figure out, I'm not going to be contacted here, and I don't know what else I can add." My eyes went to Hansen. "How do I reach you?"

He extended a card. I read it—"James V. Hansen, Bishop for Security," and a wireset number. "I think we should meet tomorrow, Minister Eschbach. Perhaps around eleven tomorrow."

"Where?"

"We could come to your suite. That might be easier."

"Fine. Eleven. Unless you find out something sooner."

"I'll have Officer Young escort you back to your room."

I nodded and heaved myself to my feet. *Fine operative you are, Eschbach. You can't even protect your own wife when you knew there was trouble.*

Dan Perkins stood outside the conference room. He'd been waiting. "No one told me, and it took a while to find someone who knew." He swallowed. "Minister Eschbach . . . I'm sorry. If I had known . . . this would happen . . . They wanted the concert . . . so badly. I just don't see." He shook his head.

"It wasn't your doing." I shook my head.

"I told them she was the best in Columbia."

"She is. But that's not exactly your fault."

"I don't know about that." He paused again. "Can I do anything?"

Somehow, I didn't think so. I had the feeling that he was probably the only honest one in the bunch, and there was no sense in getting him tangled up. "Just make sure you put together the best recording that you can."

He looked puzzled.

"I *think* Llysette will be all right. One way or another, though, the singing was important, almost everything at times, and she'll want the recording." I was trying to be positive, hoping that the kidnappers would keep Llysette alive long enough for me to ensure that she'd remain so. The fact that it was a kidnapping, rather than another assassination, gave me some hope.

"I understand." He worried his lower lip. "Are you sure there's nothing I can do?"

Something he'd said earlier . . . I frowned. "You said *they* had wanted the concert so badly."

"When Brother Jensen found out that Dame Brighton was unavailable—she'd agreed, less willingly than Llysette, to sing two of my songs—he wired me. I wasn't going to be the accompanist for Dame Brightman, you see. She has her own, some fellow named . . . I don't recall. Jensen wanted to know who the best singer in Columbia was that he could get who could also sing at least a couple of my songs. I thought of Llysette, because of James Bird."

I waited. The name was familiar, but I didn't recall why.

"He attended one of her master classes in New Bruges last year. James has a good ear, and he was impressed. I knew her by reputation, and she'd written asking for one of my arrangements. So I told Jensen all that. He asked if I would play for her." Perkins shrugged. "When he mentioned the fee, I couldn't say no, but I did push for the recording rights for us."

"Us?"

"It was in the contract. Llysette and I split them fifty-fifty. He agreed without even a murmur, and that was unusual. Then I didn't hear anything for a few weeks. He wired and sent a contract, with the notation that I'd definitely understated her ability and that the First Counselor would surely be pleased with the concert."

"I take it that such effusiveness isn't exactly normal in their past dealings with you?"

A wry smile crossed the composer's face, and I got the picture. Daniel Perkins wasn't exactly *persona grata* with the hierarchy in Deseret, but he was just well enough known that they'd had to tolerate him.

"Your songs are well received elsewhere," I pointed out. "And your operas."

"Elsewhere—that's true."

More pieces fell into place—or more confirmation of what I'd already suspected.

"I'd even bet that you haven't had much trouble lining up international distribution for the recordings."

That brought another wintry smile. "I see you understand."

"I'm getting there."

"I shouldn't be keeping you." He shook his head. "I'm sorry. But if there's anything Jillian or I can do." He handed me a card. "Anything."

"Hold good thoughts." *Very good thoughts.*

It had clearly been an inside job. Why had Llysette been given that particular dressing room? Jensen? Hansen? Cannon? Someone from the Revealed Twelve? But what did any of them have to gain? The problem was that I didn't know Deseret politics well enough. I did know one thing. More than one person was playing for high stakes, very high stakes.

25

~

THE suite was empty—very empty. The *thunk* of the door echoed hollowly, but the sound of my boots was swallowed by the thick carpet as I walked to the bedroom. I took Llysette's performing gown from the garment bag, holding it for a moment and wishing she were in it and I could hold her as well. Then I hung it up.

I walked back to the sitting area and stood by the window, looking at the points of light. Great Salt Lake City—where Llysette's career was supposed to have taken off. Great Salt Lake City—where events had confirmed, once more, that we never escaped our past, that we had to vanquish it again and again. And yet again.

I closed my eyes. That didn't help, and I opened them again.

My thoughts were whirling because nothing added up—or, rather, too much added up. Hansen was in charge of security, apparently fairly high up, although I had no idea how high a bishop for security was, and he'd been involved from the beginning. That argued that someone had been worried early on. That worry was confirmed by our Danite followers and the constant surveillance.

Yet someone had clearly bypassed everything, and Hansen wasn't happy about it. That shone through, and it argued that if it were an inside job, he wasn't on that part of the inside. The fact that Hansen had personally been half-watching Dan Perkins was another confirmation that Perkins wasn't on the inside. Besides, Perkins had everything to lose from a plot that would hurt Llysette. She was literally his ticket back to respectability and financial security.

The clippings and Counselor Cannon's words indicated that he wanted to use Llysette—and me—as a lever for closer relations with Columbia. So who didn't? The manner of Llysette's disappearance argued that someone in the power structure didn't agree with the counselor—either that or someone was awfully good at evading all the precautions set up by Jensen and Cannon and Hansen.

Among my problems was that I didn't know the power structure. Oh, Jerome had kindly provided me with names and bios, but they didn't say much. The head of the LDS church, the "Prophet, Seer, and Revelator," was Wilford W. Taylor. He was also the President of the Kingdom of God in Deseret. Then there were the Twelve Apostles—or the First Presidency—depending on which hat they wore. But the real power there appeared to be the First Counselor, who, as speaker for the Quorum of Seventy and as counselor to the Apostles and the First Presidency, wielded power equivalent to that of, say, the Speaker of the House or a prime minister. His deputy was someone named C. Heber Kimball, who, as Second Counselor, ranked something like deputy prime minister.

The other Apostles, as I recalled, had names like Smith, Young, Sherratt, Lee, Monson, Owens, and Orton. Some had biblical first names, others rather English varieties. Unfortunately, Jerome's biographies didn't provide many hints, and Cannon was the only one I'd met face-to-face—that I knew. I'd never been introduced to the pair with him at the Salt Palace. I should have asked, but I hadn't been thinking. My head had been hurting—and still ached.

With that reminder, I went into the bathroom and blotted away the dried blood . . . gently. The area around the cut was already swelling and would be very black and blue.

The bedroom was just as empty as the sitting room.

Finally, since I couldn't sleep, tired as I was, and couldn't seem to piece together much, I started assembling items, including Llysette's hair dryer.

Once I had what I thought I needed together, including fresh batteries in Bruce's calculator gadget, I undressed slowly and climbed into bed. The faint scent of Llysette's perfume didn't help me sleep.

Neither did thoughts and dreams about various terrorists I'd known. In the end, that part of me that was still Carolynne pleaded in Shakespearean quotes for me to seek refuge in sleep.

I guess I did—for a while—but I was awake with the sun, gray as it was through the inversion layer that again blanketed Great Salt Lake.

After showering, shaving, and dressing, I looked at the silent wireset, then at the door. No calls. No notes. Then, it was Sunday, and no doubt a time of worship for all good—or radical—Saints.

I was to be contacted. Wonderful. No one was going to contact me in my suite—that I doubted. So I went down to breakfast in the Refuge early on that Sunday morning. Two Danites waited in the lobby, one talking to the concierge, the other ostensibly using the wireset in the alcove off the registration desk.

I was escorted quietly to a corner booth of The Refuge. For a moment, I sat there, not picking up the menu, but thinking of Llysette sitting across from me.

Thinking about Llysette confined or tied up in some dark space or room didn't help much, nor did the waiting. Lord, I hated waiting, good as I'd gotten at it in the Spazi. But it was different when it was personal.

Special breakfast number two—a cheese and mushroom omelet—was what I settled on, sipping chocolate as I awaited my order.

"Minister Eschbach?" The dark-haired man in the continental-cut suit smiled broadly as he slipped into the other side of the booth, seemingly oblivious to the Danites three tables away. His face was familiar, and he carried a small flat case scarcely larger than a folder full of maps or papers as he sat at the table. The case went on the linen between our places as he dropped into the chair across from me.

I wanted to shake my head but forced a smile. "I should have guessed. What do you want?"

"It wasn't us, Johan."

"You didn't take her?"

"No. This was local, as you'll find out in, I'd say, somewhere over an hour or so." He smiled sadly. "Believe it or not, Johan, I had nothing to do with it. We don't deal with families."

"And I suppose you had nothing to do with the attempts in New Bruges?"

"I had nothing to do with that, either." He poured water from the pitcher into the empty glass across from me, then took a long swallow.

"Careful choice of the pronoun, Dietre."

Dietre shrugged. "I can't stay long. I'd suggest you tell the Saints that I recognized you from the concert and was congratulating you. By the way, she is the finest I've ever heard. And I have heard the finest. It is a pity that they must deal in such a . . . roundabout fashion." He paused as the waiter set down my breakfast.

"Would you like anything else, sir?"

"Another pot of chocolate, thank you."

The waiter inclined his head and departed.

"Always so Dutch you are, Johan."

"I could remark on your ancestry, but I'll refrain. Still . . . it's rather hard to believe that your . . . group . . ." I glanced toward the door but didn't see any more Danites—or any motion from the pair at the nearby table. Then, they probably had orders to watch and not act unless I appeared threatened.

"My . . . superior . . . doesn't care much for you personally, Johan, but he's no fool. Neither is his . . . leader, if you understand. They'd prefer that the present situation remain stable, but some accommodations could be made." Dietre's smile was wry. "These days, naval actions are all the rage, but some rumors have surfaced that General Lobos-Villas could have the south Kansas oilfields in less than forty-eight hours. Over the long run . . . not exactly desirable . . . except for enthusiasts of a 'Greater Europe.' Even our interests must bend to those of cultural diplomacy."

"You're not here officially." My stomach growled, and I took a small bite of the omelet, impolite as it may have been.

"In Deseret, as officially as I can be. I'm an accredited representative of FrancoPetEx." He nodded toward the folder lying on the table. "I believe you left that in the concert hall in your distress."

I looked at the plain black leather gingerly. "And?"

"I found the contents most interesting, as I'm sure you did."

"This isn't for free, Dietre. What do you want?"

"As little disruption as possible—double or nothing is the way to go." He shrugged. "I have great faith in you, Johan. So does your Minister Jerome, and quite a few others. The problem is that you solve problems, shall we say, in a rather unique way. On behalf of our . . . group, as you put it, I would like this solution confined to the recovery of your lovely bride." He nodded toward the not-so-thin leather case I held. "That will help us all."

Both my ghosts—and I—sensed that Dietre was telling the truth, and that scared me.

"And, by the way, I suspect that in the group that will contact you is someone who was tied into the unfortunate attempt in New Bruges. I don't know who that might be, but it doesn't make sense any other way."

The more I heard, the less I liked it.

"Now . . . our group did agree to pass a message to you. We're still playing both sides of the fence, much as I would prefer otherwise. You're to take a walk through the Temple grounds between one and one-thirty. Thirteen hundred Republic military time." He laughed at that reminder.

I didn't.

"You'll be contacted. You won't recognize whoever it is. I wouldn't either." With a broad smile he rose and said loudly enough for his voice to carry, "Give your lovely wife my congratulations, Minister Eschbach!"

"Thank you. Best wishes on your new venture." I stood as he left.

The Danites watched, but that was all.

I sat and took a sip of chocolate and several bites more of the breakfast I really didn't taste before opening the folder.

The thick file contained detailed engineering drawings—from what I could tell—for the stage III synthfuels plants, the materials specifications, and the highly proprietary information on the Saint catalysts. I closed the leather folder casually, and for a time I sat there forcing myself to eat and sipping chocolate, trying to sort it through.

Dietre was one of Maurice-Huizinga's top operatives. Some of what he said was false as a lead schilling—like the business of not involving families. Maurice-Huizinga had effectively held poor Miranda Miller's son hostage to get Miranda to spy on me and Llysette on behalf of New France. So I couldn't believe that somehow they had a soft spot for families or Llysette.

Yet if what he'd said were true and the plans and specifications were accurate, it meant that my first assumptions had been correct, that Llysette had been taken by agents of the Revealed Twelve.

Why the synthfuels specifications, specifications for which Reilly and his staff would have sacrificed dozens of operatives? Dietre, or, more precisely, Maurice-Huizinga, wanted something, and Dietre had said double or nothing. Then, Dietre had referred to "the unfortunate attempt in New Bruges." "The"—as in singular—and that meant, first, he only knew of one and, second, New France hadn't been involved in either. There was a possibility, as always, that he was lying, but, again, I didn't see much point in a lie on that point, although I'd have probably been hard-pressed to explain why.

After a time, I nodded to myself. Double or nothing. If I managed to pull it off, somehow, and I didn't have more than the vaguest idea of what was involved, then Columbia would have the plans that represented years of trial and error engineering based on the original Austrian research—effectively reducing over time the Saint energy and chemical monopoly.

If I didn't pull it off, I'd be dead, probably linked to spying to devastate the Saints' energy industry, with chances of Columbia getting energy supplies from Deseret close to nil for another decade—or longer.

For all that, Dietre's efforts were weighted toward helping me. Why? Altruism wasn't exactly the watchword of New France, and the sale of Deseret oils to Columbia would probably deprive someone else.

I took another sip of cold chocolate and checked my watch—still only slightly past nine-thirty. Then I swallowed. How had Dietre known I'd been in The Refuge? I shook my head. I wasn't sure I wanted to know.

That just illustrated how unclear everything was. How was Llysette's kidnapping tied into what had to be domestic Deseret politics? How would helping me resolve the problem, with a bonus of sorts, and benefit New France?

I smiled grimly. By playing messenger to the schismatics, Dietre was implying New French support, and he could build on that if they won. By assisting me, if I managed to turn the tables on the schismatics, he was implying support for Columbia and the established Deseret government. His connections to the loser would never come out.

Equally important, someone had figured out that stiff-necked Columbia hated to be in anyone's debt. But Columbia couldn't afford not to build some synthfuels plants, and Ferdinand would certainly not be pleased to see them because it would eventually reduce the effect of his control of the Arabian peninsula oil, and the Austrians planned far into the future. That was exactly how they'd taken Europe and were taking over the Mid-East.

I signed the check and stood. I had a meeting in an hour and a half and then a rendezvous. I wasn't looking forward to either.

The lobby smelled of perfume, an unfamiliar brand, as I crossed to the elevators. The concierge offered a brief smile.

Up in the performing suite, I made more preparations, ensuring the scan-proof dart gun was ready and that the blade was easily reachable. Brother Hansen arrived at closer to ten-thirty, accompanied

THE GHOST OF THE REVELATOR

by two policemen in uniform and another man in a conservative brown suit.

"Minister Eschbach."

"Brother Hansen. Have you discovered anything?"

"No. Have you been contacted?"

"Indirectly." I glanced toward the door. "I thought Counselor Cannon would be here."

"Counselor Cannon and Second Counselor Kimball are scheduled to meet us at eleven."

"I'd prefer not to explain it all twice."

"As you wish." Hansen glanced toward the bedroom door, half-ajar. "Do you mind if we look around? There might be some . . . indications."

"Be my guest." Nothing I'd put in my suitcase looked terribly suspicious, and anyone who would recognize certain items should know that I was going to need them. I hoped they wouldn't be foolish enough to make an issue out of them.

I made some of the powdered chocolate and sipped it slowly as they wandered through the suite. The chocolate was so bad I had to sip it. I couldn't have gotten it down any other way.

Hansen stepped over several minutes into their search. "Your wife is dark-haired, is she not? With long hair?"

"Yes."

"Then it's likely these are her hairs, and we'll be taking what we can find just in case."

"Fine." I didn't want to discuss the implications of "just in case."

Besides the hair, they found nothing—nothing that they wanted to talk about, at least—and that was fine with me. Close to eleven, the four gathered in the sitting room. Hansen looked at his watch. "Counselor Cannon and Second Counselor Kimball should be here before long."

Unlike the audiences at the Salt Palace performing complex, the two counselors were punctual. They came into the suite unaccompanied, but I saw at least two Danites or other plainclothes security types station themselves in the corridor outside.

Cannon looked at Hansen's three subordinates. Hansen nodded, and they bowed and left.

The four of us sat around the small table.

"Minister Eschbach," Cannon said sonorously and with concern dripping from his voice, "I deeply regret this unfortunate situation, and I want you to know that we will do whatever is necessary to ensure your wife's safety." He shrugged. "Unfortunately, we have little to go on." His eyes went to Hansen. "Have you anything to add, Brother Hansen?"

"We have some indications that the kidnappers had scouted the complex earlier. We also have confirmed that the Browning they used was stolen. It was recovered early this morning near Point of the Mountain. We have recovered several strands of dark hair that may match samples we've taken from here."

"Are there any other signs?" asked Counselor Kimball.

"Nothing that the forensics people are willing to talk about yet," Hansen said. "Would you have been in the dressing room with your wife normally?"

"Probably." I shrugged. "Probably. She wasn't too interested in listening to me talk about water reuse treatment systems, and she was tired. I usually help her after she performs."

"So, based on your actions of the first two nights of the concerts, the kidnappers would have expected you to be there?" pressed Hansen.

"Probably."

"Is there anything else that might lend support to the idea they were after you? Besides the note itself?"

The three looked at me.

"I've already had a message," I said, cradling the empty chocolate cup for lack of anything better to do with my hands.

"The gentleman who visited you at breakfast?" asked Hansen.

"Yes."

"What did he say?"

"He was an intermediary—just told to tell me where I should be to be contacted." I waited. "On the Temple grounds early this afternoon."

"That would make sense," mused Hansen. "The grounds and the park are crowded then. Did he say anything else?"

"He said that Llysette gave an exceptional concert."

"Nothing else?" pressed Hansen.

"He said to congratulate her, and that he was sorry to have been contacted as an intermediary for such a sorry situation—or words to that effect."

"Dietre Treholme," Hansen said crisply. "He's supposedly the accredited FrancoPetEx representative here. He knew you personally, Minister Eschbach. From old times, I take it."

"I have met him before. FrancoPetEx has operations in Columbia, and they had environmental concerns." All of that was true.

"He's the chief operative of the New French intelligence service here."

"I can imagine that," I answered. "He's always seemed mysterious, and he did hint that his organization had nothing to do with Llysette's disappearance, but I couldn't imagine that the state oil company would, energy politics or not."

Counselor Cannon cleared his throat softly. Hansen paused.

"Bishop Hansen, do we have any indication that this Dietre Treholme is acting as anything other than an intermediary?" The First Counselor's eyes remained warm, interested.

"No, sir."

"The note said they did not want your wife, Minister Eschbach," interjected the Second Counselor. "That would mean they want you for some reason or another."

"Either that," I answered, "or they want me to do something. Or obtain something."

"What might that be?" asked Kimball.

That had me stumped. I wasn't about to discuss ghosting and de-ghosting technology, and I hadn't the faintest idea what else they might want.

"Embarrassment," suggested the First Counselor. "If we cannot protect visiting artists and government officials in our own capital, how can Deseret be trusted to keep other agreements?"

"How can we claim . . . ," began Kimball, but stopped as Cannon eyed him.

"Exactly," said Cannon quietly.

I got the message anyway. The problem with being a theocracy is that if too many bad things happen, either God has turned away or the leaders have turned from God.

"The Revealed Twelve?" I asked, stirring the pot a little.

Kimball's face twisted. Hansen offered a frigid poker face.

"What do you know about the so-called Revealed Twelve, Minister Eschbach?" asked Cannon.

"Very little except that they exist. I've read some news clippings that suggest you've been waging a covert war or opposition to the group." I picked up the empty cup again.

"You are well-informed. I would not expect otherwise," answered Cannon dryly, so dryly it was clear he'd been well briefed on my background. "And, yes, if this effort is the creation of the Revealed

Twelve, and if it succeeds, it will cause a certain . . . reassessment of the policies of the First Presidency. Such a reassessment would not be in the interests of Columbia, I must admit."

"I had already come to that conclusion. That means I have to do what they want, especially until they release Llysette."

"We cannot accept the schismatics' terms," announced Hansen.

"I do not believe that was precisely what Doktor Eschbach proposed," said Cannon quietly.

What had I proposed? Had I proposed anything, really, except getting Llysette back? My head ached, still, I realized, and my thoughts were fuzzy. Fine secret agent and spy I was, letting my own wife get kidnapped out of her own dressing room.

"I want my wife back, safe and unharmed. So do you," I finally managed.

Hansen frowned. "We want the schismatics. Or whoever did this."

I had to look at Cannon. He nodded cherubically, and that meant I got to explain.

"You've trumpeted to the world that Deseret is a cultural capital, and that it is a modern city. Exactly how are you going to explain to the world that a world-class diva has been abducted by a group of religious extremists? And if you try to hush it up, how will you explain the disappearance of a Columbian Subminister for Environmental Protection and his wife, a world-class diva?" I waited.

Hansen still looked blank.

"That plays into their hands. You give Columbia an excuse to make demands you can't or don't want to meet. Then they divert all the headwaters of the Colorado into their Aspinall tunnel project, citing the fact that you broke the Reciprocity Agreement. The schismatic group then has you on two counts—you aren't following the Prophet, and you're bringing harm to Deseret."

Kimball turned to the First Counselor. Cannon nodded. "Doktor Eschbach has a point there. What do you suggest, Doktor?"

I swallowed. "Let me do what they *think* they want."

"Why?"

In for a penny, in for a sovereign. I swallowed. "Right now, you have a missing diva. If I can work a trade for her . . ."

"Who are you trading?" asked Kimball.

"Me." I'd thought that was obvious, but maybe it wasn't in a society that still clung to polygamy. Or maybe it was just Kimball.

"What is our advantage there?" asked Cannon quietly. "We still have a prominent Columbian in the hands of a . . . radical organization."

"If something happens to a singer, it's an outrage," I pointed out. "If something happens to a former official of a powerful neighbor, who in Deseret can fault you for taking whatever steps are necessary to bring the malefactors to justice?"

Even Kimball nodded.

"You seem anxious to do this," said Hansen.

"I'm not looking forward to putting myself in the hands of a bunch of religious screwballs." *Especially screwballs funded by either Ferdinand or someone else.* "But I'd rather act sooner than later."

Cannon smiled almost benevolently. The smile vanished with my next words.

"I'll also need a solid briefing on the Prophet and where you feel that the schismatics diverged from his teaching or whatever."

Cannon winced at the term "or whatever," but his face smoothed over.

"What does doctrine have to do with it?" asked Hansen.

"With fanatics, doctrine is everything," I answered. "The last thing I want is to say the wrong thing and push the wrong button. It also might give me some insight."

"Minister Eschbach seems determined to meet their demands. What do you want me to do?" Hansen's voice did not quite conceal a bitterness.

"Wait to see how matters develop," suggested Cannon. "Offer Minister Eschbach the support he needs."

And above all, I reflected, *keep things quiet.* But that seemed to be understood in the Saint culture. No one was going to be happy with the solution, no matter what First Counselor Cannon said.

I turned to Hansen. "I'd appreciate it if you would get together all the condensed and direct quotes of a theological nature from your first two prophets—and the current codified doctrine, or whatever you call it. I'll need it by the time I get back."

"How do you know you'll come back?" asked Hansen.

"I don't, but I have to plan as though I will." I forced the smile. "I need to get ready." I also wanted time to think.

After a nod from the First Counselor, the other three stood.

"Good luck," offered Counselor Cannon warmly as he left. "Please let us know if there is any way in which we can assist."

"I will." I hoped I wouldn't have to ask Cannon for anything, but I wasn't burning bridges I might have to cross. He'd probably give

me what I needed. After all, it was clear by his presence that a satisfactory resolution was important to him. I had the feeling that our
definitions of *satisfactory* might differ considerably.

I left the suite not much after the dignitaries, taking too long
strides toward the Temple area and trying to breathe deeply and
maintain some semblance of relaxation. While I carried a number of
items that Brother Hansen might not have approved of, I hoped I
wouldn't have to use them.

The faint odor of late fall, molding leaves, a mustiness, ebbed
and rose around me in the intermittent wind.

Despite the partly overcast skies, the Temple park was filled with
families and a large number of young couples. Were such family out-
ings where young Saints met? Or, like all young adults, were they just
taking advantage of the opportunities?

To my right, a slender dark-haired girl in a dark blue wool coat,
braided hair swinging slightly, looked down at the stones of the walk
when a sandy-haired youth murmured something. She raised those
green eyes, and he flushed slightly. Would Llysette and I have been
like those two, had we been raised in Deseret?

After a half hour or so, while I loitered reading the week's concert program posted outside the Assembly Hall, a heavyset and
bearded man in a checked brown suit that had gone out of fashion
a half-century before even in Deseret eased up beside me and peered
at the program.

"Minister Eschbach, if you wish to see your wife again, please follow me down South Temple. Keep walking until you are picked up."

"No," I said. "You need me, not her. I'm not interested in dealing until I know she's safe." I hoped my words were cooler than I felt.

His bearded jaw dropped open. "We have your wife."

"I'm sure you do. There are two possibilities: you've already murdered her, or she's safe. If she's dead, then there's no point in my
negotiating with you. If she's safe, I will."

He looked confused, and that worried me, because it meant he
was another courier or the group were amateurs, and amateurs
could do anything.

"But . . . we have your wife."

"Exactly. I happen to love her, and I'm perfectly willing to trade
myself for her. But I'm the only leverage I have, and I'm a stubborn
Dutchman. If you know me at all, or of your superiors do, you know

I keep my word. You need my knowledge, but you won't get it until Llysette is safe within the walls of the Columbian embassy."

There was silence.

"I'm perfectly willing to take a steamer to some isolated place on my own, provided it has a portable wireset or a radio. Or some other similar arrangement. Once I talk to her and know she's safe, then I'll be willing to accompany you."

"You're in no position to bargain."

"Neither are you. You don't need Llysette. You need me."

I could see the frustration mounting in his eyes—another disturbing indication.

He lunged, and I moved, my hands reacting with patterns acquired years earlier. His arm snapped, and he cradled it, eyes watering.

I stepped closer. "If she is hurt . . . even scratched, what I did to your arm will look like a pleasure cruise in the Sandwich Islands compared to what I'll do to every one of your sorry group."

"You wouldn't . . . You couldn't. . . ."

"You don't think so." I forced a hard smile. "You don't think so? Ask your superiors what I've done."

"You'll be sorry."

I already was, but that was beside the point. Already, people around us were drawing away, and silence was radiating from where I stood like ripples in a pond.

Abruptly, brown-suit turned. I watched as he headed toward the building in which the Deseret Woolen Mills store was housed, but he merged into the people once he was more than fifty yards away.

I was shaking by the time I started to walk back to the Lion Inn. Logically, I knew what I'd done was my only chance. I was the only option in town—literally—but I still shivered and sweated all the way back. What if they'd already killed Llysette? It didn't feel like they had, but I'd been wrong before—and that had killed Elspeth and Waltar.

I'd been wrong before and taken a bullet through the shoulder. I couldn't afford to be wrong again, and yet I wondered if I already happened to be—and just didn't know it.

26

HANSEN was waiting when I returned to the Lion Inn. He got on the elevator with me, and he looked as tired as I felt. His eyes were bloodshot, and he carried a heavy-looking satchel.

"I don't know," I told him after the well-dressed couple with their three blond children got off on the fourth floor. "They wanted me to come with them."

"They?"

"A bearded man in a very out-of-style brown-checked suit and a nasty temper. He tried to assault me when I told him I wasn't about to go with him."

"You said that?" Hansen raised his eyebrows, then touched the beard shaded with white.

"Look. Either Llysette's dead already"—I swallowed, even though I hadn't meant to—"or she's not. If she's not, and I go with them, then she will be dead before it's all over."

"You don't know that."

I just looked at him, and he looked down.

We got off the elevator and walked to the suite. I opened the door and held it for him, then wandered through the place. The rooms were still empty, the piano silent, Llysette's robe still draped over the stool in the bathroom she'd used.

The faint aroma of Ivoire lingered. Llysette loved it, even if it were manufactured in New France these days and cost twice what it once had. The old price had been close to fifty Republic dollars an ounce, and that had been back before the impact of energy costs had run up everything.

I went back to the sitting room, where Hansen had stacked four books on the table.

"You realize what you're saying, don't you? That there's a good chance you won't make it through whatever you have in mind."

"I have a chance. If I don't do it this way, Llysette has very little chance." I picked up one of the volumes—*Doctrine and Covenants* a fairly new printing. Did the Saints revise their theology all the time?

"You think she does?"

"Someone knows my background, or I hope they do. *If* they do, they'd know how I'd approach it. I have to hope that they do. They know a great deal already."

"How do you know that?"

"Because they clearly want me. Because they're using Llysette as the lever."

Hansen frowned. I didn't clarify that.

"Can you tell me anything more about your contact?"

"Young—early thirties, dark-haired, fair-skinned, bearded, no white or gray in the beard, pale gray eyes, thin lips, broad nose, nose once broken, I'd guess. Fine hair, thin eyebrows. Could probably be a dozen like him."

"Anything else?"

"He's amateur. He found it hard to believe I wouldn't accept their terms."

"So would I. You're a hard man, Eschbach."

"No. Hopeful, hoping, wishing, but not hard. One of the things they pointed out years ago when I was a pilot . . ." I shook my head. "Old history doesn't matter now."

"Go ahead. It might." But he didn't look at me as he spoke.

"It always made sense. If you're captured, once you do what the enemy wants, or say what he tells you to, your value is diminished. If they're honorable, they won't kill you whether you tell or not. If they're not, then withholding knowledge until you can do something is all you have. It may not be enough, but it's all you have."

I found myself pursing my lips together too tightly, wishing I'd hadn't injured the idiot who'd jumped me, but trained reactions don't always give you much choice, especially when you're emotionally involved, and with Llysette's life at stake I definitely was far too emotionally involved to be dispassionate, no matter what Hansen thought.

"What's the matter?"

"Oh . . . he also has a broken arm. I wish I hadn't, but he jumped me, and I didn't have time to think."

A moment of silence followed. "Just like that, he jumped you and you broke his arm?"

"I reacted. I didn't think, and then I had to act as though it were planned to show they'd better understand who they were dealing with." I shrugged. "You can't show weakness."

"The more I learn about you, Minister Eschbach . . ." Hansen glanced toward the window, then back at the books on the table. "There's a lot more here than anyone's saying."

"There always is, or things like this wouldn't happen." How much more I really didn't want to explain.

Brother Hansen actually sighed. "We will check the hospitals and doctors, but I doubt we'll find anything." Hansen half-stroked his beard again. "Do you think you'll be contacted?"

"There isn't much doubt about that." My only doubts were about Llysette's health.

"How soon?"

"Several hours, I'd guess. Maybe longer. I'd want to make me sweat, but they also don't want to give you—or any Deseret authority—too much time."

He nodded. "We'll keep in touch."

I was sure he would. I was also sure every wireline to the room was monitored and every hall snooped.

When Hansen left, I ordered a room service meal and really got to work, forcing myself through the *Doctrine and Covenants,* writing down passages or derivations of passages that I thought would be useful if I had to use my knowledge. The first prophet had definitely been both a man of vision and a shrewd politician, so shrewd I had to wonder how he'd gotten himself murdered. By a shrewder politician? Bad luck? Either could happen to anyone. There's always someone smarter and tougher, and luck doesn't necessarily favor the skillful or the bold, and Smith had to have been bold, whatever else he had or hadn't been.

The words *psychic proliferation* came back—Jerome's words. I felt they tied in, but I didn't know why . . . yet. I tried not to think of bad luck as I read, and noted, and, later, ate through the same chicken pasta dish I'd had earlier from room service.

Then came *The Book of Mormon* itself. Some of it I could skip, because it was historical. For my purposes, Lehi's flight from Jerusalem wasn't much use, nor was Lehi's death or the wanderings of his son Nephi in the wilderness. It was interesting to see the parallels between Nephi and Laman and Cain and Abel, except in *The Book of Mormon* the younger son prevails—in his own lifetime, anyway. There were some interesting quotes in the second book of Nephi, which I jotted down, wishing I had a difference engine as I did. Writing was always laborious.

Then came the section named "The Words of Mormon," and that was followed by another 250 pages of Saint theological and temporal history as recounted by the personages of Mosiah, Alma, and Helaman. That brought me to another book of Nephi, except it was a different Nephi. From what I could figure, racing through the text, the second Nephi, who presumably wrote the third book of Nephi, presided over a religious rebirth of the Nephites—those were the good Saints, I figured—except that the rebirth and godliness didn't last, and pretty soon there wasn't much difference between the Nephites and the Lamanites. After that, almost all the Nephites eventually perished under the swords of the Lamanites, and *The Book of Mormon* ended with a cautionary and advisory chapter from Moroni, who appeared to have buried the golden plates on which his and all his predecessors' words were inscribed and then expired in turn.

Just like that—over five hundred pages chronicling a religious history, and all the good followers of the Lord are wiped out because, from what I could figure out, they forsook him and indulged in wickedness. That meant to me, in practical terms, that the whole Saint "bible" was cautionary. It also implied that the Revealed Twelve were claiming that the current Saint leadership was like the ancient Nephites, rejecting the "true" vision of the Lord.

Of course, "truth" tends to be rather subjective, as I'd already had confirmed once again from reading the *Doctrine* book. An awful lot of what the first prophet had written could have been interpreted in more than one way, and that might have been why the Saint faith continued to rely on further "revelations"—to keep it on track.

I rubbed my forehead as I sat there at the table.

Then, the Revealed Twelve could certainly claim that later "revelations" had not come from God, but from Satan.

For a moment, I wanted to rip up everything in sight. One or both sides were playing with words and theology to gain temporal power—but that was exactly what the entire *Book of Mormon* effectively warned against. Yet each side would doubtless claim that they were on the side of the Lord. And unless there was a major miracle . . . who would know?

I also had this sinking feeling that the Revealed Twelve wanted me to create something along those lines—and that they'd gotten a little boost from Ferdinand along the way. The misplaced papers, the warmth of the difference engine—both took on a new significance, perhaps a terrible significance. Why did they want a ghost? That they wanted one seemed inescapable. That *someone* knew I could create one seemed equally inescapable. I just wasn't sure who knew—or who had told them.

I opened my case and looked at the folder with the difference engine codes and the code lines. How was I going to translate them into what I needed?

At that point, the wireset chimed. I looked at it. It chimed again. I picked it up.

"Eschbach here."

"We accept your terms. Details will be given to you on the public wireset outside the north door to the Salt Palace. Be there at eight tonight."

Click.

That left me with less than three hours to finish preparing what I needed, and all I had was several sheets full of scattered quotes, and even more scattered ideas.

Should I start on the applications side, assuming that was what my soon-to-be-captors would have in mind? I reached for the sheets of code that I had brought.

Thrap! The knock echoed through the sitting room. I closed my case, sealing away the Babbage code lines I'd hoped to be able to forget. Why was it I never had a chance to put anything behind me?

I peered through the peephole. Hansen stood there.

Even before he got inside, he spoke. "You got a call."

"Why don't you come in and sit down for a moment?" The last thing I needed was an angry bishop of security, and I needed Hansen on my side or, at least, not against me. "Can I offer you anything?"

"Water would be fine." He sank into one of the chairs. His eyes were still bloodshot, his suit rumpled, and his shoes dusty. What I looked like was probably worse.

He drained the entire glass, and I refilled it before sitting down.

"I suppose you've digested all of this?" He gestured toward the table and the books and the stacks of paper.

"No. I've got enough—or I will."

"Eschbach, you puzzle me. Why haven't you contacted your embassy?"

"What point would there have been if the kidnappers didn't agree? The embassy types would just get upset. You don't contact them until you know what you want to do. And why."

"Experience speaking again?"

I shrugged.

"Do you mind if we tap the wireset by the Salt Palace?"

"Did you find out where this call was made?"

"No. It was from somewhere in Great Salt Lake, but it was too short. The equipment can trace a call in about four seconds, but it takes a few moments to get it on the right line. The operator fumbled, and—"

"They were off."

"Right. If they have to give more detailed directions, it will take longer."

"I'm sure that they'll wire from a public set."

"They will, but what else do we have?"

"If you can tap the line without getting near it, I don't have any problem, but I'm not too keen if it means people swarming all over the area."

"We can do that. What are you going to do now?" Hansen finished his second glass of water and blotted his forehead.

"Contact the embassy. Finish my notes."

"Would you mind telling me what the notes are for?"

"Background for what I think the kidnappers want me to provide."

"Couldn't you just provide written material?" The bishop for security had a glint in his eye as he set his glass on the table.

I picked up the nearly empty and cold cup of chocolate from my dinner, then set it back down without drinking. "Actually . . . no. The material has to be applied . . . shall we say." I offered a hard smile. "It's better that I don't get too specific."

"How can we help you when you won't even tell us what the kidnappers want?"

It was a fair question and deserved the best answer I could give without endangering a lot of people. "First, I don't know what they want. They haven't said. I'm guessing, just like Counselor Cannon and you are. Second, it's dangerous enough that the fewer people that know, the safer everyone will be. Third, I'm fairly convinced that the Austrians have a hand in this, as well as a few others, but I can't prove it. Finally, to the best of my knowledge, I'm probably the only person not under government lock and key with the expertise to handle this." I paused. "That doesn't exactly answer your question, but it's why the Counselor ordered you to help. I'm probably skirting the bounds of things to say that if you knew more of the story, you might not be so willing. If you knew the entire story, you wouldn't hesitate, but I wouldn't give much for your life expectancy."

"You're protecting *me?*"

"I'd like to think so." I looked at the books on the table.

So did Hansen. Then he got up. "I think you're being more honest than many, but I cannot say I'm pleased. I intend to stay nearby. My number will get me in a few minutes or less if you need me."

"I'm sorry. I'm doing the best I can." I stood and walked to the door with him. "I really am."

Once the door was closed, and locked, I wired the embassy but could only get the duty clerk. I impressed on him the need for the First or Second Secretary to contact me as soon as possible. He promised to try to find them.

I had my doubts and suspected I'd have to storm the embassy in the morning. I tried the telephone book, but as I did not know their names, it wasn't much help.

Again . . . I should have been more assiduous in gathering that sort of information, but you don't expect to have to run down people on Sundays. You should figure it could happen, but I was out of practice and, once more, it showed. Espionage was like athletics: you have to stay in shape, and paranoia helps.

I'd have to wire the embassy again later.

I glanced at the closed case. Babbage codes or quotes? I decided on codes, at least until I had a better formulation on the structure I had in mind. My last ghost from scratch hadn't been all that successful.

In two hours plus, I had something on paper. What it would do was another question, and that assumed that the Revealed Twelve had the necessary hardware. What scared me was that I thought they did.

At seven-forty, I closed the case and left it on the table. The codes by themselves meant nothing, and I couldn't carry everything everywhere. I washed my hands and face quickly, trying to ignore the remaining scent of Ivoire, and hurried out to the elevator.

I was walking south on 100 West Street at quarter to eight. Ahead, the Salt Palace performing complex loomed like a dark abandoned ruin. Slightly behind and to the east, the Temple shone in a cocoon of shimmering white light. Personally, I'd have preferred the reverse, but that might have been my skepticism about the overall benefit of religions based on true believers.

Several figures—all Danites or Hansen's men or both—lurked in the shadows while I lounged less than a dozen feet from the public communications booth.

Finally, at three past the hour, the wireset rang, and I picked it up. "Eschbach."

"There is another wireset two blocks south of where you are." The voice was disguised and electronically resonant, and that spoke of more sophisticated communications technology than that used by an average terrorist or kidnapper. The technology level reassured me, but only slightly. "It is the only booth with a red facade. Tomorrow at eleven you will receive final instructions. You will park a steamer there, rented from a commercial establishment. We trust you will make your own communications arrangements with your embassy.

"You will be given directions where to drive and for how long. At the end of that time, you will contact the embassy to confirm your wife's safety. Then you will be picked up."

"I can accept that."

"Good. Eleven tomorrow morning."

Click.

I hung up the handset and walked back to the Lion Inn. Again, Hansen was waiting by my door. We walked inside before I spoke. "Eleven tomorrow."

He nodded.

"Any luck on tracing the wire?"

"A public set outside a grocery in South Great Salt Lake City. Right beside the south expressway. No one will be there, but I sent a steamer to check."

"Speaking of steamers, we'll need to rent a steamer in the morning."

"I heard."

"I assume there's no commercial establishment open now."

"This is Sunday, Minister Eschbach."

I wanted to shake my head. What did they do about babies, heart attacks, and other inconveniences that occurred on the holy day?

After he left, I wired the embassy again.

"This is Minister Eschbach. Have you had any luck in finding the Second Secretary?"

"No, sir. We've put a message on his service and on the system and posted it in his box. He's not at home, or he's not answering."

"Tell him it's urgent."

"Yes, sir."

"Tell him Deputy Minister Jerome thinks it's urgent also."

"Ah . . . yes, sir. I'll try again right away."

"Thank you. Both Minister Jerome and I would appreciate it."

I really didn't want to say more—not yet. If need be, I could have Hansen wait outside the embassy with a radio. He'd do it. He'd do anything ethical and legal not to have the blame for the mess dropped in his lap.

27

~

R OOM service delivered breakfast to the suite at seven. By seven-thirty I had talked to Hansen. He'd pick me up at the embassy at eight-thirty. Before eight I was dressed, wearing, among other things, the gray vest that looked like leather and was, in fact, little more than textured plastique. I had everything ready to go.

I had packed what I needed into the case—the professional papers, the code lines, the notes and quotes, and *The Book of Mormon.* I took the engineering drawings Dietre had supplied with me. Double or nothing, because if I got killed with the schismatics and they were found there'd be hell to pay. But if I left them behind they wouldn't be there when I returned, and I deserved some payoff for the mess Harlaan and Jerome and all the others had gotten us into. Besides, it was almost a matter of principle. I needed to do more than expected, and I might need every bit of leverage I had once we got back to Columbia. If we got back.

No sense dwelling on that. So I checked my watch. Eight o'clock. Of course, the Second Secretary hadn't called back. So I put in another call to the embassy.

"Ah . . . he's not available at the moment."

"This is Minister Eschbach, and I strongly suggest you find him—this moment. Or the First Secretary. The name is Eschbach, and neither President Armstrong nor Speaker Hartpence or a fellow by the name of Asquith will be very pleased if you don't. Nor will Ambassador Klein or Minister Jerome."

It took a few moments more—more than a few—on the wireset, with a few more helpful suggestions, before I put it down flatly.

"I'll be there in ten minutes to see either the First or Second Secretary."

"We can't do that."

"If you don't, you're all likely to be on a turbo to the Federal District by tonight. By the way, tell them it's Hamilton's Whiskey Revolt."

"Would you hold for a moment, sir?"

"I'd be happy to." I wasn't in the slightest happy to hold.

"This is Second Secretary Trumbull-Hull."

"Johan Eschbach. You have a condition red-two facing you. Hamilton Whiskey Revolt. Status amber, going red at eleven. I'll be there to see you in ten minutes."

"Eschbach? *The* Eschbach?"

"Yes. I'm back where I didn't want to be."

"I'll be here." He sounded less than pleased. I couldn't blame him.

Someone had clearly briefed him, however, by the time I arrived by a steamer cab—a Reo, not a Browning. The embassy was on the hill, between Deseret University and the Temple, in a huge old complex that had probably housed some former patriarch's establishment. The oak door was golden, with spotless brass furnishings, and it opened before I reached it.

Two Republic marines in blues stood back. "Minister Eschbach, sir?"

"That's me." I had out both the diplomatic passport and the government ID."

The shorter marine nodded. "This way, sir."

The Second Secretary's office was on the first floor on the back side, overlooking a garden. The conversion into an office had left an ancient fireplace, faced with blue and cream ceramic tile, with a hearth of the same tile, and a dark walnut mantel that held the picture of a handsome brunette and two children.

Trumbull-Hull was in his midthirties, taller than I was, and balding. His forehead was damp, and he stood behind an antique walnut desk as if it were a rampart under siege.

"Please have a seat." He motioned to the chair in front of the desk.

"I take it that my concerns were reinforced?" I asked pleasantly.

He nodded stiffly. "I was told to offer any assistance within the power of the embassy."

"Good. It isn't that bad from your point of view." How much should I tell him? Too much and he'd muck it up. Too little and he'd manage to obstruct everything.

"It's rather simple. A contact went bad. The wrong people got involved, and they hold my wife. They want me. I need your help in a small way in ensuring her safety and the successful conclusion of the operation."

"Your wife? The singer?" His mouth almost opened.

I nodded.

"The news media—"

"They don't know yet, and I hope they never know. So do you. If this goes right, she'll be here on your doorstep sometime after eleven—probably around noon, but the time could vary."

"Here?"

"Here."

"We'll do what is possible." His words were careful, calculated. "What, exactly, do you need from us?"

"Very little. We reached an accommodation—of sorts: Llysette is delivered here. I talk to her before going with them, but I have to be close to their reach. So what I need from you is a radio or the equivalent and someone listening constantly from eleven onward—a shortwave or similar unit that will reach from anywhere in several hundred miles to the embassy."

"You're going to do that?"

"You can't defuse a bomb long-distance." I laughed hoarsely. "Anyway, my wife is supposed to arrive here sometime after they contact me at eleven. I'll need confirmation of that, and I'll need to speak to her personally. If, and I hope this is not the case, she cannot speak, or she doesn't arrive, I want you on the other end." I smiled. It wasn't a totally pleasant smile.

"Ah . . . I think we can do that. Is there anything else?"

"Once I've resolved the situation, we both get immediate turbo passage to the Federal District and guards to the aerodrome to ensure we get home."

"And?" Trumbull-Hull asked warily.

"You may be contacted by a Bishop Hansen."

"The Saint security chief? You are moving in . . . interesting circles, Minister Eschbach."

"You can tell him one of two things—either that you have Llysette or you don't."

"Are you sure you want to go through with this?" he asked, almost perfunctorily.

"You don't want an incident, and I don't want one. I'd prefer things be kept very quiet. I was trained for this, and I doubt you have anyone acceptable." I cleared my throat. "I'm sure you people can find a cover story if something happens to me. You can't if it happens to her. Not exactly easily." That probably wasn't true. With enough effort, anything can be covered up, especially in a nation that would want it covered, but I didn't want Second Secretary Trumbull-Hull thinking along those lines.

In the end, he saw it my way, not that I really had to press much, probably because he didn't have many choices. Second Secretaries were often more self-serving and rational than the political appointees. More cowardly, often, too. The brave ones usually didn't last, as was the case in so many other fields as well.

Still, I didn't get back outside the embassy until eight-forty, lugging a small radio with a long collapsible antenna and my datacase. Brother Hansen was waiting in a dark green Browning with a young clean-shaven driver.

The day was gray and cold, and even my overcoat didn't seem that warm.

Hansen held the door open from inside, and I climbed out of the wind.

"I see you persuaded Trumbull-Hull to part with a radio."

"It wasn't too hard."

"You talk a good game, Eschbach, but do you really know what they want?"

"I don't have an absolute confirmation, but almost anything would be better than what I've prepared for." I laughed hoarsely. "Then, I'll probably find out that what they want is even worse than that. It usually works that way."

I was guessing, of course, but the kidnappers had agreed to my terms, and that meant I was the *only* one who could do what they wanted—and that was either to destroy or create a ghost. Since there were no rumors about ghosts in existence, that meant creating one, and I had a good idea what that meant.

The security limousine hissed to a stop outside a sandstone-type building. In the car park were a double handful of fresh-washed steamers. The sign read: "Deseret Rentals."

Hansen almost choked at the invoice for renting the steamer. "Three hundred . . . and not even a Browning."

"Groundnuts," I said quietly, deciding he needed a reminder of what was at stake. "You want deGaulle's Foreign Legions marshaling in Santa Fe for a quick march toward the San Juan gasification plants?"

Hansen looked puzzled and I really didn't feel like explaining, but at this point some explanation—or speculation—wouldn't hurt too much.

"Escobar-Moire and deGaulle need diesel for those fleets, and they really don't want to pay your prices. Columbia does, and Ferdinand wants a civil war here and unrest all over North America. If Llysette disappears, you'll get trouble with Columbia and problems from your schismatics. A rental steamer is cheap insurance."

Of course, that was only part of the story, but a part that was true and certainly wouldn't hurt for Brother Hansen to hear. I would have paid for it, if necessary, but with all the risks Llysette and I were taking, I preferred that the Saints, and Counselor Cannon, paid as many of the bills as possible. I'd end up paying more than my share no matter how well matters turned out, and I didn't even want to consider the costs if they didn't.

With all the paperwork—every country had it—it was almost nine-forty-five before I fired up the rental steamer, a small brown Reno, barely big enough for four people.

"Let's go back to the Inn," Hansen suggested. "We haven't finished."

He was right about that, and I worried about what he had in mind.

Because I needed to eat, we sat in the corner booth in The Refuge, which confirmed, indirectly, that Hansen had had a lot to do with our seating and that the table was probably snooped to the gills and Hansen wanted my words on record. I'd have to be careful how I said what I said.

Hansen's eyes met mine over the chocolate. "Would you mind telling me what is really going on?"

"An attempt to use religion as a weapon to alienate Columbia and Deseret forever by playing on the simplistic side of people's faith in a time when life is too complex for many of them to handle."

"My, you sound superior."

"I don't mean it that way, but that's what I see." With a sigh, I refilled my mug.

"You're saying that the schismatics have no real faith and that they're using their disputes as a cover to gain temporal power?"

"Not exactly." How could I put it? "I have no reason to disbelieve the sincerity of what the schismatics believe. I do believe that they are being supported by outsiders who see the schismatics' beliefs as more in the interests of the outsiders."

"Very politely put. One can tell you were a politician."

"A very bad politician, Brother Hansen."

"So, Deseret's . . . furor over faith . . . is being used for political goals."

"That's my guess. It's only a guess."

"And what's in this for you, since you're not exactly a Saint?"

He was right about that in both senses. "The first is obvious. I want my wife safe."

"You love her. That is obvious, and praiseworthy. I do not believe that is the only reason."

"No. I'd like to put a stop to those who would use people's beliefs in ways that aren't in their own interests."

"High-sounding rhetoric, Minister Eschbach."

"Probably, but I've noted that disruption fueled by religious disputes gets extraordinarily ugly, especially when the . . . temporal . . . stakes are high. I happen to think that Columbia and Deseret need to work out an arrangement that's less adversarial. That won't be possible if the schismatics succeed."

Hansen stroked his beard. "That makes sense, but I'm still not totally convinced."

I wasn't either. So I sipped more chocolate and had another bite of the dry ham sandwich.

"There has to be more," he prodded.

"There is. I really want to be left alone. I really want Llysette to be able to sing without fear or concern."

He nodded, and he apparently understood enough that he asked a different question. "Are you certain you don't want a close tail?"

"Look," I said. "They won't do anything until they're convinced no one is following me. That's why they want a rental steamer. I don't want a tracker or a tail."

"Then you'll have to tell us where you're headed."

I laughed. "It's all a blind. I'll be back in Great Salt Lake City by tonight. Where in Great Salt Lake City I haven't the faintest idea. This whole business is designed to make a transfer where you can't get too close. But the best place to hide remains a city."

"You don't want us too close, do you?"

"Yes and no. I'd prefer to be rescued, but the problem is that the problem won't stay solved if it's not played out." I'd only thought the problem had been played out the first time around. Self-deception can be so comforting, until you're called on it. How could I have thought Branston-Hay's theoretical formulations on creating ghosts would have stayed buried? I'd applied them. Probably Minister Jerome had people working on applying them.

"It's your neck."

Unfortunately, it was, but a lot of other necks were stretched under the knife as well. They just didn't understand that.

At quarter to eleven I pulled the Reo up beside the red-faced wireset booth. No one was using the unit, and I walked over to it. No sense in letting someone decide to use it when Llysette's life was possibly hanging on it.

At eleven-eleven the set chimed.

"Eschbach."

"Take a steamer on south on the expressway. When you get to Beehive Route Three, take it east. Once you see another steamer flying a purple banner, you may contact the Columbian embassy. When you're satisfied, get back in the steamer and keep heading east. Follow the steamer with another purple banner. Stop when it does, and you will be contacted. Do you have that?"

"Expressway south to Beehive Three. East on Three, until I see the purple banner. Contact the embassy. Confirm Llysette's safety. Then head east again. Stop when the next steamer with the banner does."

"Correct."

The line went dead.

Simple enough. What wasn't spoken was equally simple. Once Llysette was free, my life was forfeit if at any point I tried to double-cross them. Somehow, I'd feel better, a lot better, once Llysette got into the Columbian embassy.

I wiped my forehead, damp despite the chill, looked at the pitifully small Reno, swallowed, and walked back to the steamer.

It sounded simple. I got to drive a small steamer south on the expressway and then out into the Fastness of Zion, along some back road, with no one following, not closely anyway.

Once the radio confirmed that Llysette was safe and I talked to her, then I would get back in the steamer and follow the first steamer I saw with another purple flag.

I followed 300 East south for three blocks, then turned east. Another five blocks found me turning onto the expressway south.

The traffic, for Deseret, was heavy, a mix of haulers, battered steamers, and glistening new Brownings, and I had to concentrate on driving, more than I had anticipated.

Beehive Route Three almost crept by me, and I had to take the ramp at a higher speed than I'd figured. The poor Reo shuddered as I applied the brakes to make the stop at the top of the incline.

I waited for a westbound tanker bearing the logo "Deseret Fuels" and easily several dozen times the size of the Reo. Then I turned behind a gray Browning that left me in the dust of the two-lane road that angled toward the mountains.

To my right, I could see a second flat lake, surrounded by factories, with smoke and steam pouring into the chill early-winter air. The higher reaches of the mountains framed by the front windscreen were mostly white.

I drove for more than a quarter of an hour, intermittently being passed, and drawing closer and closer to the mountains, taller than I realized. A glance in the rearview mirror told me that a glistening red steamer was sweeping up behind. The road on the other side was clear, and the red Browning swept past, then slowed. A purple flag popped from the side window and fluttered there. I just watched for a moment, then finally lowered my window and waved. What else was I supposed to do?

The red Browning accelerated out of sight even before I pulled out into a wide turnout on the right side.

I glanced around. The turnout was empty, except for a painted green metal drum for trash.

After opening the door and setting the radio on the roof, I cranked up the collapsible antenna. The frequencies were already set. I cleared my throat, my heart pounding.

"Embassy, this is Eschbach. Do you read me?"

After a moment of static, an answer squawked through the speaker: "Say again, please."

"Embassy, this is Eschbach. Do you read me?"

"We read you, Minister. A little weak, but we read you. There's someone who wants to talk to you."

I hoped it was Llysette. Lord, I hoped!

"Johan?"

"Llysette?"

"*Mais oui, mon cher. . . .*" Her voice was tired, but it sounded like her voice, despite the static.

"How is Carolynne?" No one else would know what I meant, and I hoped that she wasn't too tired to understand.

"Ah, she and I are well. Did you know that once she sang for the First Prophet?"

I frowned and tried to call up a memory or an image . . . but only got a hazy sense of limelights. "I don't recall that."

"That was before she met the deacon."

"Are you all right?"

"I am tired. I have some bruises. This was not bad. This was not so bad as the Fall of France." She laughed gently. "It was not so bad as when you and I came to know Carolynne better."

"You're sure."

"*Certain* I am."

I nodded. "You take care, and stay in the Columbian embassy until this is over."

"*Mais oui.* I do not like what you do."

Neither did I. "I'll be fine," I lied.

"You must take care. You, we want you back safely."

"I wanted you back safely."

"We know. Take care, *mon cher.*"

"You, too. I'll do the best I can. Just keep yourself safe."

I finally flicked off the radio and glanced around the turnout. A battered black hauler rumbled past, its front hood wreathed in steam, then another new Browning, this one blue.

The radio antenna went down, the unit back into the seat beside me, and I eased the Reo out back onto Route Three, still headed east. All I could do was hope . . . hope that everything went right, knowing that, once again, it probably wouldn't.

I drove steadily east for another ten minutes, until I needed a side road. Abruptly a cargo hauler pulled out in front of me, a square purple banner flying from the black-painted door mirror frame. I slowed to follow the big steamhauler.

Five minutes later, the hauler turned left, back north, along Bee-hive Six, and in less than ten minutes we were back on the express-way, headed north.

Perhaps three miles farther north, the hauler slowed and

stopped under a bridge. I swallowed and stopped right behind it, then picked up the case, leaving the radio behind but triggering the transmitter with a blank signal. That might help.

I walked toward the hauler, the kind with a double cab and without windows in the back. The rear cab door on the shoulder side was open. I saw no one, and the front window was blackened.

I stepped up into the rear seat, empty, and with a partition between the front seats and the rear.

Nothing happened.

I sighed and closed the door, sitting there in gray gloom of the enclosed space, unable to see who was driving, where I was headed, and where I was going. With a hiss, the hauler eased out into the traffic I couldn't see.

28

On the narrow bench seat in the back of the hauler I bounced, occasionally steadying myself, as the vehicle turned off the expressway and began to wind through streets, presumably of Great Salt Lake City. The single door had no window. The odor of oil and heated metal seeped up around me, and the space was hot, especially with a wool suit coat and the plastique vest that didn't really breathe. Even after taking off my overcoat, I felt faintly nauseated without any fresh air.

After a time, the hauler slowed, then stopped, and a rumbling screech followed. Then the hauler inched forward and lurched to a second stop. The screech of ill-lubricated metal punctuated more rumbling. The hiss of escaping steam indicated a shutdown. I waited.

Finally, a figure in a gray jumpsuit, wearing a gauzy sort of black hood over his head that concealed all but his general head shape, opened the door. "Minister Eschbach?"

"That's me."

"Follow me, please."

Without much choice, I followed the fellow. He didn't think much of me or my abilities—or knew I wouldn't do much—because he scarcely looked in my direction as we walked through what seemed to be an industrial garage and down a narrow corridor to a door, which he unlocked.

"If you would."

I stepped into the room—more like a prison cell, I supposed. No windows, a pallet bed, a shower nozzle over a drain surrounded by a curtain, and an exposed toilet. No sink. One towel hung on a wooden bracket on the wall, a bar of soap on the back of the toilet.

He stepped inside after me. "What's in the case?"

"Material I thought I might need."

"You might. Would you open it, please, and leave it on the floor?"

I did and stepped back, trying to sniff the air, which smelled like industrial solvents and chlorine combined.

He leafed through the papers. Despite the hood, I had the feeling his eyes were half on me—alert but very amateurish. Then he stood.

"What exactly do you want?" I asked. No sense in assuming too much.

"The ghost of the first Revelator. Your skills should be sufficient to locate and recall up his ghost."

"Not Prophet Young?"

"He was the antiprophet—who turned the Saints from the true path to Zion."

I didn't pretend to know that much about Brigham Young, but I had to wonder how the prophet who had built an independent nation out of the wilderness had set the Saints on the wrong path. "I'm not sure I understand. . . ."

"They've hidden it, but it's there," answered the tall figure. He shifted his weight and stated, as if he were quoting, "Verily, verily, I say unto thee, no one shall be appointed to receive my commandments and revelations in this church excepting my servant Joseph Smith, Junior."

I waited, and I wasn't disappointed.

"And if thou art led at any time by the Comforter to speak or teach, or at all times by the way of the commandment unto the church, thou must do it. But thou shalt not write by way of commandment, but by wisdom; and thou shalt not command him who is at thy head, and the head of the church."

"I take it that means that there are no other prophets but Joseph Smith?" I tried to ask casually.

"Even an unbeliever understands that, and yet those hypocrites who strut in the Temple do not."

I couldn't imagine First Counselor J. Press Cannon strutting anywhere but kept my mouth shut.

"Even the Danites have forgotten the meaning of their motto."

"I'm afraid I don't know the motto."

THE GHOST OF THE REVELATOR ⌐ 263

"It's from the Book of Daniel: 'They shall take the kingdom and possess it forever.' President Taylor's weaknesses will turn Deseret back to the Lamanites of the south and the Zoramites of Columbia."

"And?" I asked gently.

"All that the prophet strove for will be lost. Once again, Sampson shall rise. You wouldn't know that, Gentile, but Sampson always rises again. Sampson Avard was one of the pillars of the early Saints, until the followers of Satan turned the prophet against him."

"That's all very well, but how do you expect me to locate a ghost that vanished more than a century ago?"

"You have that knowledge." Abruptly he stepped back and closed the door. The lock clicked.

I closed the datacase and set it on the foot of the pallet bed and began to study the room, or converted toolroom. The walls were cinder or cement block, the floor ancient concrete. So was the ceiling. I checked the door—metal, solid core, steel-framed, with the hinges on the outside. Not impossible to get out of in a pinch, assuming there was some steel in the bed frame or that a few things on my person might assist, but the work would be laborious and noisy. A single lightbulb was set in a bracket above the door, but no switch was visible in the room.

The area had been prepared well, and in advance. I went and sniffed around the pallet bed. No scent of Ivoire, and that probably meant they'd held Llysette elsewhere. Good for her, not so good for me.

"You have that knowledge." The certainty of those words chilled me. They weren't asking me to create a ghost. They'd been told that I could find a ghost that had once existed, a very specific ghost. That was impossible. The first Revelator's electromagnetic spirit field had long since dissipated, if it had even survived his assassination. Yet to escape, to have any chance of surviving, I had to do that. And that meant creating an "old" ghost from scratch. Subconsciously I'd figured out something along that line, but I'd thought the Revealed Twelve were political opportunists who'd wanted me to create a ghost for political purposes. Instead, I had theological fanatics who'd been set up by someone else. They still needed a ghost, but . . . fooling them would be hard, far harder than what I'd anticipated.

With a shrug I sat on the end of the pallet bed. I didn't touch the scan-transparent blade that remained in my belt or anything else. There was no reason to, yet.

Perhaps a half hour passed, and I finally checked my watch—twenty minutes. I opened the case and began to study the notes I'd taken.

Some time later, the door clicked, and a shorter figure stood there.

"If you would come this way, it's time to begin your work."

I didn't ask if the work was mandatory.

The second door in the corridor was open. He gestured, and I stepped inside. Light poured down from a bank of ceiling glow strips. The walls were generally the same blocks, and there was a large glass mirror inset on one wall. Next to the single door was a booth or shield of sorts, which was topped with two feet of leaded glass. Another figure, also in a gray jumpsuit and hooded, stood there. The side of the shield facing the difference engine shimmered.

The more I saw, the less I liked it. In the middle of the room were an oak table and chair. On the table were several items I recognized.

In fact, I had to swallow. The difference engine on the table was almost an exact clone of my own SII machine, and it was fitted with the gadgetry Bruce and I had developed—that is, the projection/collection antennae, but nothing that resembled the de-ghosting projector.

"I take it you find this familiar?" There was a laugh.

"I have to compliment you on your thoroughness."

"Take a seat, Minister Eschbach."

I saw no reason not to, even though he didn't sit, probably since there was only the single chair, except for the stool for the guard behind the booth shield.

"Let's make it simple," I suggested. "What do you want?"

"You know that already. We want you to bring back the ghost of the first prophet, the Revelator of Truth."

"That might be possible," I conceded.

"We've been led to believe that it is very possible."

"Do you have any real timetable for all this?"

"We had hoped you could bring back the ghost of the Revelator within a week."

"I'll need some help from you."

"You're the expert."

"Not on the prophet. To . . . recall . . . his ghost I'll need some help on what teachings and sayings you feel are the most important."

"Why?"

"The more information I have, the easier the location will be."
That was as close to the truth as I could get.

"That might be possible." My escort gestured toward the difference engine. "You can begin anytime. It would be more useful if
you didn't attempt to direct any of the antennae in this direction."
His hand went to the mirror set into the wall facing the difference
engine. "That is two-way glass. You'll be under constant surveillance
from at least two points."

With a cough and then a click of the door, he was gone. The
click told me another thing: it was locked from the outside as well,
locking one guard in with me.

They'd had some briefing on my background. Not only that,
but somehow, I felt they didn't trust me.

I looked around the gray room. Everything was gray or reflective
gray. There was too much money and preparation for simple fanatics, and that bothered me. It bothered me a lot.

Finally, I took out one of Bruce's pens and some paper. Then I
flicked on the difference engine. It called up my own directory. I
swallowed again, when I saw the disk case by the keyboard—with
the backups for the hidden files for ghost creation.

No . . . I wasn't dealing with just a bunch of political schismatics.
The combination of religious fanatics and an unknown political ma-
nipulator was even worse. I swallowed and looked around at the gray
once more. My forehead was very damp, and I felt flushed all over.

29

EARLY Tuesday morning found me back in front of the equipment that effectively duplicated my own, looking at a stack of my own notes and shifting back and forth between three profile configurations, with another hooded and silent guard watching everything.

The concrete-walled and -ceilinged room still smelled of ancient oil and dusty concrete and of heated synthetics being cured in the new difference engine before me.

One stack of notes blurred into another, and I massaged my stiff neck.

When I'd tried to create the first replica of Carolynne, the whole profile had collapsed. I never did really create her ghost doppelgänger from scratch—if *doppelgänger* were the term for a copy of a ghost of a singer who'd been killed a century earlier. I'd actually ended up making a duplicate of the real ghost of Carolynne. The ghost of justice and mercy had never been more than a caricature— enough to still give me shivers when he/it surfaced inside my soul, but a caricature. Now I had to create a "real" complete ghost, when I'd never accomplished that before, while pretending that I was only "finding" an existing ghost. And I had to get it done in a way in which I could walk away from the results.

Would three separate profile configurations be enough? I shook my head. Not for what I had in mind. My eyes went to the gray screen and the pointer poised there.

Finally, I called up what I'd been working on and took a deep breath, looking at the smeared mirror surface of the two-way glass across the top of the difference engine from me. All I saw was the reflection of a stubbled professor, once again in over his head.

The guard remained silent.

I started to set up the sketchy profile files for loading, but when I did try the loading, the machine locked.

The guard leaned forward. I reset the difference engine and waited. The same thing happened again. So I took out the empty auxiliary disk and studied it.

I could tell, as usual, nothing was going quite as planned, either for my captors or for me. They hadn't bothered to get SII auxiliary disks, or the generic equivalent, and I needed the auxiliaries because the equipment was designed to use both the fixed disk and the auxiliary simultaneously or actually in rapid switch succession. That wouldn't have been a problem in Columbia, but Deseret used the New French standards, with a different balance and spin rate.

Purists would say that you can vary the auxiliary disk spin rate and it makes no difference. In fact, some claim you can get better performance that way. Maybe . . . but my system—or the clone set up by the Revealed Twelve—wouldn't take standard Deseret disks. I was finding that out early on.

I reset the difference engine, cleared the screen, and tried a disk format.

"Not reading auxiliary drive" scripted out on the screen.

For a moment, I sat there looking at the machine. Finally, I turned to the guard behind the shield.

"I need standard Colombian auxiliary disks. These don't work, and I can't reformat them, and they'll only foul up the system."

"Keep working."

"I'll do what I can, but I can't finish the project without at least one auxiliary disk." I rubbed my stubbly chin. The shower, such as it was, kept me clean, but my clothes weren't getting any fresher, and I hadn't brought even spare underwear—another one of those stupid oversights. I was making entirely too many of those.

The guard mumbled or grunted.

I touched the cover of the difference engine.

"You don't need to do that," he snapped.

So . . . they didn't want me monkeying with the equipment. That also triggered my suspicious mind.

I played around with Bruce's calculator and diddled some figures, then put it back in my pocket and wrote out some more code lines to build up the profile that I'd eventually have to transfer to the disks I didn't have.

Another guard stepped into the room, and the two mumbled for a moment, low enough that I couldn't hear, before the second disappeared and the lock clicked.

I spent another hour or so building up the quote files, selectively speaking, and trying to design a structure to create parallel interlocking files that the antenna could project in close to real-time simultaneity.

Just about the time I thought I had something, the door to my small section of the blockhouse opened and a tall figure stepped inside. He didn't move far from the booth/shield.

"You said you needed more disks. Why? Why do you need them to recall a ghost that already exists?"

I managed to keep my jaw shut while my thoughts whirled. He really meant it.

"It's hard to explain," I temporized. "Let me put it this way. In our world, which is a temporal world and not primarily a spiritual one, we rely on physical structure to hold us together—our skeletons, for example. A ghost is held together by an energy structure, an energy profile. When the profile loses energy, it collapses." I cleared my throat. "I have to re-create the profile, and that means a lot of storage capacity. Once the profile is re-created and energized, the ghost reappears, but the profile has to be as accurate as possible, in order to ensure that the reenergized ghost is the correct one." I felt proud of myself—momentarily—until I realized the rest of the implications.

After a moment of silence, I pointed to the notes and *The Book of Mormon*. "You can see. I'm using verified statements of the prophet as keys to the profile."

After a long silence, the tall man spoke. "How many disks do you need?" He seemed to be the same one who had led me into the blockhouse—that's what it felt like—and who seemed to be in charge of the group.

"I *might* be able to get by with one, but three, in case of problems—"

"Problems?"

I did sigh, turning in the chair to face him. "I don't know what anyone told you, but this is a new and fairly experimental procedure. This is something where some government research laboratories have failed for years. You want me to duplicate that kind of work with minimal equipment." I didn't tell him that I wouldn't have been able to do it at all without the years of work from one of those laboratories—or the genius of the late Professor Branston-Hay.

"Why aren't you using the antennae?"

I frowned at the change of subject. "Because that's the last stage, when you project the profiles and the fields."

"How much delay will this cause?" he asked.

"Very little if you can get the disks within the next day. I would have liked to load them incrementally, but that's not absolutely necessary."

I had another thought. "If you can get an image scanner and a likeness of the prophet that you think is the most representative, those would also help."

Another period of silence, and then the mesh hood nodded and the door opened and he departed.

As the hours went by, I tended to lose track of time until I checked my watch and found that when I was thinking time sped and when I was wool-gathering, trying to puzzle out vague conceptualizations for the refinements I knew I needed, it dragged.

Every four hours or so, I got something to eat—basically a slab of meat, some bread, a piece of fruit, and some powdered chocolate in a mug. Another guard delivered it. That is, he set it on the floor, and I got it and had to put it back there when I was done.

It was close enough to the booth that I probably could have disabled the guard—but why? I still couldn't have gotten out of the place.

Someone always watched me from the booth, but seldom the same person for more than a few hours, although each wore a gray jumpsuit with no markings and one of the fine loose mesh hoods.

In working out the code lines, I made a point of apparently using one of the pens Bruce had provided and the calculator. I wanted both to be familiar to all the Revealed Twelve people.

I tried not to think about Llysette or much of anything else except what I wanted and needed to do, and that was to create the most powerful ghost image possible—the stronger and more imposing the better. That had been one reason I'd wanted to check the hardware early.

The graphics images would be the hardest, because all the Saints had an ingrained visual concept of Joseph Smith and I'd never really done that much with that side of ghost file creation. In my previous efforts I'd let the internal substance create the image, and that wouldn't be enough for a really strong ghost image of the prophet. I hoped that they'd come up with a scanner, but . . . that remained to be seen.

I took a deep breath and looked at the third—or fourth—guard. The eyes behind the veiled or mesh hood could have been open, closed, or glaring. I wouldn't have known.

After standing and stretching, I sat down again and looked at some of the quotations I had to incorporate into what I would have called the dialogue profile:

All things unto me are spiritual, and not at any time have I given unto you a law which is temporal. . . .

Behold, verily, I say unto you that there are many spirits which are false spirits, which have gone forth in the earth, deceiving the world. And also Satan hath sought to deceive you, that he might overthrow you. . . .

Wherefore, for this cause I gave unto you . . . and I will give unto you my law, and there you shall be endowed with power from on high. . . .

Then there were those that I'd modified, that I hoped would be close enough to the structure and yet would reinforce the current "regime" and its efforts. Neither I nor Columbia wanted a government in Deseret controlled by religious fanatics basing their actions on a century-and-a-half-old code that hadn't been that workable then. Like it or not, I had to support First Speaker Cannon, and I wasn't thrilled about it. I was just less thrilled about the alternatives.

As the angel Moroni said, do not anger so exceedingly that you have lost thy love, one towards another. Do not thirst after blood and revenge continually. . . .

How can a people delight in abomination—and in killing our neighbors and those who have not lifted a hand against us—how can we expect that God will stay his hand in judgment against us? . . .

For behold, a bitter fountain cannot bring forth good water; neither can a bitter man bring forth good works. . . .

Condemn not your brother because of his imperfections, neither his father, because of his imperfection, neither them who have written before him, but rather give thanks unto God that he hath made manifest unto you those imperfections that ye may learn to be more wise than we have been. . . .

Cursed is he who puts his trust in man. More cursed is he that puts his trust in a man's false interpretation of what I have said. Trust rather the Revelations of thy Father in heaven than the man who twists my words. . . .

Unto each generation cometh the Revelations of God; harken unto them, for the Lord will provide, both counsel and providence for those who listen. . . .

I had to hope that no one was going to go through thousands of lines of code, but I had this feeling that they wouldn't, that *any* image of the prophet would serve the purposes of the Revealed Twelve.

I swallowed and looked at the difference engine screen. It was going to be a long day, with at least several more to come.

30

TUESDAY, I stayed in the blockhouse difference engine room working Babbage code lines until close to midnight. Why? Because
the only way out was to create what they wanted, and more. At least,
that was the only way I saw it, and worry wouldn't allow me to sleep
until I was exhausted. So why not work?

I did, and I was so tired that the continual drip from the shower
nozzle didn't keep me from sleeping. Nor did the rock-hard pallet
bed, nor the clamminess of the de facto cell, nor just about any of the
inconveniences.

Wednesday morning, I struggled through a cold shower—the
nozzle was piped only to a cold water line. I felt grubby enough to
suffer through it before shivering dry and pulling back on dirty
clothes.

Still thinking about whether my captors could or would come up
with a compatible scanner and the SII-style auxiliary disks, I took
The Book of Mormon and began to read through it.

Parts of it struck me as strange—strange because I had to wonder. How could a barely literate farm boy who followed a vision from
Virginia backcountry to upstate New Ostend ever even transcribe a
five-hundred-page printed manuscript, let alone keep it consistent?
Or was it consistent? I wasn't enough of a biblical scholar to tell.

How did he manage to convert thousands to a new religion—or
a new manifestation of the old? Would he have managed it if things
had been different? If the English colony at Plymouth had succeeded?

I pursed my lips and blinked. Those kinds of speculations weren't exactly useful in my situation.

I had only read another few pages when the door opened and another of the hooded figures stood there, waiting.

When the lock clicked on the difference engine room, in addition to a tray with bread, cheese, and fruit on the floor, a number of objects had been added to my occupational prison.

On the table beside the difference engine was an SII scanner—used, it seemed. In addition to the scanner, the cabling, and the manual, three blank SII disks lay beside the difference engine—as if to suggest that I would have no excuses for failure. In a way, I was more worried about the aftermath of success.

I picked up the portrait of the prophet—a size that would fit entirely on the screen of the flat-bed scanner, allowing me to get it in one pass, assuming I could make the codes match, and that was a big assumption.

Although I wanted to shake my head, I didn't. The heavy gray concrete slab ceiling seemed poised to collapse on me—like everything else. For a moment, I felt very sorry for myself. All I'd really wanted after Elspeth's and Waltar's deaths had been to retreat, to gain some quiet. I'd been lucky enough to find love and respect with Llysette—and Carolynne—but my past seemed to dog me . . . and them.

Why couldn't the powers that be leave us alone? Why couldn't Llysette be allowed to perform without being used as a pawn in a four-sided—or who knew how many-sided—diplomatic and military chess game? Other retired Spazi agents didn't have their lives turned upside down. Other singers, with less talent than Llysette, got to perform and be recognized and make money without risking life and limb.

My eyes burned, and I did shake my head. Self-pity wasn't going to do the slightest for me.

So I coughed, cleared my throat, and ate most of what was on the tray. Not particularly hungry, I still ate, because I didn't think well with low blood sugar and I needed to be able to think.

I definitely needed to think, since what I was attempting was insane. If I succeeded, I'd have to create a ghost that wasn't too apparently distinguishable from a real ghost. Was there theoretically any difference? I didn't know. And if I succeeded in my wild scheme, the ghost had to support the doctrine of the current Saint church leaders, and I had to develop that right under the eyes of the leaders of the Revealed Twelve. That wasn't a problem. Escaping the Twelve would be, and then I'd have to find a way to escape Cannon. Why? Like a lot of things, I couldn't explain why, but I didn't trust the First Speaker, and I hadn't survived all those years as a Spazi agent by ignoring my feelings.

When I finished eating, I set the tray back on the floor and opened the installation manual for the scanner, ignoring the guard and the reflection of a tired and haggard-looking man who had no business doing what he was doing.

Physically connecting everything was easy enough, and so was installing the conversion programs—on a disk I hadn't seen at first.

Once it looked like the system and scanner worked, I eased the image onto the scanner and toggled the scanner on, waiting until it stopped humming and the codes had been fed to the file. Then I called up the receiving file on the screen. Half of what should have been code lines was gibberish.

When I ran the file back through a conversion protocol to get a screen image, all that popped into place was something like a blueprint.

As I had feared, obtaining a graphics image compatible with the ghost file protocols was going to be the problem. In my earlier efforts, the internal substance had effectively created the image, and that wouldn't be enough for a really strong ghost image of the prophet that resembled his image.

In the end, I reverted to doing it by trial and error, using the image scanner on gray-scale and edging the contrast as high as possible. Then I started jiggering the codes into a matrix of sorts.

By the time the midday tray arrived with beef, bread, fruit, and fifth-rate chocolate, I was still working on the codes for the top third of the image.

Midafternoon found me, after two breaks to use the facilities in my cell, with a complete set of codes for the image profile, but codes probably not defined enough. Still, I saved the file on one of the auxiliary disks, then called the image onto the screen.

What I got was a ghostly image on the screen. I compared it to the copy of the painting and shook my head. I needed more definition, and I wasn't sure how to get it.

"How are you doing?"

I jumped a foot from the chair. I hadn't even heard the tall man enter.

"You work hard."

"It's hard work."

"Why is the image so important?" He actually sounded curious.

"Because I have to recall the entire ghost," I answered, trying not to lie too egregiously. "It's hard in the case of the prophet because so many others have spoken his words." That was certainly true enough.

The hood bobbed as though he had nodded. Then he took the tray and left, and the lock clicked. I hadn't even noticed, but a new and shorter guard had taken the place of the former guard.

Sometime after what might have been dinnertime, I ran a second image. Clearer, but still, I felt, not strong enough to carry what I had to load onto it and into it.

I tried second subroutines below the codes, cross-linked, and that improved the image, but the improvement in the areas that were double-coded showed the deficiencies where I hadn't tried subroutines.

By then, my eyes burned and my head ached and I couldn't even think.

I glanced toward the guard. "I can't do anything more."

There was no response. I just put my head down on the table and closed my eyes.

Within minutes, the lock clicked and the tall figure was back.

"What have you accomplished?"

"I've got a basic image to which I can tie the recall programs." My voice was hoarse, even if I hadn't spoken much. Maybe it was rusty from disuse.

"How do we know this will work?"

"When I've got everything ready, I'll give you a test run." I took a deep breath. "Look at the screen. Is this beginning to look like Prophet Smith?"

I called up the image.

"It is similar."

"But not close enough. Well, that's what I need to work more on, but I can't even see the screen in front of me at the moment. I'm calling it a night."

He didn't object as he led me back to my cell-like quarters, and that confirmed, in my mind, a few more suspicions. I was too tired to examine the implications in any depth, and once I was on the pallet bed, my eyes closed despite the dripping from the shower nozzle, despite the odor of oil and dusty concrete.

31

I lurched awake, drenched in sweat from running through endless corridors papered in difference engine printouts, banging at doors that were only images plastered over steel walls, blood running from fingers raw from trying to claw my way through solid steel.

Sitting, breathing heavily, on the edge of the pallet bed, I rubbed my eyes and looked at my hands. No blood. Then, I studied the four walls again.

Nothing had changed. The bulb over the gray metal door still bathed my cell quarters in dim light. The shower nozzle dripped. I still smelled old oil and cement dust. My datacase stood by the side of the bed, and my head ached.

Finally I checked my watch—six o'clock Thursday morning, less than three days, and I was both exhausted and ready to murder the whole lot of them. Llysette was safe, at least, provided Second Secretary Trumbull-Hull hadn't reneged, provided . . . provided . . . I didn't want to think about all the things that could have gone wrong. That way lay even greater insanity.

Instead, I took a cold shower and washed away the worst of the stink of my own fears.

Then I forced myself to write out more codes and ideas while I waited to be retrieved for more work.

It was becoming clear, all too clear, that unless I could resolve this problem, the next one would be worse—I wouldn't stand a chance because I'd simply get potted with a sniper rifle. Then everyone would deny everything, wonder publicly, and I'd be an entry on the obituary page. Llysette would mourn—for a while—but no one mourns forever.

That line of thought made me even angrier, especially at those who had set up me, and the list included the oh-so-helpful Minister Jerome—for who else could have allowed a search of my house?—Speaker Cannon, Brother Jensen, and possibly even Harlaan Oakes. I was convinced, for some reason I couldn't nail down yet, that Cannon wanted me in the hands of the Revealed Twelve. If they killed me, then he had a civil hook, so to speak, to eliminate them. If I succeeded in somehow disrupting their plans or escaping, then that proved that God was not on their side—at the very least. And . . . miracle of miracles, if I pulled off creating a ghost that supported the existing order, all would be well for Cannon, Deseret, and Columbia . . . and who would care about the wear and tear on the poor Eschbachs?

I went back to work, grimly, and had three pages in longhand before they got me at eight o'clock. The timing confirmed yet other suspicions about their status and class—all good family men maintaining a hidden retreat manned by younger disciples. I wouldn't have been totally surprised if the entire place were locked and deserted while I slept—except for one or two of the new faithful—but I really didn't see the point in trying to escape, not yet.

My escort to the difference engine part of the redoubt was someone new, slightly more rotund—also in the gray jumpsuit and mesh hood.

The difference engine area hadn't changed either—gray concrete, shimmering booth shield, and smeared one-way glass that reflected a man whose beard was coming in mostly white. I knew there was a reason I preferred to be clean-shaven, against the Dutch tradition or not.

I wolfed down the half-breakfast while the difference engine went through its checks. Then I entered all the code lines I'd written over the hours preceding.

The prophet's image was sharper, perhaps sharp enough, because the other profile sections would further refine that image. Time to go back to text.

Sometime after midday the door opened to admit four people. The three figures behind the tall leader turned their hooded visages toward me but did not speak. All three wore dark cloaks under the hoods, so voluminous that their shapes were indistinct even under the gently unforgiving light of the blockhouse's—or warehouse's— glow strips.

"Report on your progress, Minister Eschbach." The word "Minister" was almost mocking.

I ignored that.

"I might have something. . . . Actually, I could show you something now."

"How do we know this will work?"

How many times had I heard that question?

"It will work. I could provide a demonstration."

"Good. After that, we will give you the coordinates where the prophet will be recalled."

I had to force the laugh, but I managed, and then it wasn't forced because the sheer ludicrousness of the demand became all too hysterical.

When I finally choked off the laughter, the tall man snapped, "Explain."

"Don't you understand? You can't do this from a distance. Where this equipment is—that's where the prophet's ghost will . . . reappear." I almost choked on that. "You're lucky I can do that."

"How does that allow a demonstration?"

"I'll manifest the profile, then collapse it before it recalls the actual prophet's ghost."

"Then do so."

I shrugged and began to work, checking the projection antennae and then the auxiliary disk before loading the one I wanted . . . the incomplete one that didn't draw full power. I also set up the program run to trigger only three of the eight profile configurations.

"Are you ready?" I asked after about ten minutes. They were beginning to fidget—no patience at all. If they'd known what I was thinking I'd have died three times over.

Almost immediately, at the focus of the antennae appeared the hazy patriarchal image—from the waist up, since I hadn't bothered with lower limbs on the partial disk—wavering into place, white-limned and slightly flickering, but strong enough to cast a faint reflection in the mirror of the two-way glass.

"It is the Revelator." Even the tall man's voice was hushed.

"This is only a partial retrieval, and I need to collapse it." I turned off the entire difference engine—safer and quicker that way.

The image vanished like the flame of a quick-snuffed candle. "Why?"

"You don't want the Revelator to be anchored here, do you?"

The fact that there was no answer was answer enough.

"That will not affect his ghost, will it?" His voice was almost anguished.

"The full ghost was never called. That was just the ghost profile. That's why it was hazy." That was a lie, of course. The figure was hazy because I'd inhibited the full projection. "You didn't want him locked here, did you?"

"That is not clear," rasped one of the three behind the tall man.

"Look," I explained. "I told you earlier, where a ghost is created or recalled, that's where the ghost remains. You can see that when a ghost is created by violent death anywhere in Deseret. The ghost doesn't move. If I call up the ghost of the Revelator here, his ghost will be locked here, and I don't think that's what you want." I gestured toward the equipment before me. "This has to be set up where you want the Revelator to be recalled and where you want his ghost to remain."

"Can one of us do it?"

I laughed, easily. "I know what I'm doing, and it's taken me years to get this far." That was true. It was also largely irrelevant.

Figures looked at each other.

"Then make the equipment ready. You will have less than two hours to reassemble it and call the Revelator."

They all left, except for the guard. Once again, I had the feeling that whoever had briefed them had left out a few details—like I was creating ghosts and not recalling them, like ghosts of all sorts had limited capabilities.

Why had those details been left out? Either to ensure that one Johan Eschbach got eliminated in anger or to give me a chance? Or both? Ferdinand's agent, and there had to be one in the group, wanted me dead. Maurice-Huizinga's agent—or Dietre's—wanted me to escape. Cannon wanted me to escape, and I was convinced he had his own agents in the Revealed Twelve. Any government worth its salt has agents among the dissidents, and Cannon was too capable not to. I didn't know who was who, just that they had to be there.

That was another reason why I'd pushed myself to get the ghost file done so quickly. I had to get it done before people started comparing notes, and they'd do that if I took too long.

Undoing cables and setting drives for transport was much quicker and easier than writing and checking codes. I doubt it took even a half hour.

"I'm done for today," I finally said. "Everything's ready to go whenever you are."

They led me back to my cell. I even got an earlier dinner there. But I didn't digest it very well. I knew what was coming, and there was little I could do but wait and prepare, wondering if I were really prepared, if my ghost of the Revelator would be as stunning as I'd planned.

The shower nozzle dripped, and the dim bulb shed minimal light, and I waited and sniffed old oil and cement dust—and tried not to think about all that could go wrong.

32

I actually found myself dozing when they came. It was quarter past midnight, and they didn't bother to knock. They still wore hoods, but not the gray jumpsuits—regular dark gray or navy blue suits and polished shoes.

"It's time to go."

I grabbed the datacase.

"You won't need that," said the tall man.

"Unless something goes wrong," I snapped.

"Let him keep it."

They let me keep the case, with the quotes and the engineering drawings, and the definite conclusion that they had absolutely no intention of seeing me walk away from my efforts.

For the first time, their weapons were obvious—all Lugers, straight Austro-Hungarian version, and all of very recent manufacture, and that confirmed that Ferdinand's people had placed one agent, very openly.

The tall man pointed toward the corridor by which I'd entered. "Straight ahead."

"Where's the difference engine?" I asked.

"In the hauler. You'll travel with it."

I let my steps drag slightly so that I edged back toward the guards who followed, enough so that I had a chance . . . a faint one, but one against an untrained fanatic.

The hauler wasn't the commercial kind that had brought me but a square city van, with double doors on the rear. All of us went into the cargo space, except for whoever was driving and one other figure.

The ride wasn't that long, no more than ten minutes, really, before the hauler backed up to some sort of loading dock. Someone opened the double doors.

"You carry the equipment case, Eschbach."

As requested, I picked it up, and set the datacase on top of it.

Two more slender figures carried the difference engine.

I got the faintest glimpse of white light—the Temple, I suspected—in the crack between the van doors and the loading dock doors. Even the quick breath of cold air smelled clean, compared to the way I smelled and felt and the oil and cement dust I had been breathing for days.

I followed the two men with the difference engine down a narrow staircase to a ventilation duct that had been removed. The Twelve people liked ventilation ducts, I gathered.

I didn't like carrying anything but resolved to throw both cases or drop them strategically at the slightest provocation.

I didn't have any.

Three more of them walked behind me, carrying the long-barreled Lugers pointed in my direction as we walked along the empty tunnel, leading presumably to the Tabernacle.

It had to be the Tabernacle, because the Temple hadn't been consecrated until well after the death of Joseph Smith. Hard to imagine how a Virginia farm boy ended up in New Ostend, called to a mystical hill among skeptical Dutch, proclaiming a new religion that had turned into a sovereign and powerful nation in little more than a century.

The Tabernacle made sense for several other reasons. It was open to outsiders, and thus the ghost of the prophet would reinforce their claims not just in the Temple, but to all. And of course, everyone would understand his words just as they did. I almost laughed at that but instead kept lugging the equipment box and my datacase.

The tunnel smelled faintly of dust and of a sickly-sweet odor I would rather not have identified and hoped represented the remains of smaller rather than larger animal matter. The only sounds were those of eight men breathing—strange how most armed fanatic organizations are predominantly male—and the echoes of steps in the tunnel that my head almost brushed.

At the other end of the tunnel was an ancient wrought-iron gate whose lock had been previously drilled out. How many tunnels were there beneath the Temple square? Probably not so many as there would have been if Columbia had been successful in the Saint wars.

Then, there might not have been a Temple or Tabernacle at all. Who could tell what might have been?

"Up the stairs."

The stone steps looked ancient, but they couldn't have been. The centers were barely hollowed, and the stone walls were rough. I followed the two with the difference engine, and we exited from a closet into an arched foyer, gloomy and dark.

I waited, since the others did. The tall man eased up beside me. "How close does it have to be to where you recall the ghost?"

"Five to ten feet."

There was a sense of a nod, and he stepped in front of the men with the difference engine. "Follow me."

They did, and I did, too, my booted feet nearly silent where the carpet lay over the stone floor.

In the dimness, they set the difference engine on the floor in the open space between where the Choir of the Saints normally sat in the high raised seats and the lower seats occupied by worshipers or whoever came to hear speakers or the choir.

One of the younger men laid a power cord from somewhere in the back.

With a hooded figure holding a flash wand, I reconnected the difference engine cabling and then set the antennae in place. Without waiting for any sort of approval, I flicked the power switch and monitored the machine as it self-checked.

I kept checking the positions of the various schismatics, knowing that I'd have only instants once the Revelator's ghost materialized, knowing that I wouldn't have a chance to recheck when the time came. I'd just have to act, and hope the old training held enough to immobilize those necessary to escape.

My mouth was dry as I set up the programs and profiles and laid the auxiliary disk and its backup out. Theoretically, what I had in mind would work. It had worked before, but not quite so much had been riding on it, and I'd be really pushing the power parameters with my modifications, not that I had any choice.

First I made sure all eight profile sections were keyed to be projected; then I loaded the auxiliary disk. Then I gave the execute command and prayed . . . but not for long. While the power built and the antennae almost hummed and vibrated, I eased the calculator from my jacket pocket—I'd left my overcoat behind—then waited until a ghostly shape began to appear in the darkness. Ghosts are slightly phosphorescent and far more impressive in near-total darkness than in daylight or artificial light. Glow strips, especially, tend to wash them out, but the Tabernacle was dark.

The face, and the expressive eyes, appeared first, and then the figure in antique clothes.

The difference engine began to whine, ever so slightly, and I could smell the overload, the odor of ozone and overheating plastics and circuit boards.

"Wherefore, hear my voice and follow me, and you shall be a free people, and ye shall have no laws but my laws when I come, for I am your lawgiver, and what can stay my hand?"

Even the voice was stronger than ghost-normal, except it was more like a mental voice—that was true of all ghosts. People tended to hear the kind of voice they expected, and that should help slow the reactions of those around me.

The eight stood there, stunned.

I had to admit—the ghost was pretty impressive, turning his head from side to side in midair, as if to judge them. The beard was white, patriarchal, definitely patriarchal, and the eyes seemed to burn.

I slipped the pens into the calculator and slowly stood, as silently as possible, angling to one side, so that the disassociator wouldn't impact the ghost of the Revelator.

"That if the day cometh that the power and the gifts of God shall be done away among you, it shall be because of unbelief. . . . To believe in man, any man, prophet or man, rather than in the living God and his Revelations, that is idolatry, and marks the idolator as the spawn of Laman. I did not bring your forefathers to Zion to be idolators."

I winced. That had come out more strongly than I'd expected.

Seven of the eight still looked stunned, perhaps because the ghost aura was overpowering. Number eight turned, and he had something cold and metallic in his hand.

I knew what was coming and pressed the delete key on the pseudo-calculator. Bruce's toy made no sound, but the guard, re-formed apostle, whoever he was, shuddered and lowered the Luger, but only momentarily. He staggered, and that was enough.

He was fighting ghosts, a disassociator, and me. I was fighting him and fatigue. The Luger clattered on the floor, and one of the other schismatics shook his head and turned slowly.

Beyond us, that sonorous voice rolled forth into their minds, seemingly turning their reflexes into molasses.

"The Lamanites shall destroy this people, for they do not repent. All peoples who do not follow the Revelations of the living God shall be destroyed."

I stepped inside his guard and crushed his throat with my elbow. He struggled for a time more, then slowly crumpled. People forget how deadly a well-placed elbow can be, and an elbow's good close up, extremely good.

Staggering back as the second schismatic moved toward me in slow motion, in my own slow motion, I bent and recovered the calculator, replaced the loose pen, and touched the delete key. The schismatic jerked like a marionette with spastic strings. His face smoothed, and a phantasm of white lifted from him and vanished. Another zombie.

I replaced the batteries in the calculator and focused it in turn on each of the six remaining figures who were entranced by the ghost of the Revelator. I had to replace the batteries once more in the process, and yet no one turned. Shooting fish in a barrel would have been more of a challenge, caught as they were in the power of the ghost that continued to become ever more real- and solid-looking even as the smell of burning insulation grew stronger.

In the end, there were also seven zombies and a body. The body was that of the first man, who had to have been Ferdinand's agent. I bent down and ripped off the wig, toupee, whatever you called it, and underneath was one of the flexible metallic-mesh helmets that Branston-Hay's team at Vanderbraak State had won. My guts churned. I collapsed the mesh helmet and pocketed it. That evidence would have implicated Columbia, even if it had been planted by Ferdinand, and I wasn't about to let that happen.

Behind me, the ghost intoned, "Cursed is he who puts his trust in man. More cursed is he that puts his trust in a man's false interpretation of what I have said. Trust rather the Revelations of thy Father in heaven than the man who twists my words. . . ."

Even after all I'd done, it was hard to believe he wasn't talking to me. Then maybe he was.

Sometimes age and treachery are enough to overcome skill. Anyway, this time they had been. But I wasn't done. I stripped off the vest and molded the plastique in place quickly around the difference engine, then connected the wires.

I scooped up my datacase and sprinted toward the door.

I didn't quite make it before there were difference engine parts everywhere . . . some embedded in the wooden supports for the balcony. For a moment, I leaned against the outside door and gasped, before opening it and stumbling out.

Since it might have been a good idea to yell, I did: "Help!"

Nothing happened. I yelled again.

A guard in a blue uniform hurried across the lighted stones as I stepped out into the open air for the first time in what seemed forever. Behind the guard, the light-sheathed Temple towered into the dark night sky. I could even see the brighter stars, and a faint smile cracked my lips as I took a deep breath of the city's polluted air, which seemed so clean at that moment.

"Who are you? The Tabernacle's locked. What were you doing there?" His words were cold, brusque.

"I'm Columbian minister Eschbach. I was kidnapped by . . . those people. The ones inside. You'd better contact Bishop Hansen of Saint security and the First Counselor."

"Why?" The policeman clearly didn't like my unshaven countenance.

At that point there was a second small explosion from within the Tabernacle, and I wondered what one of the zombied schismatics had been carrying. "Go see for yourself."

He didn't but waited until two compatriots arrived, and they started in on me while he eased into the Tabernacle through the smoke. I hoped some of the zombied Revealed Twelve had survived the explosion. I had no doubts that the ghost of the Revelator had.

"Can you prove you're Minister Eschbach?"

"The real Minister Eschbach is at the Columbian embassy."

I dug out my passport. "You will note, gentlemen, that I possess this passport. You will also note that it contains my picture."

Sometime around that point, Bishop Hansen trotted up. "Eschbach! Are you all right?"

The two police officers drew back and exchanged glances.

"I'm tired, and it's been a long week. I've got a few bruises, I think, but I'm in far better shape than I expected."

"Minister Eschbach was detained by the schismatics," Hansen said crisply. "Not another word."

They nodded.

I turned to him and lowered my voice. "There's some exploded equipment in there, and some very stunned schismatics. They're not going anywhere. I'd strongly suggest you get the pieces of the equipment out of there immediately and swear everyone to secrecy."

"Why?"

"There's also the ghost of the Revelator—the first prophet. You'd better see for yourself. I'll explain later. Just take care of it."

He took my arm, and we walked back through the dust into the Tabernacle. I still hung onto my datacase. Better that no one saw that, or its contents, now.

"Holy God . . . ," he murmured.

The ghost image that resembled Joseph Smith turned in midair. "Oh, the vainness, and the frailties, and the foolishness of men! When they are learned they think they are wise, and they harken not unto the counsel of God, for they set it aside, supposing they know of themselves, wherefore, their wisdom is foolishness and it profiteth them not."

The first police guard stood transfixed before us. Five of the seven zombies were still standing there as well.

Hansen swallowed and turned to me. "I knew you were trouble."

"No trouble. The Revelator—any ghost—can only say what he once said." I shrugged. "It may even convince a few people. It certainly won't help the schismatics."

"I don't know," murmured the bishop for security.

The ghost turned toward Hansen. "Unto each generation cometh the Revelations of God; harken unto them, for the Lord will provide, both counsel and providence for those who listen. . . ."

I nodded. Those words came out right, and even Counselor Cannon would like them. He'd better, the double-dealing weasel.

"I'm not sure I want to know." Hansen tapped the policeman on the arm. "Christensen! Seal the Tabernacle until we can check for damage! We don't want anyone hurt. We'll need a detail for the injured."

The ghost image winked out, then re-appeared on the far side of the open space. ". . . thou shalt not write by way of commandment, but by wisdom; and thou shalt not command him who is at thy head, and the head of the church."

I stood and listened to Hansen organize the local forces, then followed him outside and listened some more while the building was cordoned off. I almost smiled. I'd done a hell of a good job.

Before long, another entourage arrived—that of First Counselor Cannon. He almost frowned when he saw me, but I smiled tiredly.

He drew me aside, away from Hansen. "What happened?"

"I'm afraid that the prophet was too much for them." I nodded toward the Tabernacle.

"You did what they wanted?"

"I'm afraid they got what they wanted. They asked me to recall the ghost of the Revelator. I didn't have much choice, as you must know. They didn't realize that they'd get the Revelator as he was, not as they thought he should be." I had to cough. My throat was raspy, my mouth dry.

Cannon's mouth opened. Behind his shoulder, Hansen smiled tightly.

I smiled more tightly. "Seven are zombies. One's dead, maybe more. I suggest you check the dead man's background very closely. That's the one with the crushed throat. I'd suspect a certain Austrian connection. They all had very new Austrian Lugers."

Cannon stepped closer. "The Tabernacle?" His voice was more curious than upset, and that, unfortunately, didn't surprise me in the slightest.

"I'm afraid the ghost of the Revelator has returned to set straight the record. Of course, I'm an outsider, but it sounds a great deal like what was recorded in the *Doctrine and Covenants.*"

"What will happen?" snapped Hansen.

I shrugged. "I'd guess what usually happens. Most ghosts fade in time."

"You believe this is the ghost of the prophet?" asked Counselor Cannon.

"I'm not equipped to judge that, Counselor," I pointed out. "All I can say is that I'd be very surprised if the ghost says anything new or radical. Ghosts don't, as a rule."

Cannon offered a warm smile, the one I really mistrusted. "Then the people will hear and believe, as they should. And I thank you."

"As they should," I reinforced. Of course, I'd chosen what words had been taken from the *Doctrine and Covenants,* and I'd been pretty careful. Cannon wouldn't like all of them. No, he wouldn't, but . . . none of us likes everything in our chosen faiths. That's what makes life interesting for a believer. "I have a small favor to ask in return, Counselor. A very small favor."

"Even the powers of a counselor are limited, as you know, Minister Eschbach."

"This is within your power. You've already offered it, and I was unable to take advantage of it. I would like you to confirm it in writing, and by immediate message to Speaker Hartpence and President Armstrong." I forced a smile. "An invitation to bring a technical team, headed by me, to study your advances in wastewater tertiary treatment and, if you will, a strong hint that the team would not be welcome without me. I think that's only fair, after all that's happened."

It was more than fair, and it was another form of insurance. Minister Reilly *wanted* that information, and I wanted the Speaker and the president to get the impression that not only was Llysette's survival important for Columbia's future and ability to obtain resources from Deseret, but mine was also. I needed every little angle I could find, especially since it was clear Jerome had betrayed me.

Cannon touched his beard, then nodded with a slow smile. "Yes, Minister Eschbach, that is something within my powers, and in all of our interests. I might also suggest it be coupled with the next performance of your wife. She might be a tremendous draw to open the summer season at the St. George opera house."

I returned the smile. "I think we would both be delighted with that offer."

"They will have the message in the morning—or later this morning. Have a good trip, Minister Eschbach, and give my best to your lovely wife."

Hansen glanced from Cannon to me, and the shock in Hansen's eyes was palpable. I couldn't say I blamed him. He was a true believer who'd just discovered that his leader not only had feet of clay but also had trafficked with the schismatics.

I touched Hansen's arm before he could speak. "I'd like to go to the Columbian embassy. I presume that's where Llysette still is."

Hansen nodded. "Unless your people moved her." His eyes went to the First Counselor.

"Will you take me, Bishop Hansen?"

Cannon cleared his throat. "Go ahead, Brother Hansen. And thank you, Minister Eschbach. Minister Jerome had said you were a man of your word, and your actions have confirmed that."

Good of them, both. I, unlike Hansen, managed to keep from swallowing as his words confirmed both his and Jerome's role. Jerome had supplied the information about psychic proliferation technologies, just enough that it couldn't be used without me, and Cannon had had it funneled to the Revealed Twelve. Very neat, even if I didn't know exactly how.

That also confirmed that Jensen had definitely been Cannon's agent in ensuring that Llysette and I had gotten into the hands of the Revealed Twelve. Not that I had a shred of real proof, which was why it would have been a mistake to say anything, but I knew . . . and Cannon knew I knew, and neither of us needed to say a word. Sometimes, that's for the best.

Hansen and I finally walked toward the south side of the Temple, where the shining Browning was waiting, amid several police steamers and two red fire steamers.

"I'll drive, Heber." Hansen motioned for the driver to get out of the Browning. "You wait here for me. I won't be too long."

Hansen said nothing until the steamer was clear of the square. "Why did you insist I escort you? My job isn't done there."

"To keep you from cutting your throat, Brother Hansen. Just think about things for a while." I meant it. Hansen was honest, and I respected that honesty. He'd been chosen as head of security because he was honest. Cannon couldn't afford a dishonest security chief; no head of government can. But that meant Hansen had been really shocked to discover the extent to which the First Counselor had manipulated the situation and had used me and the schismatics to reinforce the current Saint regime and its efforts to reduce the conflicts with Columbia.

Hansen's eyes narrowed, but the Browning kept heading east, uphill, at least in the general direction of the Columbian embassy.

After he pulled up into the "No Standing" area reserved for official vehicles, he turned in the seat. "Why do you care about me?"

"Because you're honest and, while we'll never agree on many things, I won't be party to seeing an honest man take the blame for something. So don't. Just accept it as it appears—the schismatics were overcome by the reappearance of the ghost of the Revelator."

He frowned again. I would have, in his position, but there wasn't much else I could do except give him a chance to cool off.

We walked up the stone walk and steps to the main entrance to the embassy. The guard post in the front archway was an oasis of light in a dark structure. The marine guard looked sleepily at me, frowning at my disheveled condition.

"I'm Minister Eschbach."

To my surprise, he straightened. "Sir? You're back!"

"I'm here. Probably Second Secretary Trumbull-Hull wants to know that, and I'm certain my wife does."

"Yes, sir. She's in the guest wing suite. Ah . . . and . . . just a mo-

ment." He fiddled with the wireset at his post. "Madame Eschbach
. . . your husband, he's here—he appears safe. . . . Yes, madame. . . ."
He shook his head. "She'll be right here." Then he looked at the list
and punched out another number.

Hansen looked from the marine to me. "I think a number of
people underestimated you, Eschbach."

"If so, for that I'm quite grateful."

"Sir, Minister Eschbach has just returned." The guard looked at
Hansen, then at me.

"With Bishop Hansen of Saint security," I supplied, adding in a
lower voice to Hansen, "You need some credit in this."

"Kind of you," he said dryly.

"With Bishop Hansen of Saint security," the Marine parroted.
"Yes, sir. I'll get them right in." He hung up the wireset receiver and
used a key to open the front door. "Please step in, sir. Secretary
Trumbull-Hull will be right down. He's been sleeping in the duty
quarters."

Hansen followed me in gingerly, then eased closer. "You had the
connections figured out before you left."

"No. I only knew there had to be connections. When I saw the
counselor's face and when I realized you didn't know, it was obvious."
I didn't mention Minister Jerome. That was my problem.

He shook his head. "This . . . is going to take some getting
used to."

I felt sorry for him, but all I could say was, "This sort of thing
does." Then I added, "I left my overcoat in their blockhouse. I'd
guess it's a concrete building in the northeast warehouse district.
Where exactly, I don't know."

"Did you leave anything else there? Anything explosive, for example?" His voice was bitter, and I didn't blame him.

"No. I doubt there's much trace of anything anywhere, now."

"Convenient."

Expedient, but I didn't voice that, and didn't have to.

Llysette, with another guard leading the way, charged past him
and down the side corridor, launching herself into my arms. She
had thrown a robe over a nightgown, and she looked and felt like
diva, beauty, and queen, all in one.

I could feel the dampness on my cheeks, but my own eyes were
wet as well, and I realized that I really hadn't been sure I'd ever see
her again. I held her for a long, long time.

When I let go, Trumbull-Hull stood there, just in his shirt and trousers, barefoot, and I'd never seen a Columbian diplomat unshod.

"It's over," I said, turning but not letting go of Llysette. "Here in Great Salt Lake City, anyway. Saint security has most of the key schismatics, and I'm sure that they'll find most of the others."

"What happened?" he asked.

"The schismatics had this idea that the ghost of their prophet would lead them, and that I'd be a useful hostage. The only problem was that when he appeared, he didn't have quite the same ideas as they did, and in their confusion, I managed to put several out of commision and escape. That allowed Saint security"—I nodded to Hansen—"to collar a bunch of the others, and I imagine they'll have everything pretty well in hand in the next few days."

"We believe so," Hansen said on cue.

"It sounds rather traumatic," observed Trumbull-Hull. "Are you certain you're all right?"

"There's nothing wrong with me that some food, a hot shower, and several nights' sleep won't go a long way toward remedying," I lied—because there was still one enormous loose end to tie up before I got hung by it. I was somewhat relieved, because the loose end didn't threaten Llysette, not directly, anyway. "But we'd still like to leave tomorrow."

Both Trumbull-Hull and Hansen nodded. It was clear they'd both like the Eschbachs on the way back to Columbia.

That was fine with us.

33

THE olive drab bulk of the Republic turbojet squatted on the tarmac like a brooding eagle, being refueled. Llysette and I stood in the VIP lounge, where generals and the like waited, as, it appeared, did government ministers.

The chocolate was nearly decent, and I was on my third mug when a lieutenant in formal drabs stepped up to our escort, Colonel Borlaam, who'd been somewhere close ever since I reappeared.

"There's a blond fellow—says he's Doktor Perkins and that he'd like to see either Minister Eschbach or Mademoiselle duBoise."

"Could you let him in?" I asked Colonel Borlaam. "He was Llysette's accompanist at the concerts, and he's one of the greatest living composers. He's also been on our side."

The colonel looked doubtful.

I glared. I was tired of everyone else calling the shots—literally and figuratively.

"If you would . . ." Llysette's smile would have dissolved even the ghost of the Revelator.

The colonel nodded at the lieutenant.

Dan Perkins hurried in, silver-blond hair drooping over his forehead, but with an enormous grin. "I'm so glad I could get here." He looked from Llysette to me. "Congratulations on the commendation from Counselor Cannon. Both the *Deseret Star* and the morning news had stories about you, something about how you had helped resolve, informally, a major obstacle to talks between Columbia and Deseret."

The colonel raised his eyebrows but said nothing. Neither did I. The commendation was something I hadn't asked for, or expected, but sometimes good things happened, especially if they were in other people's best interests. First Speaker Cannon had once again pushed his media empire into releasing the story he wanted.

I held back a frown, realizing something else I should have caught earlier. Cannon had warned me about Jerome. He was too good a politician to have let Jerome's name slip. He'd wanted me to know that. He also wanted me to do something about Minister Jerome. I would have anyway, but it was reassuring to know I wasn't the only one who felt that way.

"Anyway," Perkins rushed on, turning back to Llysette and handing her the case, "I brought you the first disks from the concert. I could only get ten. We'd pressed five thousand." He shook his head. "They're gone. The distributor says there are orders with deposits for another ten thousand."

The disks showed a picture of Llysette and Perkins—one of the pictures snapped as they'd taken a bow. The title read modestly: *The Incredible Salt Palace Concert: DuBoise & Perkins.*

Colonel Borlaam leaned forward slightly, and I stepped sideways so that he could see the disk cover as well.

"It is incredible," Perkins said. "After all these years . . ."

I understood perfectly. Besides the artistic side, the disks represented freedom—for both him and Llysette.

I couldn't help but calculate. Llysette got almost a Columbian dollar for each one. Fifteen thousand dollars at a minimum, and that was without any sales in Columbia. Strangely, in a way, I felt even happier for the poor Saint composer.

"*Le pauvre homme . . . ,*" Llysette murmured after Perkins had waved and departed.

I nodded. Still, I thought things would improve.

"He's famous, isn't he?" asked the colonel.

"One of the more famous living composers," I said. "You can probably boast about it to friends and family in a few years."

That got an awkward smile, I suppose because colonels couldn't ever admit to boasting.

A figure in a flight suit opened the door to the tarmac, and the odor of distillate and hot metal wafted in.

"We're ready, Colonel."

We walked across the tarmac, through the wind, chill enough for me because I still hadn't gotten back my overcoat, and probably wouldn't, and up the steps into the middle cabin.

"This is where I leave you, Minister," said the colonel, "and head back to the embassy."

"Thank you for everything, and for taking good care of my wife in my absence."

He cleared his throat. "We've enjoyed it, but from what I've heard, Minister Eschbach, no one could take better care of her than you. She's a lovely lady." He saluted and stepped back.

I nodded, and we stepped fully inside the military VIP transport. The decor was military brown, but I didn't care. As the hatch closed, we settled into the pair of plush leather seats before a low table bolted in place—the only passengers in a cabin designed for a dozen.

"You're going to be very famous," I told Llysette, squeezing her hand and then leaning over and kissing her cheek, drawing in the scent of Ivoire again. Lord, at times over the past days I'd never thought I'd see her again.

"*Ca, ce n'est pas finis, n'est-ce pas?*"

"No. I sometimes wonder if it ever is."

"Is it Ferdinand?"

"In a way, but there's nothing we can do until we reach the Federal District." And there wasn't. I'd sent a message to Harlaan Oakes, strongly suggesting, if he valued his life and his career, he meet us. I didn't make a habit of that sort of thing, and I suspected he'd be waiting. Angry, upset, and ready to rip me apart. But he would be there, and that was fine with me.

In the words of a southern Anglicism, it was his turn to be the hunting dog.

In the meantime, I intended to enjoy every moment with my bride. I squeezed her hand again as the turbos roared and the big aeroplane rolled toward the long runway.

After a moment, her face cleared, and she kissed me.

34

HARLAAN Oakes was indeed waiting at the foot of the steps to the landing area once the Republic turbo squeaked to a lurching stop at VanBuren Field, outside of the Federal District and once we walked down the steps and into the cold misting rain. He looked at Llysette.

Her eyes were cold as she returned his glance.

Harlaan looked to me.

"No," I said coldly. "Her life has been played with enough. She knows. You and Minister Jerome's replacement are going to protect her even more than before. She's going to be doing international tours, now, I imagine. A cultural ambassador, for President Armstrong."

"You're presuming a great deal, Johan." He glanced back at the turbo.

"I don't presume, Harlaan, and I don't play games. Haven't you figured that out yet? Have you gotten the follow-up invitation from First Counselor Cannon?" I offered a smile.

He winced slightly. "Speaker Hartpence isn't pleased."

"He'll be less pleased as events unfold. The president should be happy, and that should be your concern." I paused. "I presume you have transportation for us to the B&O station. We're ready to go home after we've debriefed you." This time I was doing the debriefing, rather than being debriefed. It felt good.

"I thought it might be something like this. I have a secure limousine."

Two soldiers carried our luggage to the limousine, and I enjoyed that a great deal. I kept a tight grip on my datacase, although I had prevailed on the embassy to use their duplicating equipment to make a second set of plans, now in the lining of Llysette's luggage.

None of us spoke, not until the limousine was steaming back toward the Presidential Palace—or the B&O station on the Mall. The panel between us and the driver was closed, and Harlaan sat with his back to the front of the limousine.

I held out the flexible mesh helmet. "Do you know what that is?"

Harlaan winced, almost in spite of himself.

"I take it you recognize this. Ferdinand's agent in Deseret was wearing it. He had orders to kill me, and probably Llysette. According to Ralston's briefings," I lied, "only Branson-Hay had figured out the helmets. I never had one. I only saw them once, in his laboratory, and his research was totally funded through the Spazi. They were supposed to be destroyed, as I recall, by Minister Jerome." I pocketed the helmet.

"Johan, there could be other explanations. . . ." He paused. "What happened to him?"

"He's dead, but the Deseret security chief knows he was an Austrian agent."

"There could be a dozen explanations. . . ."

I waved off his words. "Now, the other thing is that there was a complete duplicate of my home SII system waiting for me in Deseret—in the hands of the Revealed Twelve. The system had to have been duplicated when the Spazi had my house under complete surveillance. Even the files were there, as well as some equipment duplicated from a hidden storage room in my house."

"That's a serious charge, Johan. I know the Spazi and you have not gotten on well, but that seems beyond anything anyone would expect."

I was getting tired of his explanations. "Also, the schismatics were all armed with Austrian weapons, new Austrian weapons."

"That would figure," he admitted. "It's to their interest to keep us at odds."

"Something else of interest was a pressure switch bomb that I detonated at our house in New Bruges. Jerome wired me the next morning and suggested I leave such matters to the Spazi, but the problem is that where I detonated the bomb wasn't visible to his observers. So how could they have known what it was that exploded? He didn't ask, by the way—he told me."

Harlaan's mouth twisted.

"Needless to say, Harlaan, I'm not very happy with these events, nor would I be thrilled if I were President Armstrong, because it looks like someone wanted us both dead, with a trail back to you and the president." I smiled. "There's also one other small problem."

"Oh, Johan?"

"There's a very smart head of security in Deseret who is very close to the First Counselor and who won't be very happy dealing with Minister Jerome. The First Counselor has also indicated that he would not be pleased to deal with a government whose minister of security would support Austrian agents in Deseret." I was elaborating slightly, but Cannon had conveyed almost that much indirectly.

"Why is that a problem?"

"Because if I were the president, I wouldn't be very happy if the First Speaker of Deseret were to stall negotiations because of Jerome's actions, especially given his Austrian . . . contacts. And the message both the president and the Speaker received this morning offers a far better option."

"All this is surmise."

"Come now, Harlaan," I chided him.

"Minister Eschbach, what do you want of me? I am merely an advisor to the head of state, not a cabinet minister."

"In practical terms, Harlaan, I want the Spazi to stop trying to eliminate me—and Llysette—whenever they think they might be able to get away with it." I paused. Time for another push. "There's also one other thing."

"I'm not sure Columbia can stand one more thing," he said disgustedly.

Llysette's eyes narrowed, and she smiled coldly. "You have not been in Ferdinand's prisons. You have not watched your husband sacrifice himself for his wife and his country. You, do you plan to silence me? You, do you plan to put me away for small politics? Do you wish to upset the head of Deseret? He *would* be upset, if anything happened to me." Her green eyes were as hot as the sun, as cold as midwinter eve in New Bruges, and as deadly as when she had held a Colt-Luger to my forehead.

Harlaan's forehead beaded sweat, and he wiped it. "I can't promise anything."

"Harlaan," I said gently, "you don't have to promise. Just do what needs to be done. Now, there is one other matter. I'm working out some arrangements with FrancoPetEx."

"Yes."

"It appears that there is some New French interest in Columbia becoming more energy-independent. Through some personal contacts, of the type not available to Minister Jerome, I have finalized the agreement."

"What did you agree to?"

"For services already rendered in Deseret, once they are confirmed officially, I will receive the entire plans, specifications, and design drawings, including proprietary technology, of a stage-three Saint synthetic fuel plant."

"What services?" Harlaan asked tiredly.

"The murder of Ferdinand's agent among the Revealed Twelve."

Harlaan winced again. "Just how many bodies did you leave behind this time, Minister Eschbach?"

"None that will ever be attributed to Columbia. That's all that counts, isn't it?"

"You will do what is necessary, *n'est-ce pas?*" asked Llysette, a chill smile on her lips.

The president's advisor shrugged tiredly. "Have events left me much choice?"

"No."

"*Non.*"

"When can I promise delivery of those plans?" Harlaan asked after a time.

"When the Spazi situation is resolved," I said. "I don't think my contacts would feel comfortable with Minister Jerome's attitude or position."

"You drive a hard bargain, Minister Eschbach."

I shook my head. "You and the president set the price when you drafted us. It's only fair that it be paid."

"This is going to change everything," he mused.

Even Harlaan didn't understand exactly how much, and I wasn't about to tell him. After all, the journey is the fun, not the destination. Death is always the eventual destination, so there's no point in hurrying the trip.

I smiled at Llysette and leaned back. She put her head on my shoulder, and the faint scent of her, and Ivoire, surrounded me.

35

I glanced out the kitchen window into the darkness of Saturday night. Less than three months had passed since Llysette had given a recital attended by the Deseret concertmeister, and our lives had changed dramatically.

Hartson James—the TransMedia mogul who'd been entranced at the Presidential Art Awards dinner—had indeed plugged Llysette and Dan Perkins's disk, and it continued to sell briskly in Columbia. The indications were that the trustees of Vanderbraak State University would grant Llysette tenure at their next meeting, and Llysette had three upcoming concerts scheduled—one in New Amsterdam and one a week later in Philadelphia and, of course, the opening of the spring season in St. George in Deseret. The guarantees for each were triple her annual income from teaching.

There were a few more gowns in her closet and quite a few more dresses, but the Haaren remained in the music room because "a good instrument it is, and given with love." And she was paying for our trip to Saint-Martine.

I could accept that.

Harder to accept was that Llysette had suddenly become as well-off as I, and shortly would become very well-off, I suspected, from what I saw through my activities as her de facto business manager—with Eric's assistance. My former brother-in-law's legal advice had also been most helpful.

Hartson James had recently written about the possibility of using an Irish subsidiary as the vehicle for marketing the disk in Austro-

Hungary, and if anyone could work those angles, I suspected the media magnate could. I also suspected that the royalties on a good-selling disk in a market of over 200 million people would be considerable.

"Johan, I have been thinking." Llysette slipped up behind me and put her arms around my waist.

"Yes?"

"So skeptical you sound."

I laughed.

"Was it not strange that the deputy minister, he committed suicide so soon after your return?"

"Do you really think so?" I asked.

"Suicide, it was not. *Non?*"

"No," I admitted. "Not from what I know about the Speaker and the president." Jerome's "suicide" had made it very simple for them; it had all been the deceased Spazi chief's fault. If I hadn't pressed, though, I would have been the corpse . . . and possibly Llysette, in some terrible "tragedy."

"Was he not the one who sent the bomb?"

"I think so." I looked out the window. Bruce was a little late.

"Did he not work with the agents of Ferdinand?"

"He slipped them some information about us, and that sort of thing doesn't set well even in the Federal District, not at that high a level. There's no deniability."

"Why did he dislike you so much, Johan?"

"Because spymasters dislike anyone who knows their operations and is not under some control and because Jerome was too young. He took my actions personally."

"You think Minister Oakes, he will do better?"

"At least, Harlaan understands both sides of the fence, and can operate as a bridge between the Speaker and the president. The Speaker wasn't happy about it, but given Jerome's indiscretions, he preferred it not become public, and accepted the president's compromise. Since Harlaan never wanted the position . . ." I shrugged. "The synthfuel plans confirmed that Jerome's approach was too paranoid for this new and changing world."

The world changed more slowly than our lives, but changes were coming. FrancePetEx was actually talking about a joint venture on the first Columbian synthfuel plant—designed to convert north-lands natural gas into kerosene—and with those kinds of cooperation between the North American nations, Ferdinand's rhetoric had toned down. I snorted to myself. All that meant was that the Austro-Hungarians would expand southward, rather than westward.

As the flapping of Bruce's Olds ragtop preceded the venerable steamer up the drive, I stopped mental philosophizing and hugged Llysette. We watched Bruce for a moment while the snowflakes swirled around him. He extracted a large box from the passenger side, then went to the door and opened it.

"Greetings and congratulations!" Bruce shook off the scattered snow and stamped his feet. "And happy something." He extended the enormous box, then grinned. "This should go in the music room . . . for now."

So we followed him there, after I checked the oven to make sure the green bean casserole wouldn't overbrown.

He opened the box and extracted a small box that looked like a miniature difference engine, with two disk slots. Then came two DGA speakers, relatively expensive, followed by a scanner. "There!"

"It is . . . what?" asked Llysette.

"You had mentioned the problem with accompanists for students." Bruce beamed. "This solves that problem for practice, at least. You use this to scan the music, and then you can set whatever modifications to the tempo that you need. I figured that you need to stop at any time, too, given what I know about students, and this little gadget here"—he pointed to another little box with a stick—"lets you stop and back up to wherever you like."

"Now, I know there's no substitute for a real accompanist for performing, but this might help with practicing and with students."

Llysette looked at the equipment, half-bewildered, half-bemused.

I drew Bruce aside. "How much . . . I mean . . . this was scarcely inexpensive."

"Johan," and Bruce smiled at me. "This is my treat. I get to solve a problem in a positive way and see a pretty woman smile."

I also understood what he wasn't saying, that things had changed and that we had to be equals, that he was no longer, if he ever had been, merely a contract employee.

"Fair enough." I paused. "Just a moment. I'll be right back."

Bruce's brows furrowed before I headed down to the cellar. Let them.

I brought back up six bottles.

"You liked the Sebastopol. Take these with you."

"I couldn't."

I got to grin. "If we're truly friends and not just business part-ners, then I get to give things, too."

He smiled back. "It's been a long time."

And it had been, in so many ways. Then, I had to run to the kitchen because something was overcooking, but that was life, too.